The Witch of White Lady Hollow

Cover Design by Ben Savage

ISBN: 978-1-947578-41-8

Ink Smith Publishing
P.O. Box 361
Lakehurst, NJ 08733

Printed in the U.S.A.

The final approval for this literary material is granted by the author.

All characters appearing in this work are fictious. Any resemblance to real persons, living or dead, is purely coincidental.

THE **WITCH** OF
WHITE LADY
HOLLOW

C. DAVID BELT

Ink Smith Publishing • www.ink-smith.com

For Cindy,
Who gives me the courage to tell my stories.

For Alison,
Who inspired the whole thing.

For Rachel,
Who in so many ways inspired Tabitha.

A witch ought never be frightened in the darkest forest . . . because she should be sure in her soul that the most terrifying thing in the forest was her.

Terry Pratchett

Thou shalt not suffer a witch to live.

Jehovah

Exodus 22:18

By the pricking of my thumbs,
Something wicked this way comes.

William Shakespeare

Macbeth, Act IV, Scene I

Blue Beech Ridge, Missouri: 1852

Lettie's pale lips writhed around a voiceless scream. Her knees wobbled, and her legs threatened to give way. With every trembling movement, the coarse hemp noose tightened around her white neck.

No! Please! Lettie's lips moved, but of course, no words escaped. No words ever escaped Lettie's lips.

She pulled at the rope binding her hands behind her back, but she couldn't free herself. And even that simple movement almost toppled her.

All round the great blue beech tree in the village square, the townsfolk, old and young, stood. They jeered and hooted, while Lettie pleaded silently. *Please! I ain't done nothing!* Even some of the slaves—standing at the back of the crowd, of course—had come to watch the hanging. Lettie looked frantically from face to face. *I healed you. I saved you. Somebody, please help me!*

"Go on, Elias." Hazel Chatham, a tall, gaunt woman with a face like a dried apple, waved a hand at the stool under Lettie's feet. "Kick it out and be done with the witch!"

That rickety, four-legged piece of furniture was all that separated Lettie from oblivion. *No! Let me go! Please!*

Hazel's face split into a gap-toothed grin so malevolent, it would've made Ol' Scratch himself proud. She licked her thin lips. "Burn in hellfire, White Lettie! Burn in hell, witch!" Hazel stepped closer to Lettie and spat at her. The spittle missed, and this seemed to infuriate the tall woman all the more. Hazel howled and rushed forward, her fingers curled into feral claws.

No! Lettie mouthed. *Don't kick the stool!*

But Hazel didn't touch the stool. With a lunatic shriek, she tore at Lettie's skirts, ripping a large hole in the dirt-and-blood-stained dress. The cool autumn air sent a chill down Lettie's exposed leg.

9

Then she felt Hazel's claws scrape down her bare flesh. The crazed woman gripped Lettie's white thigh, screamed, and sunk her teeth into Lettie's leg.

As the woman gnawed on Lettie's thigh, Lettie recoiled and very nearly fell off the stool. The noose tightened around her neck, and her lips quivered.

No! Please, Lord Jesus! Help me!

And to Lettie's mind came unbidden the words of the psalm—*They gnashed upon me with their teeth.*

Another woman detached herself from the mob. Evangeline Wood, short but slender, gripped Hazel about the waist, yanking the older woman back, away from Lettie.

Lettie could feel blood flowing down her leg, mingling with the dried blood on her inner thigh. She stared at Hazel in horror. Gore dripped from the ghoulish woman's mouth and chin. Hazel continued to struggle in Evie Wood's arms a moment, then grew still. She spat blood—and a tooth—at Lettie. "Burn, witch!"

Evie Wood shoved Hazel roughly to the ground, then stood with her back to Lettie and faced the mob—faced her neighbors, church-going folks Lettie had cared for over the years, now all transformed into demons howling for Lettie's very soul. "Stop this!" Evie cried. "How could you? What's she done?" Evie pointed a finger at Hazel as the woman got to her feet, not bothering to wipe the blood from her mouth. "It's like y'all're possessed!"

"Witch!" a man yelled. Lettie couldn't see who'd spoken, but the cry of "Witch!" echoed through the throng.

"Stuff and nonsense!" Evie cried. "Ain't no such thing as witches, and y'all know it."

I ain't a witch! Lettie mouthed. *Not a witch!*

"She's a witch," said a woman's voice to Lettie's left. Lettie tried to see who had spoken, but dared not turn her head.

"No, she ain't," Evie said. "Y'all are a buncha hypocrites, like them Pharisees. Ain't a one-a y'all but hasn't gone to Lettie for doctorin' over the years—you or someone in your family. Even your niggers sneak out at night to White Lettie's Hollow for healin'." Evie spoke with all the blistering conviction of a hellfire-and-damnation preacher, but if she were looking for shame or any other sensible reaction from the mob, she didn't get it. "Lettie ain't never asked for nothin' from us," she continued, "less'n it was eggs or a piglet or a bag of apples you brung as payment for her help. And even if you didn't bring nothin', she helped you anyway. She's helped all y'all. And the first time she come to us for help, we—"

"She's a witch, I tell ya!" Coralline Thibodeaux—short and very fat and standing next to Hazel's skeletal frame—had once, by all accounts, been quite pretty. But her round face was twisted into a bestial grimace, like a dog snarling over a scrap of bone. "She put a hex on my Elias!" Coralline waved a pudgy hand at her husband. "Enticed him, she did. Ain't nothin' else for it. She bewitched him!"

Elias Thibodeaux stood with head bowed, though his gray eyes peeked out from under red eyebrows. Lettie could feel those eyes on her even then, hungering for her, even as she tottered between life and death. How she hated those cold, iron-gray eyes!

In his arms, Elias held a small, blanket-wrapped bundle.

For a brief moment, Lettie forgot about the rope around her neck. *My baby! Please! Give me my baby!*

"Oh, yes," Evie Wood said, her voice dripping with scorn. "Mayor Elias Thibodeaux—bewitched by poor White Lettie. Can't be no other explanation. No, ma'am." She waved dismissively at the tall, strapping mayor and his short, rotund wife. "It ain't like your husband hasn't made indecent advances to most of the women in this town, *including* me. From what I hear, he's succeeded in bedding half the good ladies of Blue Beech Ridge. And he's a regular at the saloon in Poplar Bluff. And y'all know he ain't there for the watered-down whiskey!"

A snigger ran through the men—the unmarried men, at least—like a contagion. The married men scowled. A number of women flushed red under their bonnets.

"Why," Evie continued, "when I told our esteemed mayor to leave me be, he tried to force me. Woulda too, if'n I hadn't put a fish knife to his nethers and threatened to—"

"You're a lyin' whore, Evie Wood," said Charlotte Kilmore, one of the pretty young wives who'd blushed a moment earlier. "Elias Thibodeaux is a good—"

"Your little Davie's got red hair, don't he?" Evie said. "You ain't got red hair. Does your husband? Do any of his grandparents?"

Charlotte Kilmore's eyes went wide with horror, and she began to splutter. Her raven-haired husband glared at her.

"That's right," Evie continued. "He's got that bump on his right ear, don't he? Just like Elias Thibodeaux does."

Grim faced and lock jawed, Charlotte's husband gripped his wife by the arm and dragged her away from the crowd, even as Charlotte proclaimed her innocence for all who cared to hear.

Like a candle flame in a darkened room, hope flared up in Lettie's heart. *They believe me. Let me go! Give me my baby, please. Don't let that wicked man have my son!*

Evie Wood stared after the retreating, unhappy couple for a moment, then resumed her spirited defense. "Lettie came to us for help. She couldn't deliver the child alone. Lord knows how she dragged herself all the way from the Hollow in her condition. And when the child was born, we took one look at Lettie's baby and that bump on his right ear... and we *knew!*" Evie raised both her fists and pounded the air. "We knew it was Mayor Thibodeaux's child." She pointed a finger in Lettie's direction. "And we blame *her*? I'm telling all y'all—he raped her!"

"You shut your vile mouth, Evie Wood!" Coralline Thibodeaux looked as if she might burst a blood vessel. "She's a witch. Why, just look at that hair, them pink eyes. They's the devil's eyes, I say! And if you don't get outta the way, Evie Wood, we'll do for you too." Coralline turned her bulk from side to side, encouraging the mob. "Witch! Witch!"

I ain't no witch! Lettie's legs quivered. *So tired. I could just . . . step off this stool. End it. So tired.*

Lettie's eyes fixed on her infant son—barely two hours old—in Elias's arms. *No! Please, Jesus. Don't let that evil man take my child. Not again.* Silent tears leaked from her eyes at the memory of her only other child—lost years ago—murdered by another wicked man. *Not again!*

"Witch! Witch!" The crowd had taken up the chant like hounds baying at the full moon.

"No!" Evie cried. "It ain't right!"

Not again. Gotta prove I ain't no witch!

So, Lettie pursed her lips—pursed her lips and blew.

Evie stiffened. Surrounded by the savage cries of Lettie's accusers, Evie Wood turned slowly to face the pale woman on the improvised gallows. Evie's jaw hung open in shock, and her eyes were as wide and round as teacups. Then her face opened in a wide grin. Evie waved a hand above her head. "Listen! Listen to her!"

And to Lettie's profound relief, the mob quieted.

They listened.

"What's she doing?" asked a man in a hushed tone.

Evie Wood, still facing toward Lettie, nodded, grinning in triumph. "That's it!" she whispered.

"She's . . . She's whistling!" said a woman.

"Can she do that?"

"Well, y'all can hear her, can't ya?"

"But she's a dummy! Dummies can't talk. Nor sing."

"She ain't singing. She's whistling."

"What's she whistlin'?"

Evie Wood turned around and opened her mouth, singing along with Lettie's tune.

> "I am bound for the Promised Land.
> I'm bound for the Promised Land.
> O-oh, who will come and join with me?
> I am bound for the promised land!"

Lettie continued to whistle with all the frantic, nigh-exhausted energy of her soul.

"See?" Evie cried. "If she was a witch, how could she whistle a church hymn like that? She's a Christian woman, I say!"

Lettie finished her tune, then began to whistle "Saints Bound for Heaven." And as soon as Evie recognized the tune, she sang along, lifting her arms and her clear voice toward the sky.

> "And to Canaan we'll return
> By and by, by and by.

And to Canaan we'll return
By and by."

Lettie's eyes roamed the crowd. Some of them looked upon her with surprise and awe. Hope swelled in her thundering heart. *They believe me! Thank You, Lord Jesus!* Her gaze shifted to her tiny son, ignoring the evil man who held him. A small, mewling cry escaped the bundle in Elias Thibodeaux's arms. *My baby! Please give me my son!*

And Lettie whistled all the louder, while Evie lifted her voice in song.

"Our Deliverer, He shall come
By and by, by and b—"

Evie's voice cut off abruptly.

So did Lettie's whistling.

Lettie saw the rock—the size of an apple—roll to the ground at Evie's feet. Coralline Thibodeaux, her stout arm still extended from the stone cast, crowed in fiendish triumph. Beside her, Hazel Chatham howled like a demon from hell.

Evie spun slowly, like a weathervane in a shifting wind. Blood gushed crimson from her forehead. And Evie fell toward Lettie, toppling slowly—ever so slowly— like a tree cut down by an axe. Evie's shoulder struck Lettie on the knees, just below the wounds left by Hazel Chatham's teeth.

There was an instant when Lettie thought she could maintain her precarious footing. An instant. But then the stool tipped, and Lettie's bare, white feet swung out over empty air. Her pale lips began to writhe around a voiceless scream—until the noose snapped tight around her neck, crushing her windpipe.

White Lettie, who had never uttered a word in her life, was well and truly silent.

Near Blue Beech Ridge, Missouri: 1978

"More country music?!" Tabitha gave the Chevy Impala's radio dial a furious twist. "This place is total Sticksville!" As she turned the knob, she passed two loud blips on the FM dial. This forced her to backtrack, which did nothing to improve her already rotten mood.

"Oh, come on, Tabby-Cat." Her mother, Molly, took one hand off the steering wheel—something she almost never did when driving on the highway—and patted her daughter on the knee. "It'll be an adventure! New people. New friends. New culture."

Tabitha found the first of the two bypassed radio stations. "Gospel?" She pointed with both hands at the infuriating radio with its stunningly monotonous selection of what passed for music in the Bootheel of Missouri. "Culture? What culture? Nothing except *twangy* country or *twangy* gospel!"

Tabitha raised her upper lip and pulled back her lower jaw, imitating buckteeth. She raised her left hand and placed the right on her abdomen, plucking an imaginary banjo. "My wife, she runned away!" she howled in a jumble of notes no sane composer would ever string together. "I'm fresh outta moonshine, cuz my still done broke! And my dawg...has...*fleas*!" She uttered three yips in a fair imitation of a coonhound. "Help me, Jesus! I cheated with the floozy at the bar, but that's all right, cuz I done been saved!" She clapped her hands together and drawled, "Can I get an amen, brothers and sisters?"

Her mother, having placed both hands firmly back on the wheel, glanced over at Tabitha with a stern look. "Tabitha Catherine Moonshadow, you are being very unfair. Who knows, maybe you'll get to like—"

Tabitha plucked at her imaginary banjo and howled, "And even the fleas done ran away!"

Molly's stern expression exploded in a guffaw. In moments, both mother and daughter were wiping tears of mirth from their eyes. "It's not that bad," Molly finally managed. "It can't be."

The male singer on the radio warbled, "I'm falling in love with you."

Molly pointed at the radio. "See, that's not so bad."

Tabitha rolled her eyes. "Mom, that's the *gospel* station. He's singing to Jesus."

Molly's eyebrows lifted, and her lips curled in dismay. "Really?"

"Yup!"

"Oh...my." Molly sighed loudly. "Like I said, it'll be an adventure."

Tabitha clamped her mouth shut. *An adventure. Yeah, like that movie,* Deliverance. The hint of a wicked grin pricked at the corners of her mouth. She plucked at her air-banjo once more. "Bah-dah-bah, bah-bah, bah-bah, bah-bah."

Her mother raised her eyebrows. "Dueling Banjos?" She glanced at Tabitha and grinned. Molly countered, echoing the banjo melody. "Bah-dah-bah, bah-bah, bah-bah, bah-bah." Then Molly's grin faded. "You haven't...*seen* that movie, have you?"

Tabitha's grin drooped as well. "No, Mom." *And from what I've heard, I never want to.* "It's R-rated. Besides, it came out when I was maybe eleven."

Molly nodded slowly. "Okay."

They rode in silence, as the Missouri countryside, with its low, forested hills, rolled leisurely past. The trees gradually closed in on both sides of the highway, blocking their view.

Tabitha continued to search the radio dial for more palatable music.

And like a beam of musical sunshine piercing the dark clouds of disharmony, Barry Manilow's clear vocals shot out of the radio—"...I write the songs!"

Tabitha sighed, her whole body relaxing for the first time in the two days of travel. F*inally. First good music I've heard since we left Maryland.*

Since we left home.

To move to Sticksville.

Tabitha turned her face toward her mother. "Do they even have a movie theater in Blue Beech Ridge?" *What a dumb name for a town! Be honest—is it any better than Suitland?*

"Movie theater?" Molly cocked her head. "I think so. I seem to remember one when I was here interviewing and house hunting." Her expression brightened. "But there's another theater back in Poplar Bluff—you know, the town we passed through about ten miles back? And you saw that drive-in theater—on the other side of Poplar Bluff?"

She slowed the car and turned off the two-lane highway onto a single-lane, dirt road. The bumpy road led downhill into a dense wood of what Tabitha assumed were the eponymous blue beech trees.

Tabitha stared at the rustic surroundings with claustrophobic horror. "You've gotta be kidding me! They don't even have pavement in this armpit of a town?"

Molly smiled. "Relax, Tabby-Cat. The town is farther up the highway. This is the road to our new house."

Tabitha groaned. *Oh, goody. We live in the sticks outside of Sticksville.*

The road dipped down toward a small valley nestled in the woods. A *"hollow"*—
that's what they call this kind of place.

The harmonious and—to Tabitha, at least—soothing tones of Barry Manilow
faded, only to be replaced with the perky strains of "Afternoon Delight."

Tabitha quickly shut off the radio.

Molly glanced at her daughter, obviously puzzled. "What's wrong with that
one?"

Tabitha gave her mother a look of incredulity, mingled with disgust. "It's a dirty
song, Mom."

Molly's quizzical expression deepened into a frown. "It is? I don't..."

Tabitha tucked in her chin, turtle-like, and folded her arms tightly, as if trying to
shrink in upon herself. She said nothing.

Her mother shrugged. "Okay, honey. You're more...sensitive to those things, I
guess."

More sensitive? Tabitha suppressed a bitter laugh. *Yeah, you bet. Ever since I
had to spend an entire month with Dad this summer.* She shuddered violently. *Never
again. I swear, I'll run away if I ever have to go back there.*

At the memory, nausea rolled over her like a wave of raw sewage. She opened
her mouth to tell her mother to pull over.

"We're here!" her mother announced in a cheerful, sing-song voice as she slowed
the Chevy to a stop. "Welcome home, Moonshadow Family!"

Tabitha lifted her eyes, her queasiness subsiding at the sight of the house. Her
mother had described it as a woodland cottage, and Tabitha agreed that "cottage" was
an apt word. The house was small, with wood walls, painted white, and a prominent
stone chimney rising from the back of the cedar-shingled roof. A pair of windows,
one on each side of the door, reminded Tabitha of eyes on either side of a nose.

"Isn't it pretty?" Molly's squeal of delight sounded a little forced. She shut off
the Impala's engine.

Pretty?

"If you were to put a thatch roof on it," Molly said, "I think it'd look just like the
Seven Dwarfs' cottage."

Tabitha squinted at the house and at the surrounding woods. "You know, now that
you mention it, yeah, it kinda would." *No, pretty isn't the word. Maybe...charming?*

Molly climbed out of the car. "Ooh, just wait 'til you see inside!"

Tabitha exited the car as well. Her mom stood half-turned toward her, extending
a hand for Tabitha to hold. *Seriously? I'm not a little girl anymore.* But she sighed
and took Molly's proffered hand. *At least nobody's watching.*

Molly tugged her toward the house. "Come on, Tabby-Cat!"

Tabitha groaned and stomped a foot. "Mom, you promised!"

Molly halted her exuberant tugging and looked at her daughter with a puzzled
expression. "What?"

Honestly, the woman is brain-dead! Tabitha glared at her mom and lowered her
voice to a growl. "You promised not to call me...*that* once we got here."

16

Her mother looked genuinely confused, then her eyes widened. Tabitha could almost see the light bulb appearing over Molly's head. "Tabby-Cat?"

Tabitha nodded. "Uh-huh."

"What I actually said was, 'Not in public.'" Molly's mouth curled in a mischievous grin. "And it's just *us* here."

Tabitha's shoulders slumped. "You're gonna forget." Her voice sounded whiney, even to her own ears. "You drag me out here, all the way from Maryland, from D.C., my friends, my school...to the Armpit of Missouri—"

"Bootheel."

"Whatever. You drag me away from civilization, music. The Smithsonian, Mom! And just before my senior year too. I finally made it into Madrigals! Now I'm in this, backwoods, hillbilly...*nowhere*."

"Tabby-Ca—" Molly seemed to catch herself. "Tabitha, we came here so we could start over. So, we could...get away from..." Molly's voice trailed off, and she dropped her gaze toward the ground.

There it was—the never-spoken, never-even-whispered truth.

It wasn't about a new job, a new school, a new beginning. The truth was very simple.

They were running away.

Running away from court-mandated visits with the noncustodial parent. From Molly's ex-husband.

From Dad.

Tears welled in Tabitha's eyes, then spilled down her cheeks. She squeezed her eyes shut, bent her head, and sobbed. But she didn't let go of her mother's hand.

Tabitha felt her mom put an arm around her, pull her close, and hold her tight. Molly pulled her hand from Tabitha's and wrapped the other arm around her daughter.

Tabitha hesitated, then awkwardly returned the embrace. She felt her mother's hitching breaths.

Mom's crying? Mom never cries. Not since I was six. Not since Dad left.

But at the moment, loud sobs shook Molly. "Oh, h-honey. I'm sorry. I'm so s-s-sorry."

"It's...It's okay, Mom."

"I—I had to. The judge m-made me do it."

Tabitha shook her head in angry resolution. "I won't go back. Never go back. Never, ever."

Molly squeezed her daughter even tighter. "I know. Seven months. Then it's all over."

Seven months. I'll be eighteen. March. And I'll never have to see him again.

Abruptly, Molly pulled out of the hug. She took her daughter's face in both hands and looked Tabitha in the eye. Framed by her curly mane of black hair, Molly's expression was determined, her eyes fierce—the eyes of a lioness.

"We're going to make it, Tabby-Cat. We are."

Tabitha turned her eyes away. "He knows where we are, doesn't he?"

Molly nodded, but she held on to Tabitha's face. "I had to tell him. That's what the judge said. But no more half-the-summer visits. No—"

Tabitha shook her head slightly. "He never...He never made me...go there before."

It was Molly's turn to shake her head. "And he never will again, honey. You'll be eighteen. He can't make you go then. So, no more summers. And if he wants to visit you—"

A bitter laugh burst from Tabitha. "You mean take me to McDonald's." *Five times in eleven years. Five times. Five lunches. They don't even have a McDonald's in this town—I hope.*

"If he wants to visit you," Molly continued, "he'll have to come out here."

"To Sticksville."

Molly nodded again. "Uh-huh, to the middle of nowhere. He'll have to come on his own."

Tabitha took a deep breath and met her mother's eyes. "Okay. But if he comes here," Tabitha squared her shoulders. "I'll be off, camping with my friends."

Molly smiled. "Then you'd better hurry up and make some."

Tabitha nodded, but said nothing. Then Molly took her daughter by the hand and led her into their new home.

Tabitha shoved a bite of canned ravioli into her mouth. She continued to pore through the business sections of the two small phone books on the dining table—one for Blue Beech Ridge and one for Poplar Bluff.

She growled. "I can't believe *nobody* has pizza around here. Talk about Sticksville!"

"No pizza? Now that is a hardship!"

Tabitha looked up from both sets of yellow pages to see if her mother was joking. However, Tabitha could find no hint of mockery in Molly's expression.

"Now that you mention it," Molly said, "I could've sworn there was a Pizza Hut in Poplar Bluff."

"Pizza Hut?" Tabitha flipped through one of the phone books. "Oh, yeah. You're right. Still, not great pizza."

Molly shrugged. "Not like Shakey's. Now that was pizza! But they have an A&W in Poplar Bluff. And a Burger Chef in Blue Beech Ridge."

Tabitha scowled at her mother. "Mom."

Molly scooped up a ravioli with her spoon. "I know about you and . . . burgers, honey, but at least it's not McDonald's."

I hate McDonald's. I hate it! Tabitha growled and turned her withering scowl on the bowl of defenseless, meat-stuffed pasta in front of her, as if daring the bland comfort food to challenge her.

18

The ravioli, seemingly unaware of Tabitha's mounting ire, said nothing. Tabitha hacked a few pieces in half with her spoon.

I hate McDonald's!

Her mother laid a hand on the phone book. "Ice cream, Tabby-Cat, not just burgers. A&W has *ice cream*. And root beer."

Tabitha nodded, still focused on the pasta mayhem sitting in its own gory sauce. "Ice cream...is good."

"Tell you what—after we wash up, we'll jump in the car and head into Poplar Bluff for a couple of root beer floats. It's only ten miles each way. Won't take us that long."

A flicker of a smile played at the corners of Tabitha's mouth. With her head still bowed, she looked at her mother from under her eyebrows. "Do you think...you could talk them into making us...root beer milkshakes? I definitely feel a SNORBS coming on."

Molly raised an eyebrow. "Snorbs?"

Tabitha nodded. "Uh-huh. SNORBS. Severe Need Of Root Beer Shake."

Molly's face split in a grin. "Little drive-in like that? You betcha!"

Tabitha smiled, closed both phone books, then quickly devoured the dismembered remains of her dinner. She pushed back from the table and gathered up all the dishes.

However, as she turned and walked into the kitchen, she froze. Her gaze flitted between the mustard-colored porcelain sink and the brand-new, yellow dishwasher under the sunny Formica counter. "Uh, Mom? How do you work the dishwasher?"

Molly chuckled. "I don't know. Is there a manual? Look in the drawer next to the stove. I thought I saw something in there."

Tabitha heard her mother's chair scrape across the linoleum. "Oh, never mind," Molly said. "That'll take too long to figure out tonight. Just put the dishes in the sink, fill 'em up with water, and we'll vamoose. I'm feeling a...SNORBS coming on myself!"

Tabitha did as she was asked, running water into the dishes without really looking at them. Instead, she gazed around the kitchen in mild wonder. *Never had a dishwasher before. And everything is new—new fridge, new oven. From the outside, this place looks . . . quaint. But inside, everything is ultramodern.*

"Mom," she said. "Did you get a huge raise with this new job?"

Her mother snorted. "It's a community college, and creative writing professors never get paid a lot anywhere."

Tabitha looked around in vain for a dishtowel. *Guess they're not unpacked yet.* She dried her hands on her long skirt, then gestured around the cottage with its all-modern features. "How did we afford this?"

Molly smiled mysteriously and tapped the side of her nose in an all-too-familiar gesture. "If you only knew..."

Tabitha rolled her eyes and threw her hands up in the air. "You *always* do that! I *hate* when you do that."

Molly chuckled and grinned widely. "It was a *steal*, I tell you! I couldn't believe my luck. Every time I seemed to hesitate about buying the place, the seller kept lowering his price. And as you can see—he put in all-new...*everything*. He must've been desperate to sell."

"But why?"

Molly made a sweeping gesture around the room. "This place—this little valley here? It's called White Lady Hollow. Apparently, it has quite a sordid history." Molly put a finger to her lips and looked around as if checking for eavesdroppers. She leaned in, grinning in fierce delight.

"And it's *haunted*."

"Okay, so it isn't the *cottage* that's supposed to be haunted." Her mom's hands gripped the steering wheel firmly, but she seemed a bit more relaxed than she normally would've been when driving on a dark highway. Molly was in full "storytelling-mode," and Tabitha knew how much her mother loved a good ghost story. "No, not the house," Molly continued. "It's too new—maybe fifty years old or so. It's the Hollow. *Hollow*—ooh, doesn't that word just sound spooky all by itself?" Molly flashed her daughter a huge grin, rendered slightly macabre by the dashboard light.

Tabitha nodded, grinning right back. "Yeah! Like Sleepy Hollow." She loved ghost stories as much as her mother did.

They cruised down the two-lane highway toward Poplar Bluff, A&W, and the promised ice cream. The sun had set, and the deepening shadows of twilight were closing in. Tabitha scanned the trees on either side of the road. *If only their branches would reach over the road...that'd make this road really spooky.*

"Anyway," Molly said, obviously warming to her subject. "Back during the eighteen-forties, just after the Saints were driven out of Missouri, there was a woman called White Lettie who lived alone in the Hollow. People 'round here thought she was a witch."

"'White...Lettie?'" Tabitha asked. "I thought you said it was 'White *Lady* Hollow.'"

Molly shrugged. "You know, I'm not exactly sure. I think I've actually heard it pronounced both ways. You know how folks around here say things a little... *differently*."

Tabitha snorted and rolled her eyes. "*Vai*-enna. New *Mad*-rid. I mean, come on! Why name towns after famous European cities like Vienna and Madrid and then pronounce them like that?"

Her mom gave a look of mock severity. "You call the capital of France Paris, when you know darn well it's pronounced 'Paree.' It's not that different. So, lighten up, Tabby-Cat." Molly sighed. Then she smiled eagerly. "Anyway...about the Hollow."

THE WITCH OF WHITE LADY HOLLOW ~

"Okay-okay-okay." Tabitha spun her hands to encourage her mother to get on with the story. "What about the Hollow?"

"So, White Lettie lived out there by herself. She was a folk-healer. People would come from Blue Beech Ridge so she could fix them up. They even brought sick animals sometimes."

"Why did they call her *White* Lettie?"

"Because she was an albino. You know—"

"I know what an albino is. White skin, white hair, pink eyes, right? No pigmentation?"

Molly nodded. "Yep. But Lettie wasn't simply albino—she was also a mute. She couldn't speak. Not a deaf-mute. She could hear just fine. And folks around here thought she was a witch."

"So, *was* she a witch?"

"No!" Molly shook her head and glanced at Tabitha askance. "Like I said, she was a folk-healer, maybe an herbalist. People came to her, but they were afraid of her too, probably because of the way she looked. Because she was different."

"Why did she live out there alone?"

"Nobody knows for sure—at least according to the history professor I met when I interviewed out here. Some say she ran away from a husband who beat her. Maybe she simply liked being alone. Maybe she simply liked the quiet."

It's quiet in the Hollow, all right. It's deserted and spooky. Which is also very cool.

"Anyway," Molly continued. "Lettie stumbled into town one day. She was pregnant, in hard labor, and unable to deliver the child by herself. Nobody in the town had known about her pregnancy. How a woman in labor made it the five miles into Blue Beech Ridge… Well, it was incredible. One of the ladies in town found her and helped her turn the child—helped her deliver it."

"Was the baby okay?"

"Yes. It was a boy. Healthy, in spite of Lettie's ordeal. Not an albino. Not a mute either. Very normal, except he had a bump on his right ear." Molly paused, as if for dramatic effect. But she didn't go on.

Tabitha turned to her mother. "A bump. On his ear. So what?"

"Well, the mayor of the town, a fellow named Elias—Oh, what was the name? Tiba-something." Molly snapped her fingers before quickly returning her hand to the steering wheel. "Thibodeaux! That's it—Elias Thibodeaux."

"So?"

"Well, old Elias became obsessed with Lettie. He made any excuse to visit the Hollow. And when Lettie spurned his advances…"

No! Tabitha wrapped her arms around herself and emotionally, drew in. *Not that. Please. I don't want to hear the rest of this story.*

Molly seemed unaware of Tabitha's distress. "Elias raped her. It was Elias's child. Everybody could see that. The boy had that same bump on his ear. Like Elias. Like Elias's father before him. And so did some of the other boys in town—none of the girls—must be a male thing—but even some of the girls had the signature Thibodeaux red hair. It seems the good mayor, a married man himself, was quite the Don Juan of Blue—"

Tabitha moaned.

Molly caught her breath. "Oh, honey, I'm sorry. I shouldn't have—"

Tabitha closed her eyes tight. *Just stop talking. Please stop talking.*

Molly turned her eyes back to the dark road and drove in silence for a while as the last of the twilight bled from the sky. Faded colors leeched away to blackness.

The silence stretched on like the dark highway. But Tabitha knew it wouldn't last. Her mother didn't do well with silence. Molly had never done well with emptiness of any kind, even an emptiness of sound.

So, Molly began to hum. She filled the awkward silence with her favorite tune, the "go-to" song she whistled or hummed or sang whenever she was out of words.

Tabitha groaned. *No! Not "Moonshadow!" I hate that stupid* song! "Mom!"

Molly stopped humming and looked at her daughter. "What, honey?"

"What happened to White Lettie?" *Anything to keep you from humming that song.*

"They lynched her."

Tabitha stared at her mother in shock. "They *hanged* her? For what? For getting raped?"

Molly shook her head. "No. They said she bewitched Elias. Not just seduced him—*bewitched* him. That, combined with her appearance, her skill with herbs, her inability to speak… She was simply *different*. They accused her of being a witch. And they hanged her."

"That's awful!"

"Yeah." Molly lapsed into silence again.

Up ahead, lights glowed in the darkness. Molly pointed off to the left. "That's where we'll be going to church."

The chapel was tiny, definitely the smallest Tabitha had ever seen for a Latter-day Saint chapel. "We have to come here? Not Blue Beech Ridge?"

"Uh-huh. The Poplar Bluff Branch. It's just a tiny branch, but it includes Blue Beech Ridge."

"How many kids my age?"

"When I attended here a couple of Sundays back in June, I only counted two girls your age. I think there was only one boy your age—one priest."

One priest-age boy? "So much for dating," Tabitha muttered.

"I'm sure there are some nice boys at the high school," her mom said. "Nice Christian boys who have our same standards."

Tabitha gave her a disgusted look. "Mom, *nobody* has our standards. They *say* they do, but…"

"You didn't used to be so picky. What about that nice Tommy Mariucci back ho— back in Maryland?"

"I broke up with him, Mom." Tabitha scowled. "Or didn't you notice?"

"I know you broke up with him when we moved—"

"I broke up with Tommy before that."

Molly shrugged. "I liked him."

"I liked him too, until he tried to put his hand up my skirt."

Molly tapped the brake and almost swerved the car. "He did what?!"

Tabitha wrapped her arms around herself. "You heard me."

Molly pulled the car over to the shoulder of the road. She put the vehicle in Park and turned toward Tabitha. "Honey, why didn't you tell me?"

Tabitha fought back tears. *I will not cry! Not over Tommy.* "Because...I handled it. That's all. Nothing happened. I...didn't let it happen." *Tommy, why? Why did you do that? You knew what my standards were. You knew who I was—who I am. Why did you have to ruin everything?*

Molly put a hand on her daughter's shoulder.

Tabitha flinched.

But Molly kept her hand on Tabitha's shoulder. "I'm sorry, honey. I...Tabby-Cat, is...is that what happened...with...with your dad?"

Tabitha jerked away from her mother's touch. "I told you, Mom! How many times do I have to tell you? He...Dad didn't touch me. Nobody touched me."

Molly nodded quickly. "Okay, honey. I believe you. But something happened. I wish you'd tell—"

"I don't want to talk about it!" Tabitha squeezed her arms more tightly around her chest. *Not now. Not ever. Not to you. Never to you. You sent me there. You made me go.*

It's not her fault, said a small voice inside her. *She had to let you go. She had no choice. You know that.*

I don't care!

Without another word, Molly put the car in gear, signaled, and pulled back out on the highway. They rode the rest of the way to the A&W in awkward silence.

Molly didn't even hum.

Molly took a long draw on her milkshake. "This is so-o-o good. How's yours?"

The Chevy's headlights provided the sole illumination as they drove back toward the Hollow. No stars were visible through the overcast sky. However, Tabitha could discern the ghostly hint of a full moon behind the clouds.

Tabitha swallowed her own mouthful of rootbeer-flavored milkshake. She licked her lips contentedly. "Really good. SNORBS completely satisfied." She paused. "You...really came through."

A sad smile lifted the corners of Molly's mouth. "Every once in a while."

Tabitha took another small sip of her shake. She wanted to make it last all the way home. At the same time, she didn't want it to completely melt.

I should say I'm sorry.

But she just couldn't. The feelings were still too raw, too close to the surface—too ready to leak out of her eyes again. She couldn't apologize, but she could do the next best thing. She could change the subject to something safe—something they shared. Something that didn't make Tabitha's insides ache.

"So, is it Lettie's ghost that's supposed to haunt the Hollow?"

Her mother smiled, and Tabitha knew Molly had caught the unspoken non-apology-apology. "You'd think that'd be it, wouldn't you? A woman wrongfully accused of witchcraft and lynched by an angry mob? But, no. When I asked the old fellow who sold us the house, he said, 'Just ghosts. Sometimes folks say they've seen 'em dancin' by the light of the full moon.'" Molly grinned wickedly. "A full moon"—she raised the pitch and volume of her voice, warbling like a banshee—"like we have tonight!"

Mother and daughter laughed. It was a small laugh, but it did the trick, relieving the tension between them like water spilling over a breached dam.

Tabitha gazed out the window at the blackness. "Do you think they have something like 'Midnight Chiller Theater' or 'Elvira, Mistress of the Dark' around here?"

Molly sighed. "I hope so. It would be nice—just like the old days. We could stay up late on Saturday nights, make popcorn, watch *The Bride of Frankenstein*, and huddle under a blanket."

Tabitha chuckled. "And laugh and scream like idiots!" *Yeah. I'd love that. Just like the old days.*

Before this summer.

"Okay," Molly said. "I think we're getting close. And I don't want to miss the turn. Help me watch for the turn-off. And watch out for animals. I don't want to hit a dog or an opossum or something."

"Roger, Dodger! No possums!" Tabitha stared out the windshield, scanning for the elusive turn-off. But she could see nothing but the deserted road and the ever-present trees lining it. "Don't they believe in streetlights around here?"

"It's a country road, Tabby-Cat. No lights out this—" Molly let out a yelp and slammed on the brakes. The car swerved and skidded to a stop. "Did you see that?"

"Mom!" Tabitha yelled, startled and frightened. "What was it? An animal?"

Molly lifted a hand off the steering wheel and pointed straight ahead with a shaking finger. Her mouth hung open, and she appeared genuinely terrified. "Look!"

Tabitha looked.

A white figure, vaguely human—head, arms, long torso—no legs that Tabitha could see—floated up ahead, just to the right of the road. As Tabitha stared in mounting terror at the spectral shape, a second and a third white figure appeared. One of them lifted a white arm and pointed toward the car, toward Tabitha and her mom.

Then the ghostly shapes appeared to link hands, levitated into the air, and vanished into the night.

3

"Where the *hell* did I put that gun?" Molly stomped over to yet another moving-box and savagely ripped it open. She rifled through the contents, tossing items everywhere onto the sofa, the coffee table, on top of other boxes, as she conducted her frantic search. She looked up frequently to peer out each window, into the blackness outside.

Huddled under a blanket, sitting on the sofa next to a pile of varied, tossed-aside belongings, Tabitha eyed her mother. Fear gnawed at her like a rat eating its way out of her gut. She had never—not once in her entire life—heard her mother swear. And on top of the terror over the phantoms, Tabitha didn't know which frightened her more—the swearing or the revelation that her mom owned a firearm. "I didn't know you even had a gun."

"Of course, you didn't," Molly snapped. She paused her anxious search and gazed at her daughter. Misery and fear were plainly written in Molly's dark eyes. "I'm sorry. That was uncalled for. I got it when your dad…when he took you this summer."

Tabitha stared at her mother in shock. "You were gonna shoot Dad?"

Molly's jaw dropped, and she shook her head quickly. "No! No, honey! I just... It seemed like a good idea at the time—you know—in case . . ." Molly looked around the room, anywhere but at Tabitha. She wrung her hands. "I was just worried he would take you…and run."

Molly wove between the boxes, rushing toward the sofa. Throwing her arms around Tabitha, Molly said, "I just felt so—so powerless! I wanted to feel like…I had some control, like I could…protect my little girl."

Tabitha loosed an arm from the folds of the blanket and awkwardly patted her mother's back. "It's okay, Mom. You said we're going to be okay."

Molly nodded. Then she bolted upright and snapped her fingers. "Underwear!" She scrambled toward her bedroom door and disappeared inside.

Tabitha gaped at the bedroom doorway for a moment, then found herself hurriedly looking out each window—searching for white shapes floating outside.

"Found it!" Molly emerged from the bedroom, waving a dark, metal object in triumph. "It was in my underwear box!"

The newly found gun was a semiautomatic with a short barrel, the kind used in cop shows—usually by the bad guys—rather than the long-barreled six-shooters from the cowboy movies. "Mom! Be careful!" Tabitha was already terrified out of her gourd. Seeing her crazed mother waving a loaded pistol around freaked her out all the more.

Her mom chuckled nervously as she carefully lowered the weapon. "It's okay." She pointed at the gun with her left index finger. "My finger's not on the trigger. See?" She shrugged. "Sorry I scared you, Tabby-Cat."

Tabitha made a sour face. "Sure." She glanced out one of the windows. *Ghosts outside, and a lunatic, gun-toting Mom inside.* "That thing's not going to work against ghosts, you know."

Molly went to the closest window. She kept the gun lowered as she stared out into the night. She appeared calmer at the moment. "They're not ghosts." Molly sounded sure of herself, resolute. She shook her head. "No such thing as ghosts—except in stories."

Tabitha stared at her mom, still trying to process the idea of Molly owning a firearm. *I could've sworn Mom hated guns. But she does look like she feels in control.*

Molly cupped a hand beside her mouth and shouted at the closed window. "You hear that? I'm armed and I'm not afraid of you! So, just go away if you know what's good for you!" She then proceeded to move from window to window—some more than once—and shouted a variation of, "I've got a gun and I'm not scared!"

But Tabitha observed a tremor in the hand holding the weapon. *She's still scared. Still scared, but…she's standing between me and the darkness—between me and… whatever's out there.* A fountain of warm affection and grudging admiration welled up in Tabitha, threatening to leak from her eyes. *Protecting me.*

Molly came away from the window and sat next to Tabitha on the sofa. "Not ghosts. Probably just—I don't know—men in white sheets." She let out a shuddering breath. "Probably just a KKK rally or something. This is the South…sort of. They have the Klan around here, don't they?"

Tabitha shook her head slowly. "Those things—whatever they were—Mom, they *flew*. We both saw it. Then they vanished. Maybe they just disappeared into the trees, but we saw them *flying*."

Her mom shrugged. "We don't know what we saw. It was dark. It could've been a trick of the light."

Tabitha leaned closer to her mother, seeking safety and comfort. *Even if you are nuts.* "I don't know. Maybe." But Tabitha didn't believe her mom's explanation. Not for a New York minute.

Molly laid the gun on the coffee table, then put an arm around Tabitha. "Men in white sheets," Molly said. "That's the most likely explanation. Occam's Razor—

simplest explanation is the most likely."

Doesn't explain the flying, Tabitha thought. "I don't think the KKK is big around here."

"That doesn't mean—"

A scream from outside cut her off, and both mother and daughter jumped. Molly snatched the gun from the coffee table, thumbed a sliding switch on the side forward, and lumbered toward the window.

A cold sweat broke out on Tabitha's skin, and she shivered. "What was—"

"I've got a gun!" Molly yelled. "I'm not—"

The screech was repeated, followed by an answering cry—softer, farther away.

Molly began to laugh—a sound of welcome relief. She lowered the weapon, sliding back the switch on the side. She placed a hand to her heart and patted it. "Just an owl. A blasted screech owl."

Tabitha let out a breath she didn't know she'd been holding. "Just an owl? An *owl*? How cool is that?" She laughed along with her mom, a soft hooting echoing in the trees.

An owl. Well, we certainly didn't have those in Suitland!

Her mom laid the pistol on the coffee table again and flopped down on the sofa beside Tabitha. Molly put her arms around her daughter. "Just an owl. Scared the living snot outta me, though!"

Tabitha snuggled closer to her mom and grinned. "Me too." She stared at the gun on the coffee table. "Do you even know how to shoot that thing?"

Her mom pulled Tabitha close. "Sure, I do. Your grandpa was a cop. He taught me to shoot when I was ten."

"But you hate guns," Tabitha reiterated. "I thought you said a gun killed grandpa."

Molly shook her head. "No, honey. A horrible man, a pimp named Big Jim Jolly, killed my daddy. He shot him…in the head…when Daddy was trying to rescue one of Big Jim's girls." She sighed. "No, it wasn't a gun—it was an evil man—a creep who sold women for his own profit. He sold those girls like slaves."

Tabitha looked at one of the windows…and saw nothing but a reflection of the box-strewn living room. She glared at the curtain-less windows, wishing they had a way to block out the unknown terrors of the night. "But those women…those prostitutes—they sold *themselves*."

"Oh, Tabby-Cat. It's never that simple. Even if they start off that way—and most of them don't—a man like Big Jim finds them on the street, hungry and alone. He sweet-talks them, tells them he loves them. Then he says, 'Hey, baby, if you love me, you'll do this for me.' And if they don't, he beats the crap out of them—but never on the face, never anyplace that'll show."

Tabitha felt sick.

Her mom continued, "He gets them addicted to heroin, then sends them out to hook for him. And then he takes all their money. And after a couple of years, when they're all used up, they die. Those girls are no more than slaves and cattle to bast—

to men like that."

Molly paused as if thinking something over. "The cops got Big Jim…eventually. He got the chair. But your grandpa? My daddy was a hero."

My grandpa—hero cop. "Mom?"

"Yes, honey?"

"When Dad left us, when he…went away…and you divorced him . . ." Tabitha hesitated. She'd asked this question a number of times before, but her mom seemed to never give her a straight answer.

"What, Tabby-Cat?"

Tabitha sensed her mother already knew what she was going to ask. *Maybe this time.* "When you changed our last names. Why didn't you…?"

"Why didn't I change it back to my maiden name? Cloyce? Your grandpa's name? Why Moonshadow of all things?"

"Uh-huh?"

Molly sighed. "I suppose I was still mad at him. I was still mad at my daddy for dying and going away. For leaving me. It wasn't his fault, but well, I was just mad. Mad at him. Mad at your father. Mad at all men." Molly chuckled. "Yeah, well…I picked a new name—a *hippie* name." She shrugged. "Pretty stupid, huh?"

Like that dumb song! Tabitha shrugged as well. "Yeah. Pretty stupid." She looked up at her mother and frowned. "You do know how much teasing I've gotten all my life, don't you?"

Molly chuckled again, hugged her daughter more tightly, but didn't look at her. She kept staring out one window or another. "You and me both, kiddo."

"Yeah, well," Tabitha said, "maybe Molly Moonshadow sounds like a hippie name. But *Tabitha* Moonshadow? Let's just say, every Halloween, all the kids expected me to dress up like a witch."

Her mom smiled. And that time, she did look at Tabitha. "You want to know something funny?"

Tabitha sighed, melting into her mother's embrace. "Yeah. I could use a good laugh right now."

"Well, maybe not *funny*-funny, but…ironic. You remember all that genealogy I did a couple years back?"

"You mean when you were dragging me off to look at old microfilm in some dusty library, and I was bored out of my freaking mind?"

Molly nodded. "Yep. That's it. Well, get this—I found out we're descended from an actual witch."

Tabitha sat up at that. "Really?"

"Uh-huh. One of the Salem witches. Sarah Towne Cloyce."

"Wow." *Now that's cool.* "Did they hang her? Like White Lettie?"

"No. She and her two sisters were all arrested and charged with witchcraft. The *sisters* got hanged, but Sarah was eventually cleared. She spent the rest of her life trying to clear her sisters' names. They weren't exonerated until after Sarah's death, though. Still, it's an interesting story—part of our family history."

Tabitha scowled at her mom. "And you waited until now to tell me this? Something this cool?"

Molly gave her a dubious look. "You always hated genealogy!"

"But *witches*, Mom! The. Salem. Witches! That's just plain cool!" Tabitha hugged her mom. "Guess there's something cool about oldy-moldy microfilm after all."

A grin curled Molly's lips. All the weariness and fear of the evening seemed to melt away in the warmth of that grin. The ghosts weren't forgotten—they just seemed to have no place in the safety of her mom's smile.

They sat, mother and daughter, snuggled on the couch for several minutes, sharing warmth, comfort, and a secret knowledge. Surrounded by the noises of the night—the soft hoot of an owl, the occasional calls of other night birds, and the fiddling of crickets—Tabitha and Molly Moonshadow slowly drifted off to sleep.

Molly woke with a start. The room was still brightly lit—she hadn't bothered to turn off the lights. She looked around the living room, trying to clear the cobwebs from her brain. Nothing seemed obviously amiss, but she felt something was wrong.

And then she heard it—the sound that had awoken her—an irregular, dull thumping.

"Do you hear that?" she asked. "Tabitha? Do you—"

And she realized what was wrong. Her daughter was no longer beside her on the couch. She was nowhere to be seen.

"Tabitha? Tabitha!" *Where is she? Please, God, where is she?*

Molly snatched up the gun, thumbing off the safety. "Tabitha!"

The only response was the continued arhythmic thumping. It was coming from the bathroom.

Molly hurried to the bathroom door. The thumping was definitely louder there. And with each thump, the door shook. "Tabitha?"

No answer.

Molly tried the doorknob. *Locked!*

As Molly fought to control her panic, images of her daughter being assaulted behind that door—fighting for her life—filled Molly's mind.

She pounded on the door. "Tabitha!"

The thumping ceased.

"M-Mom?"

A shudder of relief shook Molly from head to toe. In that instant, she was grateful her daddy had taught her how to hold a loaded gun—with her index finger down the barrel, not on the trigger. *I could've shot my blasted foot off. Or shot Tabitha.*

"Honey?" Molly called through the door. "Are you okay?"

She heard sounds of movement from inside the bathroom.

"Uh, yeah," Tabitha replied. "I'm fine."

Molly took a deep breath to calm her voice. "Tabby-Cat, can you unlock the door please?"

"S-sure."

The bathroom door opened to reveal her daughter, looking disheveled, her hair mussed, as if Tabitha had just woken up.

Molly pushed the door all the way open, still holding the gun—her trigger finger still safely pointed down the barrel—and glanced around the bathroom.

Nobody else was hiding in there. Her daughter was alone. Exhaling in relief, Molly lowered the weapon, toggling the safety on once more. "Are you okay?"

Tabitha ran her fingers through her long black hair, a sure sign she was upset. "Yeah. I'm...I'm fine."

Molly glanced around the bathroom again, noticing for the first time a crumpled blanket lying on the floor.

"Honey?" Molly tried to catch her daughter's dark eyes, but Tabitha kept her gaze on the floor. "Were you sleeping in here? In the bathroom?"

Tabitha bit her lip. "I guess."

"Why were you sleeping in the bathroom?"

Tabitha said nothing and kept fiddling with her hair.

"Tabitha," Molly repeated with just a touch more firmness, "why were you sleeping in the bathroom?"

Her daughter shrugged. "I was scared." Tears spilled from Tabitha's eyes. "Mom?" Tabitha threw herself into Molly's arms.

Molly clasped her daughter to her breast, carefully holding the secured gun behind Tabitha's back.

Sobs shook Tabitha's thin body.

Sleeping in a locked bathroom. Because she was scared. Nightmare. She must've been kicking the door in her sleep.

Fighting to remain calm, Molly smoothed her daughter's hair. *What in the world happened at Jerry's house? What did that man do to her? I've asked and asked. But she won't talk about it. And if I push her too hard . . .*

Molly took a deep, cleansing breath. Then she took another. *This can't go on. It can't.* "Tabitha, honey. Tabby-Cat. What happened at your dad's?"

"Nothing." The response was immediate, like a defensive reflex.

"Honey," Molly spoke slowly, forcing a calm that belied the growing knot of sick horror in her gut. "I know that's not true. You've never lied to me. But something happened."

"Nobody touched me."

There it is again—that mantra of defense. A wall she's built to hide behind.

"Okay," Molly said, stroking Tabitha's hair. "I believe you. I do. Nobody touched you. But something happened. Something bad."

Tabitha sobbed, but said nothing.

"You know, Tabby-Cat, there are many, many kinds of abuse. Many ways to hurt someone. It doesn't all have to be with fists or hands or . . . or other body parts. It can be with words, ideas, neglect." She paused, biting her lower lip. *Please, Tabitha. Please tell me.* "Something scared you. Something hurt you. Something or someone. Honey, was it your father?"

Tabitha froze, shuddered, and let out a long, sobbing breath.

"You can tell me, honey. I'll believe you. I promise I will. And whatever it was it wasn't your fault."

It wasn't my fault either. I had to let her go with him. I had no choice. Keep saying that, Molly. Maybe if you say it enough times, you'll start to believe it. "Was it your father?"

Tabitha slowly shook her head.

"Okay. Was it someone else?"

Tabitha hesitated, then nodded. The movement was so timid, so slight, it was almost imperceptible.

"Was it . . ." *Oh, what is that horrid man's name? Chuck? Charlie?*

"Randy." Tabitha shuddered again, more violently than before. "It was Randy."

So, Jerry's got a new one. "But Randy didn't touch you?"

Tabitha shook her head. "Not . . . really."

"Randy—that's a man, right?"

Tabitha nodded slightly. "But he likes to dress like a . . ."

Oh, my. "He dresses in drag? This Randy is a drag queen?"

Tabitha nodded again.

Anger, disgust, and an ancient pain she thought long dead twisted Molly's gut. "You said he, Randy, didn't touch you. But you said, 'Not really.'"

Tabitha shrugged, and Molly felt Tabitha's renewed ragged breathing. *She's crying again.* "Honey, tell me what happened."

Tabitha squeezed Molly tight. "He…He came home one night, all dressed up. He was…He was drunk. He unlocked my bedroom door." She trembled. "I locked it! I know I did!"

Cold dread seized Molly's spine as she stroked her daughter's hair again. "I believe you, Tabby-Cat. I do."

"He got into bed with me..."

Oh, no! Heavenly Father, please, no! Not that!

Tabitha trembled. "It woke me up. I jumped out of bed. I-I ran to the bathroom. Locked the door. But he p-p-pounded on the door. I was scared he was gonna break it down. He called me…He said terrible things. Dirty things. I had to h-hold the door closed. All night." Her voice became suddenly very quiet. "Every night."

Molly forced herself to be composed, to keep the magma of rage and the glacier of hatred out of her voice. "Did you tell your father?"

Tabitha nodded. And that nod was emphatic. "He laughed at me, called me a *liar*." Her thin body shook with anger. "I'm not a liar! I *never* lie! I. Don't. Lie!"

Molly's heart shattered, and tears spilled from her eyes. "Oh, honey. Oh, honey. I'm so, so sorry."

Tabitha barked out a bitter laugh. "Dad said I could go ahead and sleep in the bathroom—with my foot against the door—if I wanted to."

"I'm so sorry, honey." *Jerry, you bastard. How could you?*

"I hate him." Tabitha's body stiffened. "I hate him! I *hate* him!"

BOOM!

The whole cottage shook as if with an explosion, and Molly yelped in surprise and terror. The very air seemed heavy with suppressed energy.

BOOM! BOOM! BOOM!

Mother and daughter shrieked and jumped apart. They stood trembling.

Tabitha's eyes were wide with terror. "They're here!"

The pounding—some of it, at least seemed to have come from the front door.

From where they stood, Molly could barely see the front door. With a trembling thumb, Molly toggled off the gun's safety. She pointed the weapon at the front door and took a step toward it. She forced her hands to stop shaking—at least enough to shoot if necessary.

"I-I've got a gun! Go away!"

But the booming noise had ceased. The night sounds of birds and crickets had ceased as well, as if the thunderous cacophony had startled the whole world into silence.

The only sounds were Molly and Tabitha's rapid breathing.

Molly waited a moment, repeated her warning, and listened.

The night answered with silence.

Molly glanced quickly around the living room. All the windows were still closed. None were broken. *What was that?*

Keeping the gun aimed in the general direction of the front door, Molly looked over her shoulder at her daughter. "Are you okay, honey?"

Looking anything but "okay," Tabitha nodded quickly.

Molly saw something out of the corner of her eye—something that struck her as wrong, out of place—but she couldn't put her finger on what it was.

She focused again on the front door.

Still nothing.

But the feeling of *wrongness* persisted, like a snake writhing at the back of her brain.

Tabitha came to stand behind Molly.

"It's okay," Molly said. "An earthquake. Believe it or not, they get earthquakes around here." But it didn't feel like an earthquake. More like explosions. *Kids setting off cherry bombs, maybe?*

Molly glanced back toward Tabitha to show her daughter what she hoped was a reassuring smile.

And then she saw it—she knew what was wrong.

The bathroom door—it was closed.

I didn't close it. Tabitha's not near enough to close it. But the bathroom door was closed.

Did one of those booms come from the bathroom?

With her left hand, Molly pulled her daughter behind her as she turned toward the bathroom.

"Mom?" Tabitha sounded as frightened as Molly felt.

Molly aimed her weapon at the closed bathroom door. Chest high. Just as her father had taught her. *Aim for the chest.* "You!" she cried. "You in the bathroom! Come out. Come out with your hands up."

Silence.

How'd someone get in there? Couldn't get through the window—too small.

Molly took a cautious step toward the bathroom. Her trembling hand turned the doorknob and shoved the door open. She stepped back quickly and pointed her gun into the open doorway.

Empty.

Cautiously, she edged closer. But the bathroom was vacant. The only thing that didn't belong in there was Tabitha's crumpled blanket.

She checked the small bathroom window. *Closed. No wind.* "Tabitha, did you close that door?"

"Not me!" Tabitha sounded terrified. "Who closed the door? Mom, what's going on?"

"You've got to be kidding me," Tabitha muttered, just loud enough for her mom to hear. Standing in the short hallway, just outside the double-doors of the Poplar Bluff chapel, Tabitha inclined her head toward Molly. "This place is *tiny*." *There's maybe room for eighty people here. And all on folding chairs!*

She clutched her scripture case in one hand and locked her other hand in a death-grip on the strap of her shoulder bag. She scanned the small linoleum-floored room as if she expected a redneck mugger to spring out from behind the undersized sacrament table or the ancient upright piano.

Molly squeezed Tabitha's arm a little harder than necessary, as if to say, *Mind your manners, Tabby-Cat*. What Molly actually said was, "Told you—it's a small branch. Let's try to make a good first impression, shall we?"

Tabitha forced a smile she hoped looked genuine. *I'm an actress. I can do this. I can fake it, at least.*

But it's so small. So ridiculously small. And just one priest. Just one boy of dating-age. Maybe he'll be cute. Please, Heavenly Father, let him be cute. And nice. And intelligent. And not a creep. Please?

"Welcome, ladies!"

The voice came from behind them—a deep, rich baritone, slightly accented, but pleasant enough. Tabitha jerked her arm out of her mother's grasp and spun around.

The owner of the pleasant voice *was* cute—black hair, blue eyes, chiseled jaw, gorgeous smile—and about a decade too old. He turned his bright smile on her mom, then extended a hand. "Sister . . . Moonshadow, isn't it? We met back in June."

Molly grasped the cute guy's hand and shook it. "Molly. Molly Moonshadow."

Tabitha glanced up at her mom, noting her mother's wide grin. *Easy, Mom. Too young for you.* Then she snuck a glance at the guy's left hand. *Not taken, though. Maybe not too old...*

Dream on, girl.

The blue-eyed stranger cocked his head, still grinning. "Moonshadow. Not a name I'm gonna forget easily. I'll try to remember *Molly*, though. Nice flow to that— Molly Moonshadow. Just trips off the tongue, doesn't it?"

Her mother flushed crimson.

She's blushing? He's not that—

"And is this your lovely daughter?"

Tabitha found herself staring up into the handsome face with the chiseled jaw and the disarming smile. And she suddenly found herself completely incapable of forming coherent words, much less sentences.

She opened her mouth once, twice, but couldn't force anything past her gaping lips.

"I'm Brother Kilmore." He thrust his huge hand into hers. His grip was firm, strong, but not hard—the perfect missionary handshake. He seemed to flinch, then tilted his head slightly and raised one eyebrow, regarding Tabitha as if in surprise or curiosity. "You feel that? It's like…static electricity or something." He winked. "That's quite a handshake you've got there, young lady!"

Tabitha grinned like the proverbial village idiot.

Then she giggled.

Giggling? Say something! He's gonna think I'm a space cadet. Say something!

But all she could do was smile brainlessly and continue to shake hands.

Say something! Anything!

"This is my daughter, Tabitha."

Thank you, Mom!

The disarming smile broadened, and the blue eyes twinkled with a mischievous light. "Tabitha," he said. "Tabitha Moonshadow. Almost like…"

Don't say it. Please don't say it!

Cute, single, maybe-not-too-old Brother Kilmore cocked his head again. "Almost like that old TV show. Bewitched, right?"

No! Let me just die. Please, linoleum floor, just open up and swallow me.

All Tabitha could do was try to keep some semblance of a smile pasted on her face.

"Actually," Molly said, "the name is Biblical."

The twinkling eyes shifted away, toward Tabitha's mother. "Really?"

And Tabitha realized she was still holding the man's hand—holding it with a palm, slick with sweat.

She pulled her hand free and surreptitiously rubbed it on her long skirt.

"Yes," Molly continued, "New Testament. Tabitha—whom the apostle Peter raised from the dead."

Brother Kilmore nodded. "Oh, yeah! Now I remember. Didn't she have another name?"

Oh, no! Not that! Not—

He snapped his fingers and grinned from ear to ear. "Dorcas! That was it! Such a funny soundin' name too, don't-ya think?"

Any surviving vestige of Tabitha's forced smile was swept away like a sandcastle before a tidal wave—a tidal wave named Dorcas. *Please, just let me die!*

Perhaps seeing the horror and devastation on Tabitha's face, Brother Kilmore's expression transformed completely. The grin and twinkle vanished, replaced by a look of genuine concern. "Oh, now, don't you fret yourself, girl!" He placed a hand on each of Tabitha's shoulders. "No, no, don't you trouble yourself. Your secret's safe with me." He looked Tabitha right in the eye. "Trust me, Tabitha."

Tabitha's breath caught in her throat. *His eyes—so blue.* She opened her mouth. She was going to say something, wasn't she? *I trust you. Was that it?*

He broke eye contact, and Tabitha remembered to breathe. The man leaned toward her and whispered in her ear. "Just between you, me, and the fencepost, *Seven Brides for Seven Brothers* is one of my favorites. And that Julie Newmar? Ooh, she was an absolute *fox* as Dorcas. And Catwoman too."

Tabitha finally found her voice. "Thank you."

Thank you? For what? For understanding? For being wonderful? And perfect? And single? And maybe, just maybe, not too old?

Brother Kilmore looked her in the eyes again, winked, and smiled. "Welcome to the branch, Sister Moonshadow."

He turned back to her mom and shook Molly's hand once more. "So'd you buy that place down in White Lady Hollow?"

Molly nodded. "Yes, I did."

"Pretty little place." His brows creased in concern. "You ladies had any trouble out there?"

Trouble? Tabitha tried to keep her expression neutral.

Her mom gave an utterly unconvincing smile. "Trouble? What kind of… trouble?"

The man searched her face. "We think it's just kids messing around. We heard about some bonfires out in the woods. You see anything?"

Molly and Tabitha glanced at each other with questioning, doubtful looks that seemed to say, *Should we tell him?*

Molly looked back to the handsome face, which showed both concern and a no-nonsense, businesslike hardness. Molly shrugged. "We saw something. I think it was just some owls. You have white owls around here, don't you?"

It wasn't owls. That wouldn't explain…everything.

Brother Kilmore's eye twitched slightly. "Owls? Yeah. White . . . ish." His smile reappeared, wiping the hardened look away as if it had never been there. "Well, if you see anything that concerns you, just call. Ya hear? Call me directly. You have my number."

Molly's smile returned as well, and she nodded. "I will."

He turned his radiant grin on Tabitha again. "Your mom's got my number. Call me if there's any trouble. Any trouble at all."

Call you? Mom's got your number? Why does Mom have your number? Am I . . . jealous?

But his eyes and his smile captivated her once more.

Maybe you'll be our home teacher. My home teacher.

Visions of handsome Brother Kilmore calling at the cottage filled her head—him standing, framed in the door—when her mom wasn't at home.

Why, yes, come in, Brother Kilmore.

He shook Tabitha's hand again, raising an eyebrow. "Quite a handshake! Welcome to the branch, Sister Moonshadow. Welcome to both y'all!"

And that broke the spell. *First "y'all" of the day!*

Maybe not so perfect after all.

But her eyes still followed the man as he turned and walked away.

"He's a counselor in the branch presidency," her mother whispered, "I can't remember which one—first or second."

Tabitha sighed as if she were a balloon deflating. *Definitely too old.*

"He's also a cop, a deputy sheriff." Molly's voice dropped even lower. "Quite a hunk too, isn't he? Oh, I love a man in uniform!"

Tabitha's jaw dropped, and she gave her mother a scandalized look. "Mom!"

Her mother shrugged and smiled, with a faraway look in her eyes. "Maybe he's *older* than he looks."

Or maybe younger. But if he's a cop, that might explain why she has his number.

"Ladies! Ladies! Lay-yay-yay-dees!" The loud, thickly accented voice made Tabitha jump.

She turned toward the source of the irritating sound.

The voice's owner was short—almost as short as Tabitha. His dark blonde hair was curly and looked as if either he'd deliberately oiled it or hadn't washed it in weeks. His eyes were blue, but Tabitha's own eyes were drawn to the huge, angry whitehead under one eyebrow. The pimple glared at Tabitha like a pustular third eye—an eye that might burst at any moment.

The boy's toothy grin—below a thin mustache—appeared feral, wolfish. *Fresh meat!* it said. "And what would you two *fine* ladies be doing here today?"

Please tell me this is not the priest! The only *priest?* Tabitha swallowed and attempted a weak smile. "Uh…going to church?"

"Well, of course, y'all are goin' to church! What else would y'all be doing?"

Tabitha choked down a nervous laugh. *Doesn't he remember he was the one who asked the question?*

He extended a hand toward Tabitha. "I'm Buster! I'm at PB High."

Tabitha looked down at the hand as if checking for fleas. *He is. He's the only boy of dating-age in this backwater branch.* Then she grasped the hand and attempted to turn her grimace of disgust into a pleasant smile. "I'm Tabitha." She pointed at Molly. "And this is my mom."

The blue eyes and the greenish-yellow zit turned toward her mom, but their owner didn't let go of Tabitha's hand.

Molly smiled sweetly. "Hi, Buster." She offered him her hand, and the boy took it, reluctantly. "I'm Sister Moonshadow."

He gawked at her. "Moonshadow? Moonshadow? No kidding."

"I remember you," Molly said. "You *passed* the sacrament last time I was here."

Tabitha almost gasped aloud. *Passed the sacrament? He's* not *the priest. He's younger.* She took another look at the fuzzy, too-thin mustache. *Maybe a lot younger. There's hope yet.*

The meaning of Molly's significant morsel of information wasn't lost on the boy. He appeared crestfallen for the space of a breath. He glanced at Tabitha with far less confidence than a moment before. "Yeah," Buster said. "I'm still a teacher." Then he grinned hopefully. "But I'll be sixteen in January! Then I'll be a priest."

Oh goodie. At least I'm safe 'til January.

"I already got my dang learner's permit." Buster leaned in closer and cupped his hand to his mouth as if he were going to whisper.

But he didn't lower his voice one decibel. "But my daddy's been letting me drive the tow truck 'round our salvage yard since I was eleven." He pointed at Brother Kilmore's back. "Just don't y'all go tellin' the fuzz."

Buster scrunched his eye into a conspiratorial wink. However, Tabitha's own wide eyes were transfixed by the straining-to-burst pustule above that wink.

It's gonna blow! It's gonna explode all over me, and I'm gonna puke and...

Involuntarily, Tabitha took a step back. "Well, uh, that's really something."

"Excuse us, Buster," Molly said, gently gripping Tabitha's elbow and pulling her out of the pimple splash-zone. "We're going to take our seats now. Nice to meet you."

Thank you, Mom! Again.

A look of panic crossed the boy's face. "Uh, okay." Then his eyes lit up as he grinned. "We got a drive-in movie place. I'd love to show it to ya in the spring. It ain't open in the winter."

Tabitha forced her eyes away from the puss Vesuvius. She forced a small and— she hoped—noncommittal smile. "Nice meeting you, Buster."

Exit stage left!

Then she and her mom made a beeline to the far side of the chapel, a distance of little more than a dozen yards, as far away from the sacrament table as possible. They took their seats, and Tabitha inclined her head toward Molly. "Did you see the size of that thing? I mean, you had to, but—"

Molly's lips curled into an enigmatic Mona Lisa smile. "Honey, people who live in glass houses..."

No!

Horror gripped Tabitha as she fumbled in her purse for her compact case. With trembling hands, she flipped it open and searched her own reflection in the tiny mirror.

And she saw it.

Right at the side of one nostril.

No!

The pimple wasn't *huge*, but it was definitely a whitehead. Definitely noticeable.

"Mom!" she whispered. "Why didn't you say something?"

38

"I just noticed. It's not *that* bad."

Tabitha snapped the compact closed, shoved it into her purse, and placed a concealing hand over the offending side of her face.

She leapt to her feet.

Bowing her head so she could avoid eye contact and introductions with the folks filing into the chapel, Tabitha regretted their decision to sit on the far side of the room.

Which way to the ladies' room? Left or right? Did I see it on the way in?

As she scurried as discreetly as possible toward the chapel doors, she saw Brother Kilmore entering.

Oh, please don't look at me! Please! Not now! He's probably seen it already. I don't care! Tabitha's inner monologue fought.

But he did notice her. He smiled and held up a finger to catch her attention. "Sister Moonshadow. Tabitha! If I could—"

Tabitha turned her head away, like the disfigured Phantom of the Opera avoiding the lovely Christine's curious gaze. "In a minute. Ladies' room?"

He nodded and pointed to Tabitha's left. "That way."

"Thanks."

She passed him, turned left, and cast about, searching for the elusive restroom door and the safety it promised.

Where is it? This little place can't have that many doors.

She spied the desired portal with its welcome sign, "LADIES," assuring a refuge from the eyes of boys and men. With the feminine sanctuary in sight, Tabitha fought the urge to sprint the few remaining yards.

Once safely inside the bathroom, she quickly glanced around—two stalls, both inconveniently occupied.

Just my luck.

She glared at the mirror above the single sink. *I guess you'll have to do.*

She scanned the room once more, ensuring she had as much privacy as possible. She set her purse on a small metal shelf beside the sink. Then she reveled in the savage glee known only to a teenager vanquishing a fiendish whitehead.

But such victories leave scars, and this victory left an angry, red spot in the crook of her nostril. So, Tabitha fished in her purse for her tube of cover-up and her powder compact.

During her few years of high school theatre, Tabitha had garnered plenty of experience at hiding youthful eruptions on her own face and on those of others. And she did a creditable job of burying the evidence of that one as well.

She smiled at her reflection.

Mirror, mirror on the wall, who is the fairest one of all? Her smile morphed into a smirk. *Well, it ain't you, honey. You might be kinda pretty, girl, but you're no Farrah Fawcett. Boys go for blue-eyed blondes, not raven-haired girls with soulful, black eyes.*

Hearing the sounds of toilet paper rustling in one of the stalls, Tabitha decided to make her escape.

That's my cue. Exit stage right!

When she reentered the chapel, she noted about half the chairs were filled, and a few more people were still meandering in. Some of the churchgoers stared at her. *Nothing to see here, folks. Just the awkward new girl.* But Tabitha's attention went to the man with the blue eyes and the wide smile. Brother Kilmore's ever-present grin broadened as he laid eyes on her.

And Tabitha's heart skipped a beat as he hurried over.

"Sister Moonshadow!"

She grinned. "Yeah. That's me." *I sound like an idiot! Doesn't matter. He's smiling at me. At me.*

"Good!" he said. "I'd hate for you to be anyone else."

Tabitha felt heat rise in her cheeks, but she didn't drop her gaze. She stared into his eyes, and for one brief, delirious moment, she imagined the handsome man asking her to a movie or to dinner. She imagined sitting across from him as they sipped root beer shakes.

"So," he said, "your mom tells me you play the piano."

And for the second time that morning, Tabitha sighed like a deflating balloon. She dropped her eyes, then gave her mother a withering, sidelong look.

Molly waved, smiling sweetly.

Not funny, Mom.

Tabitha grinned up at Brother Kilmore with considerably lessened enthusiasm. "Sort of. I can play only four hymns." She grimaced and shrugged. "But that's it."

Brother Kilmore's smile never faltered. "Hallelujah! You see, our regular pianist, Sister Hardy—she isn't here. She's a sweet old gal, but she sometimes…well, just doesn't show up. It's nice to finally have a backup."

Tabitha shook her head. "I'm not very good or very fast."

"You'll do fine! So, what do you know how to play? You know—so I can tell the chorister, and announce it from the pulpit?"

Tabitha felt heat rising in her cheeks again. "'Silent Night' . . ."

Brother Kilmore chuckled. "It being August and all, that'll go over like a turd in a—uh, I mean, like a lead balloon. What else y'all got?"

Tabitha chuckled nervously. *I really don't want to do this.* "'Come, Come, Ye Saints'."

"Okay. That one's good."

"'Come Follow Me' and 'Abide With Me'."

Brother Kilmore nodded. "Those'll work just fine."

"That's really all I know."

"But you'll do it?"

Tabitha gave him a nervous, hesitant smile, then nodded.

"Super!" He grabbed her hand to shake it again, then flinched. He stared at her hand as if puzzled. "Girl, you have one shocking handshake. That's three times now, and each time. It's almost like you're rubbing your feet on carpet somewhere. But we don't have any carpet in this building."

Tabitha stared at his hand in hers—his large, strong, very masculine hand. *What is he talking about? I never felt a shock.*

She chuckled nervously, released his hand, and pivoted toward the ancient piano. She gave the instrument a determined, hostile glare as if it were an enemy to be vanquished.

Then she sent her mom an if-looks-could-kill stare. Her mother smiled back at her, then mouthed, "Good luck!"

Mom, you are so gonna pay for this. Why'd you have to tell him? I'm gonna mess it up. I just know it!

Tabitha took her seat on the piano bench. The tattered, blue hymnal on the piano had certainly seen better days—the spine was so broken and threadbare as to be virtually nonexistent. *At least it'll stay open while I'm playing.* Tabitha sighed in resignation and offered up a silent prayer. *Please, God, don't let me mess it up.*

She bit her lower lip. *Please, please, don't let me mess it up.*

She growled softly at the hymnbook. *Oh, well. Let's play a prelude to warm up.*

She turned to 'Come, Come, Ye Saints,' poised her fingers over the keys, and struck the first chord.

And messed it up.

Way to make a good impression, Tabitha.

"Is it always this hot here?" Tabitha glared out the car window as they sped home. She wasn't complaining about the heat so much—although it *was* hot—but she just couldn't take the silence. Her mom hadn't said two words to her after church.

She'd meant to chastise her mother for volunteering her to play the piano in sacrament meeting—it hadn't gone that badly after the first few chords of the prelude, but still. Her mother had been in a good mood when they'd separated for their Sunday school classes—Tabitha going with the young men and young women to a small classroom, and her mom staying with the adults in the chapel. But afterward, it was more than obvious her mother was upset.

Molly's fingers gripped the steering wheel at "ten and two" with a determination borne of anger—not her typical nervousness while driving. A frown emphasized the lines in her face. Tabitha's mom didn't look that old, normally, but her anger seemed to add a decade of wrinkles.

"If you don't like the heat," Molly snapped, "you don't always have to wear those long skirts! Honestly, Tabitha, you can wear knee-length skirts to church. It's okay for men to see your *ankles* once in a while. Why do you always have to—" Molly's voice cut off as if she were being strangled.

Tabitha stared at her mom with shock and pain.

Her mother glanced at her with a stricken expression of horror. "Oh, Tabby-Cat.

41

I'm...I'm so sorry." She shook her head. "I was out of line. Of course, I know why you—"

Tabitha turned her head away from her mother and wiped at sudden, hot tears. She felt her mother's hand on her knee. And she flinched away.

"Tabby-Cat. I'm sorry."

They rode in silence for an eternal minute. But as angry and hurt as she was, Tabitha disliked *that* silence even more than the previous one. *She apologized. And she wouldn't have done that, said that if something weren't eating at her.*

She brushed away a final, errant tear. "So, what happened?"

Molly uttered a mirthless chuckle. "What else? I couldn't keep my big mouth shut. Always seems to get me in trouble. Especially—well, you know."

Especially at church. Especially when certain subjects *come up.*

Molly laid a hand on Tabitha's knee again, and that time, Tabitha didn't pull away. Molly squeezed. "I'm sorry, honey."

Tabitha blew out a long breath, buzzing with her lips, then turned her face back to her mom. "So, what was it this time?"

"Oh, you know—the usual."

"Women's lib? The ERA?"

"Not you too!" Molly pursed her lips in frustration. "You know darn well, I'm *not* a women's-libber—at least not in the way most people think about it—I have *never* burned a bra, I *don't* support the Equal Rights Amendment, at least as written—the prophet made the Lord's position on that very clear. And that's the end of that, as far as I'm concerned. I'm *not* going down that road."

Tabitha raised an eyebrow. They'd had this discussion before. And it always sounded just a tiny bit as if her mother was trying to convince herself of her own words. "Well, it was *something*," Tabitha prompted. "You said, 'the usual.'"

Molly pursed her lips again. "Some jerk started spouting off with, 'Eve's sin caused the whole human race to fall, and that's why women don't have the priesthood.' I just couldn't take it!" She gritted her teeth. "I just couldn't let that one go by."

Oh my! No wonder. Then a horrible thought struck Tabitha. "Who said it? Was it..."

Her mom shook her head. "No, it wasn't the branch president."

"That's not who I..."

Her mother cocked her head and glanced at Tabitha sideways. "No. It wasn't that hunky Brother Kilmore either."

Tabitha breathed a sigh of relief.

Molly turned her attention back to the road, at least outwardly. "They weren't even in there. Maybe if one of them had been. No, it was that Brother Chatham, I think is his name. You know—the older guy who seemed like he couldn't read all that well when we were singing, he only got like one word out of three?"

Tabitha shook her head. "Honestly, Mom, I was so focused on not screwing up on the piano."

"Well, anyway," Molly continued, "it was him, the old goat. But the real problem is nobody corrected him. Nobody contradicted him."

Tabitha gave her mom a half-smile. "Nobody but you, you mean."

Molly rolled her eyes. "Well, I couldn't just let a whopper like that one go!" She exhaled sharply. "But then, everybody, at least all the men in Sunday school, lit into me. They turned on me. Then old Brother Chatham says"—Molly dropped her voice an octave—"'Women ain't supposed to talk in church. It says so in the Bible. Women gotta just keep their dang traps shut. That's what God says! All y'all know that.'"

Tabitha felt fury rise in her like steam about to lift the lid off a kettle—outrage on behalf of her mom, plus more than a little for herself. "That's horrible! No, that's just sick and—and—and wrong! And nobody stood up for you?"

Molly shook her head. "Nope. Not a soul. Not a living soul."

Tabitha folded her arms, trying to hold in the rage boiling inside her. "I'm never going back there. Ever!"

"Oh, stop being so dramatic," Molly said. "It's just a bunch—"

"Stop being so dramatic? Mom, how could you let them treat you like that? It's so wrong! It's so ignorant! It's so…so unfair!"

"Yes, it is. It's wrong. It's unfair. And they're wrong and they're ignorant, but—"

"But what, Mom? But what? Eve wasn't….and women aren't¬—We can't go back. We just can't!"

"And do what, Tabitha? Just go inactive?"

"Maybe. For a while."

Molly shook her head. "It's never just 'for a while.' I've watched too many women go inactive over this. They almost never come back. Some end up fighting against the Church."

"But it's as if men don't even appreciate us. Women have *no value* in this church! What are we supposed to do, Mom? Just take it?" She lowered her voice an octave. "'Sit down and shut up, woman! Go make me a sandwich!'" Tabitha threw up her hands in exasperation. "What are we to them? Breeders? Sex objects? To some men"—*like Dad*—"we're not even good enough for that!"

Molly said nothing for a long moment. When Tabitha opened her mouth to continue, her mom raised a hand in a silencing gesture. "You know something?" Molly's voice was preternaturally calm. "It's sobering—no, it's frightening, sometimes—to hear my own words come out of my daughter's mouth."

"Mom, you know it's true!"

"Tabby-Cat, please let me finish."

Tabitha folded her arms. "Sure. Go."

Her mom took a deep breath. "It is true. To *some* men, even in the Church, women seem to have no value, nothing to contribute. It might even seem like the majority of men, sometimes, but not all. However, if we lump them all together, we're guilty of the same sin we think we see in them." Her lips curved in the hint of a smile. "Why beholdest thou the *zit* that is above thy brother's eye, and considerest not the *zit*—"

"Mom!"

Molly chuckled. "Okay. You get the point. Anyway, it's not *all* men. I sincerely believe the prophet, President Kimball, is not one of *those* men. I hope President Roylance isn't one of them either. Did you meet him?"

Tabitha nodded grudgingly. She'd met the branch president—a pleasant, friendly, older man with snow white hair, twinkling gray eyes, grandfatherly jowls, and an infectious grin. "He was . . . nice. But—"

"I'd bet my bottom dollar that handsome Brother Kilmore isn't one of them either. At least I hope not." Molly sighed. "He is dreamy, isn't he?"

"Mom!"

Molly shrugged. "A girl can dream, can't she? Anyway—"

But Tabitha's frustration had reached its limit. "Mom! That's not the point! How can we keep going to a branch where we're treated like this...like—like second-class...baby factories and house slaves?"

Molly nodded slowly, deliberately, as if she were trying to formulate exactly what to say. "Tabitha, there are jerks everywhere."

"But in the Church, Mom?"

"Yes, honey. Even in the Church." Molly smirked and shook her head. "*Especially* in the Church—and that makes it worse, because they should know better."

"But if that's what the Church teaches—"

"Oh, honey." Her mother sounded tired, utterly worn out. "It's not what the Church teaches."

"But today—"

"Today, yes. Today, a jerk said something stupid and ignorant and terrible."

"But the others!"

"Yeah, the others sided with him. At least some of them did. But not everybody was in there. You can't lump everyone together, just because of a few jerks. That'd be like lumping all men together, just because of your father."

"But how can we go back?"

Molly sighed, sounding as if the burden of Atlas were carried in that sigh. "'Then Simon Peter answered him, Lord, to whom shall we go? thou hast the words of eternal life.'"

"What?" But Tabitha recognized the scripture.

"When some of the disciples were offended. Many of them went away, and Jesus asked, 'Will ye also go away?'"

Tabitha wrapped her arms around herself and sulked. "Not fair."

Molly chuckled. And that time, there was real mirth in it. "You said it, Tabby-Cat. Not fair. But true."

"Men are jerks!"

Molly shrugged. "Well, old Brother Chatham certainly seems to know how to act the part."

As they turned off the highway and onto the dirt road to the cottage, one aspect of Molly's misadventures finally pricked at Tabitha's memory. "Mom?"

"What?"

"You said his name was…Chatham?"

"Yeah. That's right."

Tabitha rolled her eyes and shook her head. "Well, that might explain it."

"What?"

"What?"

"Oh, it's just…well, the *one* priest—you know, the *only* boy of dating-age?"

"Yeah? What's he like? I saw him sitting at the sacrament table with one of the missionaries. He looked cute enough. Did you talk to him?"

Does it matter anymore? "Yes, ma'am." Tabitha affected her southern accent. "I sure as heckfire did."

Molly raised an eyebrow. "Uh-oh. Doesn't sound like it went so well. What'd he say?"

"Well, ya see. It were just like this. I talked. Yes'm. I sure did. Him? Well, he didn't so much as give me the time o' day. No, ma'am. He didn't say nothin'. He just acted like I wasn't even thar!"

Molly looked at her. "Really? Oh, that's too bad."

Tabitha made an exaggerated, tight-lipped frown. "Well now, I ain't so sure o' that. No, ma'am. Ya see, I figure it's genetic and all."

"Genetic?" Then understanding dawned in Molly's eyes. "No!"

"Yes'm. It seems that thar boy's last name is…"

Molly sighed and shook her head. "Chatham."

Tabitha gave her a sardonic grin. "Got it in one. Give the purdy lady a Kewpie doll!"

"Oh, Tabby-Cat, I'm sorry." Her mom sighed, then chuckled. "Well, so much for first impressions."

"Well," Tabitha said, dropping the mocking accent, "at least this day can't get any worse."

Molly held up a warning finger. "Don't say that. Don't you *ever* say that. It's like a jinx." She slowed the car to a stop in front of the cottage. She stared straight ahead with wide eyes. "Tabitha, did you leave the front door unlocked?"

"No. I locked it my—" Tabitha's voice trailed off as she turned her gaze to the cottage door. *Oh, no!*

The door hung wide open.

And inside, white figures moved in the shadows.

Molly slammed the car into reverse and stomped on the gas.

The engine died.

Molly shoved the transmission lever on the steering wheel into Park, pumped the gas pedal, and turned the key. The starter motor churned. The engine coughed, then stayed dead.

Flooded it! Molly thought.

She tried the key once, twice more, but no luck.

"Mom?" Tabitha's panic and fear echoed in that one word.

Molly tried to strangle her own panic. "Tabitha, get down." Molly reached past her daughter for the glove box. "Lie down in the seat, honey."

"Mom? What?"

"Do as I say. Now." As Tabitha complied, Molly pulled the semiautomatic gun from the glove box. "Stay down 'til I tell you it's safe." Molly unbuckled her seatbelt. "Try to stay behind the engine. Best protection."

She opened the door and stood behind it. "It'll be okay, honey." She thumbed off the weapon's safety and pointed the gun at the ghostly figures in the cottage.

She put her finger on the trigger—lightly. *I'm prepared to kill. I am.* "You in there! I've got a gun! Get out of my house!" She was mildly surprised neither her voice nor her hands shook. For good measure, she added a dramatic, "Come out with your hands up!"

Her policeman-father's words ran through her mind. *Never point a gun at someone unless you're prepared to kill him. You can shoot him if he comes into the house, but not outside. Outside . . . the law gets murky. But if your life's in danger, you shoot anyway.*

Just as her dad had taught her, Molly steadied the gun by cupping her left hand under the butt of the weapon. She sighted down the barrel and aimed at the figure framed in the doorway. *I'm prepared to kill. Protect my daughter.*

In the shadows, the intruders—Molly was sure there were at least three of them—continued to move and shift, almost as if they hadn't heard her.

"I said—" she began, but shouting from inside the house interrupted her.

Molly could hear multiple voices. She saw a flurry of movement within the cottage. Then one voice emerged loud and clear. "That's right! You heard the lady. Get the hell out of here!"

Confused, Molly pointed the gun down toward the ground and removed her finger from the trigger. She extended her trigger finger down the barrel, ready to move it back and fire at the first sign of danger.

BANG!

Molly yelped, jerking the weapon up, almost firing it. *Not a gunshot. Not a gunshot. What was it?*

Two figures, robed in white, sprinted from the back of the cottage into the surrounding woods.

Backdoor? Slamming open as they ran?

"That's right!" yelled the voice from the cabin. "You better run. And don't you come back, you white-trash sons of . . ." A pause, and then, "Don't shoot, ma'am! I'm coming out!"

Panting as if she'd just run a hundred-yard dash while wearing heels, Molly aimed the short-barreled gun at the doorway. But she kept her finger pointed down the barrel. "Come out slowly, with your hands in the air."

"Yes, ma'am." A man, tall, muscular, and dark-skinned, emerged from the doorway. He held his hands high. His black face split in a wide, cheerful grin. "Please don't shoot, ma'am. I'm on your side." He stopped just outside the doorway.

And he was most definitely not wearing white.

Dressed in jeans, sneakers, and a red-and-blue basketball jersey with the "BBRHS" of Blue Beech Ridge High School and the number "11" proudly emblazoned on the front, he said, "I don't have a weapon."

A kid. Just a kid. "What were you doing in my house?" *And I almost shot him.* A tremor ran through her.

The youth's smile widened, showing a mouth full of very white teeth, then he lowered his eyes, as if embarrassed. "I was just . . . Well, you see, ma'am, I was hiking in the woods, and, well, I saw the door sitting open and . . . and those creeps inside and . . ." He rolled his eyes and shook his head. "I guess I thought I could play the hero or something. You know, like Shaft. Go in and kick some cracker—"

Molly shook her head doubtfully. "And I'm supposed to believe you were just . . . *wandering* in the woods and *happened* on my house—just a good Samaritan in the right place at the right time?"

He shrugged, or rather tried to—a difficult feat with his hands still in the air. "Sorta. Well, we were—my girl and me—we were . . . Well, the Hollow is . . . our *spot*, you see. We meet down here. Just to talk, mind, but . . ." His smile vanished. "Oh, please don't tell anybody! We'll be in so much trouble."

"We?"

"Yes, ma'am. Me and my girl. We can't—"

"Where is she?"

He shook his head adamantly. "Please, ma'am. We don't want any trouble."

Quickly, Molly scanned the woods. She could see no sign of the robed intruders or the young man's girlfriend. *Assuming his girl wasn't one of the intruders. Assuming he wasn't one of them.* "Where is she?"

The boy looked visibly upset. "Please, don't tell anybody. We're in love, but—"

"Please don't hurt him!" A young woman broke from the trees. She was dressed in jeans and a T-shirt. She was blonde, pretty, and obviously very Caucasian, her eyes were wide with terror. She wrung her hands like Lady Macbeth trying to wash away blood. "Joey's just protecting me. Don't shoot! Please, don't shoot him."

Black boy dating a white girl? In Missouri? Might explain the skulking about in the woods. Molly kept half an eye on the young man in the jersey. "Joey, huh? I'll ask you again, Joey. What were you doing in my house?"

"We just saw the door open," the girl said. "A-a-and those people inside. Joey told me to hide in the woods. He went to—to chase them out. He's so brave!" She smiled at Joey with obvious pride and affection.

"What were you doing in the woods?"

"Just walking . . . you know, talking." Joey nodded his head toward the woods— in the direction the intruders had run. "I live up yonder." He smiled sheepishly. "Can I put my hands down?"

Molly glanced toward the woods again. *No sign of the others.* "Okay, but go step over there with"—she nodded in the girl's direction—"your girl." She paused. "What's your name, young lady?"

"Beulah, ma'am." She dipped her head in the suggestion of a curtsey. "Beulah Martineau." She looked at Joey, and an expression of shock drew across her pretty features. "Oh, Joey! Your eye!"

Joey had already lowered his hands and was walking quickly toward Beulah. "Oh, this thing? So, I got a black eye." He grinned impishly. "It's not like anyone'll notice." He took her hand in his, interlacing his dark fingers with her pale ones. He turned his face to Molly, and, for the first time, Molly noticed a darker patch of swelling below his left eye. He shook his head, and his expression became serious. "I didn't mean any harm. I saw them rummaging in there. And them wearing robes like that. I thought they were Klan wanna-bes."

Molly lowered her gun again. "Tabitha?" She glanced toward the car, only to see her daughter standing right beside her. Molly jumped again, then gritted her teeth in annoyance. "I thought I told you to stay in the car."

Tabitha shrugged. "Didn't seem like there was any danger anymore."

I need to be able to trust you—be certain you'll do what I tell you. But Molly didn't voice her thoughts. She knew it was mostly fear and nerves behind her irritation. Mostly. *Besides, I'm not about to berate you in front of strangers.* "Tabitha, go inside and call Brother Kilmore. His number's right by the phone."

Tabitha nodded. "Okay." She turned to go.

"Wait a minute," Molly said, calling her back. "I'll go. I need to check and make sure the house is safe." She motioned to her daughter. "Come here, honey. You hold the gun and I'll—"

"Mom! I don't know how to shoot a gun."

Molly grunted in frustration. "Of course. We'll have to remedy that soon, won't we?"

Tabitha rolled her eyes.

Molly turned her attention back to the tall boy and his girl. *What am I supposed to do with Romeo and Juliet here?* She sighed. "We're all going inside the house. Then I'll call the sheriff."

The blonde shook her head vehemently and clung to Joey. "No, please! You can't! If the sheriff finds out, my daddy'll find out. And if my daddy finds out . . . well, he'll skin me. That's what he'll do! And he'll kill Joey." Terror was written plainly across her pretty face.

"It's true, ma'am," Joey said. "Beulah's daddy won't approve. He'll . . . He's a powerful man in these parts. Please don't call the sheriff. Or at least, let Beulah go. Don't involve her in this. Please, ma'am?"

How do I know you weren't both involved? "Who's your father?"

Beulah glanced at Joey. The boy nodded. Beulah looked down at the ground. She mumbled something that Molly couldn't hear.

"What? Please speak up, young lady."

The girl raised her eyes, straightened her back, and looked at Molly. "He's the pastor of the Assembly of God Church in Blue Beach Ridge."

A pastor? Assembly of God. Aren't they Pentecostals? What's their view on this sort of thing? "I thought your church was pretty tolerant of interracial marriage."

Beulah rolled her eyes. "What Daddy says in church is one thing. What he says . . . and does at home is . . . well, something else entirely. I'm telling you, he'd be mightily pissed if he found out."

What do I do? Molly grimaced, then nodded. "Go on, young lady. Get out of here. But *you* need to stay, young man. You're a . . ." She groped for the right word. "You're a witness."

Joey's face lit up with a wide grin. "Thank you, ma'am. Thank you so much."

Joey and Beulah turned to each other. They kissed, the smooch lasting long enough to make Molly a bit uncomfortable. Then Joey caressed Beulah's cheek. "You go on. I'll be fine."

Beulah almost smiled at that. Almost. She glanced at Molly. "He's a good guy." Then she turned and sprinted into the woods.

"And now, young man . . ." Molly said. "What's your last name, Joey?"

He smiled. "Parsons, ma'am. Joey Parsons"

Mr. Parsons—dating the parson's daughter. "Well, Mr. Parsons"—Molly gestured toward the house with her gun—"if you'd care to come inside? We'll put some ice on that eye."

He smiled again, bent slightly at the waist in an almost courtly bow, but his eyes remained on hers. With his bright brown eyes, chiseled features, and disarming smile, he was quite handsome. "Thank you kindly, ma'am. You're a lady of wisdom *and* beauty, if you'll permit me to say so. I'm most pleased to accept your gracious invitation."

Ooh, you're a charmer.

But then, once upon a time, Jerry was a charmer too.

I'll be watching you, Mr. Parsons.

The corner of Molly's mouth twitched in the hint of a smile. "It's Ms. Moonshadow. And I'm not inviting you to tea."

"We got you, *boy*." The burly deputy sauntered, circling the dining table in the cottage kitchen where Joey Parsons sat. "Got you dead to rights on breaking and entering. What you got to say to that, *boy*?" The deputy managed to cram two distinct syllables, along with centuries of bigotry, into the word.

Still holding a makeshift icepack to his eye, Joey gave the lawman a beatific smile. "Actually, Deputy Thibodeaux, sir, while I did enter—just being a good neighbor and all, just trying to protect Miss Moonshadow's property—it's not breaking unless somebody broke in. And the door was already open when I got here. So, you see, sir, it couldn't be breaking and—"

WHAM!

Deputy Thibodeaux pounded a brutish paw on the table, making his Smokey-Bear hat bounce. His broad face twisted in rage, and he pointed a meaty finger at Joey's nose. "Don't get uppity with me, boy!"

Tabitha, sitting in the living room with her mom, jumped. Heart thumping like a rabbit in a snare, she glared at the sheriff's deputy with unabashed disgust. *Creep. Redneck. Pig.*

Joey's smile, however, never faltered, but his visible eye narrowed ever so slightly. "Wouldn't dream of it, sir."

Thibodeaux lowered the finger and sneered at the kid. "That's right, *boy*."

"No, sah." For the first time since Tabitha had encountered Joey, his speech assumed a "black" *patois*. "I knows mah place. Yes, sah, Massah Thibodeaux, sah."

The porcine lawman's face reddened. He raised his hand as if to backhand Joey across the cheek.

Tabitha and her mom gasped.

Joey stared back, his smiling face utterly devoid of fear.

"Thibodeaux!" The voice hadn't been loud, but it bore the unmistakable force of command. Still in his Sunday suit, but wearing a gun belted at his hip, Brother Kilmore stood silhouetted in the front doorframe.

Deputy Thibodeaux's hand snapped contritely to his side, as if the appendage itself was ashamed it had ever threatened violence. "Lieutenant! I was just…"

Kilmore stepped into the muted light of the cottage. "I think I know what you were just about to do, sergeant. I'm sure Mr. Parsons knows, too. And I'm very sure the two ladies know as well." He inclined his head slightly in the direction of Tabitha and her mom. Gone was the kind, friendly man from church. This was a man with an expression of stone, a man who could stare down a raging bear.

Or a wild boar.

Thibodeaux blinked at him with beady, stupid eyes. Sweat broke out on the man's pale face. "Lieutenant—"

"Wait outside."

Thibodeaux opened his mouth as if to protest, but Lieutenant Kilmore cut him off. "Now."

The deputy bowed his head, but his eyes shot daggers of hate at Kilmore. Without a word, Thibodeaux sulked past his superior.

Brother Kilmore stepped aside, allowing the bulkier man to pass through the doorway. Kilmore waited a moment, took a deep breath, and released it. He inclined his head to Tabitha and Molly. "My apologies, ladies."

Tabitha could see no hint of a smile. But even without the charm, the man was an imposing and breathtaking figure.

Tabitha realized her palms were sweating.

You could arrest me anytime.

Stupid thing to say.

Lieutenant Kilmore turned toward the table. The commanding demeanor melted away as he took a seat opposite Joey. For his part, Joey eyed the man with a steady eye and an ambiguous smile.

"And to you, young man, on behalf of the Butler County Sheriff's Department, I offer my sincerest apologies. He had no call to treat you that way." He smiled. Charming Brother Kilmore was back. "Please forgive the deputy."

Joey grinned. "Apology accepted." The accent was gone. He shrugged. "Besides, he's a Thibodeaux. I don't think he knows any other way to act."

Brother Kilmore chuckled softly. "You're a very insightful, well-spoken young man, Mr. Parsons. And, if you'll permit me to say so, you're a marvel on the basketball court. Not bad on the football field, either."

Joey grinned broadly. "You should see my math and science grades."

Kilmore nodded in appreciation. "A man of many talents, eh? A Renaissance man?"

Joey folded his arms and sat back. "You could say I'm aiming to be known as the black Leonardo da Vinci someday."

Kilmore gave Joey a thumbs-up. "Sounds like a good goal. But you know what'd be a better one?"

Joey shook his head slightly, confusion dampening his smile. "What's that?"

"Forget the *black* part. Just be the modern-day Leonardo. Don't let the color of your skin or anything else define you. The only things that should matter are your brains and your talents."

Joey's grin broadened. "I like that. You're okay, Mr. Deputy."

Brother Kilmore set both his hands on the table. "I just have a few more questions, if that's okay."

Joey shrugged. "Okay, but I have one of my own."

The lieutenant nodded. "Fair enough. Shoot."

"How come you're interrogating me here? Why not take me down to the sheriff's office?"

Brother Kilmore pursed his lips and squinted at Joey. "Do you *want* to go down to the sheriff's office?"

"Not particularly. I have a funny feeling that if I *did* go there for... questioning, the good deputy would find some excuse to lock me up or rough me up. Or both."

"Just between you, me, and the fencepost, I agree with you. But I'm working to change folks' attitudes around here."

The young man chuckled mirthlessly. "Yeah. Good luck with that."

"Rome wasn't built in a day. How's the eye?"

"It doesn't hurt. Not one bit, thanks to Miss Moonshadow and her lovely daughter."

Tabitha felt her cheeks flush at the compliment. *He's just being polite, but...*

Brother Kilmore nodded. "Anyway, we both owe these lovely ladies a huge debt of gratitude for allowing us to turn their kitchen into an...impromptu interview room." He turned his face toward Tabitha and her mom and graced them with a dazzling smile.

Joey turned and smiled as well. "Much obliged, Miss Moonshadow." He inclined his head to each of them in turn. "Miss Moonshadow."

Cute, smart, and polite, Tabitha thought. *I can see why—Now what was her name? Beulah? I can see why Beulah likes him.*

Her mom squeezed Tabitha's hand.

Maybe Mom's thinking the same thing. I like him. I hope he wasn't one of the . . . others.

Tabitha didn't have a name to apply to the intruders.

She glanced at her mother, then took a harder look. *Nope. She's not even looking at Joey. She only has eyes for him.*

And for his part, Brother Kilmore favored Molly with his best, most dazzlingly perfect smile. "Now, ladies, if you would be so kind, I really should conduct this interview in private." He gestured toward Tabitha's bedroom. "If you wouldn't mind waiting in there, please? This shouldn't take long."

In reality, it didn't take all that long, but to Tabitha, waiting with her mom in the bedroom felt like an eternity. Neither of them spoke as they sat on the edge of the bed. Perhaps they kept silent because they were both trying so very hard to listen to whatever might be going on in the kitchen—not that either of them could hear a comprehensible word.

They could be strangling each other in there for all we'd know, Tabitha thought.

Days could pass. Years. Eons. As she conjured up images of violence, Tabitha conveniently ignored the fact that the afternoon sunlight shining through her window had barely moved across the floor.

When at last the knock came at the bedroom door, both Tabitha and her mom jumped, like naughty children caught listening at a keyhole.

"You can come out now," said Brother Kilmore through the door.

Tabitha was the first to the door. She opened it to find the handsome lieutenant standing there. His brow creased as if he were consumed by deep thoughts.

"Well?" Tabitha looked past him, searching for Joey. *Oh, no!* "Did you arrest him?"

Brother Kilmore focused on her face in confusion. "Arrest . . . Joey Parsons?" The corner of his mouth lifted in a half-smile, and he shook his head. "Naw. I sent him home. I offered to drive him, but he insisted on walking."

Molly came up behind her. "What about that other deputy?"

Brother Kilmore's half-smile blossomed into a full, mischievous grin. "Still cooling his heels outside. I made it crystal clear—in terms even a Thibodeaux can understand—if the Parsons kid so much as stubs his toe, I'll be on the sergeant like stink on sh— Well, you get my meaning." He chuckled to himself. "You know, you can take the country boy out of the Bootheel, but somehow, as soon as he comes back, all that Bootheel... *charm* just comes seeping right back in."

Is he talking about himself?

"Anyway," he continued, looking directly at Molly. "Do you have any idea what they were after?"

"After?" Her mom sounded confused.

Tabitha snorted. "Of course, they were after something. They broke in, didn't they?"

Brother Kilmore smirked, closed one eye, and shook his head. "That's just it. They didn't—break in, that is." He scratched behind one ear like a man working out a riddle.

Tabitha was reminded of a dog scratching at a pesky flea. *Not the most attractive image.*

"What do you mean?" Molly asked.

He hesitated as if considering whether to answer. He looked back at the front door, shrugged, and turned his attention back to Molly. "They came to the window. There're footprints—nothing I can take a casting of, mind—but the footprints go from the woods to the window over there." He pointed at one of the living room windows on the side of the cottage. "They stood there for a bit. The prints are deeper and more defined there. Then they went to the front door and right in. If they'd stood there long enough to turn the knob and open the door, there'd be two matching footprints, side by side. But, no. They didn't even pause to open the door, from the looks of it, they walked right in."

"I locked the door!" Tabitha was on the defense. "I know I did! I remember—"

Brother Kilmore held up a hand. "I believe you."

"You do?" *I remember locking it.*

He nodded. "You see, when you're new to a home, everything's unfamiliar. You're not careless yet. You lock and double-check your doors, even your windows sometimes."

Tabitha's mom opened her mouth to say something, then closed it.

Tabitha fought to keep a scowl from her face. *I knew she didn't believe me.*

Brother Kilmore smiled at her. "So, you're off the hook, Tabitha."

He called me Tabitha. Not Sister Moonshadow. Is that a good thing?

"So, they have a key to our house?" Her mom's voice was raised in alarm.

"I—" he shook his head. "I don't think so. They walked right in, remember? They stood at the window, but then they walked right in as if the door was standing wide open." He looked over at the door again. Then he looked toward Molly's bedroom door. "Then they went straight in there and went through your chest of drawers. They rummaged through a few more things—they didn't touch your jewelry box. Almost as if they weren't really interested in robbing the place. And what's with the white robes, I wonder?"

"The KKK?" Molly ventured.

"Mom!" Tabitha said. "I told you the Klan isn't around here." She turned to Brother Kilmore. "Are they?"

He shook his head. "I would've heard. Besides, not one of y'all has mentioned pointy hoods. They had hoods, but more like—I don't know—*ghosts* or something."

Both Tabitha and her mom stiffened at that.

Brother Kilmore didn't seem to notice, however. "But ghosts don't leave footprints—not that I've ever met one, mind." He grinned. "A ghost, that is. I've never met a ghost. But I'm pretty sure they were searching for something specific. It's like they knew what they were looking for, and more importantly, where to look. They dumped out your . . . uh . . ." The man actually blushed. "They dumped out your underwear drawer. That seems to have been their target."

Tabitha and Molly gasped.

And this time, Brother Kilmore noticed. "What? What were they looking for in there?"

Molly cleared her throat. "They must have been...looking for my gun. I had it with me, so they didn't find it."

Tabitha caught her mom's eyes. They didn't need to speak out loud, but both mother and daughter knew what the other was thinking.

They knew exactly where to look for it. That night, the night we saw them flying… They were right outside our house. They overheard us talking about the gun.

6

"Well, Señor Boyardee, I reckon this here town just ain't big enough for the both of us." Tabitha's hands trembled only slightly as she aimed the gun at the ravioli can. She cupped her left hand under the grip to support and steady the heavy gun.

The tin menace—long bereft of its yummy meat-stuffed pasta and bland-yet-comforting cheesy-tomato sauce—was now fit only for the trash or target-practice. Boldly, it sat upon a rock near the ruins of an ancient cabin, daring Tabitha to shoot it just one more time. The day after the encounter with Joey, Beulah, and the ghosts, Tabitha and her mom had hiked into the woods, going deeper into the Hollow, to find a spot deserted enough for Tabitha's first shooting lesson.

The afternoon sun dipped toward the horizon, casting long, sinister shadows from the trees across the clearing. It bestowed upon the lonely spot an aura of mystery and gloom.

"Don't hold your breath, Tabby-Cat." Her mom's voice came from behind her. "Take a breath, and then take the shot about halfway through your exhale. And *pull* the trigger—don't squeeze it."

"Yes'm," Tabitha replied in her best gunslinger accent. "Don' hold yer breath. Pull, don' squeeze. I reckon you done told me that 'bout a hun'rd times already. But this here coyot' ain't long for this world, I reckon, seein' as how I'm 'bout to pump his yella hide full o' lead." In spite of her bravado, Tabitha wasn't at all confident she could hit the target. At ten paces, she'd managed to put a few holes in Chef Boyardee's smiling face, but the can was double that distance away now.

I can't even see the evil Chef's face. Tabitha stared hard at the can. *Is there really a Chef Boyardee? An actual person?*

"Focus, Tabby-Cat," Molly whispered.

Tabitha exhaled slowly, letting about half the volume of air out of her lungs. In that instant, halfway between life and death, between heartbeats, the front sight at the end of the gun barrel halted its wiggling and centered neatly inside the rear sight.

The target was dead center.

Tabitha pulled the trigger.

The gun jumped in her hand, the barrel jerking up slightly.

And the can flew backward off its rock perch, landing inside the ruin of the old cabin.

"Yes!" her mom cried. "Good shot!"

Tabitha was more than halfway tempted to raise the barrel to her lips and blow the smoke away. *It'd look really cool, but I'd probably blow my nose right off my face. Even if that was the last round. Always assume the gun is loaded—Mom's safety mantra.*

"I reckon I showed him. That thar varmint ain't gonna be botherin' us no more."

Her mom laughed. "I reckon you're right, Tex. It took a good fifty rounds, but that was a fantastic shot. An MP-25's not that great for accuracy, but you're a natural, Tabby-Cat."

"I'd rather be a natural at tap dancing." However, Tabitha still grinned at the compliment. It wasn't that she hated or feared guns—it was simply that the cold, deadly weight of the firearm made her uneasy. *Instant death in my hands.* She set the weapon's safety switch from "F" to "S" and gratefully handed the gun, grip-first, to her mom. "I just hope the high school doesn't do a show that requires tap or ballet." As soon as the gun left her possession and was safely in her mom's control, Tabitha's right hand began to tremble. She gripped her right hand inside her left to calm it. *Glad that's over.* "I've got two left feet when it comes to anything more than a waltz." She glibly pattered on, attempting to cover her discomfort. "With my luck, they'll do *Guys and Dolls* or something crazy." She stifled a whole-body shiver with a sigh. "What I wouldn't give to do *Camelot* or *Fiddler on the Roof* or"—she sighed wistfully—"*My Fair Lady*. At least the dancing would be simple."

Well, at least simpler.

She watched as her mom popped out the clip and reloaded the weapon. *Oh, can't we just be done already?* Tabitha forced a sweet smile. "I thought we were going back." She tried to keep the frustration and disappointment out of her voice.

Her mom snapped the clip with its deadly cargo of ten bullets back into place, then double-checked the safety switch. "Yeah. I think fifty rounds are enough for one day. Besides, if you really do need to use this thing, your target will probably be a lot closer and a lot bigger." The corners of Molly's mouth lifted, forming a smile which didn't reach her eyes. "You know the basics. That should be good enough for now."

"Yeah." A vision filled Tabitha's mind—a white-robed figure with a crimson stain blossoming on its chest. Tabitha swallowed, fighting down a sudden wave of nausea.

Molly placed the gun in her purse. "I really don't think they'll come back. But just in case." She patted her bag. "I'll feel safer when you're home alone if you have this around. You remember…?"

Like I could forget. Tabitha nodded. *In the kitchen drawer with the phone books.*

They hadn't named the hiding place aloud, but her mom had shown Tabitha the new spot using gestures, all the while chit-chatting about trivialities—just in case the ghosts were somehow listening again.

"Yep," Tabitha said, trying not to think about a loaded gun being kept in their kitchen. "Hopefully, there'll be auditions for a show soon. Once rehearsals start, *you'll* get home before me." She paused. "If I make it."

Her mother chuckled. "School starts tomorrow. I doubt they'll have a show that soon. And *if* you make it in? They'd be nuts to pass up a true talent like you."

"As long as there's no dance audition." *I've got to make it in. I need a show! I need something to take my mind off...all this. I just need to be on stage.*

Molly offered her hand. "Shall we head home?"

Yay! No more shooting. Tabitha felt as if a weight had been lifted off her shoulders. "I'll get the can." She grinned. "'Give a hoot. Don't pollute!'"

"Okay, Woodsy Owl." Her mom grinned and winked. "Hurry up."

As Tabitha walked, almost skipping, toward the well-mutilated can, she hummed the tune from the overplayed Saturday-morning Public Service Announcement. The inane words ran through her mind.

Smokey Bear has got a friend
Who is always on the prowl.
Woodsy is his name you know.
He's the anti-pollution owl.
Give a hoot.
Don't pol—

With a growl, she forced herself to stop humming the annoying jingle.

Dumb song. Stuck in my brain.
All hail the power of advertising!

The ravioli can lay like a tin corpse inside the decaying rectangle of the old cabin. The roof of the structure was long gone. Only the shallow remnants of the wall—marked by a few rotting logs—and part of the hearth remained. A broken piece of slate, along with a dozen or more stones indicated the location of the old fireplace.

"Okay, so the wood rotted away," Tabitha said, surveying ruins. "But what happened to the chimney and the fireplace? Even if it fell down, wouldn't the stones still be here?"

Her mom joined her, stepping over a log to set foot on the dirt floor of the house. "Maybe somebody carried them off?"

"Why would they..." Tabitha gasped, an electric thrill of awe running up her spine. "Is this White Lettie's cabin?"

Her mom grinned, turning around to take in the entirety of the ruin. "Maybe! Maybe folks around here carried off the stones. Maybe they thought they were—"

Bouncing on her feet, Tabitha clapped her hands together in delight. "Magic!" She spun around, searching the dirt and rotting leaves with eager eyes. "Maybe there's something else left here—something really cool!"

Her mom turned over one of the rocks with her foot. "Not much. You know, this place is tiny! What? Maybe ten feet square? I suppose that's okay for one person."

Tabitha knelt beside the old hearthstone. She pursed her lips in annoyance.

"Nope. Not much here." She scraped at the dirt floor near the remains of the fireplace. "Barely one log left on another." She ran her fingers over the rotted log which terminated where the chimney had once stood. "The logs aren't all that thick. I thought log cabins were made of great, big logs."

"People use what's around," her mom said. "The trees here aren't that big or they're not straight enough. No tall pine trees, you know. And if this was Lettie's place, and she built this by herself, I doubt she'd have been able to handle anything huge."

Tabitha felt along a smaller piece of wood lying next to the wall. It was straight, but very skinny. "This one's just a stick." *A very straight stick.* "Maybe it's an old tool or something. Like a shovel or a hoe, maybe?"

She dug her fingers into the ground, forcing them around and underneath the object. Taking a firm grip, she tugged.

It moved slightly.

She dug around the stick with all the enthusiasm of a dog digging up a favorite bone. Soon, she had exposed most of the ancient wood. Unlike the logs of the walls, the stick felt hard and sturdy to her touch—no sign of rot.

Her mom knelt beside her. "What have you got there?"

"I don't know." Tabitha tugged at the wood, and it slipped out of its earthy grave. She stood, holding her prize aloft in both hands.

Heavy. Too heavy.

"It's a pole," her mom said. "I wonder what it was for."

The artifact was straight as a spear, a little more than an inch in diameter. Tabitha rose to her feet and stood the pole on one end. It came up to her chin. "This can't be just wood." She ran one hand along the shaft. "It feels like wood, but it's so heavy."

Her mom stood and extended a hand. "May I?"

Tabitha nodded and passed the stick to her mother.

Keeping the pole pointed at the ground, Molly lifted it a few inches. "Wow. You're right." She peered down at the end. "Maybe it has a metal core—you know, like a fighting staff." Molly handed the object back to Tabitha.

"So, what are you saying? You think Lettie was into karate or kung-fu or something?"

Molly shook her head. "In Missouri? In the nineteenth century? I doubt it. But that's what it looks like. You know, I once dated a guy who was into this stuff...long, ago—you know, back when dinosaurs roamed the earth." She grinned at the old joke. "That's what this looks like. He called it a *bo* staff." Molly examined the pole more closely. "Look at this." She put her finger on the end of the pole.

Tabitha examined the spot at the pole's end. It was darker than the rest of the stick, and it appeared to be pocked as if with tiny craters left by dust-sized meteors. But it definitely did not have a wood grain.

"This feels like old iron." Molly removed her finger. "See the dark patina? That's not rust. It's like the oxidation layer that forms on really old metal. Here. Feel it."

Tabitha put her finger on the dark spot. The instant she touched it, she felt light-headed, dizzy. The sensation of vertigo was fleeting, lasting no more than a couple of seconds.

Whoa. That was weird.

She pulled her finger away and then slowly, gingerly touched the spot again. The disorientation returned for a second, then was gone. She frowned, glaring at the spot.

It does feel like metal, but it feels funky.

She tapped her finger on the spot a few times. Eventually, the sensation of dizziness she experienced with each touch diminished until it vanished altogether.

Must've imagined it. Just tired.

"Hey, look at this." Molly pointed to a spot an inch or so below the top of the pole.

Tabitha's eyes followed her mom's finger. "What?"

"This." Her mom scraped at the spot with a fingernail, then traced the circumference of the pole. "This discoloration. It goes all the way around. Like something was strapped here or tied on." Suddenly, Molly grinned and her eyes lit up. "I know what this is!"

"What?" Tabitha could at last see the mark, but she couldn't divine its meaning.

"It's a broom!" Molly ran her finger around the lighter band again. "This is where the straw was tied on. This was a broom."

"But it's so heavy! It makes no sense. Why make a broom out of a—a weapon?"

Molly shrugged, but her grin would've done the Cheshire Cat proud. She bobbed her eyebrows up and down and whispered conspiratorially. "Maybe to disguise what it was—to hide a weapon in plain sight."

Tabitha lifted the pole off the ground again, still marveling at its weight. "The witch's broom!" She bounced on her heels in her excitement. "This is *spooky* cool!"

She grasped the old broomstick with both hands and slid the end of it between her legs. She squatted until she was sitting astride it. "Whoosh!" Then she sighed wistfully. "If only I really could fly with this!"

"In your dreams, Tabby-Cat." Molly smiled at her daughter playfully. "Still, this is quite a find."

Tabitha turned her eyes to her mom. "Can I take it home?"

Her mom shrugged. "I don't see why not."

Tabitha smiled at her prize, clutching it to her chest as if the broomstick was an archeological treasure as valuable as legendary Excalibur. "Cool."

As they strolled back to the cottage, Tabitha experimentally touched the dark spot over and over.

Nothing.

She extended the broomstick toward Molly. "Hey, Mom. Touch the dark spot on the end, will you?"

Her mom gripped the pole and put a thumb on the end. Tabitha watched Molly's face for any reaction, any sign of a flinch.

Nothing.

"Yeah?" her mom said. "What?"

"Does it feel weird at all to you?"

Molly's face twisted in confusion. "It feels cold—cooler. Why? Does it feel weird to you?"

Tabitha shook her head and pulled the broomstick out of her mother's hand. "No. Colder—like you said."

She touched the metal end once more. *Colder. Metal absorbs heat. That's all. Just my imagination.*

Later that night, after cannibalizing their only good broom and after making many solemn promises to replace it at the first opportunity, Tabitha sat cross-legged on her bed, carefully wrapping twine around the straw bunched about the end of the broomstick. It had taken her several frustrating attempts, but Tabitha had finally gotten the straw strapped onto the pole in a fair approximation of a broom. She tied off her efforts, then held the restored combination weapon and cleaning tool upside-down, admiring her handiwork.

"Not bad, if I do say so myself," she said. "You know, if this whole acting thing doesn't work out, Tabitha, old girl, I'd say you have a bright future as an old-timey broom maker."

Tabitha unfolded her pajama-covered legs and stood. She turned the broom over. Gripping it with both hands, she made a few experimental sweepings across the floor. Nothing in particular moved. *If the floor were dirtier, maybe...* "Seems okay. At least none of the straws broke or fell off." *Still really heavy for a broom.*

That's 'cause it's also a deadly weapon, my dear. The better to clonk you over the head with, my dear.

She sat on the bed again and laid the broom across her knees. "Cool."

Tabitha had avoided touching the iron center of the broomstick since they'd returned home—whether consciously or unconsciously, she wasn't sure. But at that moment, her restoration labors complete, she eyed the end of the broomstick with a creeping trepidation. The memory of vertigo—psychosomatic or not—made her uneasy.

I imagined it, didn't I?

Only one way to find out.

A wicked grin plucked at the corners of her mouth. She lowered her voice, channeling her inner Boris Karloff. "Go on, child. Touch it. Touch it! If you dare... Mwa-ha-ha-ha-ha!"

She gripped the shaft near the top of the broom, held her thumb poised above its tip, hesitated...

And pressed her thumb down.

The room whirled around her. Her breathing came in short gasps, as if she couldn't draw enough air into her lungs.

Let go! Let go!

60

THE WITCH OF WHITE LADY HOLLOW

But her hand spasmed, locking itself tight around the broomstick, keeping her thumb firmly planted on the iron. Tabitha felt limp, weak, as if all the strength in her body, in her whole soul, was concentrated in her hand, draining through her thumb into the iron, into the witch's broomstick.

The room spun faster and faster, colors blending together—red, blue, green, yellow, brown, merging into white. She couldn't focus, could see nothing clearly—nothing, except white.

And then the white resolved into clear images.

Into vivid memory.

Her husband raised his fist, ready to strike her again. He staggered drunkenly, reeling is if he were back on the deck of his ship.

Her left eye was already swelling shut. Her mouth tasted of blood. Cowering on the floor, she raised a pale arm to ward off the coming blow.

"Why?" he bellowed. "Why do ya rile me so? Why, Lettie? Why?"

She shook her head, sobbing mutely. No! she mouthed. Rupert! Please! No!

But Rupert wasn't even trying to read her lips. With a roar, he swung his fist. The blow caught her above the left ear.

White, blinding pain exploded in her head. For a moment, she could see and hear nothing. Then his voice pierced the fog of vertigo and pain. " . . . with them devil eyes o'yourn. Always starin'. Drive a man mad, 'twill."

She rolled onto her side, struggling through her agony to get away, to avoid the kick she knew must come next. As she rolled, her good eye fixed on the face of her son.

Jonah, barely two years of age, lay motionless on the dirt floor. The child's body was twisted, broken, his neck bent at an impossible angle. His blank, dead eyes stared accusingly back at her. Why didn't you protect me, Mama? his sightless eyes seemed to say.

But she'd been powerless, unable to save him from the monster who'd sired him, then beat the life out of him. She'd tried. Oh, how she'd tried, but she'd been utterly…Powerless.

My baby. My precious son!

"That's yer doin'," Rupert growled. "Ain't nobody's doin' but yourn."

The kick caught her in the back. She felt a rib break.

"Ya made me do it, damn ya!"

Strong hands seized her and rolled her onto her back. Then, as if she weighed nothing, Rupert gripped her arms below the shoulders and hauled her quickly to her feet. He held her there, glaring at her, shaking her like a ragdoll. His eyes were wide and bloodshot with drink and fury. And madness. His teeth were bared and spittle flecked his lips like a rabid dog's.

With a bestial roar, he shoved her backward. She crashed into the wall. The impact drove a new spear of agony through the broken rib.

She barely kept her feet.

Rupert stood, swaying, staring at her with an insane grin on his face.

And then he began to laugh. The sound began low and soft in his throat, like the grunting of a hog. Then it rose in pitch and volume, 'til it became the lunatic howl of a wolf.

Leaning against the wall, she groped for something, anything at all she might use as a weapon. Her fingers closed on the staff, the heavy one her husband had brought back from the Japans.

She pulled the staff from where it leaned against the wall and held it in front of her, gripped in both hands.

Her husband's mad howl transformed into an inhuman scream. He lunged at her.

She swung the end of the staff down, putting all her strength behind it and the blow struck his head.

He stopped, then staggered back, clutching at his forehead. Crimson flowed between his fingers. He stared at her in shock. Then he lowered his hands and gazed upon the blood. He seemed confused, as if he couldn't comprehend where the bright red fluid had come from. Then, through a veil of gore, his features twisted in rage. With another howl, he lunged at her again.

But she was no longer powerless. She struck him harder.

He fell, crumpling at her feet. He lay twitching, as a grew about his head.

With one last, longing, horrified glance at the corpse of her son, she fled out the door and into the night, clutching the staff—her deliverance, her power—to her breast.

The broom dropped from Tabitha's hands and onto the rug. She gasped loudly, sucking air into her lungs as if she'd been drowning. Her heart thundered in her chest like some timpani played by a madman.

What was that?

She stared at the broom, lying on the floor at her feet.

White Lettie?

Panting like a winded dog, Tabitha glanced quickly around her bedroom, expecting to see White Lettie's ghost floating in the air.

Or Rupert's.

But there was nobody—no apparition, no blood. Nothing.

There was only White Lettie's broom lying on the floor.

The witch's broom.

Deputy Sergeant Daniel H. Thibodeaux took a long draw on his Marlboro, savoring the potent taste of unfiltered smoke. He preferred his cigarettes unfiltered. *Real men don't need filters*, his daddy used to say. Old Daddy, who'd smoked four packs of unfiltered cigs each and every day, was healthy as a Poplar Bluff mule—at least, until the night he'd plowed his pickup into a tree. Word was, Old Daddy'd had a black gal and a half-empty bottle of whiskey in the truck with him. No sir, it wasn't the cigs that'd killed Old Daddy Thibodeaux. It was the combination of stiff Jack Daniels, sturdy blue beech tree, reliable Chevy, and a sweet bit of brown sugar.

Ain't the cigs as'll get ya. Cars, whiskey, and whores, maybe. But not the cigs. Besides...

"Filters are for fags," Thibodeaux muttered, repeating one of his father's oft-spoken nuggets of wisdom. He tapped the cigarette against the patrol car's ashtray, then raised the Marlboro to his lips again, the cigarette's glowing tip providing the only light in the vehicle. The moon was long gone, and few stars shone through a partially overcast sky to illuminate the highway. But that was just fine—black night suited Thibodeaux's mood.

"Leave the Parsons boy alone." Thibodeaux grunted in disgust. Even to his own ears, the sound was unnervingly piglike. He growled at himself, then grinned. *There. Least that sounds more like a hound. Ain't nothin' wrong with a good ol' hound dog.* "I'd rather be a bloodhound than a pig," he sang softly, changing the words of the old song to suit. "Yes, I would. If I only could, I surely would. Mm-hm."

He grunted again. "Don't you lay a damn finger on the Parsons boy. The Parsons *boy*."

All righty, Lieutenant Pretty-Boy. Think you're so high-and-mighty, you holier-than-thou, nigger-lovin', big-city, Mormon son of a bitch. I won't lay a finger on the boy.

Thibodeaux took another long draw on his cig.

Not the boy. No sir.

Although, he would most certainly have enjoyed beating the tall, lanky black boy. Yes, indeed, he would. He'd beat him 'til Joey Parsons vomited blood. Thibodeaux closed his eyes for a moment and indulged in a lovely fantasy of kicking the kid— kicking with his regulation, steel-toed shoes. And how he'd relish the almost erotic sound of cracking ribs. Then, just for good measure, he'd stomp on the boy's fingers, crushing the delicate, skillful bones beyond repair or recognition. "You think you're so good, *boy*? Such a damn star? Well, good luck dribbling a basketball with no fingers, *boy*." He opened his eyes, still grinning at the scene so lovingly painted in his mind. "Yeah, *boy*, then a dozen or so well-placed kicks 'tween your legs, and you ain't never gonna—"

A point of light winked in his rearview mirror. He took a quick draw on his cigarette, set it in the ashtray, then stared intently into the mirror.

The light drew nearer.

He smiled. *Right on time.*

He expected the single light to separate into two as it approached. However, the growing light stubbornly refused to do so.

His smile faded. *Just a damn motorcycle?*

He listened for the telltale roar of an approaching cycle.

Nothing.

Nope! No motorcycle. Just a busted headlight. He smiled again like a hungry wolf, licking his lips in anticipation. *Making it too easy.*

He stubbed out his Marlboro and waited for the car to pass.

As soon as the aged Pontiac rolled past with its single working headlight and an engine chugging on only five working cylinders, Deputy Thibodeaux started his own engine, purposefully left his own headlights off, and pulled the cruiser onto the almost-deserted highway.

He drove casually at first, following the older car from a distance. He loved the anticipation of the chase, the savage joy of the hunt. *Like sneaking up on a doe. Don't let it know you're even there. Not 'til the last second...*

His pulse and his breathing quickened as he began to close the distance.

The Pontiac's right-turn signal blinked, the brake lights shone red, and the car slowed. Thibodeaux followed the vehicle as it turned off the highway and onto a dirt road.

He laughed softly. *Still don't see me, do ya?*

He waited until he was absolutely certain they were out of sight of the highway, counted ten seconds more...then flipped on both his headlights and the red flasher atop his cruiser.

He left the siren off.

The Pontiac jerked and swerved slightly as its red brake lights flared. It rolled to a quick stop in the middle of the dirt road. With only a single, narrow lane, there was nowhere else to stop, nowhere to pull over.

Nowhere to run.

Thibodeaux halted his own car a few yards behind the Pontiac, put the transmission in park and waited. A thrill ran through his large body, from the top of his head with its close-cropped hair to his steel-covered toes. He imagined the fear wafting like sweet musk off the driver of the other car. He could almost smell it from where he sat.

The manifestation of his own power and authority. He loved it, craved it like good whiskey.

When he pulled the suckers over, he always let them sweat—let them wonder, *What'd I do? Speeding? Forget to signal? What'd I do?*

"Oh, sugar," he whispered. "You gonna wish that was all your trouble."

He opened the door of his cruiser, climbed out, and stood with his trooper's hat in hand. Placing the wide-brimmed hat on his head, he closed the door, stuck his thumbs in his gun belt, and sauntered over to the Pontiac.

As he pulled the flashlight from his belt, he sniffed the air.

Yes! There it was—the sweat, the terror.

He stopped beside the driver's window and stood, drinking in the moment. He grinned wide, placed one hand on his revolver and shone the flashlight into the car. "Evenin', Miss Parsons. How y'all doin' this fine, fine night?"

In the light of the flashlight, Joey Parsons' mother shivered, but not from the cool night air. She gripped the steering wheel with both hands, squinting and blinking up at him.

Thibodeaux kept the light squarely in her eyes.

"O-O-Officer?" She squeezed her eyes shut, forcing tears of pain out at the corners. "I wasn't speeding or anything."

At the sight of her tears, Thibodeaux's heart almost skipped a beat. *So damn sweet.* "No, ma'am. You wasn't speedin'. No, ma'am."

"I . . . signaled when I t-turned off the highway." Her voice trembled. "I did. I know I did." But she didn't sound as if she were quite sure herself.

"Yes, ma'am. You certainly did signal." Oh, he was enjoying this. Yes, indeed he was. Almost as much as what was coming after.

Almost.

She opened one squinting eye and tried to look at him. "S-so why'd you stop me?"

The deputy looked her over. *Might've been pretty once,* he thought, eyeing the lines in her face and the womanly curves of her chest, *for a darkie. Pretty enough to get herself knocked up, at least. But then, all them black girls get themselves knocked up when they's just girls. That's what they do, ain't it? Breed like damn rabbits. That's right. Damn jungle-bunnies.*

"Your headlight's out, ma'am."

Her entire body shuddered, and her head dropped. "Oh." She let out a nervous chuckle. "Is that all? I-I thought I was in trouble." She swallowed hard, then nodded. "I'll get it fixed. Right away. Tomorrow."

Thibodeaux leered at her. *You think you're outta the woods, don't ya, bitch?* Her temporary relief would make it all the sweeter. "Now, Miss Parsons, that ain't the way this works."

She shuddered again—and that time, it wasn't from relief. "W-what? I-I said I'll get it fixed t-tomorrow."

The sweet aroma of fear-sweat filled his nostrils. It seemed like the darkies sweated more than white folks. *Yes, indeed they do. 'Specially the bitches.*

"You been drinkin', Miss Parsons?"

She shook her head firmly. "N-no. I haven't been drinking."

"When I pulled you over, you swerved a bit. Like you been drinkin'."

"No. I haven't b-been drinking!" Her voice shook with fear, but there was a touch of anger too.

"You been smokin' dope?"

"No! I don't do that stuff! Never done that stuff."

"Get outta the car, Miss Parsons."

She froze, looking straight ahead. She took a deep breath, closed her eyes, and bowed her head.

"Get outta the damn car."

She nodded slightly. "Yeah."

"Slowly, now." He backed away just enough so she could open the door.

She climbed out of the car, then closed the door. She stood with head bowed and her hands raised.

Thibodeaux gripped her arm roughly and dragged her over to the rear of her car. He spun her so she faced the trunk. "Assume the position."

Without a word, she bent at the waist, placed both hands on the trunk, and spread her feet apart.

Thibodeaux stared at her, taking in the shape of her behind. The lights of the cruiser—the bright, white headlights and the slow-strobing red of the flasher— allowed him to see her perfectly. She wore her waitressing uniform, consisting of a knee-length dress and white sneakers. She wasn't wearing the customary white apron, though. He'd imagined, fantasized about her wearing that little apron. She'd worn it many times as she'd served him at Sambo's.

Served him pie.

Sweet pie. Musta left it at work. That's okay. The dress makes it so easy.

"I don't have any drugs." Her protest sounded weak, resigned.

He licked his lips. "Still gotta search ya."

He sidled up behind her, reached forward, and began to pat her down. He started at her shoulders, ran his hands down her sides, to her waist. There he lingered. Then he slid his hands down the luxuriant curves of her hips.

And stopped.

"You wanna stay outta jail?" he said, his voice thick and husky with hunger. "You wanna keep workin', supportin' that *boy* of yours? You wanna keep that *boy* of yours outta jail? Bad things'll happen to him in jail. Real bad things. You don't want that. Now, do ya?"

A sob shook her. "N-No."

He grinned. "Well, that's just fine. I'm glad we come to an understandin'. So, here's how this is gonna work." He began to pull up her skirt, slowly gathering it in his sweaty, sausage-like fingers. "Y'all ain't gonna tell nobody. But y'all *are* gonna tell that *boy* of yours Sergeant Thibodeaux says…*Howdy*." He imbued that last word with all the menace he could muster. "Y'all understand me, Miss Parsons?"

She nodded her head, then shuddered with loud, pitiful sobbing.

Sweet music to his ears.

Leaving one hand on her hip, fingers tightly curled in her skirt, he loosened his gun belt with the other hand and lowered the belt to the ground. He unbuckled his trousers belt, unfastened and unzipped his pants, and let them drop to pool around his ankles.

He leaned in close to whisper in her ear. "And y'all ain't never gonna know when's the next time I'll pull y'all over for another bit of—"

He was jerked backward, then thrown to the ground. He landed hard, the impact knocking the wind out of him. He fought to breathe.

"Go," said a deep voice, cold and commanding. "Go home. Tell no one."

Desperate to pull air into his lungs, Thibodeaux clutched at his ample belly. He saw the Parsons woman turn and stumble out of the light.

"Th-th-thank you," she said between sobs. "Won't t-tell anyone. Nobody!" And then she was gone.

Moments after that, her car door slammed.

Gravel from the Pontiac's spinning tires struck Thibodeaux on the face, but he barely noticed.

All that mattered was *air*.

The pressure on his lungs was agony, like a Mack truck resting on his chest, crushing him. *Breathe*! His vision blurred at the edges. *Breathe*!

And then he sucked in air. Sweet air.

He took three gasping breaths, seizing the air with his lungs, his diaphragm, his entire body.

Only then did he think of his gun.

He reached for it at his waist, but his hand met only shirttail and boxers.

He kicked his legs, feeling the weight of the gunbelt still miraculously caught around one ankle. He tried to sit up and failed. He rolled on his side, bent, and pulled his knees up in a desperate attempt to get to his weapon.

He groped with his fingers, trying to reach the gun. One finger brushed against the holster.

Almost got it!

He could see it, lying in the clump of trousers, gun belt, and shins. He made another grab at the weapon and was lifted up. Up into the air. High into the blackness. He squealed then. Like a pig.

He floated in the air, kicking and flailing his arms and legs.

Looking down, he could see the police car ten feet below him, its red flasher still spinning, the headlights illuminating the dirt road and the trees on either side.

And just out of the direct beams of the headlights, he saw a half-dozen figures standing in a circle. They appeared to be connected to each other, as if holding hands: white and mostly shapeless.

Like ghosts.

"Help!" he screamed, his voice as high and shrill as a little girl's. "Help me! Hel—"

His mouth clamped shut. He couldn't open it. Try as he might, he couldn't force his mouth or even his lips to move.

He whimpered. The pitiful, frightened mewling came out through his nose, punctuated by bubbles of snot.

He sucked in a wet, gurgling breath through his dripping nostrils. And he smelled the unmistakable, pungent odor of fear-sweat—his own fear-sweat.

His arms slammed against his sides, and his legs were forced together. He felt no pressure, no invisible hands holding his body rigid. There was nothing—nothing at all holding him there, and yet he floated as if lying face-down, high in the air, staring at his car...and the ghosts.

One of the figures tilted its head up toward him, and Thibodeaux saw a glint of gold where the thing's face should've been.

Then Thibodeaux looked straight down—at the ground impossibly far below.

Gonna fall. Gonna fall. Please, don't drop me! Please!

As if in answer to his unspoken entreaty, he began to descend—slowly, almost gently it seemed—floating lazily toward the ground. A sliver of hope stabbed through him. *Gonna live!* Tears of relief fell from his eyes. *I'm gonna live!*

As he descended into the beams of the headlights, he tried to twist his head to better see the phantoms. But he still couldn't move his head, only his eyes.

He caught a glimpse of sheets or robes, like Old Daddy used to talk about whenever he'd wax rhapsodic about the glory days of the Klan.

Ain't ghosts. Just people. Klan. Brothers. I'm one o'y'all! He tried to say it, but his mouth still refused to open. *One o'y'all!* But what came out was a terrified, porcine squeal.

Just before Thibodeaux reached the ground, his knees and hands were forced into new positions.

He came to rest on the dirt road, face-down, with his legs slightly parted, and his hands pinned in front of his groin. He couldn't move. He couldn't budge. All he could do was whine through his burbling nose.

I'm one o'y'all! Please! Lemme go!

"Daniel Thibodeaux." A new voice, female and cold as a killing frost. "You have sinned."

A woman? Ain't no women in the Klan! And the Klan can't do magic. Who the hell are they?

"Sinned," said another female voice. "Sacrilege."

"Sacrilege." A younger voice—a girl's. "Against womanhood. Blasphemy against the Divine Feminine."

"Sacrilege," repeated several voices, as if in chorus—as if chanting in ritual. "Sacrilege against womanhood. Blasphemy against the Divine Feminine."

"And you shall pay." The cold, commanding voice again—a decidedly masculine voice.

Thibodeaux whimpered, almost screaming through clenched lips. *No! Please!*

"Have you any last words?" the male voice asked.

Suddenly his mouth and lips were loosed. "P-p-please!" he blubbered. "I-I didn't d-do nothin'!"

"You were going to rape a woman," said the man.

A laughing, choking sob burst from Thibodeaux. "I was j-just funnin'! That's all. Just funnin'. 'Sides, ain't no woman. N-nigger bitch. That's all. Just a d-damn nigger bi—" His mouth clamped shut again.

"Woman," said one of the girls. "Sacred. Holy. Divine. Woman. Goddess."

"Magnus," said the cold-as-frost female voice. "Shut off that flashing light. If we want to make it look like he just stopped to take a piss, he wouldn't have that red light on."

Take a piss? What?

"As you command, my dear," said the male voice.

The red strobe vanished.

Then Thibodeaux heard the sound of tires—tires rolling on dirt. The headlight beams moved, growing brighter and smaller, as if the car—his car—was rolling...*at me!*

No! He screamed through his nose. *Please! Stop!*

He felt heat radiating off the engine, then the cold rubber of a tire as it rolled between his feet.

No! Stop!

"You should have left Julia Parsons alone," said the male voice. "Joey Parsons is under my protection."

And just as the front tire of the police cruiser rolled up onto Thibodeaux's thighs, pinning them, smashing them, tearing his flesh, he thought he recognized that voice.

No! Didn't touch the boy!

STOP!

The car rolled onto his buttocks, crushing his hips and his trapped hands. It continued to roll slowly, pulverizing his spine, splintering his ribs. The vehicle stopped as it came to rest on his back, snapping what was left of his neck.

When his heart finally exploded, he felt very little pain.

In the last moments, as the synapses in his oxygen-starved brain fired in random patterns, Deputy Sergeant Daniel H. Thibodeaux heard the voice of Old Daddy—a nugget of wisdom to send him off to hell.

Ain't the cigs as'll get ya.

History's gonna suck.

History was one of Tabitha's favorite subjects. Actually, she loved history. She savored learning about how people lived, loved, and fought, how they failed and triumphed. She'd been looking forward to taking U.S. history during her senior year. In Maryland, it'd been a college-level class.

But not in Blue Beech Ridge, Missouri. No, the local school board, in all its infinite wisdom, had determined U.S. history should be taught as a freshman-level class.

It's going to be all names and dates and places. No motivations. No stories. In other words…

"Boring as snot," Tabitha muttered as she stared at the walls from her desk at the back of Mrs. Henrietta Wardle's first-period history class. There was the obligatory American flag, and taped on either side of it were colorful, somewhat cartoony posters of George Washington and Abraham Lincoln, both wearing disinterested, almost severe, expressions. These contrasted with the photo of Jimmy Carter, flashing teeth as he grinned like a jackal…or a politician.

And then there were the portraits of Robert E. Lee and Jefferson Davis on either side of a Confederate flag. They too were part of history, but Tabitha wondered just how much the leaders of the Confederacy might be revered in that part of the world.

Be fair, girl, she thought. *If you pre-judge these people, doesn't that make you prejudiced?*

But she didn't want to be fair. She was tired and irritable…and frightened.

What's happening to me?

Life had become topsy-turvy, first with the move to this backwater town with a house that had doors slamming on their own, break-ins that weren't exactly break-ins, ghosts or whatever they were stalking around outside—not to mention there were no boys to date, no friends, and she had seen an impossible, violent flashback that didn't belong to her.

And the rotting cherry on top of this crap milkshake is being stuck in this history class, surrounded by freshmen and a teacher who practices monotone as an art form in a cheesy classroom.

The walls were adorned with the obligatory pictures of the Mayflower, Washington crossing the Delaware, and a dozen other incidents from history. Even the classroom door, which stood open, sported a picture of John F. Kennedy on its glass window. The room felt overdecorated, and the effect reminded Tabitha more of an elementary school classroom than a high school.

Of course, her foul mood wasn't helped one bit by her lack of sleep.

The vision, seen through the eyes of White Lettie—the brutal beating at the hands of her psychotic husband, the broken corpse of her little son—had left Tabitha sitting, quaking on the bed, staring at Lettie's broom. She hadn't called for her mom. She hadn't done anything. She didn't even pray.

She had curled up into a fetal position and wept. She wasn't even certain why she was crying. For Lettie? For love turned to madness and brutality? For a child she'd never known, but somehow grieved over just the same?

For herself?

Eventually, when she was cried out, drained of emotion, Tabitha had uncurled her body. She had sat up on the edge of the bed and stared once more at the broom. She had stared at the thing for a long time.

Then, acting on an impulse she didn't understand or want to analyze, she'd gotten off the bed, plucked up the broom, and jammed her thumb down on the cold iron tip.

And felt and saw nothing. Nothing, except the by-then-familiar moment of vertigo and weakness.

Fleeting weakness, but no vision.

Several of the very young-looking freshmen boys stared at her with varying degrees of boldness. Tabitha studiously avoided their eyes. It wasn't that she was taller than any of them—no, she was on the short side—and she'd love to have believed they were staring because she looked so much more mature and pretty. But she guessed the truth was probably much less flattering.

They probably all went to junior high together. I'm the new girl, the stranger, the interloper. The Yankee. Watch one of these fourteen-year-old little boys try and ask me out.

Maybe her attitude wasn't helping, but Tabitha suspected the first day of school was off to a hopelessly bad start.

Mrs. Wardle, a gray-haired, bespectacled, and rotund woman who looked as if she was long overdue for retirement—or an appointment with the undertaker—sat at her desk, droning on about the contributions virtually all of her ancestors had made to the grand and glorious history of the good ol' U.S. of A. To hear her tell it, Mrs. Wardle's progenitors had settled virtually every state east of the Mississippi and south of the Mason-Dixon Line and had fought in every battle of every war in

American history.

As she listed their heroism, pluck, and fortitude, she didn't seem to be going in any particular order. Her ancestral boasting jumped haphazardly from World War I to the French and Indian War to the American Revolution to the Civil War and back again.

"…uncle Justin Hancock landed at Normandy on D-Day, June 6th, 1944. Killed himself at least twenty Nazis…"

Her voice carried no enthusiasm whatsoever. Nada. Zip. Zero. She could have been discussing the weather or bass-fishing or pulling the wings off flies, rather than great events in history where men and women lived and died, loved and struggled, raised families and buried children.

" . . . great-granddaddy Ezekiel Clark fought at the Battle of Haun's Mill on October 30th, 1838. He shot himself a dozen Mormons—"

What? Tabitha's mouth dropped open. *What did she say?* Tabitha raised her hand, but she didn't wait for the teacher to call on her. "Did you say, 'The *Battle* of Haun's Mill'? The *Battle*?"

Mrs. Wardle blinked stupidly, resembling nothing so much as an enormous toad that couldn't comprehend why a juicy fly had gotten away. She glanced around the room as if confused. "Who said that?"

"I did." Tabitha's heart raced, the blood pounding in her temples and in her ears. She fought to control her breathing and the righteous outrage burning like a nuclear reactor inside her.

"You're the new girl." The corpulent woman tilted her head down, peering over the rims of her glasses at Tabitha. The gray bun on top of her head bobbled, threatening to come undone. "Moonshadow, am I right? What kind of a hippy name is Moonshadow, anyway? Hmm?"

"Yes, ma'am." When Tabitha was confronted with rudeness, she tended to respond with exaggerated politeness—politeness barely holding back simmering anger. "Moonshadow is my name. But Mrs. Wardle, you called it the *Battle* of Haun's Mill? You mean the Haun's Mill *Massacre*, don't you? When an armed mob of two hundred and forty Missourians attacked the tiny Mormon village of Haun's Mill?"

Mrs. Wardle's thin, crimson-coated lips opened, and she bared her yellow teeth in a toadlike grin—that is, if toads had teeth like a wolf's and lips like a cheap hooker. "You a Mormon, missy?"

Tabitha nodded fiercely. "Yes, ma'am. I am indeed. I'm a Mormon." Tabitha slid out of her desk seat and rose to every inch of her five-foot-three stature. "I'm a Mormon. And proud of it. But you said your great-grandpappy was there? At Haun's Mill? And you're *proud* of that?"

The toadish-wolfish-whorish grin widened, excess red lipstick smeared like blood on yellowed teeth. "You're a Mormon, are you, missy? Well, guess what, Miss High-And-Mighty Mormon Moonshadow? You get a F in my class, ya hear? For the whole year." The grin vanished, replaced by a scowl. "Now sit down and shut your yap."

THE WITCH OF WHITE LADY HOLLOW ~

Tabitha did not comply, and her yap refused to shut itself. "Your great-grandpappy murdered a *dozen* Mormons, did he? That's quite a feat, considering there were only *seventeen* men and boys who were slaughtered. Were the other two hundred and thirty-nine cretins just really bad shots, then? Tell me, did your great-grandpappy rape most of the women too? Because he and his pals did that, you know. Are you proud of that? Are you, you sick, bloated, old—"

"Sit your ass down and shut—" she paused, and Mrs. Wardle's large eyes had narrowed to slits behind her spectacles, "—up."

But Tabitha had no intention of backing down. "They hacked the bodies up, some of them while they were still alive. They threw the bodies down a well and *pissed* on them."

Tabitha took two steps toward the vile creature squatting behind the desk.

The teacher shrank back, like an old she-wolf trembling before a feral rabbit. "Sit down and shut up, ya damn Mormon—" she spluttered as if trying to find a word foul enough to suit her fear, but in the end, all she could spit out was, "—missy!"

Tabitha shook her head slowly, deliberately. "No thank you, ma'am." Then she took another step forward, halfway to the wooden desk behind which the old toad cowered. The nuclear fire inside Tabitha had reached critical mass. "Your great-grandfather was nothing but a raping, murdering coward!"

BOOM!

Several of the girls—and a few of the boys—screamed.

Tabitha jumped, and her head snapped to the right, toward the classroom door. It'd slammed shut. The glass window in the door had cracked. As if shot by an assassin's bullet, the picture of President Kennedy had fallen, replaced by a spider web of cracked and jagged glass.

"Now all y'all calm down." Mrs. Wardle seemed to have regained her composure, somewhat. Though breathing heavily, at least she wasn't cowering behind her desk anymore. "Just the wind."

Tabitha glanced from the teacher to the windows. All the windows were shut. She could see several of the other kids eyeing the windows dubiously as well. *There was no wind.*

"Now, you, missy!" The old woman had risen to her feet, though she leaned on the desk with both fleshy hands. "Sit down and shut up."

Tabitha wasn't listening to her. *No wind. The door just slammed shut. All by itself. Like the door at home.*

A chill like an icy claw seized her spine, and she trembled from head to foot. *Just like the door at home.*

"Little Miss Mormon, if you don't sit down right now, I'll send you to the office."

Tabitha turned toward the teacher and glared daggers at Mrs. Wardle. "Please don't trouble yourself, ma'am."

Tabitha spun around, tromped over to her desk, and snatched up her books and her shoulder bag. Holding textbooks and bag to her chest like a shield, she strode up the aisle between the desks, directly toward the squat, toadlike figure.

Tabitha stopped in front of the teacher's desk. The old woman opened her mouth as if to speak, to say some last cutting remark before Tabitha made her exit. But she snapped her red lips shut under Tabitha's withering stare.

A classic line from *Macbeth* popped into Tabitha's mind. The line seemed appropriate. Tabitha dropped her voice into a low and menacing tone, employing her best Cockney accent. "By the pricking of my thumbs," she paused and leaned toward the hag cowering behind the desk. "Something *wicked* this way comes."

Let her stew on that for a while. If she can even remember it.

Then Tabitha turned on her heel and strode to the closed door. She turned the knob and pulled. For one brief, alarming moment, the door didn't budge. Then, with an almost ghostly groan, it swung open.

As Tabitha forced herself to walk—not run—down the hallway, she thought, *I can't believe I did that.*

Her steps faltered as a wave of regret washed over her. *I shouldn't have done that. It was...* She searched for the right word. *Wrong? Inappropriate? Not Christlike?*

Then Mrs. Henrietta Wardle's voice came screeching after her like the wail of a distant banshee. "Y'all get a F, missy! Ya hear? Y'all get a F!"

Both Tabitha's expression and her resolve hardened, and she marched to the school office.

Fifteen minutes later, armed with a note from the office, a changed class schedule, and a somewhat aggrieved sense of justice, Tabitha walked slowly back down the hallway toward Mrs. Wardle's classroom. She would have to walk past the door with its cracked glass. She really didn't want to confront the woman again, so she attempted to tread quietly.

Her long skirt—she always wore long skirts lately and, for once, wished she hadn't—rustled as she walked. To her ears, the rustling seemed far too loud.

Don't be stupid. She can't hear your skirt. She can't.

She kept her ears open for Mrs. Wardle's droning monotone, but heard nothing. Tabitha imagined the old woman crouching inside her domain, ready to pounce on her as she passed. In Tabitha's mind's eye, Wardle's bun had unraveled, and her gray hair hanging down one side of her head like a lopsided ponytail, drool spilled from her lips, and her beady eyes were as yellow as her teeth.

Waiting to pounce.

Tabitha shuddered at the image.

As she passed the open doorway, she risked a glance inside. All the students were bent over their desks, apparently reading from their textbooks. Wardle herself sat at her desk, head turned as if staring out the window.

However, it was the door that caught Tabitha's eye and held it. The picture of JFK had been taped to the door window again, but the cracks in the glass wreathed his head as if with white lightning.

It wasn't the wind and you know it.

Tabitha hurried past the door and out of sight.

A few yards farther, she breathed easier. *Safe.* Then she scowled. The vice-principal's words had left her frustrated and angry.

"Let's get you transferred to a different class," he'd said, taking his pen and a preprinted slip of paper in hand.

Tabitha couldn't believe her ears. "She should be fired! She can't just brag about killing—"

"Listen to me." He looked up at her and smiled broadly. His eyes, however, held no warmth. "A couple of years ago, she could've had you expelled. So, we're just going to move you to a different class, okay?"

Tabitha's mouth dropped open. "Expelled? For what? For calling her on her bullcrap?"

His smile faltered. He took a deep breath, then said, "For being a Mormon. It's not right, but that's the way it was. There're lots of folks around here who're still bitter about the Trouble Up North."

Tabitha blinked. "Trouble up north?"

He nodded and then went back to filling out the Class Transfer paper. "What your people might call the Mormon War."

Tabitha shook her head. "Never heard of it. You mean the persecutions? When the mobs drove the Mormons out of Missouri. The Extermination Order?"

He nodded again. "Yep. The very same." He shrugged. "Like I said, it's not right, but that's how it is." He handed her the slip of paper. "Miss Tulane's a fine teacher. You'll like her." He winked. "And she's not from around here, if you understand what I'm saying."

"But what about Mrs. Wardle? What're you going to do?"

He shrugged again. "Nothing to be done. You can't change people's hearts with the stroke of a pen. Not even Governor Bond can do that. He's the one who rescinded the Extermination Order a couple of years back. That fired a few folks up."

"But—"

He shook his head. "Get along to class, Miss Moonshadow."

Tabitha stood in the open doorway of Miss Suzanne Tulane's U.S. history class. The room was modestly adorned, compared to Mrs. Wardle's classroom—the pictures were less cheesy, and there was no red-white-and-blue crepe paper.

Miss Tulane stood in front of her class, talking with an animation and enthusiasm that was the polar opposite of Mrs. Wardle's droning. She was pretty, if not quite beautiful, but wore too much makeup, especially around her eyes. Her red hair was long and fell in waves to her waist. She wore a green blouse, black knee-length skirt, and black heels.

Heels? At school? Isn't that a bit much?

Who are you to talk, Tabitha Catherine Moonshadow? You wear long skirts everywhere.

Touché. But I have my...reasons.

"...not enough to just know who, where, and when," Miss Tulane said in a rich alto voice, lively and full of inflection. "The most important thing is *why*. For example, *why* did Washington, a man whose military command experience prior to the Revolution included a surrender and a friendly-fire skirmish *that he lost? Why* did he, of all people, volunteer to lead a rag-tag army against the full military might of the British Empire? *Why* would anyone appoint him to such an important job? *Why*? That's the important question! We need to know the *why*. And the *why* is what makes history so much fun!"

Tabitha smiled. *I like her.*

The teacher turned toward Tabitha. "May I help you? Are you lost?"

Tabitha stepped into the room, extending the Class Transfer slip toward Miss Tulane. "Actually, I'm in your class."

The teacher took a step toward her. She was tall for a woman, but then, everyone seemed tall to Tabitha. She smiled at Tabitha, then took the paper. "A senior, huh?" She gave Tabitha a quick appraising look, then returned her attention to the paper. "Tabitha Moonshadow." She looked Tabitha in the eye and smiled, her grin full of warmth and a touch of mischief. "What an interesting name. I bet there's a story behind it." She winked at Tabitha. "I like stories."

With a welcoming smile, the tall, pretty teacher pointed toward an empty desk at the front of the room. "Have a seat, Miss Moonshadow. I hope you like history, because I love it."

Tabitha returned the smile and took her seat, ignoring the many inquisitive, eager, and appraising stares from the freshmen.

She felt a surge of hope for the first day of school at Blue Beech Ridge High.

Maybe history's not gonna suck after all.

9

I hate gym class, Tabitha thought. But hate was far too mild a word to encompass Tabitha's feelings toward physical education—not the subject itself, just her personal participation. Not hate. Loathe would've been more accurate. And if she'd stayed in Suitland, Maryland, for her senior year, she wouldn't have had to take gym again at all.

Blue Bech Ridge school board strikes!

As she sat brooding on one of the very top bleachers, she saw a girl, her blonde hair in a ponytail, wearing a skimpy red-and-blue cheerleader uniform, break away from a small crowd of similarly dressed girls. They had been sitting several rows down, giggling together like a gaggle of twelve-year-olds. The blonde began to ascend the steps, and in moments, to Tabitha's amazement, it became obvious the cheerleader was climbing toward her.

Tabitha glanced around quickly, but there was nobody else up there with her.

Tabitha felt no particular animosity toward the girls who flounced and jiggled, wearing barely-there miniskirts, waving pom-poms, doing flips and handstands, and whipping crowds into a frenzy. They could somersault and form pyramids and cheer to their hearts' content. They could bask in the undisguised ogling of adolescent boys and their middle-aged fathers all they wanted. Tabitha enjoyed masculine attention, of course, but not in that way—not as a result of putting her body on display.

The cheerleader waved at Tabitha and Tabitha raised a tentative hand back.

And then she recognized her. *The girl with Joey Parsons! The secret girlfriend.*

Beulah stopped one row below Tabitha. Her smile was all teeth and pink lipstick. "Hi. Do y'all remember me?" Her southern accent was strong, but not obnoxiously so.

"B-Beulah?"

The cheerleader's smile widened, and she nodded, pleased. "That's right! Beulah Martineau. But we were never properly introduced." Still grinning, she shook her head. "This is a trifle awkward, but I'm afraid I never got your name." She extended a hand toward Tabitha.

Feeling much more than a trifle awkward, Tabitha shook hands. "Tabitha, Tabitha Moonshadow."

Beulah stepped onto the bleacher and into Tabitha's row. She motioned at the spot next to Tabitha. "May I?"

Tabitha shrugged. "Sure. Uh, please."

Beulah sat, assuming a ladylike, almost prim pose, with her back straight, her knees together, and her hands folded in her lap. Every inch a proper southern lady, in spite of the miniskirt. Her face took on a thoughtful expression. "Tabitha Moonshadow. What a pretty name. It's like that old TV show…"

Tabitha suppressed the urge to roll her eyes.

"…and that old song, right?"

Tabitha nodded. "You got me."

"Pretty name," Beulah reiterated. She gave Tabitha's shoulder a companionable pat. "Welcome to BBR High." When she said the initials of the town and school, it came out as "bee-byar."

"Thanks."

"So, Tabitha Moonshadow, my new friend—I'm gonna have to assume you're my friend, since you're keeping my little secret. Mine and"—she lowered her voice to a conspiratorial whisper—"Joey's."

Tabitha grinned. "Your secret's safe with me. Mum's the word." She mimed a zipping motion across her lips.

"So, how do y'all like it here?" Beulah shook her head suddenly. "No, that's not fair. I can only imagine how hard it is to come here in your senior year. So, don't you answer that. I hope you'll like it here." One corner of her mouth lifted in a mischievous grin. "In spite of Ol' Waddle."

Tabitha didn't bother to hide her confusion. "Old Waddle?"

Beulah winked. "You know. Miss Wardle? The history teacher? Ol' Waddle?"

"You *know* about that?"

"Girl, half the school knows. And the other half'll know by lunch."

Tabitha hid her face in her hands and groaned.

"Don't do that! What you did was really cool, standing up like that to the old bat. I wish somebody'd told her off years ago! Believe me. She had it coming."

Still with her face hidden behind her hands, Tabitha felt an arm around her shoulders.

"Really," the other girl said. "Y'all did good. Well. Y'all did well." Beulah pulled her arm away. "There I go again. You'd think English was my second language or something."

Tabitha chuckled softly as she lowered her hands. "Thanks, for making me feel welcome. I don't exactly feel like I…fit in here."

"Well, you have at least one friend here."

Tabitha smiled, biting her lower lip as she did. "Cool."

Beulah's welcoming expression changed to one of curiosity. "So… y'all're a

Mormon?"

Tabitha froze.

"It's okay. I heard all about it. It's just, well, I know y'all have a church over in Poplar Bluff. Daddy—he's a pastor—says y'all ain't Christians and all y'all are going to hell, but I don't believe a lot of what Daddy says over the pulpit. I figure, way he acts, Daddy doesn't believe much of it himself." She chuckled and shook her head. "I can't believe I said that out loud." She shrugged. "Anyway, I don't think I've ever met a Mormon before."

Tabitha forced a hesitant smile. "There are at least three of us in this school."

Beulah looked surprised. "Huh. I don't know any others. And I figure I know just about everybody. Anyway, is that why y'all're wearing that lovely skirt? That a Mormon thing?"

Tabitha blinked in confusion. "My skirt?"

"I overheard you arguing with Coach Smith. You know, about wearing sweatpants instead of shorts for gym? That a Mormon thing, keeping your legs covered?"

Tabitha scowled and shook her head. *I don't want to wear shorts. I don't want to take gym again. I thought I was done!* "No. That's a...Tabitha Moonshadow thing."

Beulah nodded, her expression thoughtful once again. After an awkward silence, she whispered something which Tabitha couldn't catch.

"What?"

Beulah looked embarrassed. "Are you...Are your legs ...ya know...scarred or something? I really shouldn't ought to ask. It's none of my business, really. Maybe y'all just forgot to shave your legs or something. I'm sorry if—"

Tabitha shook her head. "No. It's nothing like that. It's just..." *Am I really going to tell her? This stranger? This kind, friendly stranger in a town where I have no friends?* "I had a bad...a really bad summer. There was..."

Beulah gasped, a look of horror on her pretty face. "Oh my! Were you... *assaulted* or something?"

Tabitha shook her head and pursed her lips. *Not physically.* "Not that. I had to spend the summer with my father. My parents are divorced, and my dad, he's..." *Gay. Women have no value in his eyes. I have no value.* "Well, there was this man"— Randy—"this guy there, at my dad's. He was always..."

"It's okay. Take a deep breath. You can tell me."

Really? I can't even tell Mom. "He was always...making fun of me, of my legs, my body." *My chest. My hips. My butt.* "It was constant." Tabitha could still hear Randy, the drag queen boyfriend, mocking her—*I'm more woman than you, honey. Just look at my—*

"Oh, honey," Beulah said, throwing her arms around Tabitha from the side, "I'm sorry. Men are such *pigs*."

Men? Even your Joey?

Tabitha awkwardly patted the other girl's arm. "It's okay. I'm just more comfortable"—*safe*— "wearing something...modest."

Still hugging her, Beulah nodded. Tabitha thought she heard a sniffle.
She's crying? For me?

"I'm sorry." Beulah broke the hug. She wiped quickly at her nose, then dashed away a tear, somehow without smearing her eyeliner or mascara. "It must've been awful. Men. They can really…" She smiled again, wiping away another tear. "It really is a lovely skirt. Who knows? Y'all might start a fashion trend." She shrugged, laughing softly.

Tabitha returned the laugh. "Oh, that's not going to happen!"

Beulah lifted her shoulders, sighed, seeming to take control of herself. "I think you and I will be good friends."

Tabitha grinned. "I'd like that. I could use a friend here."

"So, who've y'all got? For teachers, I mean? I know you don't have Ol' Waddle anymore." She winked.

Tabitha opened her binder and showed her new friend the revised schedule.

"Oh," said Beulah. "Y'all got Tulane. Well, that makes sense. We've only got two history teachers. She's nice."

"Yeah. I like her."

"Better than Ol' Waddle, anyway. Y'all've got Moreland for…calculus. Calculus? I'm impressed. You must be a brainiac."

Tabitha shrugged, inwardly pleased at the compliment.

Beulah shook her head. "I gave up after trig. Moreland's fine. Except for his mustache is just too dang big."

The two girls exchanged a look and a giggle.

"Y'all have Smith for PE, obviously." Beulah paused. "MacDonald for physics." She turned her suddenly serious face to Tabitha.

"Is that bad?" Tabitha asked.

Beulah shook her head. "Not bad. In fact, it's good. Real good. Just…well, y'all gotta know how to handle him. I had him for chemistry last year, you see."

"Handle him?"

Beulah gave her an impish grin. "Yeah. The old guy's in a wheelchair. World War Two veteran. Got himself paralyzed in a car crash, so I heard. His first name is Fergus, of all things! Funny name, Fergus."

Tabitha raised an eyebrow. *Fergus? What about Beulah?*

"Anyway," Beulah continued, "he really likes pretty girls. I mean, he *really* likes pretty girls. He has to shake the hands of every girl when he first meets them. He shakes the boys' hands too, but he pays a whole lot more attention to the girls. It's kinda creepy, but it's okay. Just go on and shake his hand. Then, if y'all ever need him to, you know, put off a quiz or a test for a day, or give y'all an extra day for an assignment, just ask him. He'll do it! Well, for *one* day, at least, he will—but only if a cute girl asks him. Boys don't count."

Tabitha looked at the other girl dubiously. "You've gotta be kidding."

Beulah shook her head. "Nope. Serious as a heart attack. It really works! Cross my heart and hope to die."

"Okay…"

Beulah turned her attention back to Tabitha's schedule. "Choir with Miss Hargrove."

"I have to audition for that over lunch. If I don't make it in…"

Beulah pursed her lips and waved a hand in dismissal. "Oh, you'll make it. I know y'all will."

"But, you've never heard me sing! How do you know if I—"

Beulah shrugged again. "I don't know for sure, but… Well, I just have a feeling, you know? Were y'all a singer back home?"

Tabitha drew her lips into a tight line and nodded. "When we moved, I'd just made it into Madrigals. That's the special a cappella choir. I…well, I was pretty upset about missing out on that."

Beulah tapped her nose. "See? I knew it. You'll love Miss Hargrove. *Everybody* loves Miss Hargrove."

"Miss Hargrove? Aren't any of the teachers married?" *But didn't she call Mrs. Wardle Miss Wardle?*

Beulah waved her hand dismissively again. "That's just a southern thing. Everyone's 'Miss' 'round here." She grinned. "Except the men, of course." She looked down at Tabitha's schedule once more. "And last period? Miss Goldsmith for Shakespeare. Well, I don't know her at all. She's new too. I think she's that new drama teacher. Not that we have an acting class, mind, but when the school does a play—"

"Drama?" Tabitha could barely contain her excitement.

Beulah cocked her head. "Is that your thing? Acting?"

Tabitha nodded vigorously. "That's what I want to do—be an actress."

Beulah put an arm around Tabitha's shoulders and gave her a squeeze. "Well, sounds like y'all lucked out!"

The bell rang, signaling the end of third period. As the two girls rose to go, Beulah said, "Remember what I said about Ol' MacDonald. Shake his hand and smile pretty"—she flipped her ponytail—"and he'll be putty in your hands." She smiled wickedly, then pointed a warning finger at Tabitha. "But don't y'all dare even *whistle* that song—you know—*Old MacDonald Had a Farm?* He hates that. Anyway, welcome to Bee-Byar High, Tabitha Moonshadow." She leaned in and gave Tabitha a quick hug. "We're gonna be good friends, you and me. I just know it!"

Then she turned and left.

Tabitha smiled as she watched her go. She rose to her feet and started down the bleachers, whistling *Old MacDonald* as she went.

Any thought of agricultural nursery tunes was driven from Tabitha's mind as she realized there would simply be no escaping Mr. Fergus MacDonald and his reportedly creepy handshake—not if she wanted to actually *enter* the physics class.

Like a paraplegic commando waiting in ambush, Mr. MacDonald had stationed his wheelchair and himself at the door of the physics and chemistry lab, leaving barely enough room to squeeze by. The gray-haired man's face was thin, almost gaunt, but his cheery, toothy grin stretched from ear to ear, deepening the grandfatherly wrinkles around his keen blue eyes. He wore a white lab coat over an avocado shirt and sported a plaid bow tie. His tan slacks did nothing to disguise the skeletal condition of his legs. His brown penny loafers looked too big, giving the impression that perhaps his feet had not withered as much as his legs.

A dozen students, male and female, stood in a line stretching from the door, each waiting their turn to gain admittance into the classroom by submitting to the ritual of shaking the old man's hand. Mr. MacDonald took the time to greet each student, welcoming them. He hailed returning students with warm words, recalling each by name. New students were greeted with joy and wonder as if their very presence was a gift. But as Tabitha observed the old teacher, she saw he definitely lingered with the girls, especially the prettier ones, holding their hands noticeably longer than he did with any of the boys.

Tabitha held back until the end of the line. When it came time to present herself, the old man's eyes lit up at the sight of her. He extended a larger-than-expected hand.

"Well, aren't you a pretty little thing?" His voice held just a hint of Missouri drawl. He clasped her hand in a surprisingly firm grip, though his hand twitched a bit.

"Uh…" Tabitha was so taken aback by the old man's words that her tongue refused to cooperate with her brain.

"What's your name, young lady?"

"Uh…T-Tabitha Moonshadow."

He gave her hand a squeeze. "Welcome to MacDonald's Sanctum of Science. I'm so glad you're here, Miss Moonshadow."

He winked. It was no more than she'd seen him do with any of the girls before her, but Tabitha felt suddenly more than a little creeped-out by the old man's smile. Her palm became slick with sweat. "Uh…thanks?" She made an attempt to extricate her hand from his, but he held her fast.

"Take a seat, please." In spite of his words, he still clasped her hand. With a final squeeze, he let go.

Tabitha lowered her eyes and awkwardly stepped through the narrow gap between the wheelchair and the doorframe. All the desks were taken except for two—both of them in the front row. Forcing her face to remain calm, suppressing a sigh of resignation, she chose the farther one and took a seat.

As she bent to pull her physics book, notebook, and pencil from her bag, she observed out of the corner of her eye Mr. MacDonald wheeling himself toward the teacher's desk. She also saw a pair of legs and feet, clad in blue jeans and high-top sneakers, approaching the vacant desk next to hers. The newcomer sat, and Tabitha heard a somewhat familiar voice. "We meet again."

She looked up and was greeted by the smiling, handsome face of Joey Parsons.

"Moonshadow, right?" He winked at her, and Tabitha could definitely see the darker patch beneath his bruised eye.

She nodded. "Tabitha." She extended a hand. "And you're Joey, right?"

"That's right." Joey grasped her hand, then flinched. "Whoa, girl! I mean, uh… Tabitha. That's some handshake you've got." His grin widened, showing gleaming white teeth contrasting with his dark skin.

Tabitha withdrew her hand. *I didn't even squeeze hard. And his hand's so big.* She chuckled nervously. "I guess it's…a Mormon thing. You know, firm handshakes and all."

He lifted his eyebrows. "Uh-huh. Firm. That's it." He turned to face the front of the room. Then he leaned toward her. "You and your mom doing okay? No more break-ins?"

It wasn't a break-in, exactly. "Nope. And we're fine." She paused, suddenly embarrassed. "Thank you. You know, for…stopping them."

Still looking straight ahead, he beamed. "You're most welcome. I didn't—"

"Mr. Parsons!" The teacher eyed Joey with a stern expression fit for a Marine drill sergeant. "If you please, young man, my classroom is not to be used as a nightclub for you to pick up hot chicks!"

Joey swallowed and nodded quickly. "Yes, sir. I mean, no, sir, it's not."

Tabitha raised a hand. "I'm sorry, Mr. MacDonald."

The teacher's fierce expression transformed instantly to a kindly smile. "Yes, Miss Moonshadow?"

The rapid change in the old man's mood sent a shiver through Tabitha. *Jekyll and Hyde. Only which one's which?*

She lowered her hand. "I was just thanking Joey for, uh, coming to my rescue a few days ago. It's my fault."

Mr. MacDonald winked at her. "Well, in that case, no harm done." His blue eyes twinkled, and he wore an amused grin as if he were chuckling at a secret joke.

Beulah was right—he backed right down when I asked him.

She opened her notebook and wrote in large letters:

DOESN'T HE LIKE YOU?

She lifted the notebook and discreetly showed it to Joey.

Joey responded in the same manner:

HE LIKES ME JUST FINE. HE JUST LIKES YOU A LOT BETTER.

Why? Because I'm a girl? Because he thinks I'm pretty?

She looked up at the teacher. Fergus MacDonald was staring right back at her as if his eyes had never left. Surely, he'd seen the two of them writing notes.

He doesn't seem to care. Can girls get away with anything in here? Is he simply some dirty old man who has the hots for teenage girls?

The old man in question winked at her again, then said, "Welcome back, Disciples of Science. Galileo once said, 'Mathematics is the language with which God wrote the universe.' Physics is, in large part, the translating of the world around us back into that primeval language. In other words, together we're going to learn what makes the universe tick and what makes the wheels on the bus go round and round." At last, he turned his piercing, amused gaze away from Tabitha. He made an expansive gesture with his hand, taking in the entire room of students. "And it's going to be fun!"

Tabitha shuddered, feeling vaguely unclean. B*ut he's in a wheelchair. Even if he is a dirty old man, he's harmless, right?*

Tabitha emerged from the cafeteria lunch line, clutching a compartmented tray populated with mac and cheese, patty o' mystery meat, lettuce wedge—*Not even salad dressing. I mean, who eats just a wedge of lettuce?*—applesauce, and chocolate milk. She searched the large, raucous room for either an empty table or a familiar face. She spied one of the girls from church sitting at a table with an empty seat. Tabitha scoured her memory for the girl's name, but the name eluded her. After a long moment's hesitation, she took a tentative step in that direction.

The girl, tall, with brown hair and a pleasant—if not pretty—face, looked up from her lunch as Tabitha approached. The girl's eyes grew wide as she caught sight of Tabitha, then narrowed to forbidding slits. Her lips stretched into a thin line, and she shook her head quickly but definitively, warning Tabitha off.

Seriously?

Pursing her lips in annoyance, Tabitha felt somewhat deflated, though she wasn't exactly sure why. After all, the girl hadn't been exactly friendly on Sunday. But then, none of the youth—except the obnoxious Buster—had been overly welcoming.

Welcome to church, Sister Moonshadow. It's so nice to have you here. Yeah, right. I'm the new girl. New girl. New school. New town. New ward—no, make that new branch. But still...

"Tabitha!"

She scanned the room, searching for the source of the voice.

"Tabitha! Over here!" Beulah Martineau, still dressed in her cheerleader uniform and surrounded by several other members of the squad, waved enthusiastically at Tabitha.

Tabitha grinned and carried her tray toward the cheerleaders' table. *This is so weird.* Not that she'd ever craved the company of the pep squad, but she wasn't about to refuse her new friend.

Before she could even set her tray down, Beulah was on her feet. "Well, don't keep me in suspense, girl! How'd the audition go? Did you make it?"

Tabitha shrugged noncommittally and sighed. "Yeah. Soprano." Her mouth opened in a bright grin.

Beulah took the tray from Tabitha's hands and set it on the table, beside her own. Then she turned toward Tabitha and hugged her tight, squealing and bouncing with delight. "I just knew it! Congratulations."

"Thanks."

Beulah withdrew from the embrace and held Tabitha by the shoulders at arm's length. She eyed Tabitha with concern. "Y'all're happy about it, right? It's what you wanted?"

Tabitha nodded, still grinning. "Yep."

Beulah gave her shoulder a playful poke. "Well, good. Y'all better be happy about it and all, since y'all missed my pep rally for those *silly* auditions."

"Pep rally?"

Beulah rolled her blue eyes. "Of course! Welcome-Back Pep Rally? Beginning of lunch? It was announced in home room."

Maybe that explains why she's been wearing the uniform all day. "Oh, yeah." Tabitha sat. "Sorry." *Not really. Definitely not my thing.*

"But y'all made it into choir," Beulah reiterated. "That's really cool."

Unsure what she could say that wouldn't sound conceited or self-congratulatory, Tabitha took a bite of mac and cheese. As soon as she'd shoved the bland pasta and reconstituted cheese powder into her mouth, she regretted it. *Ask her about something she thinks is important. It's not all about you.* She swallowed quickly. "So, how was the pep rally?"

"Fantastic." Beulah struck a pose which Tabitha assumed was meant to be provocative. "What else?" Beulah asked, then plopped herself down, beside Tabitha. "See, the main point is to get the freshmen excited. They're new and—"

"You mean the freshmen *boys*," said a redheaded cheerleader with a lascivious grin. "They don't know what to do with us."

"Oh, they know what they'd *like* to do with us," said another cheerleader. She giggled, and the rest of the red-and-blue clad girls giggled along with her.

Seriously? Tabitha felt her cheeks grow hot, and in that moment, she wished she'd found an empty table after all.

"Uh, ladies," Beulah said, "I think that's enough of that. We're making our new friend uncomfortable."

"New friend?" asked the redhead. "Why, Beulah Martineau, shame on you. You haven't introduced us."

Tabitha looked up from her food and adopted a smile she didn't feel, as Beulah introduced the other girls.

"So, you're the Mormon girl!" The redhead, Patsy Moody, declared loud enough for the entire student body—at least those still in the cafeteria—to hear. She clapped her hands in delight. "What y'all did to Ol' Waddle! I heard she pissed her bloomers. Classic!"

Tabitha's cheeks reddened afresh, but her eyes were drawn to the girl from church, the one she'd originally meant to sit with—the girl who'd warned her off as if embarrassed to be associated with Tabitha. *Carrie-Anne. That's her name.* Carrie-Anne was, at that moment, beating a hasty exit, like a small brown mouse scurrying away while the cats are momentarily distracted by a new plaything.

"She said you broke her door, you slammed it so hard," said another girl in red-and-blue.

"That ain't the way I heard it," said Patsy. "She called you a witch—a Mormon witch. Said you broke it with your witchcraft."

Tabitha felt panic rise in her throat. "I—"

"Are all Mormons witches?" asked another girl. "I mean, folks say like all y'all are goin' to hell."

"Wasn't White Lettie a Mormon?"

"Lettie wasn't no Mormon."

"She was a witch, though."

They seemed to have forgotten Tabitha as they chattered on about witches and Mormons. Absurdly, a song from The Music Man ran through Tabitha's brain...

Pick a little, talk a little,
Pick a little, talk a little,
Cheep-cheep-cheep,
Talk a lot, pick a little more...

If Tabitha hadn't been scared out of her gourd, the clutch of cheerleader hens clucking away might have actually been funny. She took a deep breath and stood up. She stared straight ahead, not looking at any of them directly. "Yes, I'm a Mormon." They stopped talking and stared at her. "No, I'm not a witch. Mormons are"—she choked down bitter words that welled up in her mind—"as Christian as you. And I didn't break the stupid door."

Am I sure?

"I was nowhere near the door." Tabitha balled her hands into fists. "I couldn't have broken it."

I couldn't have.

Beulah shook her head, smiling. She put an arm around Tabitha's shoulders. "Of course, y'all didn't break the stupid door. What a silly thing to say."

"Hello, ladies!" said an increasingly familiar voice.

Tabitha looked up into the beaming, roguishly handsome face of Joey Parsons. His brown eyes sparkled. Tabitha noticed all the girls were grinning back, and most of them were wiggling or posing or otherwise attempting to attract his attention.

"Hey, Joey," said Patsy, fluttering her eyelashes.

Batting your eyes, Patsy? Seriously?

Several of the girls said a word or two of greeting. Beulah, however, merely favored him with a knowing smile.

Joey's eyes flickered in Beulah's direction, but there was no other outward sign of their special, secret connection.

He turned his radiant grin on Tabitha. "I do hope you ladies are making our Miss Tabitha Moonshadow feel welcome here at Bee-Byar High. There's no prettier spot in the Bootheel"—he winked at Tabitha—"and no lovelier ladies."

Is he flirting with me? Or does he just flirt with all the girls?

Tabitha heard two of the girls sigh. One of them actually purred. Tabitha was almost certain it'd been Patsy who'd made the feline sound.

Definitely make that "flirts with all the girls."

"Mr. Parsons?"

The vice-principal, the infuriating man who'd glossed over Mrs. Wardle's disgusting conduct, stood behind Joey. The man wore a grim countenance.

Joey turned around, still grinning as if life were the grandest adventure imaginable and he, Joey Parsons, were the unrivaled and well-accolaed hero. "Vice-principal Hardin! How're you doing this fine afternoon, sir? And how'd you know it was me, seeing me just from the back and all?" He ran a hand through his short, kinky hair. "It's the haircut, am I right? Maybe I should get it cut differently so I blend in better."

Hardin's mouth twitched, and his eyes tightened. "Mr. Parsons, there is a Lieutenant Kilmore, from the Sheriff's Department, who wishes to have a word with you."

Tabitha's heart skipped a beat at the mention of the handsome Brother Kilmore. A collective gasp rose from the other girls.

Joey's smile vanished. "Am I…Am I in some kind of trouble?" Then his eyes grew wide with alarm. "This isn't about my mama, is it? She okay?"

Beulah laid a hand on his arm, and Joey placed his hand atop hers.

His mom? What's going on with Joey's mom?

The vice-principal shook his head, and his expression softened a bit. "He didn't say anything about your mother. He simply said he wanted to ask you some questions."

Joey's shoulders slumped in relief, and he let out a shuddering breath.

Mr. Hardin put his hand on Joey's shoulder. The vice-principal, though not a short man by any measure—but then again, just about everyone seemed tall to Tabitha—had to reach up to administer the comforting gesture. "I didn't mean to scare you, son," Hardin said. "Is something wrong with your mama?"

Joey closed his eyes and shook his head. "No. She…had a scare last night. Wouldn't tell me about it. I thought…" He opened his eyes and smiled once more, but it wasn't the joyous, amused smile he always seemed to wear. This smile seemed plastic. "Sure. I'll go talk to the man." Then his grin blossomed, organic humor returning to the brown eyes. "I mean, I'll go talk to the *Man*!"

Several of the girls tittered at his joke.

The vice-principal pursed his lips, apparently not amused. He withdrew his hand from Joey's shoulder and tilted his head in the direction of exit. "If you'll come with me, Mr. Parsons?"

Joey turned his beaming countenance upon the girls. "Catch you later, ladies." He mimed catching a football and pulling it to his chest. "And I do hope to *catch* some of you later." He winked, and although his smile might have been directed at all the girls, Tabitha had the distinct impression his wink was directed at her alone.

As Joey strode away beside the comparatively diminutive vice-principal, Tabitha looked over at Beulah. The pretty blonde watched her secret boyfriend go, then glanced at Tabitha. Seeing that Tabitha was looking back, Beulah gave a small smile, but the edges of her grin seemed pinched. Her shoulders raised in the barest shrug.

It's okay, that shrug seemed to say.

Tabitha shrugged back. *He flirts with all the girls. I've got exactly one friend in this whole school. I don't want to lose her over a stupid wink.*

Besides, he's not LDS.

"Hey!" Beulah's face suddenly brightened. "After cheer practice, me and the rest of the squad were going to head over to Sambo's in PB for milkshakes. Wanna come?"

Tabitha nodded vigorously. "That'd be cool."

"He's dead! Dead!" Joey Parsons had rarely known real terror in his nearly eighteen years, but he was scared at that moment—scared of the man sitting in the shadows of the darkened room. "I thought you were just going to frighten him, not kill him!"

"Danny Thibodeaux was a waste of skin," said the figure in the dark. "Besides, he was in the act of—how shall I put this delicately—*assaulting* your mother."

"Mama? He *raped* my mama?"

"No. He was about to. We arrived just in time. I saved her. Or rather, the Circle saved her. I was merely the instrument of—"

"Cut the crap, Magnus!" Rage, fear, and loathing fought within Joey, squirming through his guts like a tangle of vipers. "I *know* how this works. But my mama—she's okay?"

"Yes, she's unharmed." The man known as Magnus smiled, and from the shadows, only his eyes and his teeth were visible. He could've been wearing the golden mask for all that could be seen of his face—but he wasn't. There was no need to conceal his identity. Joey knew exactly who Magnus was behind the mask. Yes, Joey knew who led the Circle—Joey and only one other were privy to that secret.

"Thibodeaux died"—Magnus's grin widened into a savage display of teeth—"horribly. And no one will suspect it was anything other than an unfortunate accident." Magnus chuckled, and the sound sent waves of nausea washing through Joey. "An unfortunate *pissing* accident. The man died with his pants around his ankles."

"Yeah." Joey choked down bile. "And a Ford on his back."

Magnus laughed a bit louder. "Oh, yes. A very clever touch that was, if I say so myself." His grin diminished, but didn't vanish altogether. "But that isn't why I wished to speak to you."

Joey clenched his teeth, still battling the urge to vomit. "Yeah." He nodded curtly.

"Tabitha Moonshadow."

"Yes. She is *very* special." The grin in the blackness widened once more. "Very special indeed."

"Uh-huh. But you knew that already. I mean you touched her well before I did. That was"—Joey quivered at the memory—"oh, man, that was incredible. I never felt anything like it. Her power must be..."

"Beyond anything we have known," Magnus finished with an ecstatic shudder of his own. "Perhaps greater than the entire Circle combined. And the broken door! I... *We* must have her."

"Yeah." Joey's nausea and fear were nearly subsumed by a sudden desire—a nearly overwhelming lust—to touch that power, to possess it again, however fleetingly.

And it was never enough.

"Cultivate her, Joey. Cultivate our Miss Moonshadow."

"I'll try, but she may not—you know—go for me. She already knows about Beulah and me. And besides, you know all about Mormons. She'll be so straitlaced when it comes to sex..."

"Perhaps," said Magnus, "but one never knows when it comes to Mormon girls—they can be...*pliable* with the right...pressure." He whetted his lips. "Oh, yes, indeed. They can." Magnus paused, closing his eyes. He emitted a shuddering sigh. "But she's new in town. And it would seem she has no friends among the youth at church. She's isolated and vulnerable. However, if overt seduction doesn't work, then friendship will have to suffice. We'll use a two-pronged approach." Magnus extended his left hand to the only other person in the room, the only other who was privy to his secret. "Won't we, my dear?"

A slender, feminine hand took his, the fingers interlacing intimately. Magnus rose to his feet. He took a step toward the girl and traced his free hand down her cheek in a sensuous caress.

She moaned softly at his touch.

Fresh nausea knotted Joey Parsons's guts—nausea and loathing. *For her? Or for him?* Joey wasn't sure.

The girl bared her teeth in a grin that would've been right at home on a wolf— assuming such a beast also sported a blonde ponytail and pink lipstick. "Don't y'all fret none," said Beulah Martineau. "I'm already on it."

The cottage door burst open. Heart pounding, Molly leapt from the sofa, clambering madly toward the gun hidden in the kitchen drawer. But at the sight of her daughter, Molly halted.

Tabitha twirled through the open door, high on her toes, like a ballerina, and singing at the top of her lungs.

"I could've danced, danced, danced all night!"

With her arms flung wide and her head tilted back, Tabitha held the last note, drawing it out and building it to a dramatic crescendo. This gave Molly a chance to recover a bit from her moment of stark terror. She calmed her breathing, but not her thundering heart.

"Does this mean?" Molly didn't dare finish the question. She knew how much this meant to her daughter. Molly had been offering up silent prayers all day, even kneeling a few times in her tiny office at the college, pleading with the Lord.

Tabitha beamed and clasped her hands together. "I got it!"

"Eliza Doolittle?"

"Yes!"

Molly squealed with delight, and Tabitha dropped her school bag to the floor. Mother and daughter locked in a hug worthy of a pair of wrestling grizzlies. Together, they bounced up and down, dancing and swaying and laughing with joy.

"Oh, Tabby-Cat!" Molly managed when at last their joint celebration slowed a bit. "That's wonderful! I'm so happy for you."

Tabitha pulled out of the hug, then grasped Molly's hands in hers. Tears of joy spilled from Tabitha's eyes. "I can't believe it! They posted the cast list today. I didn't dare look. I was sure I was too short, that they'd pick some other girl, somebody they knew better, somebody prettier. Beulah auditioned. She's good. And she's pretty and she's tall. She wasn't mad, though. She's gonna be Mrs. Pierce. I actually felt bad for her, but…Mom! I'm gonna be *Eliza Doolittle*!"

This set off a new round of girlish squealing and jumping.

When that second bout had spent itself, Molly dragged her daughter over to the couch. They both sat, exhausted, but still brimming with excitement. Molly put an arm around Tabitha. "So, who's going to play Professor Higgins?"

"Billy Hammond."

"Do I know him?" Molly was fairly certain she didn't, but remembering names was not one of her native talents.

"I don't think so."

"Do you like him?"

"Mom!"

"I just want to know if you're going to be okay working with him." *Not the whole truth, but...*

Tabitha shrugged. "He's okay. He's in choir and Shakespeare with me. He did an awesome Macbeth monologue."

"Can he do a decent British accent?"

Tabitha nodded. "Yeah. He's really good. I saw his audition."

"Is he cute?"

"Mom!"

"Just asking." Molly paused a moment. "So, is he?"

Tabitha shrugged again. "Yeah. Cute enough. But he's not Mormon."

"Oh, honey—"

"Mom, I'm not having this discussion with you *again*." Tabitha's expression darkened, and she looked straight ahead, away from Molly.

"Okay." Molly couldn't suppress a small grin. *I'm glad you're keeping your sights high, Tabby-Cat.* Then her grin bled away. *I just don't want you to be lonely. Like me.* Molly and loneliness were old and bitterly intimate companions.

Molly cleared her throat. "Well, I've got some good news of my own. And it's every bit as important as yours."

Tabitha turned her face to her mom. "What?"

"In fact, it's colossal."

"Come on, Mom! What is it?"

"Guess what's on at midnight..." Molly said in a sing-song tone.

Tabitha's eyes brightened. "What?"

"*Dracula.* The one with Jack Palance!"

Tabitha's jaw dropped. "Really?" She shook her head, but grinned fiercely. "I actually *liked* that one! It's gonna be hard to make fun of it."

"Oh, forget that, silly! We'll turn off all the lights and have a good scare!"

Tabitha bobbed her eyebrows up and down. "Coo-ool!"

"And I bought root beer and frozen pizza for dinner. It's not tea and crumpets, but we'll celebrate in *style*!"

At that, Tabitha's countenance fell.

"What's wrong?"

Drawing a deep breath, Tabitha grimaced. "I, uh, was hoping to go to a wienie roast tonight. Beulah was getting together a bunch of friends—no boys, just girls—

and no beer or anything else. We were gonna celebrate…"

Molly took a moment, trying to compose herself, attempting to conceal her disappointment, to shove aside the loneliness clawing at her. *She's growing up. She has friends. She's pulling away. Next fall, she'll be gone, and I'll be all alone in this wretched town.*

Tabitha searched her mother's face. "But I'll be home by midnight…"

Molly managed a smile. "Sure. We'll have our celebration later. And I'll save the pizza for another time."

"Thanks, Mom. You're the best!"

The clutching specter of loneliness twisted its claw, but Molly had other concerns. "You've…um…been hanging out with Beulah a lot lately. Did she give you a ride home?"

Tabitha shook her head, and her cheeks reddened. "No. Joey did."

"Joey?"

"Yeah. He lives out this way, and the coach cancelled football practice today on account of—"

"Oh."

Tabitha eyed her mother. "Is something wrong?"

And in an instant, Molly was on her guard. She knew she was treading on dangerously thin ice. "No. It's just…"

Tabitha folded her arms across her chest. "Just what?"

Molly shrugged, trying to adopt an air of nonchalance she most certainly did not feel. *How do I express what I can't explain even to myself?* She changed her tack. "I thought…I thought Beulah and Joey were…a couple—a *secret* couple, but…"

Tabitha visibly relaxed, unfolding her arms. "Yeah. They are, but…well, it's complicated."

"Complicated?"

Tabitha screwed up her face into a grimace. "I guess Beulah doesn't want her dad to know about Joey, so-o-o-o…she *dates*. A lot. Other guys, I mean. And I hear stories. None of them very nice. I don't believe them."

But Molly suspected Tabitha *did* believe them, to some degree at least. Molly held her tongue—just letting Tabitha continue at her own pace.

"And then there's Joey. He is the biggest flirt! He even flirts with me." Tabitha gave her mother a sidelong glance. "And before you ask—"

Molly's lips drew into a thin smile. *Wouldn't dream of it. Well, I would…but I won't.*

Tabitha sighed. "He's even asked me out. Several times." Tabitha paused, as if waiting for Molly to ask the obvious question, then continued. "I turned him down. I told you—I'm done dating guys who don't have our standards." Looking straight ahead again, she narrowed her eyes and muttered, "I'm practically a Mormon nun."

Molly gave Tabitha a gentle tug, and her daughter snuggled against her. "I'm sorry, Tabby-Cat." *I'm sorry about so many things. Your father. The branch—the way they shun you. The way they shun us both.*

Except for Mike Kilmore. A smile twitched at the corners of her mouth, and she suppressed a wistful sigh. *Especially Mike Kilmore. Not that he thinks of me that way. Dang it.*

Tabitha put her arm around Molly's waist, hugging her mother gently. "Anyway, Joey dates too…if you can call it that. They don't go to the movies or to the A&W— no white girl's dad is gonna let his daughter date Joey—not around here—but… well, there're lots of nasty stories there too. I mean *half* the cheerleaders! At *least* half. And there are a few others—not cheerleaders, I mean. And they all know about each other. And they don't seem to care. It's like Joey has a harem. Only, I think they actually call themselves 'the Circle.' It's like a club of Joey's girls or something. I mean if the rumors are true. He seems like such a nice guy. I don't wanna believe what I hear."

Molly cleared her throat, then spoke slowly and softly. She could almost hear the proverbial ice cracking beneath her. "But you accepted a ride with him. Alone."

Tabitha hesitated, then nodded. "Yeah." She shrugged and tightened her hug a bit. "Pretty dumb. But," she shrugged again, "in spite of everything I hear, all the flirting, I feel like I can *trust* him. He doesn't touch me. He's never *tried* anything, except—" She tensed, pulled her arm away, and sat up. "He…It's so weird."

What? What? Calm, yourself, Molly. Let her say it. Whatever it is . . . She's going to say it. Just be patient. Please, be patient. She bit her tongue. Be patient.

"He…He likes to…shake hands."

"Shake hands?" Molly couldn't hide the surprise in her voice.

"Yeah. He likes to shake hands. And he holds my hand like that for a long time." Tabitha hunched her shoulders. "Maybe it isn't that long, but it *feels* like it, you know? Just a little bit too long."

"Tabitha, honey, I…" *Am I really going to say this?* "I have a bad feeling. I would say, a prompting, but I don't know how to say this."

Tabitha folded her arms and hunched her shoulders, drawing in on herself. "Mom," she said through gritted teeth, "these are my friends. My only friends."

"Yes, honey, I know."

"You dragged me to this armpit of a town."

"Yes, honey, but you know why I…"

"Away from home, away from—"

"I know. I'm, well, I'm *not* sorry—not really, but I know it's been hard."

Tabitha closed her eyes, pressed her lips closed, and breathed noisily through her nose.

She's not listening anymore. Can't get through to her, not when she's like this. Not right now.

Tabitha's tensed lips parted slightly. "So, can I go?"

No. Stay here. Stay safe. Stay safe, here, with me. Let me protect you. But if I push too hard... Molly sighed. "Be home by midnight?"

Tabitha smiled and opened her eyes. She turned her face to her mom, and Molly searched for triumph in her daughter's eyes.

And found none—just simple relief. It means so much to her.

An impish grin spread across Tabitha's face. "Jack Palance as Dracula? Wouldn't miss it for the world!"

Molly returned the grin, but her sense of unease remained.

Can't win this one. Right now, I have to get her to trust me again. And that means letting go—a little. You let her go and spend the summer with Jerry, and look what happened, her innermost thoughts yelled. *I had to. I had no choice.*

Molly squeezed her daughter's knee. "I'll have the popcorn popped, the lights out, and the blanket ready."

"I'm gonna do it." Tabitha lifted the pair of blue jeans from her dresser drawer. "I am."

Except for the indignity of gym class with its mandatory wearing of short shorts, Tabitha had worn nothing in public but long, modest skirts—both to cover her legs and to emphasize her womanhood.

Not since the summer.

Randy can go hang. Dad too.

In her head, mention of her father was an afterthought—casual, barely worth noting. *He is an afterthought,* she'd told herself countless times. Dad was simply a man who'd rejected all women. Not worth her time.

But in her heart—deep down in the lightless caverns at the pit of her soul, where the black demons of self-doubt lurked on wings of loathing—the thought of her dad was a wound that simply would not heal. Because he had rejected *her.*

Instead of protecting her, he'd thrown her to the wolves—to one wolf at least—to Randy.

Men.

Somehow that one word contained the sum of her fears, her pain, her yearnings.

Who needs them?

She stared at the blue jeans. They weren't simply pants. They were a statement—of what, Tabitha wasn't sure. Rebellion? Independence? Courage?

"A skirt's just not practical in the woods." It was the argument she'd been using to work herself up to this moment of decision—over a choice which should have been trivial—less than trivial.

Still staring at the jeans in her hands, she no longer saw the pants. Instead, her mind filled with the image of Tommy, her last boyfriend. The only boy she'd ever kissed—off-stage, at least. Their last date.

Their last kiss. Her breath coming in ragged tremors, blood pounding in her ears. Tommy's hand sliding up her leg, pulling up her skirt...

She'd slapped him then. Hard. And that had been the end.

Tabitha found herself lying on her bed, clutching the pair of jeans to her chest. Weeping.

94

Tommy, why? You ruined everything!

Angrily, she scrubbed away her tears. And put on the pants.

I get to be Eliza Doolittle in My Fair Lady. *I should be happy. I am happy. Men can all go hang.*

She checked her watch. Five-seventeen. *Too soon to head over there.*

Beulah had offered to pick her up, to drive her over to the clearing, the spot in the woods. They'd all hung out there before. They would build a campfire, roast hotdogs, make s'mores, and listen to a portable radio. Beulah had promised there'd be *no* country music. And at the time, for the briefest of moments, Tabitha had wondered why Beulah and the others—the Circle—had been so accommodating.

But Tabitha had declined the offer of a ride, at least on the way there. She'd let Beulah drive her home. The clearing wasn't far—a hundred yards beyond the ruins of White Lettie's cabin—and Tabitha wanted to walk. At least that was the excuse she'd given. She'd said she wanted to be alone with her thoughts for a bit.

But that's not the whole truth, is it? You just want another excuse to walk through the Hollow. To linger in her place.

She'd told her mom about Beulah's offer of a ride, but had omitted the part about not accepting. There'd been no more encounters with the "ghosts" since the break-in-that-wasn't-a-break-in, but her mom was still wary. She didn't like the idea of Tabitha being alone in the woods—without the gun, at least. But for herself, Tabitha wasn't worried about the white-robed intruders. At least not in the daylight.

They got caught. They won't be back, at least, that was what she told herself.

Tabitha had been to Lettie's Hollow on several occasions during the afternoon hours between school and her mom's return from work.

And she'd always taken the broom.

Tabitha reached for the broom—*the witch's broom*—now accoutered with longer, more rustic, more authentic bristles. She hefted it, savoring the weight. *So heavy. Not just a broom. A symbol of power, a weapon.*

Faces, male faces, swirled through her mind like a perverse carousel in a demented carnival of pain and terror: Tommy. Dad. Randy. Joey.

She wanted to shut them out. Forget them, for a time at least. Shut out the anguish, the fear, and—in Joey's case at least—the confusion.

Joey confused her.

He was handsome, sure. And charming. Funny. Not quite humble, but self-deprecating. Confident. Smart. And so-o-o not Mormon.

And her best friend's boyfriend. Tabitha didn't want to think about him at that moment. Him or any man.

Especially Brother Kilmore. *Dreamy Mike Kilmore.* The one man she wished would notice her…in that way.

Give it up, girl. He's never going to think of you as anything but a kid. Men! At least there won't be any men there tonight.

But the gathering—and the escape it promised—seemed so far off.

"I could have danced all night…"

THE WITCH OF WHITE LADY HOLLOW

But even that image involved men. Tabitha knew one way at least to escape. For a time.

She sat on the bed, laid the broom across her lap. She fixed her eyes on the end of the broomstick, on the tip of its dark iron core. Deliberately, she pressed her thumb against the iron.

The first sensation, as always, was weakness, as if all her strength, all her vitality—all of *Tabitha*—had been drained out of her.

Then the room spun about her, dissolving into a swirling maelstrom of colors—all blending into white.

She carefully poured the dark powder onto a clean cotton rag. She gathered the corners of the rag and tied them. The result was a small bundle, containing dried, ground-up yarrow leaves from her herb garden. She placed the medicine bag in Sally's hands.

The slave woman's skin was black as pitch, but the palms of her hands were nearly as light as any white woman's—any normal white woman's.

Nobody's skin was as white as Lettie's.

"Dis cool da fever?" Sally's eyes were wide with fear. "Dis save my baby? He so hot, Miss Lettie. So hot."

Lettie combined a shrug with a compassionate smile, trying to communicate cautious hope.

It was so hard with the black folks, with anyone, for that matter, black or white, who couldn't read—so hard to communicate.

She mouthed, I hope so.

Sally nodded. "Thank ya, Miss Lettie. Thank ya! Lord Jesus bless ya."

Lettie nodded. She threw her arms around the tall woman and embraced her. So tall. So strong. Slave-owners breed them like horses—for size and strength. And they treat the horses better.

After a brief hesitation, Sally returned the hug. "Ain't never got hugged by no white—"

Tabitha pulled her thumb off the tip of the broom. She inhaled sharply—a shuddering but cleansing breath. The bedroom coalesced around her as if a fog had dissipated.

A good memory. A pleasant memory.

Through practice, she'd learned she could yank herself out of a vision if she separated herself from the iron. She wanted—no, yearned to know more about White Lettie, but Tabitha had no desire to relive the horrors that stained Lettie's past.

She was a good woman. So wise. So loving. So caring.

But the men in her life...

Lettie's father and her brothers had all mistreated her. But her husband! He was by far the worst of a bad lot.

But this...this is a nice memory.

THE WITCH OF WHITE LADY HOLLOW

Tabitha placed her thumb on the iron once more.

"—woman afore."

Lettie squeezed her more tightly, then patted Sally's back. Barely more than a girl, Lettie thought. And she's got two babies. One of them by her master.

May God curse Elias Thibodeaux, smite him with the French disease. And the insanity that comes of it.

A Latin proverb sprang to her mind. Quos Deus vult perdere, prius demantat— Whom God would destroy, He first makes mad.

"Lord Jesus an' all the li'l baby angels bless ya, Miss Lettie. Ain't got nothin' to give ya this time. No chicken. No cornpone. No squash. No nothin'. Next time, maybe. Next time, I brings ya somethin'."

Still holding Sally close, Lettie shook her head. I don't heal folks for payment. If folks had something to give, that was all well and good, but Lettie had all she needed in the Hollow. She healed because it brought her peace—peace and escape from the shadows of the past.

Lettie took Sally's black face in her too-white hands, pulled it down, and kissed the slave woman's forehead.

Then Lettie took a step back and mimed mixing the herbs with water, boiling it, then drinking the tea.

"Stir it? With water?" Sally asked. "Make a tea?"

Lettie nodded, then bestowing a kindly smile, she motioned for Sally to go.

The slave woman grinned, wiping tears from her big eyes. Then she turned and trotted out the cabin door, clutching the tiny bundle of herbs like a treasure to her ample breast.

Lettie snatched her broom from where it leaned against the cabin wall—she never left the safety of her cabin without her heavy broom—then followed Sally out the door. She watched the tall woman disappear into the woods at the edge of the Hollow.

Then Lettie knelt on the ground, holding the broom like a talisman across her thighs. She bowed her head and offered up a mute prayer for Sally's little boy.

God in Heaven, spare Sally's little Thomas. Heal him in thy mercy. Let my herbs—the herbs thou gavest me—let the herbs do him good. Let the fever abate.

But if he should die, Lord . . . If he should die, take him to Thy bosom. Hold him close to Thy bosom.

Hold him close . . . beside my precious little Jonah.

Lord, please tell Jonah I love him. Tell him not a day goes by, but I think of him.

Tell him I'm sorry I couldn't—

Grief exploded within her, bursting from her as a silent, choking sob. Like a summer cloudburst, the anguish had come on her unexpectedly, overwhelming her, clouding her senses.

She bent forward, doubled over in a visceral agony of loss.

Jonah!

She mouthed her son's name again and again.

Jonah! My Jonah! My little—

Strong hands seized her from behind.

She was slammed onto her back, then pinned to the hard ground by a great weight. Her broom, her only protection, rolled out of her hand. She scrabbled at it with grasping, desperate fingers.

No!

And above her—

—the leering face of Elias Thibodeaux.

Lust like the madness she'd wished upon him burned in his devil eyes.

God! Please! Help me!

But the Heavens were silent.

And as Elias crushed his lips against hers, his breath invading her mouth—foul, smelling of rotting things—Lettie's own lips writhed around a voiceless scream.

Tabitha tore her thumb off the cold iron. She fell back on her bed panting, still clutching the broom to her chest.

Not that one! Not that memory!

And Tabitha wept. She wept for Lettie.

That horrible man! That evil, sick...man! And there was nothing, nothing Lettie could've done to save herself!

Elias had been too strong. Lettie had been alone—alone and utterly defenseless.

Not even her broom could save her that time.

Tabitha's grief twisted inside, frothing up into rage—rage at Elias Thibodeaux. Her dad. Randy. Tommy.

Even God.

Why? Heavenly Father, why?

Why didn't you listen? Why didn't you save her? She was alone and afraid and helpless! What did she ever do to deserve that? Any of it? All her life? What did she ever do?

Why did you let those men hurt her?

Why didn't you protect her?

"Why?" she snarled through clenched teeth, amid a deluge of angry tears. Her legs kicked out, as if of their own volition, kicking against a locked bathroom door which wasn't there, as if to keep Randy and his vile threats outside.

"Why didn't you protect me?"

Molly couldn't shake the gnawing feeling of dread. *It's just a wienie roast. No booze. No drugs. No boys.* Molly sighed.

The "ghosts" or whoever they were haven't been back. Probably scared off. I hope. And Tabitha won't be alone. Tabitha's almost an adult, and she seems to be handling herself well enough. Most of the time.

But she's still my baby. My only baby. And I'd do anything—anything to protect my baby.

My little Tabby-Cat.

Molly sat at the dining table, staring at Tabitha's bedroom door. Occasionally, she would glance in the direction of the kitchen drawer.

I could send it with her. In her shoulder bag.

Molly shuddered at the thought.

She's pulling away. Too soon.

Molly got up and paced the floor. She wandered around the living room, into the kitchen, and back.

It's ust a wienie roast. I went to wienie roasts as a kid.

Don't let her go. Keep her safe.

But I already said yes.

Who's the mother here? Who's the adult? Just put your foot down and—

Jerked out of her thoughts and back in the real world, Molly was startled to realize where she was and what she'd been about to do. Her hand was gripping the doorknob to Tabitha's bedroom.

She recoiled from the knob and stepped away from the door. Even had she been about to confront Tabitha, to take back her permission, she should knock first, not just barge in.

Is that what I was going to do? Just barge in and say, "You can't go." Was that it?

She wheeled around and resumed her pacing, which took on a more frenzied aspect. When she found herself unconsciously reaching for the doorknob again, she froze.

Stop it! Either you trust her to go or you don't.

I trust her, but the others?

Heavenly Father, what should I do?

And the words came to her mind: *Remind her who she is.* The inner "voice" was very much like her own, so much so that Molly couldn't be sure the words weren't her own.

Molly pondered that. Remind her who she is.

Then, acting on impulse—or prompting, she wasn't sure which—she strode to her own bedroom. Standing in front of the dresser, she lifted the lid on her jewelry box. The box itself was nearly as old as she was, a gift from her daddy when she was a little girl. Like most of the objects it held. The box wasn't expensive, but neither was it a box made for a child. It was one of the few things she still had from her father. In addition to her jewelry, the box contained her small treasures—a seashell she'd picked up during a vacation to the California coast, a porcelain thimble that had belonged to her grandmother, a pebble from the banks of the Mississippi, and a small, dark metal disk, about the size of a half-dollar, round on the outside, with a square hole in the middle.

She pulled the disk out of the box and held it between her thumb and forefinger. It wasn't much to look at. In fact, it was ugly—pitted and darkened by the passing of years. It felt rough and cold to the touch.

She heard Tabitha's door open, and she turned in time to see her daughter emerge from her bedroom. Tabitha wore a thick turtleneck sweater...and pants.

"Tabby-Cat?"

Tabitha turned to her and smiled. "Hey, Mom."

To Molly's eyes, her daughter's smile seemed weary, almost sad. Tabitha's eyes were red, as if she'd been crying. "Honey, you okay?"

The smile brightened a little. "Sure. I'm off, so..." Tabitha waved and turned toward the front door.

"Tabby-Cat? Before you go..."

Tabitha turned back to face her mother. "Yeah?"

Molly swallowed, struggling to find the words. "Um, it's...I said you could go—and you still can, of course—but I want you to. Well, remember who you are."

Oh, good going. Very profound.

Tabitha's face twisted into a confused grimace. "Remember who I am?"

Molly nodded. "Yes. You are a daughter of God. You are *my* daughter." *My baby. My only child.*

Tabitha shrugged. "Of course. I know that. How many times do I have to tell you this? I know what the standards are, Mom. I'm not gonna...you know."

"I know, but." Molly took a step toward her daughter. "I know it's hard here, especially with the branch—the kids at church—the way they treat you"—*and me*—"but—"

"Mom, I really don't have time for this. I've gotta—"

I'm blowing it! Think of something! "I . . . I want you to have this." Molly extended the metal disk toward her daughter.

Tabitha's eyes went to the proffered object. "What is it?"

"It's a washer for a railroad spike."

Tabitha raised an eyebrow and looked at her mother askance. "A washer?"

"You know—you put a spike through it—see the square hole—to help hold the spike in place."

Tabitha made no move to take the disk from her. "Ohhh kay. So what?"

"Well, it belonged to your grandfather—to my dad."

"I thought your dad was a cop, not a railroad worker."

"He was a cop." Molly pointed to the small dining table. "Honey, can we just sit and talk for a minute? I didn't hear a car outside. Is Beulah here already?"

Tabitha hesitated. "No. I was just going to... Okay, but just for a minute." She took a seat.

Molly joined her. "My dad was a cop. He was a hero."

"Yeah, I know."

"Well, one day, there was a train derailment. Passenger train. It was bad. Lots of people were killed. Lots were hurt. Your grandfather was the first responder on the scene. One of the cars was on fire—the dining car, I believe. My dad went into the flames and carried five people to safety. He"—Molly's voice broke—"got burned pretty badly. Scars on his arms and back."

As Molly talked, her daughter's expression softened, and a tear threatened at the corner of one eye. "That's awful. But it's also pretty cool—that he did that, I mean."

Molly smiled sadly at a bittersweet memory of running her small fingers over the scars on her daddy's arms. A tear fell from her own eye. "My daddy was a real hero. He was selfless." She cleared her throat. "Anyway, he took this washer home as, as a memento. He gave it to me. It's one of my greatest treasures." She wiped the tear away and smiled. "Next to you, of course." Molly offered the disk again. "I want you to have it. To help you remember who you are, who you're supposed to become."

Tabitha looked from her mother's face to the disk and back again. "Are you sure?"

"Yeah, honey. I love you so much. And I'm so proud of you."

Tabitha extended her hand, palm up, and Molly dropped the iron disk into her daughter's open palm.

Tabitha gasped sharply, and her hand snapped into a closed fist around the disk. Her eyes rolled up until only the whites showed. She slumped in her chair as if every muscle in her body had turned to Jell-O—every muscle, except those in her fist, straining around the iron washer.

"Tabitha!" Molly scrambled out of her chair and around the table. She grasped Tabitha's shoulders and shook her. "Tabitha!"

Tabitha was unresponsive. Her mouth gaped ope but she was as limp as a rag doll. Or a corpse. Molly stared at the rise and fall of her chest: Tabitha was breathing,

Molly let go of Tabitha's shoulders and pried her fist open, peeling back the fingers with supreme effort, terrified she'd break them.

As soon as the disk was exposed, Molly ripped it out of Tabitha's hand, and dropped it onto the table.

Tabitha gulped in air like a resuscitated drowning victim. Her eyes rolled down 'til her dark pupils were visible once more. She sat bolt upright and stared at her mother.

Stark terror was written all over Tabitha's face. A sob ripped from her throat and tears flowed down her cheeks. "Oh, Mom!"

Molly threw her arms around her daughter. Tabitha clung to her, trembling like a lost and frightened child.

Molly herself quaked with fear. "Honey, what's wrong?"

Tabitha sobbed. "Mom! I'm so s-s-sorry!"

"What is it? What happened?"

"It's so—so awful!"

"What, Tabby-Cat? What?"

"D-Dad. What he s-said." Tabitha took another gulping breath.

"What? What are you talking about? Did he call?" *He doesn't even have our phone number, does he?*

Tabitha shook her head so hard, tears flew from her cheeks in tiny droplets. "No. What he said when he l-left."

"What?" *What is she talking about?* "You mean when I picked you up at your dad's place this summer?" *Jerry didn't say a word to me.*

"No. When he told you he was l-leaving you." A sob shook her again. "Leaving us."

Molly patted Tabitha's back. "But that was years ago, honey. You weren't even there. You were at school that day."

"All those disgusting things sick things he wanted you to do. But you wouldn't. You couldn't. It was horrible! And he called you, he called you, the Frigid Bitch of the West."

The air froze in Molly's lungs. The Frigid Bitch of the West. Jerry had called her that only once—eleven years ago—on the day he told her he was gay—on the day he walked out.

How could Tabitha possibly know that?

11

"Well, butter my butt and call me a biscuit!" Beulah stared, mouth agape. "Tabitha Moonshadow! Is that you?"

Tabitha's cheeks flushed crimson, though she doubted anyone could see in the light of the dancing campfire. Should've just worn the skirt. She grinned sheepishly and waved at Beulah, then at the rest of the girls.

The Circle, as they called themselves, sat around the fire on logs or stones. All of them were in possession of long sticks. Some sticks skewered a hotdog or marshmallows and were held over the flames or near the coals. Other sticks poked idly at the fire. Tabitha counted quickly. *Ten.* Uncertain of just how many members there were in the informal—at least she *assumed* it was informal—club, she couldn't tell if anyone in particular was absent. *That's pretty much everybody.*

"I've never seen you in pants, girl!" Patsy slapped her own knee. "See, y'all! She *does* have legs—outside of gym class, I mean!" She elbowed Cassie—one of the few non-cheerleaders. "Girl, you owe me five dollars. Five dollars!" Patsy extended her hand toward Cassie and greedily rubbed her thumb against the tips of her first two fingers. "Pay up!"

Please stop making a big deal out of it! Tabitha felt a strong urge to turn and run—run back to her mom, who she was sure was still waiting and would be, at least for a few more minutes, in the car up the dirt road leading away from the clearing. *If I go back, she'll think I can't handle this on my own—that I'm still all shook up.*

But you are, her inner voice said. *You're still rattled.*

The vision, coming as it had without warning, had ripped through her like lightning through a tree. Her mom had told her the trance had lasted only a few seconds, but to Tabitha, it'd seemed to go on and on. She'd seen through the eyes of her mom—becoming her mom for a time—feeling her mother's anguish, her horror, her revulsion. And then came the loss, the ultimate rejection.

Mom! How could you bear it?

Tabitha had seen her dad as she'd never known him—as her mother had known him. Molly had loved him, desired him, trembled at his touch, trusted him. And Jerry had betrayed her, abandoned her. Destroyed her. He'd taken everything from her—safety, security, love, virginity—everything except her daughter. Well, she'd given him love and her virginity—everything she had to give. And in the end, he'd thrown it all away. He'd thrown Tabitha away as well, discarding her like something putrid and unpleasant stuck to the bottom of his shoe.

They'd talked—Tabitha and her mom—for nearly an hour. Tabitha had confessed about the visions. *What choice did I have?* Her mom, although understandably shocked and ashen-faced at the revelations, had been sympathetic and accepting, never indicating the slightest doubt at Tabitha's implausible story.

And in the end, they had embraced, and Tabitha felt as if an unbreakable bond had been forged—or at least strengthened, like a steel chain tempered in the fires of loss and pain.

Mom believes me.

Night had enveloped the Hollow by the time they were done, and her mother, after reluctantly giving her consent once more for Tabitha to attend the gathering, had insisted on driving her there—or at least to the last bend in the dirt road. Tabitha, after faithfully promising to get a ride home with Beulah and to be home by midnight, had been allowed to walk the remaining distance to the clearing.

Sitting among her friends, Tabitha felt a wave of longing sweep over her. She ached to be home, in her mother's arms.

I shouldn't have come.

"Earth to Tabitha Moonshadow! Come in, Tabitha Moonshadow!"

Tabitha blinked, clearing her head of the befuddling images. With White Lettie's visions, Tabitha had little difficulty separating herself from the other woman's memories, but with her mom . . . *Maybe we're just too close. I know her. More than I ever wanted to.*

Tabitha fought back tears.

Mom, I'm sorry.

"Seriously." Beulah laid a hand on Tabitha's shoulder. "You okay?"

Tabitha shook herself. "Yeah. Sure." She forced a grin. "Why wouldn't I be?"

Beulah took her by the hand and led her to a log. Patsy sat there, but she scooted toward one end to make room for Tabitha. "Well," said Beulah, "there is the fact that you're an hour or so late to this here shindig. There's the fact that you went all *Twilight Zone* on me." Beulah sat on the log, and Tabitha joined her. "And…there's the inescapable fact of your so-not-Tabitha-Moonshadow fashion statement." She pointed at Tabitha's jeans, and mouthed with exaggerated enunciation, "You're wearing pants!"

Tabitha chuckled at that. "Yeah, well. What can I say?" *So pathetic. Such a refined and erudite lady I am.*

Beulah handed her a stick with a hotdog impaled upon it. "You can say, 'Thank you, Beulah, my best and truest friend, for excusing my inexcusable tardiness *and* for saving me one of Oscar Meyer's finest.'"

Tabitha's grin was genuine, and she winked as she accepted the stick. "Oscar Meyer, huh? Ooh, we are high class!"

"Why, yes, Miss Tabitha. Only the best the Sniders IGA had to offer." Beulah gently gripped Tabitha's wrist, guiding her stick toward the fire. "We even have Wonder Bread buns!"

"Oh, my word!" Tabitha adopted an accent to match her friend's. She tilted her head back and made an exaggerated show of fanning herself. "How will I ever bear my return to the real world?"

"You know, girl, y'all do the Bootheel proud—that's for sure—but that's the wrong accent, especially tonight." Beulah lifted her voice. "Okay, y'all, how about a round of applause for our own Eliza Doolittle!"

The other girls clapped or slapped their thighs—mindful of their hotdog- or marshmallow-laden sticks—and called out words of congratulations.

Tabitha smiled, nodding timidly at first. Then her grin widened. She lifted one corner of her mouth, determined to dazzle them with her Cockney accent. "Why, thank ye, ladies. You are most kind. Most kind indeed."

This elicited a fresh round of applause and cheers.

"And did y'all know," Beulah said as the accolades died down, "that she *already* knows the *entire* play? All the songs?" She nudged Tabitha. "Ain't that right?"

Tabitha lowered her head. On stage, she could easily bask in applause, but up close, where she had to meet another's gaze, such praise embarrassed her. "Yeah. Pretty much." She paused. "It's always been my dream to play Eliza. I've had the script for years."

A part of Tabitha was still amazed Beulah showed such grace in being beaten out of the part herself. She'd had the lead in the school musical the previous year. And the year before that.

Beulah patted Tabitha on the back. "That's what you told me."

Tabitha looked at her friend. "I did?"

Beulah nodded. "The first week of school, when you heard we were going to do *Guys and Dolls*. It was pretty obvious you weren't happy about that one." She tapped the side of her nose with two fingers. "Something, as I recall, about not being able to tap-dance."

Tabitha nodded, flushing at the memory. "Yeah. Fumble-Foot-Tabby—that's me all over. And you asked me what show I'd wish for if I could do any show in the world."

"That's right."

Tabitha shook her head. "I'm still amazed we got to do *My Fair Lady* at a high school. It had a revival on Broadway until just last year. I mean, the royalties alone must've been . . . astronomical!"

Beulah nodded. "More'n likely. But don't y'all worry about that. From what I heard, an anonymous and wealthy benefactor stepped forward and footed the entire bill—royalties, costumes, sets, and all."

Really? It's almost as if they changed the show just for me.

Tabitha shivered as if an ice cube had been dropped down her back. *They wouldn't do that, would they? And if someone did, why?*

Don't look a gift horse in the mouth, girl.

Pay no attention to that man behind the curtain . . .

Stop it. You get to be Eliza Doolittle.

But all she said out loud was a noncommittal, "Huh."

Her thoughts shifted back to her grandfather's railroad washer. *Iron. It must be iron. When I touch iron... But why Mom's memory? Why not Grandpa's?*

Patsy elbowed Tabitha. "Y'all gonna eat that hotdog or just char it to a cinder?"

Tabitha pulled the blackened Oscar Meyer from the fire. Upon examination, the hotdog still appeared to be edible. Crunchy, but edible. Tabitha shrugged. "Eat it, I guess."

Patsy elbowed her again. "Good choice."

One of the girls, Wanda by name, cranked up the volume on a largish portable radio and tape player. "Ooh, I love this one!"

The strains of the Eagles singing "Witchy Woman" permeated the clearing.

Normally, as far as Tabitha was concerned, the music of the Eagles was okay, but this particular song was not one of her favorites. *At least it's not country.*

When the chorus came around, all the girls of the Circle joined in, lifting their faces to the moon and howling out,

"Whoo-oo-oo-oo, witchy woman!

See how high she flies!"

Something about the wild abandon of the singing made Tabitha uneasy—as if something was crawling across her neck.

They're my friends. They accepted me when no one else would.

No one else.

Not even the kids at church.

Holding the gun pointed toward the ceiling, Molly stood at the side of the door. She had her index finger pointed down the barrel. After Tabitha's confession about the visions, Molly was so spooked, she didn't trust her finger on the trigger. She took a deep breath, attempting to control and calm her trembling. *Too early for Tabitha.* "Wh-who"—she paused, taking another deep, calming breath—"Who is it?"

"It's Mike Kilmore."

Molly's body sagged with relief as the tension flowed out of her like water through a sieve. "Just a minute."

Stilling her trembling, she set the safety on the gun, then rushed over to the kitchen and stowed the weapon in its drawer. Then she strode quickly to the door.

Mike Kilmore. Not Brother *Kilmore.*

Suddenly, she was trembling for an entirely different reason.

Her palm moist from nervous sweat, she opened the door to the night.

Bathed in the cottage's light, Mike stood there—tall, handsome, built like a rock, and smiling. At her. "Evening, Miss Molly. May I come in?"

Molly returned his infectious grin. "Absolutely."

He was dressed casually—blue jeans, denim shirt, and Western boots.

What a hunk! I can't believe I keep using that word. But if the cowboy boot fits…

His handshake was firm and warm, and if he noticed the sweatiness of her palm, he didn't mention it. "We missed y'all at the branch social tonight."

Molly sighed. *Not a social visit after all. Just a home teacher checking up on one of his assigned families. Well, what did you expect? To be asked out on a date?* She led him to the living room. "Yes, well, I…we don't…"

He clicked his tongue and tilted his head. " . . . don't exactly feel welcome?"

Molly nodded. "Yes, that's one way to put it." She sat on the love seat, indicating he should sit on the sofa.

"Thank you, ma'am." He took his seat. "Um, I do get that impression. Yes, I do. And I'm sorry 'bout that. Most folks in the branch, well, they don't accept… newcomers all that well. 'Specially folks who, well, uh, that is…"

"You mean, women who can't keep their mouths shut?"

He chuckled, tilted his head again, and winked at her. "That's about it. You're a very perceptive lady, if I may be so bold, Miss Molly. And you're not afraid to speak your mind."

Molly forced a sagging smile. *Oh, well.*

"Is your lovely daughter at home?"

Molly's smile drooped even more. *Am I actually jealous of my daughter? And just how old are you, Mike Kilmore?* She surreptitiously cleared her throat. "No. Tabitha's out with friends."

"Well, then, Miss Molly…"

"Molly," she corrected. "Please."

He grinned and nodded. "Yes, ma'am. Well, *Molly*, would you have dinner with me tomorrow night?"

"Yes." The word came out unbidden, without consideration, seemingly of its own volition. Molly swallowed.

He just asked me out? He sure did. And I just accepted.

Heat rose in Molly's cheeks.

"Well"—his bright, infectious grin seemed to split his chiseled face from ear to ear—"that went a lot easier than I expected!"

Molly discovered she was giggling. And immediately stifled her girlish laughter. "Um, what time?"

"You tell me. I'll be at your disposal all evening. And what d'y'all like to eat? Steak? Ponderosa ain't that fancy, but I know the manager. And I know how to get him to cook a T-bone ju-u-ust right."

"You know what I hate, I mean, absolutely *despise* about that play?" Beulah poked at the fire with her stick. Sparks flew up and died in the crisp autumn air.

The sparks reminded Tabitha of the "ghosts" she'd seen on their first night in the Hollow. She suppressed a sudden urge to look around for white-robed figures hovering in the air. "The play? *My Fair Lady?*"

Beulah nodded. "Uh-huh."

"What?"

"It's all the anti-women crap. I mean, they joke about it, but There's 'Why Can't a Woman Be More Like a Man?' and at the end, after all Henry Higgins has done, Eliza goes back to him. I mean, don't you think it's a bit much?"

Tabitha was stunned. *That came out of the blue.* "I think it's romantic."

"Romantic? Girl, he's a bully. Men—they're all bullies. They think, just because they're bigger and stronger, they can make us do anything they want. They want us to be soft and pretty and to cook and clean and jump into bed at a moment's notice." She raised her voice. "Am I right, ladies?"

Her words were met by a chorus of assent.

She nudged Tabitha. "Am I right?"

Tabitha dropped her gaze to the dirt, but said nothing. The parade of male faces marched through her head. *Dad. Randy. Tommy. Joey.*

Brother Kilmore.

Cassie raised her stick into the air, wielding it like a spear of challenge. "And what do we get in return, huh? A black eye, that's what!"

"Men suck!" called another girl—Tabitha didn't know the girl's name. This epithet was also met by a chorus of agreement.

Beulah nodded, frowning. "Yes, indeed. Men do suck." She poked at the fire. "The whole rotten sex." She spoke quietly, evenly, almost dispassionately. "They can all go straight to hell."

After what she'd seen through her mother's eyes, Tabitha was almost ready to agree with her. Almost. She whispered, "Uh, what about"—*Brother Kilmore*—"Joey?"

Staring at the dancing flames, Beulah shrugged. "Joey's different."

"How? How is he different?"

"Because Joey appreciates me."

"But," Tabitha knew she was treading on dangerous ground. They, the two of them, had never discussed this, not directly. "The way Joey, I've heard stories. He's not…"

Beulah turned her head and gave Tabitha a sidelong look. "Not faithful to me? He cheats on me? Is that it?"

"Yeah."

The blonde turned her face back to the fire. "That's just sex. That doesn't mean anything."

It means something. It means a very big something. To me.

"Besides"—Beulah chuckled, shaking her head ever so slightly—"it's not like

I'm not getting mine. What's good for the gander's even better for the goose, honey."

"You know it," Patsy said. She elbowed Tabitha again. "Or you would if you weren't such an uptight Mormon virgin. You *are* a virgin, right?"

Get up. Go. Get out of here!

Tabitha started to get to her feet, but Beulah put a firm hand on her thigh, pushing her back down. "You know, I did some reading about y'all's church. I read it's a misogynist patriarchy. Men control everything. Men hold y'all's priesthood."

"Yeah, but…" Tabitha tried to rise once more.

Beulah gripped Tabitha's thigh with well-manicured claws. "They make all y'all women wear dresses and learn to be house slaves and legal whores. That's what being a wife is, you know—nothing but legal prostitution."

"You got that right!" Patsy said.

"You tell her, Beulah!" said another.

Tabitha realized Beulah, little by little, had been raising her voice 'til all the Circle could hear.

"I bet," said Beulah, "they don't even let y'all talk in church."

They don't. Not here. We're not appreciated, not valued at all.

Nobody gives two cents about what we think, how we feel—

"You know what I heard?" Beulah's voice filled the clearing as if she were an actress on a stage.

Or a preacher at a pulpit.

"Tell us, sister!" More than one girl had said it—not exactly together—but the whole scene reminded Tabitha disturbingly of a rowdy southern Pentecostal service. "Tell us what you heard!"

"I heard our Miss Tabitha Moonshadow was asked to play the piano. At a special church meeting. A meeting just for *men*! They were gonna have in some priesthood bigwig from outta town. "

"Stop it!" Tabitha begged, appalled. "Don't tell that story!"

Beulah, however, paid her no heed. "Seems none of them worthless Mormon men can play the piano. No, ma'am. So, they asked Miss Tabitha—as a special favor, mind—to play for their men-only meeting. And she practiced for weeks! And when she showed up to play—" Beulah paused for dramatic effect.

"Stop!" Tabitha hissed. "It was a secret!"

"When she showed up to play, some high mucky-muck from *Utah* told her, 'Thank you, but no thank you, *sister*. Go on home where y'all belong!'"

Tabitha's cheeks burned, and tears, bitter as acid, spilled from her eyes. "Beulah, you promised!" But the memory itself hurt far worse than Beulah's broken promise.

It'd been President Roylance who'd asked her, telling her it was an important meeting, and there'd be an "exception" so she could play. And she *had* practiced for weeks—just to play two stupid hymns. And when she'd been politely, but firmly dismissed, President Roylance had just sat there on the stand, not saying a word. Afterward, he'd apologized profusely—in person—begging her forgiveness.

As if any apology could make up for her humiliation, for being treated as if she didn't matter. As if she were inferior.

Tabitha had avoided speaking to the branch president ever since.

Mike Kilmore hadn't been there that night. Tabitha wanted to believe he hadn't known about it. He'd never said anything, but…

"I know," Beulah said, still not lowering her voice one bit, "I promised. Yes, I did. But, girl, they had no call, no *right* to treat you like that, like you were somehow *lower* than them. Woman is not lower than man!"

"That's right!" said Cassie. "Woman is the source of life."

"Man comes out of Woman," said Patsy in an almost reverent tone. Then she grinned wickedly. "And he spends the rest of his miserable life trying to get back in."

"Woman is life," said another girl.

"Woman is power," said another member of the Circle.

"Woman is magic," said yet another.

The words possessed a ritualistic sound, like a religious litany, sending chills through Tabitha—and at the same time, thrilling her with a sense of empowerment. A sense of worth. A sense of belonging.

"Without Woman, man is nothing," said a familiar voice. A masculine voice.

Tabitha looked up into the smiling face of Joey Parsons, his eyes and teeth shining in the dancing firelight. "Joey? When? How?"

Joey took her right hand, then pulled her to her feet. "And with Woman, *some* men—those who know Her and worship who She truly is—*some* men, in Her divine service, can do…*anything*."

Still clasping her hand, Joey wheeled away from Tabitha. Beulah grasped Tabitha's other hand.

And with a start, Tabitha realized the entire Circle—plus her and Joey—now stood, holding hands, in an unbroken ring around the fire. The girls—every last one of them—seemed to be grinning.

Terror clawed up Tabitha's spine. "Beulah, what's going on?" She tried to pull her hands free, but Joey and Beulah tightened their grips.

"It's all right," Beulah said. "Joey, show her what she truly is. Show Tabitha her *power*."

A tremor ran from Joey's hand to Tabitha's. His bright smile widened. He seemed to convulse with a shuddering sigh. "As you command, my dear."

Tabitha felt a tingle, a pleasant rippling wave flowing through her. It seemed to come from Beulah's hand, through Tabitha's hand, and into her body. There it intensified, multiplying exponentially as if her body were a capacitor for some primal joy. And that joy and that power flowed into Joey's hand.

"Yes!" he hissed.

A sudden wind roared around them, whipping Tabitha's long hair as it rushed into the center of the circle. Fed by the gale, the campfire flared brighter. The flames wound into an ascending spiral, a dozen feet high.

Tabitha yelped, trying desperately to free her hands, but Beulah and Joey held her fast.

And in an instant, the wind was gone, and with it went the fire. The flames died down to glowing coals as if all the wood had been consumed. The air became deathly still heavy, like the atmosphere of a cavern.

"H-How—" Tabitha's voice froze in her throat as the wave of pleasure returned. With a vengeance.

And Tabitha and Joey and Beulah and the entire Circle lifted slowly into the air, rising into the night sky.

See how high she flies.

Dracula simply wasn't holding her attention. Tabitha tried. She really did; because at that moment, Tabitha craved any semblance of normalcy. Oh, she went through the motions. She squealed and shrieked and clung to her mom just as she always did during any decent—or even not-so-decent—horror flick, but her mind was elsewhere.

They were the "ghosts"—Beulah and Joey—and the rest of them. They were the ghosts.

They didn't have to break in. They could just unlock the door.

They can do anything.

I can do—

"Did you see that?" Her mom pointed at the TV. On the small screen, Jack Palance's Dracula, in a rage of grief and loss, had just tossed over the coffin of Fiona Lewis' Lucy. "Lucy moved! She moved her arm!"

Pointing out the goofs in a B-movie was always part of the fun. But Tabitha had missed the "finally dead vampiress" putting up an arm to protect herself. "No! I missed it!"

As the movie faded to black and a commercial began, Molly said, "That was hilarious! Wish there was some way to go back—you know, like rewinding a cassette tape?"

"Rewind a TV show?" Tabitha chuckled and shook her head. "That'd be the day!"

"Yeah." Molly ran her fingers through her own hair. "It'd be like rewinding the radio." She got to her feet. "I want more hot chocolate, even if it does make me pee all night. How's that sound? The hot chocolate, I mean—not the peeing."

"Sure." Tabitha pulled the blanket around herself, staring blankly at the commercial—something about fishing and racism? Tabitha didn't care.

We flew through the air. I flew.

Beulah had given the commands, but it was Joey who seemed to be directing;

controlling what they did.

They'd soared up, out of the woods, high above the trees. Faster and higher, but always together, always linking hands in a circle.

In the Circle.

The girls laughed and smiled...and moaned as if with physical pleasure.

Tabitha felt that pleasure too, the waves—ebbing and flowing—of primal, visceral joy.

"What? H-how?" she cried. I'm flying. I'm flying!

How come I'm not scared? She looked down, between her feet, at the ground and the trees below. I should be scared out of my gourd!

Beulah squeezed her hand. "We're doing this. You're doing this."

"Me?" Tabitha looked up at the waxing moon. It looks so big from up here! "I'm not doing anything!"

Joey laughed. "Of course, you are! So damn strong! Never felt anyone so strong!"

"The Power." Beulah closed her eyes and tilted her head back, sighing as if she were floating in a giant, warm bubble bath rather than on the cold night air. "It comes from within us. It comes from within Woman.*"*

"Woman is divine," said Joey. "The Power, it comes from the Divine Feminine. It comes from you, Tabitha Moonshadow."

Tabitha gazed in wonder at the stars, the dark, rolling hills below, the lights of two towns—Blue Beech Ridge on one side and Poplar Bluff on the other. "We're flying! I can't believe I'm flying!"

Beulah laughed. "I know! Ain't it just out of this world?"

"Welcome, sister!" called Cassie.

"Welcome, sister," intoned the others in unison. "Welcome to the Circle."

Tabitha shivered, in part due to the temperature of the black sky, in part because those words of welcome had sounded like a chant.

Like a ritual.

And the Power flowed through her, electric, warm, delicious.

"Joey," said Beulah, "that's high enough. Take us down."

"As you command, my dear."

Their dizzying assent slowed, crested, and gently reversed. As they descended gradually toward the blackness of the earth below, like a circlet of feathers floating on a windless night, Tabitha felt like a little girl on a Ferris wheel. She'd ridden on a Ferris wheel once with her dad when she was young. It was one of the very few memories she had of the time before—one of the rare good ones. And just as she had on that night so long ago, she kicked her feet in childlike glee.

And felt her shoe loosen.

With a cry, she snapped her feet together in a vain attempt to catch it. But the errant sneaker slipped off. It arced toward the center of the circle and down, almost out of sight.

113

Then Tabitha gasped as she saw the shoe rise up out of the night, ascending toward her, growing from a dim and indistinct speck to a full-sized sneaker.

"Stick your foot out," said Joey.

"S-stick my foot out?" she said.

"Otherwise," said Beulah, "he can't see."

"Can't see?"

Beulah squeezed her hand again. "To put it back on, silly. Put your foot out."

Tabitha lifted her knee and extended her foot.

Unbelievable.

As the shoe floated toward the extended foot, something tugged at her foot—something invisible—pulling it a few inches higher.

Her breath caught in her throat. He's moving my foot.

The shoe slid into place on her foot, then she tried to lower it. But it wouldn't move. She had no control. Then, unbidden, her foot dropped back beside the other.

He was controlling my foot. Controlling me.

And that thought terrified her.

" . . . at the college."

Tabitha became aware that her mom was speaking from the kitchen. "What'd you say?"

"Video tape? They can record and rewind the TV shows they make in the college studio."

"Okay."

"I just thought maybe someday we might have TV tape players at home. Then we could record shows at home and rewind them."

"Okay." *What's she talking about?*

"That'd be weird, don't you think?" her mother continued. "To be able to record TV?"

"Oh. Yeah." Tabitha shrugged. "I guess."

"And if you could rewind, you could also go forward really fast. You could skip these stupid commercials." Molly handed Tabitha another mug full of hot chocolate. "Here you go, honey."

Tabitha took the warm mug. The chocolate smelled delicious. Normal.

"Thanks."

She held the blanket aside as her mom sat down with her own mug. In moments, the two of them were snug beneath the blanket, sipping hot chocolate. And not saying a word.

Tabitha nestled closer, careful not to spill the contents. She felt a wave of warmth that had nothing to do with the cocoa. *Mom. She's always been there for me. Always. I can trust her. I can tell her.*

On TV, a man in a plaid sports coat prattled about used cars. Molly exhaled, not quite a sigh, but a breath heavy with portent. Tabitha knew her mom was about ask something—something important.

"So, Tabby-Cat, I do admit this hot chocolate is amazing and could easily absorb all your attention, but...well, you haven't exactly been *chatty* since Beulah dropped you off." She waited as if expecting, or perhaps hoping, Tabitha would volunteer something on her own.

But Tabitha kept her peace.

Molly took another sip, then cleared her throat softly. "So, what happened tonight?"

"So, the...the Power—the 'Divine Feminine,' as you call it—comes from women, but only a man can wield it?" Tabitha wrapped her arms around herself, striving to control the tremors which ran through her. The campfire was dying down, and she felt chilled. And scared.

And excited.

Beulah laid a hand on Tabitha's back and rubbed gently. "We can't control it. But we all have our tics."

Tabitha looked up at Beulah, at her friend. And though Beulah was smiling her familiar grin, she seemed, at that moment, more like an amiable stranger—someone who was cordial, but whose intentions were unclear.

Or all too clear.

Tabitha and Beulah sat alone. Joey sat on the other side of the fire, chatting quietly with some of the other girls—the Sisters of the Circle. He talked to them. But his eyes never left Tabitha.

And there was an unmistakable hunger in those eyes.

Tabitha felt an answering hunger, too. The power she'd felt, the pleasure—and then the absence of it. Once the Circle had been broken, she'd been left feeling hollow and weak.

Tabitha cleared her throat. "Tics?"

"Uh-huh. Little things we do—but none of us control. They seem to come out when we get excited or nervous. Or pissed." Beulah spun her free hand around. "Knockin' over a soda can or a waste paper basket. Causin' a sudden chill in a room." She pointed at Cassie. "Cassie's pencil or pen just seems to snap in half, usually in the middle of a test. Now, mine?" She shrugged. "My hair just frizzes up, like static electricity and all. How worthless and random is that, I ask y'all? Ain't that just random and useless? Like tits on a bull."

Tabitha swallowed, then chuckled nervously. "Yeah."

Beulah winked and patted Tabitha's back. "Yours seems to be slamming doors."

Tabitha tensed, and her guts felt as if they were twisting into an approximation of the Gordian Knot. "Is that how?"

Beulah nodded. "Y'all were mad at Ol' Waddle, weren't ya?"

And at home—the bathroom. Tabitha felt dizzy. She hadn't felt the slightest trace of vertigo when they were flying, but now her pulse pounded in her ears, and she felt as if she might topple off the log and into the fire.

And burn.

115

Like a witch.

Beulah shrugged. "My hair just frizzes up—especially in the middle of sex. It's so annoying."

Tabitha felt as if she might be sick. She fought to refocus, to calm the roiling in her stomach, and to steer away from moral lines she didn't want to cross.

But what do those lines mean anymore, after…all this? What does the Church, what do Heavenly Father and Jesus have to do with this? *"Uh, but a* man *can wield the Power?* Our *power?"*

"Not just any man. That talent is extremely rare. Extremely rare." She turned her face toward Joey and smiled. "I told y'all—Joey is special. I only know him . . . and one other who has the talent. But a man with the talent can't do anything by himself. He needs us. We have to give him the Power. We have to let him touch and administer the Divine Feminine."

Tabitha almost had her breathing and her stomach under control. Almost. "But all girls have it?"

"Not girls. Women. The Power doesn't develop until we are fully women. It doesn't start with puberty. It only comes later. When we're fully ripe. When we come into our divine potential."

Tabitha took a deep, shuddering breath, held it for a second, then let it out. "But all women?" Even Mom?

Beulah nodded. "To some degree or other. Most? No more than a thimbleful—hardly nothin' to speak of. But all women have the power to absorb and control the energy in a room, to calm things down—if they want—or to get everybody riled up. You've seen it yourself, haven't ya? I mean, mama walks into a room and every eye turns her way. If she's happy and graceful, her divine presence calms and fills the room with her energy. If she's bitchy, well, everything just seems to explode. You know what I mean, right?"

Tabitha said nothing, but her expression must've been enough to communicate her doubts.

"And there are some women," Beulah went on, "who can do more than that. Like the Sisters of the Circle. Like me." Beulah moved her hand to Tabitha's shoulder and gripped it firmly. "Like you.*"*

"Me?" Tabitha shook her head. "I'm not so special."

"You?" Beulah laughed and shook Tabitha's shoulder. "Girl, you are a witch. Like me." She swept her hand in an expansive gesture, taking in the rest of the Circle. "Like all of us. We are all witches. We are strong in the Power. And joined together in the Circle, we are greater, so much greater, than just the sum of our parts. We are witches—or goddesses, if you prefer—and Joey is our priest."

"Priest?" The very familiarity of the word, used in such an unfamiliar con-text, troubled her. Priests serve God. They *worship* God. *"Priest? As in he…"* She couldn't bring herself to say it.

"As in," Joey said, making her jump—she hadn't seen him approach—"I worship you." He knelt on one knee at her feet and raised his hands, palms up as if in

offering, or prayer. "How may I serve you, my goddess?"

"Tabby-Cat," her mom said, "you've never lied to me. You've kept your secrets, but you've never told me a falsehood. And I appreciate that so very much. I know I can trust you. But I, I sense that something…happened tonight."

Tabitha tried to relax her body, to mask the tension vibrating through her as if she were a piano wire stretched to near breaking. *I can trust her. And it's not like I did anything wrong.* "Mom, can we talk about this during the next commercial?" *It's not like I did anything sinful.*

Right?

After the slightest hesitation, Molly nodded. "Okay."

Tabitha shrank away from Joey. "Don't call me that."

Joey lowered his hands and nodded, but kept his eyes fixed on her. "My Lady, then."

Tabitha shook her head. Heavenly Father…if You're still there…If You were ever really there…Help me, please.

I don't know what to do anymore.

I don't know who I am anymore.

I don't know *what* I am.

I can't be a witch. I can't!

But I flew.

"My Lady," Joey persisted, "I love you, and I will worship you 'til the end of my days. Please allow me to serve you."

Tabitha shook her head all the more vehemently. "No. It's all…too much. Please. Just stop. I—I need to think."

Joey bowed his head. "As you wish, my dear."

"I…" Tabitha looked around, seeking an escape. "What time is it?"

Beulah angled her watch toward the failing campfire. "Eleven-thirty."

Tabitha almost sobbed in relief. "I gotta go. Gotta go home. I promised my mom I'd be home by midnight. Beulah, can you take me?"

Beulah smiled, but there was a hint of sadness in her face—a touch of disappointment. "Sure. Whatever y'all want." She gripped Tabitha by the shoulder again. "But, girl, you must promise me somethin'."

"What?"

"This is our secret—yours, mine, Joey's, the Circle's. Y'all must promise not to tell anyone what you saw tonight. Not even your mama. We're Sisters now. Right? Y'all can't tell anyone about the Circle. Okay?"

Dracula's snarling face, replete with fangs and a trickle of blood, dissolved to black and was replaced by an image of Ronald McDonald with a painted-on red smile. Tabitha groaned.

The dreaded commercial break had come.

What am I going to say? I can't lie. And I can't tell her what happened.

Not yet. I need time to think. Time to feel normal again. But I can trust her. I can. She'll believe me. She believed me about the broom and Lettie.

But you promised Beulah. You can't betray her confidence. But she's my mom. I can trust her. I can.

"Tabby-Cat?" Her mom laid her head on top of Tabitha's. "What happened tonight? Whatever it was, you can tell me."

Tabitha drew in on herself, wishing she could hide in her own skin. *She thinks I did something. Something bad. Sinful.*

"Okay," Molly said into her daughter's silence as the television droned on. "I'll start off. Make things easier. How about I tell you, my secret."

She has a secret? Did she do something? Does she know? Did she spy on me?

"What secret?"

She felt her mother relax a bit, and realized her mom must've been as nervous as Tabitha herself.

"Well," Molly said, "it's not a secret, so much as it is news."

"Good news?"

Molly inhaled deeply, then exhaled slowly, blowing her breath out between pursed lips. "I think so." She paused. "I hope so. Oh, boy, do I hope so."

Tabitha sat up, pulling away slightly so she could see her mom's face more clearly. "What?"

Molly flashed her teeth in a happy grin. "I have a date!" Her delighted squeal was worthy of any five-year-old girl.

"Really?" Tabitha couldn't help but grin.

Molly's nod was so enthusiastic, it shook the sofa. "Yep. Tomorrow night!"

"Wow, Mom! That's cool! Who is it? Do I know him?" She paused and adopted an expression of mock severity. "It's not old Brother Chatham, is it?"

Molly rolled her eyes. "No. And yes, you do know him."

"Who? Don't keep me in suspense."

Molly's jaw dropped in awe and wonder as if she couldn't believe the words she was about to utter. "Mike. Kilmore."

Tabitha's breath caught in her throat. "Brother Kilmore?" *No! Please. Not him! Who are you kidding, girl? He would never go for you. You're just a kid to him. And Mom hasn't been on a date in years. Yeah, but not with him. Not him.*

I should be happy for her.

But Tabitha wasn't happy. It was as if all her illusions, every single bubble of every dream or hope she'd cherished had been burst in one night. In one evening, she'd gone from the Everest summit of exhilaration and triumph to the Marianas Trench of desolation and doubt. Everything she'd ever believed, every bit of faith she possessed had been challenged, shredded, perhaps beyond recognition.

She couldn't even trust gravity anymore.

And then this betrayal.

It's not her fault. She didn't do it on purpose.

A few hours before, possessed by the iron railroad washer, Tabitha had seen with her mother's eyes—felt her pain, her desolation. Her loneliness.

Her mom wouldn't be lonely anymore.

I should be happy for her.

But at that moment, she didn't care.

Not with him.

Tabitha forced a smile. "That's cool, Mom."

Molly's sigh reeked of happiness. Then, staring at yet another commercial iteration featuring the same used-car salesman, Molly asked, "So, what happened to you tonight?"

Tabitha hesitated for a single, Momentous heartbeat.

And she did something she had never done before.

Tabitha lied to her mother.

The tall redhead approached on high-heeled shoes. These weren't the thick-heeled or platform styles so popular among the disco set. No, these were black stiletto heels, almost too formal for day wear.

Maybe she's got a date later, Molly thought. *She's certainly dressed for it.*

Molly smiled at the thought that she, herself, had a date that night—with Mike Kilmore, no less.

The approaching woman wore a flattering, pastel green, mid-length dress, tastefully accessorized with a black leather belt and just enough jewelry to bespeak casual elegance, rather than gaudiness.

How can she afford to dress like that on a teacher's salary?

Maybe she's independently wealthy.

The woman walked at a brisk, authoritative pace, but somehow still managed to sway her hips. Her annoyingly long auburn hair swished on either side of her waist.

Molly waited for Suzanne Tulane to get closer, pretending not to see the woman. Instead, she made a pretense of perusing the exhibit of varied—and mostly atrocious—student art displayed in the long hallway outside the BBR High School auditorium. But Molly wasn't the least bit interested in the posters and papier-mâché sculptures moralizing on the hot topics of the day—from nuclear disarmament to women's liberation. She *was* interested in learning more about her daughter's favorite teacher.

And, of course, by loitering just a bit longer outside Tabitha's first rehearsal for *My Fair Lady* and by listening carefully, Molly could just barely hear the cast as they did their first read-through of the script. However, any hope of hearing her daughter belting out, "The rain in Spain stays mainly in the plain!" was dashed by the approaching click of Miss Tulane's spike heels.

Molly had met the history teacher on Parents' Night, a few weeks after the school year began. And although her impression of the woman had been very favorable, Molly had been struck right away with three things about Suzanne Tulane—three things that *should* have been superficial—her makeup, her hair, and her voice.

The teacher was pretty enough, but her makeup was overdone, her pastel green eyeshadow too blatant, her rouge too pink, and her lipstick too red. *Not exactly hooker-ish—just a bit much. Like she's trying too hard.*

Molly envied the woman's hair, which fell in rich, auburn waves to her waist. *If only I could grow my hair that long.* Molly's mother had managed luxurious, lengthy hair all her life, but Molly couldn't pull it off like her mom…or Suzanne Tulane. *Tabitha got the long-hair gene, not me.*

The teacher's voice was a rich alto. And though she spoke with animation and bright enthusiasm, Molly got the sense that everything Miss Tulane said was spoken with control and precision, almost as if she'd rehearsed each and every syllable to achieve the perfect tone and inflection. *Like an orator…or an actress.*

Don't judge a book by its cover, Molly.

Especially since, by all reports, she's an excellent teacher.

Tabitha certainly likes her.

The sound of Suzanne's heels clicking on the linoleum floor and echoing through the empty hall grew louder, then stopped.

Molly knew exactly what the woman was going to say before she opened her too-red lips.

"I'm sorry," Suzanne said with a pretty, yet apologetic smile which exposed perfect, white teeth, "but this is a *closed* rehearsal."

Molly had resisted the impulse to recite the anticipated words right along with the woman. *Word for word.* She turned to face the history teacher. Molly extended her hand and smiled. "I'm Tabitha's mother."

Suzanne took Molly's hand and shook it. Her grip was light, and the shake itself was feeble—a girl's handshake, lacking the firmness and warmth of a typical Mormon greeting. However, the smile seemed genuine. "Miss Moonshadow! Yes, of course, I remember you. How are you?"

Molly resisted the urge to wipe her hand on her pants. Female handshakes had always felt slightly creepy to Molly, and Suzanne Tulane's *epitomized* girly. "I'm doing quite well, thank you. Please call me Molly. And I know the drill. This isn't Tabitha's first show. So, of course, it's a closed rehearsal. I'm just"—she inhaled deeply, then let out a dramatic sigh—"lingering. I'm so happy for Tabitha."

Suzanne nodded. "Molly it is, then. And please call me Suzanne." She beamed. "You must be very proud. Your daughter's quite talented!"

Molly gave a modest shrug. "I can't say she gets it from me." This, however, brought up unwelcome thoughts of Jerry. So, Molly hurried to add, "And this role is a dream come true for her."

"I watched the auditions. Tabitha outshined them all. But—"

"So, you're connected with the show?" Molly wasn't stalling—not really.

"I'm designing the costumes. And officially, I'm the assistant director. Although Angelica Goldsmith should do just fine without me. She's our new drama coach."

Molly nodded. "Yes, Tabitha's in her Shakespeare class. My daughter speaks

THE WITCH OF WHITE LADY HOLLOW ~

highly of her." She paused just a second too long before hastily adding, "She speaks highly of you too. In fact, you are most definitely Tabitha's favorite teacher."

The woman flushed, although the color wasn't easily visible through the woman's flawless foundation makeup—at least, she seemed very pleased. "That's very sweet of her to say. And she is an excellent student—so enthusiastic about history! I just love her to bits." She leaned in and whispered conspiratorially. "Even if I'm not supposed have favorites."

Molly found herself liking the woman more and more. *Even if she does have perfect hair. And perfect teeth.*

The sound of a confidently played piano wafted through the closed doors of the auditorium. Molly recognized the introductory bars of "Wouldn't It Be Loverly?" She pressed her hands together in a pleading gesture. "Please! Just let me hear this one—just from out here in the hall. I promise I'll leave after that."

Suzanne winked. "If you promise, y'all can stay." Suddenly, Suzanne's eyes went wide in shock, and her breath caught. Then she smiled, although with just a hint less warmth. "But just that long." She turned toward the closed doors and shut her eyes as if listening to the music.

What was that all about? And suddenly, it occurred to Molly she'd never heard the history teacher ever use even a hint of a Missouri accent. But she just said, "Y'all." *Was that it? Is she trying to hide her southern roots? Why would she do that?*

Then Molly heard Tabitha singing. "All I want is a room somewhere..." And in that moment, all speculation about Suzanne Tulane's cultural background vanished from Molly's mind. She too closed her eyes and drank in the resonance of her daughter's clear, strong voice.

Tabitha was in her element, and Molly reveled in vicarious joy.

"Why, Miss Moonshadow!" The interruption was untimely and unwelcome. "Is that you? I was hoping to see you this morning. I had a feeling y'all'd be here. And Suzanne! How utterly delightful."

Ripping herself away from the singing, Molly turned to look back down the hall, the direction from which Suzanne had come. She spied the new intruder.

The science teacher, Fergus MacDonald, wheeled himself toward them. In contrast to Suzanne, MacDonald was dressed more casually than he had been on Parents' Night. Gone were the lab coat and the bow tie. He wore a T-shirt, jeans, and sneakers. His bare arms were impressively muscled. His torso was well proportioned. His legs, of course, seemed withered, especially in comparison to his upper body. His face was all grandfatherly wrinkles, with keen blue eyes, and a wide, toothy grin, framed by well-groomed gray hair. From the waist up, he was an impressive physical specimen, especially for a man his age.

However, from Tabitha's tales about MacDonald and Molly's own single experience, one word perfectly summed up the man in the wheelchair—creepy.

He reminded Molly of a magician she'd seen when she was fifteen. The Amazing Aldo was handsome—in a slightly Snidely Whiplash sort of way—enigmatic, brilliant, *amazing*—after all, his name declared him to be so. He had commanded all the attention in the room. But his almost nonstop comments about his "lovely assistant" had carried just enough innuendo, and his "handsy" manner with female volunteers from the audience—including Molly herself—had made Molly squirm. She'd left the performance feeling vaguely unclean. But in all other ways, the Amazing Aldo had lived up to his name.

In spite of MacDonald's creepy demeanor, Molly could sense a keen, inquisitive mind. Molly also recognized something to which she could personally relate—a passion for teaching, for shaping, enlarging, and inspiring young minds. From what Tabitha had told her, in spite of his dirty-old-man persona, Fergus MacDonald was a driven and effective teacher.

However, passion and creep-factor aside, at that moment, the old man was preventing Molly from hearing her daughter sing. Molly adopted a smile that belied her irritation. She'd had to focus to hear Tabitha's song, but now she couldn't spare the attention. The intruder cheerfully demanded all of it. "Mr. MacDonald, isn't it?"

The man slowed his wheelchair to a stop right in front of the two ladies, wiped his large hand on his baggy jeans, and extended it. "Fergus! Please, call me Fergus! Mr. MacDonald was my father!"

What a tired line. Molly took the proffered hand. In contrast to Suzanne's tepid handshake, MacDonald's grip was as firm and enthusiastic as that of the greenest Mormon missionary.

"How nice to meet you again, Fergus." When the man didn't release her hand, Molly added, "And you must call me Molly." She immediately regretted this. *There's friendly, and there's too friendly.*

With a wink which bordered on being lascivious, Fergus gave Molly's hand another squeeze, then released it. "I can see from whence comes your daughter's beauty." He extended his hand to the history teacher. "And, Suzanne, my dear, it's always a pleasure to see you too. I'm so looking forward to working with you on this production."

Suzanne's smile was tight-lipped as she bowed her head in greeting. "Fergus." But she did not take the man's hand.

MacDonald's eye twitched once, but his grin never faltered as he lowered his hand to the wheelchair armrest.

Apparently, it's not just Tabitha and the other female students—and me—who think this guy's creepy.

"I need to get back inside," Suzanne said. "If you'll excuse me."

Oh sure! Leave me alone with him.

MacDonald waved. "I'll be along shortly. Let me know if you need any help taking the kids' measurements!"

Suzanne rolled her eyes, and Molly could have sworn she heard a soft growl. "Honestly, Fergus." Suzanne turned on her high heels and slipped inside the auditorium.

The old man leered after her.

But Molly ignored him as, for seven all-too-brief seconds, she heard Tabitha singing, "Wouldn't it be loverly?" Then the door closed.

Molly sighed. *Well, I did promise.* "I really must be going."

MacDonald's countenance drooped. "So soon? I was hoping we could chat for just a bit."

Molly almost shuddered at the prospect. "It's a closed rehearsal." She tapped the side of her nose. "And I know the rules about that."

The old man's grin returned, and he winked. "And we wouldn't want to break the rules, now would we? But seriously, Molly—you did say I could call you Molly—I've been meaning to chat with y'all 'bout your charming daughter."

Of course, it'd be about Tabitha. It's always about Tabitha. For one brief second, Molly felt a surprising twinge of jealousy. *Why would I care what the pervert thinks?* "I thought she was doing well in your class." *She should be doing well in every class.* In her entire academic career, Tabitha had received precisely one grade that was not an A—a single, solitary B—in typing.

And that one B still rankled the girl.

MacDonald waved a dismissive hand. "Of course. Of course. Tabitha is an exemplary student. The brightest star in my class, in fact."

So, why are you wasting my time? I missed her song! "I'm glad to hear it." Molly barely succeeded in keeping the irritation out of her tone.

"I have not the slightest doubt in my mind that Tabitha owes much of her success to her lovely and talented mother." He winked again.

Now he's flirting with me? "So, what is it you wanted to speak to me about?"

"Yes." He nodded. "Down to business. I have some concerns about your Tabitha. But . . ." His smile disappeared as if it had been a mask, and MacDonald's face became very serious. He glanced in both directions, up and down the hall, as he reached into his breast pocket. The grin returned, but it drooped at the corners of his mouth, as if forced. "I would prefer to discuss it in a less public setting. And I really must be getting inside as well. I'm designing the sets, you know!" He extended his hand again as if to shake her hand, however, his thumb was pressed against his palm, and under the thumb was a folded slip of paper. He winked again, but the wink itself seemed less flirtatious than it did *portentous.*

Molly closed her hand around his, then came away, holding the note tight in her fist. She thought of opening the paper and reading it right there, but MacDonald's almost imperceptible shaking of his head stopped her.

She nodded. "Well, I'll . . . make an appointment then."

His grin perked up. "Excellent! Now, if you'll excuse me,"—he wiggled one eyebrow—"perhaps Suzanne will need help taking the girls' measurements after all!"

He turned his wheelchair. "I know I shouldn't ask it of a lady, especially one so lovely and enchanting as yourself, but would y'all be so kind as to get the door?"

The note in Molly's hand made her fingers itch. She was dying to read it. "Certainly."

When she pulled the door open, Molly was disappointed to hear dialogue between Professor Higgins and Colonel Pickering. Molly recognized the scene—Tabitha wouldn't make her entrance anytime soon.

Besides, at that moment, she needed to read that note.

"So nice to see y'all again, Miss Molly!" Fergus MacDonald wheeled himself inside the auditorium.

As Molly let the door close behind the old man and his wheelchair, she caught a glimpse of Tabitha. Her daughter was easy to spot, with her long, raven hair and full-length, gray skirt. No jeans that morning, and that fact made Molly all the more curious as to what had really happened the night before—and why Tabitha had chosen not to share anything. Molly was certain Tabitha wouldn't lie to her—Tabitha had never lied, and Molly trusted her—but her daughter was holding something back, keeping her secrets. That in itself wasn't unusual, but after the extraordinary incident with her dad's old railroad washer and Tabitha's vision, Molly had been certain, or at least hopeful, the two of them had breached a barrier.

But old habits, like old secrets, aren't vanquished overnight.

Tabitha and the rest of the cast were seated in a ring of folding chairs on the stage. A piano was strategically positioned down on the floor in front of the stage. Molly recognized the choir teacher at the piano, and she also recognized the English teacher in the circle with the students. Everyone seemed to have their noses buried in a script.

Everyone except Tabitha. Her script lay open in her lap, but Tabitha wasn't looking at it. If Molly knew her daughter at all, she was certain Tabitha already had most, if not all, the dialogue memorized. She certainly knew all the music by heart.

Molly smiled. *She has dreamed of this role her whole life.*

Then the door closed with a puff of air, and, like a candle flame, all thought of the play was extinguished. Molly gripped the note in her fist and hurried toward the door.

When she reached the relative privacy of her car, she got inside. Then she locked the door just for good measure.

She unfolded the small scrap of paper, torn from a spiral notepad. The first line of the short message, hand printed in small block letters, seized Molly's guts like a claw of ice—seized, then twisted.

TABITHA IS IN DANGER.

"How's our star this fine morning?" Beulah took a cautious sip of coffee from her Styrofoam cup. She glanced around as if to ensure no one else was within earshot. She leaned in close to Tabitha and whispered, "Wasn't last night just amazing?"

Tabitha kept her face expressionless. Using a plastic spoon, she stirred hot chocolate mix into her own cup of steaming water. She stared at the swirling granules, most, but not all of them, dissolving, turning the water a rich, fragrant brown.

Amazing? Yes! And terrifying. Earth shattering.
I am become death, destroyer of worlds.
Where did that come from? Heard it somewhere.
"Well," Beulah prompted, "wasn't it?"
Say something. She's waiting for you to say something.
"Yeah," Tabitha said, her voice barely more than a whisper and utterly devoid of inflection. "Amazing. That's one word for it." Having finished mixing her hot chocolate, she focused her eyes on the snack table. In addition to the drinks, the snacks had consisted of brownies, homemade by Miss Goldsmith, and sugar cookies baked by Miss Tulane. And both sets of goodies had been speedily and greedily devoured by the cast, all except for one lonely cookie. Dark, moist crumbs were scattered across several otherwise-empty paper plates. The only evidence that brownies had ever actually existed.

"Well," Beulah whispered, "if I weren't the world's-best best friend"—she gently elbowed Tabitha—"I'd think y'all were avoiding me."

I am. I am avoiding you.

Tabitha shrugged, still focusing on the crumbs. "I'm sorry. I'm just…" *Scared. Confused.* And without warning, tears threatened to spill from her eyes. *I don't know who I am anymore.* She swallowed hard, then took a deep breath. "It's just a lot to take in."

Beulah put an arm around her shoulders and gave her a friendly squeeze. "I know. I know. When Magnus first showed me my divine nature—"

"Magnus?" Tabitha turned to look at her friend. "Who's that?"

The corner of Beulah's mouth twitched, and her eyes tightened slightly. "Well, there I've gone again, running my mouth." She looked around again, then put her lips to Tabitha's ear. "You haven't met him—yet. He's our High Priest."

"High priest? I thought Joey—"

"No, silly. Joey's just our Priest. He's small-fry compared to Magnus. What Joey did last night, with our Power? Why, he's never been able to lift the Circle more than a dozen feet off the ground before. But with Magnus, we could always fly—just like last night."

"But last night," Tabitha said, "we did. We flew. We flew so…high."

Beulah grinned from ear to ear, displaying very white teeth, and her eyes were bright. Like a wolf with pink lipstick. "Girl," Beulah said, "that was all *you*." She shrugged. "Well, mostly you. But it was the rest of us too. Each woman we add to the Circle increases our power. It's not like addition or even multiplication. It's like when you multiply the same number over and over. Expo…somethin' or other."

"Exponential?"

Beulah nodded. "That's the word." She squeezed Tabitha again. "But, girl, you take the cake. Y'all're something special. Y'all pushed us up to a new level entirely. I can't wait to see what"—she glanced around again—"Magnus can do with y'all in the Circle—with our Power, of course. It'll be amazing. It'll be out of this world!"

"When will I get to meet…Magnus?" The name sounded pretentious. And vaguely sorcerous. *That can't be his real name, can it?* And Tabitha wasn't at all sure she wanted to meet this High Priest of the Circle.

"We're meeting again tonight. In the Hollow. Another 'wienie roast.' You in?"

Tabitha hesitated. She took a sip of her hot chocolate, savoring the taste of something that felt normal, buying herself time. "I don't know. I can't be out late."

"Y'all doing something with your mom?"

Tabitha shook her head. "No. She's got a date." With Mike Kilmore. She narrowed her eyes and nodded curtly. "I'm in." *I'm so in.*

Beulah beamed at her. "All right! I can't wait. It's gonna be amazing! Beyond anything we ever dreamed."

You keep using that word. "But seriously, I have to be home by midnight."

"Another scary movie with your mom? I thought you said she had a date."

"She'll be home by then. But tomorrow's Sunday—you know, the Sabbath. And I've got church."

Beulah sighed and waved a dismissive hand. "I've got church too. Gotta go pretend to listen to Daddy preach another of his sermons. He doesn't believe a word of it. He's an old hypocrite, an outdated symbol of male tyranny." She rolled her eyes. "'Sides, he just uses being pastor to get himself rich. And chase some congregational tail. The stories I could tell!" She paused, pursed her lips. Then her eyes hardened. "Men been doing that since the dawn of time. Now, it's *our* turn, *our* time. We're gonna turn the whole damn patriarchal order on its ear."

Beulah shook herself as if coming out of a fugue, then she sneered. "Y'all know we got a rock band in church? No foolin'—drums, electric guitars, and everything. Even got a saxophone. Daddy has 'em rock out while the plate is passed. He jumps around and shouts, 'Hallelujah!' and, "Can I get a amen?" like some black preacher. Trust me—he can't pull it off. Y'all don't have a rock band in y'all's church, do ya?"

Tabitha almost chuckled at the thought. Then she envisioned Mike Kilmore, shirtless, playing an electric guitar. She shook herself, dispelling the image. *He's interested in my mom.* "No. Our church is pretty sedate." *Boring.* "We sing a few hymns. Mostly, we just sit and listen."

"Sounds dull as lead. Why do you go?"

I used to know. But now? "Why do you go to yours?"

Beulah's face became unreadable. "Because Daddy makes me go. Because he has ways to punish me if I don't."

Tabitha shuddered. She didn't want to know how Beulah's father might punish her.

"Someday," Beulah said, her voice flat and dead, "someday, I'll show him who's really in charge. I'll show him just what punishment is."

Tabitha shuddered and took a step back. *What have I gotten myself into?* She bumped into someone behind her.

And squeaked like a terrified mouse.

"Sorry!" said an alto voice.

Tabitha wheeled around.

Miss Tulane stood behind her. The redhead smoothed her skirt with well-manicured hands. "I was just coming to tell you girls we're going to do another read-through. Didn't you hear me calling you?"

Tabitha gave her a sheepish grin. "Sorry, Miss Tulane. I guess we just got talking—"

"And the world just faded away," said Beulah. With a wicked grin, the blonde snatched the last sugar cookie from the table. "These cookies are out of this world, Miss Tulane!" Then she sauntered back toward the stage.

Tabitha took a step to follow Beulah, but the history teacher put a hand on her arm, stopping her.

"Let's get your measurements really quick," Miss Tulane said. "I can pull most of the others out of the read-through, but you're in it almost the whole time. So, if you'll come with me?"

Tabitha followed her favorite teacher to a small table where she'd seen other students being measured. She'd seen Mr. MacDonald hanging around, but Miss Tulane had shooed him away. *Thank heavens.* Miss Tulane indicated where Tabitha was to stand. Tabitha set her cup down, then stood obediently in the indicated spot. The teacher took some measuring tape from the table and started by encircling Tabitha's head.

"Your mother's very proud of you, you know," Miss Tulane said as she scribbled Tabitha's name and a number on her notepad. "Very proud." She took a measurement of Tabitha's neck. "It must be so nice to have a mother who loves and supports you. You're very lucky."

"Your mother didn't love you?"

Did I just say that? That's really personal.

The redheaded teacher sighed. "I suppose she did; in her way. But she didn't understand me. She didn't understand who I am. She didn't even try. She didn't support me in my dreams."

"I'm sorry." *Mom loves me. I know she does. But she wouldn't understand about the Circle. She wouldn't understand what I'm going through.*

I can't tell her.

And I lied to her. I lied to my mom.

It's almost like I committed some great sin. And I'm trying to pretend like nothing happened. And it's not working.

"Tabitha. Tabitha." Miss Tulane sounded slightly impatient. "Can you lift your arms a little, please?"

Tabitha complied. "Sorry."

Miss Tulane wrapped the tape around Tabitha's bust. "Off in your own world?"

"I guess."

"So, Beulah has recruited you too, has she?"

Tabitha froze. *She knows.* "Wh-what do you mean?" She looked at the teacher, but Miss Tulane didn't meet her eyes. The teacher seemed absorbed in her work, as if she were discussing something no more momentous than the weather in a far-off country.

"The Circle." Miss Tulane measured Tabitha's waist. "You can put your arms down now."

Tabitha lowered her arms. "You know about that?"

"You girls think you're so clever, so good at keeping secrets." Miss Tulane wrapped the tape around Tabitha's hips. "Loose lips sink ships and all that. And nobody has loose lips like a teenage girl."

"I—I just…Last night. I— What do you know?"

From the ring of chairs on the stage, Beulah waved at Tabitha.

Tabitha forced a grin and gave a small wave in return.

"Hold this here." Miss Tulane pressed the tape at Tabitha's waist. When Tabitha took the end of the tape, keeping it in place against her belly, the redhead knelt and took her final measurement. "I've picked up a few things here and there. I don't know everything, but I know it's all about womanhood and *magic*."

She stood, a full head above Tabitha, looked down, and locked eyes with her. She smiled and put her hands on Tabitha's shoulders. "And I want in."

TABITHA IS IN DANGER.
SHE WILL BE SAFE AT REHEARSAL,
SURROUNDED BY FRIENDS.
MEET ME AT SAMBO'S
IN POPLAR BLUFF AT 1:30.
TELL NO ONE.

The small note in Molly's hand screamed at her. The black letters resembled tiny poisonous spiders, ready to leap off the white paper and sink their venom-filled fangs into her flesh.

Tabitha's in danger!

Molly had passed the last couple of hours in a waking nightmare of anxiety, punctuated by moments of terror where she could barely catch her breath.

My baby's in danger!

She sat in her car, glaring at her watch, willing the tiny hands—hour, minute, and second—to move faster. Then she scanned the parking lot of the Poplar Bluff Sambo's. She had no idea what kind of car Fergus MacDonald drove. But she hadn't seen him arrive—or leave, for that matter—since she'd parked in front of the all-day-all-night diner half an hour earlier.

She closed her eyes, but unbidden came the memory of ghostly figures on a dark, deserted road, pointing at her.

She checked her watch again.

1:25

How would he know? He's just a science teacher. Just a creepy, dirty old man. How would he know? Unless this is his idea of a sick joke. Please, Heavenly Father, let it be just a sick joke!

But Molly couldn't take that chance, not where her daughter's safety was concerned.

The windows were fogging up again. Molly started the Impala, and the defroster blew hot air onto the windshield, with just enough of the heat spilling onto the side windows to keep them clear as well. The engine hadn't cooled since the last time she'd run it—less than five minutes ago.

Where is he?

1:27

That's it. I'm going in. I'll wait for him inside.

Molly crumpled the warning note with its ominous and maddeningly vague message, then shoved it into her purse. Not for the first time, she wished she'd brought her gun. She didn't have the vaguest notion of what she'd do with it if she had brought it, but the heavy, ugly weapon might've given her a small measure of courage.

She shut off the engine and climbed out of the Chevy, locking the door. She'd lived in the D.C. area too long to leave her car unsecured.

Searching the parking lot with a frustration that was building toward anger, she almost ran to the restaurant door. Once inside, she ignored the cheesy wall murals of the little, dark-skinned boy with his Indian turban and plate of high-stacked pancakes, facing off against a comically menacing tiger. She ignored the sign which requested her to "Please wait to be seated." She almost ignored the attractive, middle-aged, black waitress who asked her if she required a table for one. Instead, Molly scanned the tables for a gray-haired man in a wheelchair.

"Table for one?" repeated the waitress.

Molly forced a quick smile. "Actually, I'm waiting for someone."

"Oh." The woman in the orange uniform and white apron nodded.

Molly looked directly at the waitress for the first time. The woman, whose nametag read, "Juliette," appeared to be about Molly's age. *Maybe she's got a child in high school too. She could be Joey's mother.* Molly wasn't aware of any other black kids in BBR High, and although she was in Poplar Bluff at the moment, not Blue Beech Ridge, Molly knew Joey's family lived somewhere in the Hollow. Molly worked in Poplar Bluff. It wasn't out of the realm of possibility Joey's mother worked in that town as well.

The waitress—Juliette—tilted her head. "Are you Miss Moonshadow?" She sounded like Joey—no hint of accent.

Molly nodded. "Yes. How'd you know?"

Juliette grinned, showing a mouthful of very white teeth. "Well, Mr. MacDonald said you'd be coming in. I was to take you to him." She pointed to a back wing of the dining room. The area wasn't as garishly lit as the rest of the place, and Molly realized her eye tended to slide off that wing. She spotted Fergus MacDonald at the only occupied table. The old man waved to her from his wheelchair.

She turned to go, resisting the urge to dash between the tables.

"You're Tabitha's mother, aren't you?"

Molly stopped, turning back to the waitress.

The woman grinned. "Well, with a name like Moonshadow, who else would you be? I'm Juliette Parsons—Joey Parsons's mother." She extended a hand.

Tabitha's in danger! Molly wanted—*needed*—to go, to talk to the old man. She had no time for niceties.

Juliette Parsons's countenance fell, and she lowered her hand and her eyes. "If you'll follow me, Miss Moonshadow."

She's going to think I'm a bigot. But Tabitha's in danger. She's safe where she is, among friends. MacDonald said so. Molly clung to that thought as if to a life preserver on an angry sea. *Tabitha's safe where she is.*

Molly extended her hand, grasping awkwardly at the other woman's hand. Molly shook it and smiled as warmly as she could. "Yes, of course. So nice to meet you."

The black woman's face lit up like a lighthouse in the night. "So nice to meet you, Miss Moonshadow."

"Molly. Please." Molly said. "If you'll excuse me, I really must talk to Mr. MacDonald."

"Sure, Molly. This way." Juliette Parsons turned and led the way to the back room.

Fergus beamed as they approached. "Howdy, Molly. Punctual." He winked at Juliette. "I told y'all she'd be punctual." He pointed to the seat next to him. "Molly, I'm so glad you came."

Ignoring the indicated chair, Molly took the seat opposite the old man.

Juliette set a menu in front of Molly. "What can I get you to drink, Miss, uh . . . Molly?" Juliette had produced a pad and pen from her apron pocket. With her pen she pointed at the steaming cup in front of Fergus. "Coffee?"

MacDonald reached up and patted the waitress on the elbow. "No, my dear. No coffee for our Miss Molly. She's a Mormon. No coffee. No, no, no. How about a large mug of your delicious hot cocoa with a touch of cinnamon and a mountain of real whipped cream? Hmm?"

Juliette tilted her head, grinned, and nodded. "It *is* good. I make it up *special.*"

Molly smiled back, though she didn't want anything to eat or drink at the moment. Her stomach was already struggling to digest her anxiety. "That'd be nice."

Juliette's smile broadened. "I'll whip it up right away. Back in two shakes." She pocketed her pad and pen and was gone.

MacDonald smiled after her as she walked away. He sighed. "Nice woman. And pretty too, don't you think? I do so admire a pretty woman."

"Fergus!" Molly hissed. "You said Tabitha—"

"Just a moment." The old man's grin didn't falter, but he dropped his voice to a whisper. "She'll be back in just a moment. Then we can talk in peace."

Molly opened her mouth to object, but MacDonald cut her off. "Here she comes now."

"There you go." Juliette set the mug down. "My special hot cocoa. Shall I give you more time with the menus?"

Molly shook her head. "No thanks. Just the cocoa for me."

Fergus handed Juliette both menus. "I'll take a short stack with blueberry syrup and two strips of bacon. Not too crisp, mind."

Juliette noted the order on her pad. "Got it. Holler if you need anything else."

The old man winked at her. "What I need…" He reached as if to pat her bottom.

The woman deftly stepped out of his reach. She narrowed her eyes and aimed her pen at MacDonald. "Watch it, Mister. I've got my eye on you." Then she winked.

The old man winked back. "And I've got both my eyes on you. Especially when you walk away."

She pursed her lips and wrinkled her nose. "Ooh, Fergus. You take the cake. You really do." She leaned toward Molly and said in a whisper a bit too loud to be truly confidential, "You watch yourself, Molly. This old hound dog is tricky." She spun and walked away.

And true to his word, with a leer, Fergus MacDonald watched her go.

"Fergus," Molly said, "if you please…" *Tabitha's in danger.*

The old man's lascivious expression vanished as surely as if it had been a mask suddenly yanked away. He turned his whole attention on Molly, and though he wore a gentle smile on his lips, his eyes hardened. "It's as if I'm invisible."

Molly swallowed the words of rebuke she'd been about to say. *Invisible?* "What?"

"They don't see me. They don't see me at all."

"Wh-what are you talking about?"

He cast a quick glance back the way Juliette had gone. "The dirty-old-man shtick—it's camouflage. All they see is creepy Mr. MacDonald, the dirty, old geezer in a wheelchair. Harmless. They don't think I matter at all. I'm invisible."

Confusion and a dawning understanding chased each other in and out of Molly's brain. "Who are 'they'?"

"The people around here. Blue Beech Ridge. Poplar Bluff. The whole blasted county. They all see me, but they dismiss me. But I'm not invisible to *you* now, am I? Not anymore."

Molly shook her head slowly. *It's all a façade?*

The old man bared his teeth in a joyless grin. "And I *hear* things too. When you're old, people assume you're deaf as well. So, they talk around me, often in hushed voices, but they talk. And there's nothing whatsoever wrong with my ears. Or any of the rest of me, for that matter—besides my blasted legs, of course."

Molly stared at Fergus MacDonald, as if she'd been relieved of blinders or clouded glasses. *Through a glass darkly.* No longer was he a perverted, old cripple. She observed the hard, keen eyes, the powerful arms, the muscular chest. Her eyes slipped to the withered legs, and for just a moment, the old image—the creepy-old-man image—reasserted itself in her mind.

But she dismissed it, brushing it away like a cobweb with a broom. "You were in the war, weren't you? World War II? You were a sailor, they say."

MacDonald sat up taller, and Molly could easily imagine how tall he would've been without the chair. "Miss Molly," he said with a fierce pride in his voice, "I was a Marine. I still am. Once a Marine, always a Marine." He paused. "In spite of the damnable chair."

"Were you…injured in the war?"

He uttered a grim laugh. "Many times. I have so many Purple Hearts, so many scars, I stopped counting. I was at Pearl Harbor. Guadalcanal. Others. But I was like a Timex. Took a lickin' and kept on tickin'." He pointed at the chair. "But this? This happened after the War. It happened right here. Well, in Blue Beech Ridge. Drunk driver. Mowed me down. Left me…broken."

"I'm sorry." *Stupid, wholly inadequate thing to say. This man helped save the world from Hirohito and Hitler. And all I can say is 'sorry?'*

"My girl, my Junie, she still married me…after I got better, or as good as I could be. A couple years later, we had a daughter, my little Violet. We were so happy."

A daughter? "You had a child? So, you…adopted?"

He shook his head and smirked at her. "You know that's the hell of it? The wheelchair, even the dirty-old-man persona? People assume you're not…capable. I told you. It's just my legs."

"I'm sorry."

MacDonald waved dismissively. "Don't be. You're not alone. Everybody else makes the same mistake." Then he grinned showing a mouthful of gleaming, slightly crooked teeth. There was a bitter ferocity to his expression which Molly found slightly unsettling. "And that's why I hear things, why I see things."

The old man's face softened, and he nodded. "Yes. Of course." He laid a strong hand on hers, and Molly managed not to flinch at his touch. He looked Molly straight in the eye. "Did you know that *My Fair Lady* was not the musical play the school originally intended to do?"

Molly jerked her hand back. "What? What does that have to do with—"

"It was only after your Tabitha expressed disappointment in the original show, *Guys and Dolls*, and said it was her fondest dream to someday perform the part of Eliza Doolittle in *My Fair Lady*—only then did the school abruptly change course. Did you know the royalties alone for that particular show were, shall we say, astronomical?"

"I—don't understand. I still don't see—"

"Miss Molly, how in the world does a small-town high school afford to do a world-class production like that? And you haven't seen the budget for costumes and sets. It's out of this world."

"But how…"

MacDonald shook his head, and clucked his tongue. "Don't you see? This was all done for Tabitha. All of it. To please her. To gain her favor."

Molly felt the blood drain from her cheeks. "But who? Why?"

"Why? I have no earthly idea. Who? I can't be certain. If this were a decade ago, I would've said it was one of the Thibodeauxs for sure."

The Thibodeauxs? "You mean…"

The old man nodded slowly, and his lips turned down in a scowl. "Yes. The old family that used to run Blue Beech Ridge. They used to run everything. And they would've been the only ones with the money to do it."

Molly blinked in confusion and denial. "Used to?"

MacDonald laughed bitterly once. "Used to, yeah. Once upon a time, they controlled everything around here. And they were *untouchable*. Seductions. Rapes. Murders. Madness. Lives destroyed." He paused. "You've heard of Elias Thibodeaux, the founder of BBR?"

Molly nodded.

"Well," Fergus continued, "did you know he spent his last years in chains in the attic of his mansion, psychotic and raving?"

Molly could only shake her head. *Who cares about old Elias? What about Tabitha?* But she sensed the old man was coming around to his point in his own way. And she forced herself to wait just a bit longer.

"It was a Thibodeaux who ran me down, put me in this chair. Randal James Thibodeaux—Jimmy to his friends. Fourteen years old and drunk as a skunk. And one of their lawyers—with the help of a hefty bribe to a judge—got the little schmuck off. And four years later, another one of them, the putz's uncle, Josiah Alan Thibodeaux, went stark, raving mad. Syphilis, they said. Syphilis seems to be all too common in that family. One day, he took a pump-action shotgun and stormed old Willard's grocery store, raving about witches and White Lettie. Killed eleven people. Eleven." He took a deep breath and blew it out slowly. "Including my Junie and my Violet."

Molly put her hand atop his. "Oh, Fergus. I'm so, so sorry."

"It was a long time ago. He's dead, at least. Sheriff's deputy shot him at the scene. Thibodeauxs didn't have a chance to cover that one—" MacDonald looked up abruptly, and his face utterly transformed.

The mask had returned.

"Here you go, Fergus!" Juliette Parsons set a plate of pancakes and bacon in front of him. A generous pat of butter melted atop the short stack of pancakes smothered in steaming purple syrup.

The smells of blueberries, butter, and bacon wafted into Molly's nostrils.

And she felt as if she might be sick.

Someone is after my baby.

"Can I get you anything else, Molly?"

Molly snapped her attention to Juliette's dark and pretty face. She shook her head and forced a smile. "No thank you. I'm fine." *Please, just go away.*

"If you need anything, holler!" And then the waitress strolled away.

Unlike he had done the previous time Juliette had departed, Fergus MacDonald didn't bother to follow her with his eyes. He turned his whole attention back to Molly. "But it's not the Thibodeauxs now. Not likely, anyway. You see, about ten years back, Bradley, the heir to the Thibodeaux dynasty, came of age, inherited the family fortune, emptied the family bank account, and vanished without a trace. Within six months, all the stocks, bonds, and family business holdings had been liquidated through some high-priced law firm out of St. Louis. Without all their money, the family disintegrated, lost all their power. There've been poor-relation Thibodeauxs around here time out of mind, but almost overnight, they were *all* poor-relation Thibodeauxs. They're mostly a joke now in this county. But they left their legacy. They left their scars."

He dropped his eyes. "And some scars never truly heal."

He didn't point to his wheelchair, but Molly's eyes were drawn there all the same.

However, as much pity and even sympathy as she felt for the old man, Molly couldn't wait any longer. "Fergus, what about Tabitha?"

He nodded and met her eyes again. And in his eyes, a fire burned. "Yes. Your Tabitha. Well, as I said, I've been picking up things here and there. And what I hear is, 'Tabitha Moonshadow is special.' I hear that a great deal. A great deal."

Molly was seized by an almost irresistible urge to run home, get her gun, grab her daughter, and run. "Who, Fergus? Who says that?"

He shrugged and shook his head slightly. "I hear it at the school. From faculty, students. I hear it at church. I'm an elder at the BBR Assembly of God, you know. Anyway, I hear it from folks there who, I'm certain, have never even met your daughter. But they know her name." He paused as he quickly shoveled pancakes into his mouth.

"But why? What makes her so special?" *She is special! She's my baby!*

"I don't know," he repeated. "I've told y'all everything I know and most of what I've guessed. Someone with more money than God, if you'll pardon the expression, has taken an interest in Tabitha. I, for one, believe that interest cannot be healthy. Take it from a man who everyone assumes is a pervert."

As the old man devoured the last of his meal faster than a Mormon deacon breaking his fast on Fast Sunday, Molly felt bile rising from her empty stomach. *We'll run. We'll go. Somewhere nobody can find us.*

"I know what you're thinking." MacDonald swallowed the last bite of bacon. "You're thinking y'all can just run away. After all, that's what brought y'all here."

Molly gasped.

He reached out to pat her hand, but she recoiled.

"Don't be too surprised," he said. "I told y'all, I hear things."

"But—"

"That one shouldn't be surprising. BBR's a small town. Gossip's like a wildfire—far too easy to start and nigh impossible to contain. And nobody's all that good at keeping secrets. Especially teenage girls, high school teachers, and Pentecostal church ladies."

"But—"

"And y'all can't run. Two reasons." He held up a finger. "One, Tabitha won't go. She's got her dream right here. Eliza Doolittle in *My Fair Lady*. And if you try and force her, she'll run away. She wouldn't have to go far—only as far as a friend's house. And there's nothing y'all can do about it. Good luck getting a judge in this state to side with a Mormon mother against a teenage girl who wants to go live with

THE WITCH OF WHITE LADY HOLLOW ~

a good Christian family. That judge'd see it as a heroic gesture—he'd be helping her escape the cult, if you'll pardon the expression. And unfortunately, in this state, in Missouri, it's too close to the truth."

One moment, Molly couldn't seem to catch her breath. *Too close to the truth.* The next moment, she was hyperventilating.

The old man raised a second finger. "And two, whoever is behind this, as I said, has great financial resources. There's nowhere on God's green earth you can go where he can't find you."

Molly gasped. "He?"

Fergus nodded. "Yes. I'm sure it's a *he*. I've heard a name—just a name. I've only heard it twice, mind. Just whispers I wasn't supposed to hear. The first time, I wasn't sure I'd gotten it right. But the second time, I know I heard it correctly."

Molly seized MacDonald's hand and squeezed it with a strength born of terror. "Who?"

The old man placed his other hand atop hers. "It's all right, Molly. I may be an old, crippled Marine, but I'm still a Marine. I'll help y'all. You've got an ally in this war, Miss Molly. Together, we'll protect your precious Tabitha."

And Molly felt her breathing ease just a bit. For the second time since meeting with Fergus MacDonald in that slightly darkened room, she looked at the old man in the wheelchair with fresh eyes. *I have an ally.* She squeezed his hand. "Who? What was the name?"

The old Marine's eyes narrowed, the lines around them deepening, hardening. But the fire in them burned all the hotter. "Magnus."

Beulah's hair was frizzy.

And unfortunately, Tabitha knew exactly what that meant.

Yuck.

Beulah's long, blonde ponytail had transformed into a puffball so curly, it resembled a golden afro attached to the back of her head.

Beulah fairly bounced as she strolled back toward the theatre, coming from the direction of the gym. Her pink lips curled in a huge smile. Tabitha observed her friend's lipstick was slightly smudged, as if she'd touched it up hastily. Her skin glistened with a light sheen of sweat, though her T-shirt showed not a hint of damp.

She waved at Tabitha as she passed. "Hail, Sister." Beulah hadn't raised her voice in greeting, but Tabitha glanced around nervously. None of the other kids in the hall seemed to have noticed anything strange.

Beulah's wave became a wave of dismissal. She stopped right in front of Tabitha. "Don't y'all worry about it. Nobody here knows what that means, 'cept us."

Nevertheless, Tabitha glanced around again. *Don't be so sure of that, honey.* Miss Tulane, however, was nowhere to be seen. "Uh, your…your hair." Tabitha pointed sheepishly at her own long black hair.

The blonde girl seemed puzzled for a moment, then she grinned and shrugged. "Oh, that. It happens every time. It'll be gone in a minute. I told you. That's my *tic.* When I have sex, my hair—"

"I remember." Tabitha didn't want to know, didn't want to hear about it. Except…part of her *did.* "Who? Where?"

Beulah giggled. "Joey. Behind the bleachers." She pointed back toward the gym.

Tabitha frowned in distaste. "How romantic," she muttered.

Beulah shrugged. "It was quick, but it was goo—"

"Please!" Tabitha shut her eyes and shook her head, barely resisting the urge to cover her ears. "Don't tell me." *I don't want to know.*

Beulah put a hand on one hip. She cocked her head and raised an eyebrow. "Girl, you asked."

"I know—I know." Tabitha groaned. "Can we change the subject, please?"

Beulah smiled impishly. "Well, certainly." She ran her fingers through her puffy ponytail. The tight, frizzy curls had begun to relax a bit. "What time's your mama gonna be out on her date?"

"She's getting picked up at seven." *Mike Kilmore is picking her up at seven. Mike. Kilmore.* "I'll head over to the clearing a few minutes after that."

Beulah grinned, and a disturbing image flashed through Tabitha's mind—a wolf with pink lipstick and a blonde fuzz ball on the top of its head. "That'll be just fine."

"And," Tabitha lowered her voice to a whisper, "Magnus will be there?"

"That's right. But he won't be there 'til later. He usually doesn't come 'til 'bout midnight."

"But I told you, I can't be out—"

Beulah put up a placating, halting hand. "Calm yourself, girl. I know. I told Joey." She winked. "And Joey will get word to him. So, he'll be there early. Not too early. But well before the witching hour." She chuckled at her own joke, then put a hand on Tabitha's arm. "Well, I'm all done for the day. How much longer y'all got, you and your co-star, Billy, after this break?"

"Another hour or so, probably. I have to call my mom when this is all done so she can come and get me." Tabitha didn't mean it as a hint. Not really.

But Beulah appeared to take it that way. "Sorry, girl! I'd stick around and give y'all a ride home, but I got an early date in an hour. Don't fret, though—I'll be done before the Circle meets." A wicked grin appeared on her face. She pointed to her ponytail, which had almost returned to its usual, straight texture. She breathed out a dramatic sigh worthy of Hamlet's Ophelia. "And just when my hair was getting back to normal!"

Her eyes suddenly flicked to the right. "Hey! Petula!" She waved frantically at someone behind Tabitha. "Wait up, girl!" She patted Tabitha's arm, then trotted off.

Tabitha stood, rooted where she was. *She was just…with Joey, and she's planning on meeting another boy? In an hour? For more sex?*

A part of Tabitha wanted to throw up. *Is Beulah that desperate for attention?*

A part of her wondered, how she avoided getting pregnant. *She must be on the pill.*

Another part of Tabitha, a small, scary, dark part of her, deep down in her wounded soul, made her wonder what her dad di to her. The way she talked about him, the pastor… *What's he maybe still doing to her?* Tabitha shivered.

"Hey, Tabitha!"

Tabitha tore herself out of her dark thoughts, grateful for the distraction. She looked down the hall.

Joey Parsons, his white teeth gleaming and brown eyes shining in his handsome black face, waved at her as he strode in her direction. Striding from the direction of the gym.

He was just with Beulah. He just had sex with Beulah. In the gym. Behind the bleachers.

She waved back—a timid, noncommittal wiggle of her fingers. "Hi." She felt a smile creeping up the corners of her mouth, anyway. Before the events of the previous night, Joey had made her feel many things—confused, scared, flattered, and sometimes a little light-headed.

But at that moment, the memory of the physical sensations she'd experienced in the Circle came thundering back. When Joey had held her hand, his hand had been strong and powerful, but oh so gentle. That memory alone made her tingle a little. But it was the thrill of the Power that had surged through her—the sheer unfamiliar, frightening, ecstatic joy of it—that memory made her quiver.

Joey could unleash that power, that joy within her.

Her smile blossomed.

In a heartbeat, he was standing in front her, towering over her. Smiling down at her.

She tilted her head back slightly to look up into his eyes. Her heart felt as if it might hammer its way out of her chest.

"You know," he said, "you have a gorgeous smile. Anybody ever tell you that? Your smile could light up the whole world."

With her head tilted back, and her knees beginning to wobble, Tabitha felt as if she might fall.

But Joey would catch me.

He just had sex with Beulah.

She swallowed her smile and took a step back.

Feeling a bit steadier, she said, "I have to get back to rehearsal."

His smile softened to a cocky, self-confident grin. "Okay, but you're on break, right?"

She nodded.

"I just need to talk for a minute. You got a minute, don't you? Or maybe two? I just need two minutes."

She hesitated. He just had sex with my best friend. But she's off to be with some other boy in an hour. Like it means nothing. Like sex is no big deal to her.

"Sure," she said. "Go ahead."

He shook his head slightly, though his grin widened. He winked. "Not here." He grabbed her hand and pulled her toward the gym. "Come with me."

As she hurried along with him, her hand in his, she felt more than a little let down. There was no tingle, no surge of pleasure, no throb of joyous, miraculous Power.

Because he isn't channeling.

But she went with Joey down the hall anyway, through double-doors, and into the gym.

The empty gymnasium felt cavernous, lit only by outside light filtering through windows near the vaulted ceiling. To Tabitha, it certainly didn't seem like the ideal setting for an intimate chat, much less a tryst. She felt exposed and vulnerable, almost as if she were on a stage before an audience hidden in the gloom, unseen—alone on a stage in an unfamiliar play, and she didn't know the lines.

She glanced nervously at the bleachers.

Her hand, in Joey's, felt suddenly moist.

You wouldn't really go back there with him, would you? If he asked? Would you? Of course not.

Are you sure?

"Joey, I don't—"

But Joey didn't pull her toward the relative privacy of the bleachers—and the forbidden mysteries and pleasures they promised. He halted, just barely within the bounds of the basketball court. Joey wheeled around, never letting go of her hand. He locked eyes with her, and his brow creased as if with concern. "Tabitha, ever since last night…I need to know…" He took her free hand in his free hand and squeezed both hands gently. "You see, it's like this. Last night…It was beyond incredible."

Incredible. That's one word. "Yeah."

"And…" Suddenly he looked uncomfortable, unsure of himself. "Well, it hasn't ever been like that before."

Tabitha had never seen Joey like this. Towering above her, he seemed small, like a little boy. Lost. "Joey, I don't—"

His hands twitched. And Tabitha realized with a jolt that his palms were sweaty as well. "Listen, Tabitha. As long as I have Beulah and Patsy—both of them—with me, we can fly. Not high, you see. But we can fly a few feet."

Tabitha swallowed. "That was you. You and Beulah and Patsy that night." *The ghosts, flying into the trees.*

He nodded. "Yeah. That night on the highway."

"Oh, boy. I was so scared."

"I'm sorry. We shouldn't have gone as far as the road in our robes. But that's not what I need to see—what I need to ask you."

Is this it? Is he going to ask me to…? She couldn't even force herself to think it. "What? What is it?"

Joey shook his head. "I'm not strong in channeling the Power—not like⌐⌐—"

"Magnus?"

His eyes went wide. "You know? Beulah told you?"

Tabitha shrugged. "Yeah."

"Well, I'm not strong like him. Not like Magnus. But you. You're so strong. I've never felt anything like it."

Me neither.

He bit his lower lip. "I've never been able to take the Circle so high, so fast. Not like last night."

And suddenly, he wasn't towering over her anymore. He was kneeling, his hands still holding hers. "Please. I gotta ask. I gotta see. May I, fly with you? Please, goddess, allow me to use your Power."

Tabitha looked around the empty gym. "Here?" She turned her eyes back to him.

"Now?"

He nodded gravely. "Please, my goddess?"

"S-sure."

He sighed, and it seemed as if a great weight had slipped from his shoulders. "Thank you."

He rose to his feet, and then Tabitha felt warmth surge through her, starting from her belly and radiating outward.

And it was delicious.

She felt herself rising off the polished hardwood floor. And Joey was with her.

Carefully holding one of her hands, thus maintaining constant skin-to-skin contact, he released Tabitha's other hand. His free arm encircled her, his hand pressing against the small of her back, holding her against him. He gazed into her eyes. And the two of them swayed in the air.

Like dancers.

Like lovers.

And like a couple dancing a waltz, they floated and twirled around the empty space above the gym floor.

Tabitha laughed with joy. The night before, she'd been scared. But she wasn't scared at that moment, not with Joey.

He was so warm. His chest so firm.

They floated on a sea of air, slow-dancing on a warm ocean of delirious pleasure, throbbing through her and into him.

"This is amazing." He seemed out of breath. "I can't do this—not with anybody else. Not with Beulah. And she's the strongest. With the whole Circle—before you joined—I could take us a few feet in the air. I have to be careful. I'm so afraid I'm gonna drop us all." He shook his head. "But with you, Tabitha. With you, I don't need anybody else."

He bent his head, hesitating for a moment.

And in that moment, Tabitha felt as if she couldn't breathe, as if she didn't need to breathe. All she needed, all she wanted at the moment was what she hoped, what she prayed would come next.

Joey kissed her.

And she kissed him back.

And the Power surged through her. Sweet. Electric.

Honeyed lightning.

And they both laughed, spinning and swooping through the air, glorying in ecstasy and power.

Neither of them saw the girl below, the girl who had stepped quietly back into the gym. She was blonde, her hair in a ponytail—straight, without even a hint of curl to it anymore.

But she saw them. She saw them flying. And she heard their laughter.

And she heard Joey's words.

The girl in the shadows hugged herself as she shook. Then she turned and fled the gym, dashing angry, bitter tears from her eyes.

"Molly, have you ever been frog gigging?"

Molly's fork paused just short of her mouth, the medium-rare bite of well-seasoned—though barely touched—porterhouse steak hovering in front of her lips. Her eyes focused on Mike Kilmore's. "What?"

The fine lines around his blue eyes crinkled as if in amusement, and he wore his nearly perpetual smile. "Frog gigging."

Molly set her fork and the morsel of beef back on her plate. "Frog-what-ing?"

The muted roar of nearby conversations, the clinking of glasses, and the tinkling of flatware in the Ponderosa Steakhouse seemed to close in around Molly like a sonic fog, clouding her senses and her mind. Even without the noise, she was finding it difficult to concentrate on anything except the danger to her precious daughter. *What in the world is he talking about?*

Mike chuckled. "Frog gigging. It's not a topic of dinner conversation I'd normally employ when trying to impress a dinner-date, especially on a first date—especially one as enchanting and lovely as yourself. And if I may be so bold, Molly Moonshadow, you are a *vision* tonight."

Mike Kilmore. You are such a charmer. If only I wasn't so worried about my baby. But worried or not, she was unable to suppress a smile. That had to be at least the third time he'd complimented her on her appearance that night. *Maybe he really means it.*

His grin broadened. "There you go. That's it. That's the smile that brightens my Sabbath mornings."

Molly felt heat rising in her cheeks. She lowered her eyes, but her smile stayed put. "You're sweet. I bet you say that to all the girls."

He winked. "Maybe. But to tell the truth, Molly, I haven't been out on a date since I moved back to Blue Beech Ridge. Forgive me for saying so, 'cause I don't want to sound too forward—not too forward, mind—but I have my heart set on a temple marriage. And as I'm sure you're aware—heck, you can't've failed to notice—there aren't too many eligible women in the branch. Like none, other than yourself."

Oh, great. Molly's smile vanished. *I should've just canceled tonight. If Fergus hadn't told me to go on with life as if nothing were wrong.* "Only dame in town, is that it?"

He shrugged. "Maybe so. Less'n I want to go robbing the cradle. But honestly, I've never been so enchanted in all my life. And that includes all the dating I did back at BYU. I would count myself extremely lucky to be marooned on a deserted island with you, Molly Moonshadow, assuming, of course, your name was Molly *Kilmore*, and we were married. Otherwise, I'd be the most frustrated, miserable son-of-a— uh, miserable man in creation!"

Her smile crept back.

"Heck," he continued, "if that were the case, I'd have to start my own island country, declare myself president or king or Grand Poobah or something, and make my own laws. Just so I could legally marry you." He slapped the table, making the silverware jump and the glasses of root beer totter precariously. "We'd call it Queen Molly Land! You know what? That's not a half-bad idea, if I do say so myself!" He reached across the table and grabbed Molly's hand, grinning mischievously. "Whatcha say, pretty lady? Shall we? Off to Queen Molly Land! We can stop off at the temple first, though. D.C. Temple okay? That's the closest one."

He started out of the booth, then stopped, grinning from ear to ear, his eyes twinkling, like a grown-up Peter Pan—full of mischief, adventure, and charming impracticality. "Too much? Too soon?"

Molly began to chuckle.

"Dang!" He frowned. "I knew it!"

Her chuckle blossomed into a muted laugh, and the laugh into one of those full-blown belly laughs which momentarily wash away all cares, like a baptism—a baptism, not by water, but by honest, mirthful tears.

Mike sat down, releasing her hand. He let out a dramatic sigh, looking thoroughly—if jokingly—dejected. "And here I was, trying with all my might to impress a lovely lady, and she *laughs* at me."

Molly laughed all the harder. Perhaps it was the strain of the day, with its dire warnings about her daughter. Perhaps it was the fear that'd been gnawing at her gut since she first read Fergus MacDonald's note. It was as if Molly had never needed to laugh so badly in all her life, and a laugh the size and strength of a Mt. Vesuvius eruption burst from inside her.

Mike threw his hands in the air in a gesture of mock despair and defeat. "All day, I've been telling myself, 'This Molly Moonshadow—she's one foxy lady, not to mention classy. Make a good impression, Mikey, old boy. Don't y'all dare blow it!'" He gestured at her with both hands. "But I done gone and blown it, now ain't I? Huh, classy lady?"

Molly's sides were beginning to ache as if she'd been running back-to-back marathons, rather than enjoying cathartic laughter. And judging from the bubble of snot she was suddenly forced to wipe from her nose, she was anything but a "classy lady" at the moment.

Mike Kilmore's dramatically woeful expression morphed into a wide, happy grin. "Well, if this whole police-thing doesn't work out, maybe I can find work as a stand-up comic." He winked, then sighed, still grinning. "Problem is, I'm not really joking. I really like you, Molly Moonshadow. I really do."

As her laughter slowed and then stopped, Molly was almost consumed with a sudden urge to clamber across the table—dress, heels, and all, scattering plates, glasses, and flatware—in order to plant a big kiss on that disarming masculine smile of his. In fact, she was actually starting to work out the logistics of such an ungainly, unseemly, and utterly unladylike maneuver, when Mike said, "So, back to my question. You ever been frog gigging?"

The abrupt change in topic halted her impulsive calculations. For the moment. *If you lean in for a good-night kiss tonight, mister, I'm going to plant a kiss on you so cosmic, it'll blow your mind. I hope you do. I really, really, really hope you do.* "No, Mike. And by the way, I really like you too. But"—she shook her head—"I have never been frog gigging." Then she smirked sheepishly. "I don't think."

"Well, if you had, you'd know it. Like I said, it's not actually a great topic for dinner conversation on a first date—or ever—but..." He shrugged. "It's a way of hunting frogs. Bullfrogs. To eat. Frog legs, you see."

Molly made a face. "Ew."

"Well, they're quite popular in France and down in Louisiana." He shrugged again. "Personally, I've been frog gigging once—as a Boy Scout—but I never could bring myself to eat any of the poor critters.

"Anyway, what you do is you go out at night and find a pond where you can hear them croaking and singing. Then you shine a flashlight in their eyes. Then you stick 'em with a gig. That's like this long, skinny, two-pronged spear."

Molly's appetite *had* been coming back, but now it vanished completely. "Okay."

"Anyway," Mike said, waving a hand dismissively, "that's not the point. The point is when you shine the light in their eyes, they just sit there. They don't move. You've heard the expression, 'like a deer in headlights,' right?"

Molly nodded, still wondering where he was going and why he couldn't just get back to the I-really-like-you part.

"Well, a deer in headlights is scared, petrified. They don't know what to do. With frogs, it's not like that. The frog just stares as if its brain has shut down, like it isn't thinking at all—not even thinking little froggy-thoughts. It just sits there until you stick it with the gig."

Weird. Gross. "Okay..."

"Well, Molly, I hope you'll pardon me for saying so, but you were staring just like that—like you weren't here, like you were...somewhere else. And I know even with such stimulatin' conversation as I can provide, with my keen wit, my rugged good looks, and my unimpeachable humility." His mischievous grin faded. "Well, until you 'bout busted a gut laughing just now, I was afraid, well, that you just weren't interested."

Molly sighed. "It's not that. I *am* interested." *Very interested.* "It's just…"

"It's just you got something eating at you. Listen, I've interrogated enough suspects in my time. There, I've done it again. Used the wrong blasted word. You're not a *suspect.* What I'm trying to say is I'm usually pretty good at reading people. But tonight, well, I guess, this was just too important, too personal for me. And I could see you just weren't into it. So, Molly, what's eating at you?"

Molly hesitated. *Fergus said not to tell anyone, especially the police. Go on like nothing's wrong. That way Magnus—whoever he is—won't know we're on to him.*

But I can trust Mike, can't I?

He's such a good guy, a solid priesthood holder. Leader in the Church. I can trust him. I know I can. But what if I'm wrong? What if Mike isn't as perfect as he seems? What if this is all just a mask?

Mike cleared his throat. "It's okay. You don't have to tell me. Look, if I was getting too fresh just now, I'm sorry."

No. I liked it. Do you know how long it's been since a man—a decent man—a decent, Mormon man—a decent, Mormon, utterly handsome man looked at me the way you look at me?

An ache that Molly had kept buried so deep inside her for so long, a need she'd convinced herself was long dead, came thundering back to life, pounding in time with her heart, thudding with the blood in her ears. It wasn't just a yearning for the attentions and affections of a man. It went deeper than that. She needed to be able to *trust* a man.

She needed to trust *Mike.* She needed to tell him.

And she did.

She told him everything except the part about Tabitha's visions and about Fergus. She left the paranormal business and the crippled Marine out of it. "But I just can't tell you who told me about all this. I shouldn't be telling you now, but…"

He reached across the table again and placed a hand atop hers. He squeezed gently. "It's okay. I'm glad you did. I'm so very glad you trusted me." Gone was the grin. His eyes bored into hers. It felt as if he was baring his soul with his eyes the way she had bared hers with her words. "You can trust me, Molly."

Tears spilled from her eyes, running down her cheeks. *Ruining my makeup. Don't care. Not important.* All the same, she dabbed carefully at her eyes and cheeks with her napkin.

"Go on," Mike said. "You eat. You're gonna need your strength. For your daughter. Worryin' is hungry work. Go on. Eat."

She gave him a weak smile. Reluctantly, she picked up her fork and put a now-cold bite of steak in her mouth. As she chewed, she realized she was ravenous. *Worrying is hungry work.* She swallowed. "Thank you."

"Now, while you eat, I'm gonna tell you how I can help."

She smiled and dug into her steak. It was really good, if a little cold.

"Here's what I can do," he said. "I'll ask around. Discreetly. I can't go checking bank records without a warrant, so I won't be able to trace the 'mysterious donor'—not directly. At this point, I don't even have any probable cause a crime has been committed. So, this won't be official sheriff business. But I can ask some questions. I do have a contact or two on the school board." He took a sip of his root beer. "So, where's Tabitha right now?"

Molly put a hand to her mouth to cover it while she spoke around a mouthful of food. "With friends. Beulah Martineau and Joey Parsons. Some other kids."

Mike nodded. "Those two seem like good kids. Well, good enough. Nobody around here keeps *our* standards. Heck, not even some of our own. Never mind about that. But if Tabitha's in a group of kids, this Magnus character is unlikely to approach her directly."

He shook his head and let out a mirthless chuckle. "But this trap this Magnus guy has laid for her—and that's what it is for sure—a trap. Well, it's diabolical. And it's pure genius. She's not gonna let you take her away from what she's dreamed of all her life. So, here's my advice for now. Cultivate her trust. Does she trust you?"

Molly shrugged and shook her head. "She used too, but I don't know, lately."

"She's a teenager. We were both teenagers once. So, you know what it's like. You know it's not gonna be easy. But she needs to know she can trust you. That she can come to you."

"You know she's sweet on you."

Mike blinked. Then he nodded. "Yeah, I kinda figured. But I'm way too old for her. Besides, I want a *woman*, not a girl. Like I said, I'm not interested in robbing the cradle."

Speaking of robbing the cradle. "Just how old are you, Mike Kilmore?"

His impish grin returned, making her heart twitter. "Now, if I'd asked you that same question." He let his voice trail off.

Molly narrowed her eyes. "Now, don't you tell me you don't already know my age. You've seen my membership record, I bet. So, how old, Mister?" She bit her lower lip, dreading his answer.

He shrugged. "Well, yeah, I must confess—I have seen your membership record. I'm thirty-five. Just three years younger than you."

Molly suppressed a shudder of relief. *Close enough.* She rolled her eyes dramatically, then she grinned. "Well, I'll try not to hold your youth and inexperience against you."

One side of his mouth curled into a lopsided smile, and he winked at her. "I ever tell you how sexy—"

A loud crackle interrupted him, along with a series of electronically distorted sounds which might have been words. His expression was instantly very serious. He reached below the table and pulled up a police radio.

Molly realized with a start she hadn't even noticed him wearing one.

He held up a finger. "One minute."

He put the radio to his ear. "Bravo-Charlie-Two. Go."

He listened for a several seconds, then "Copy. I'll be over in a bit." He looked at his watch. "Give me an hour." Then, "Copy that. Bravo-Charlie-Two out."

He lowered the radio, then sighed. "Molly, I'm really sorry, but we're gonna have to cut this short. Sadly, duty calls."

As he drove her home, back to the cottage in the Hollow, they talked. At first, they talked of trivial things. They didn't talk about Tabitha or Magnus or anything serious. It was the sort of clumsy boy-girl chit-chat Molly hadn't engaged in since she was dating. Dating Jerry. But Molly didn't want to think about her ex-husband. *Mike's not like Jerry. Nothing like Jerry. Mike Kilmore would never betray me.*

Eventually, the talking faded away into an awkward silence—a silence filled with an almost delicious tension.

Mike reached across the seat and brushed her hand tentatively. In response, she edged her hand below his. Then they were holding hands. Like teenagers. Or an old married couple.

And it was sweet.

And when they were standing in front of the cottage, in the yellow, bug-repelling glow of Molly's porch light, Molly was dearly hoping—hoping with all her might—that Mike would lean in for a kiss.

He looked into her eyes and his grin faded away as his expression took on an intensity she had never before seen in him.

This is it. Do it. Please.

Instead, he spoke, and the words coming out of his mouth were nothing Molly expected. "Would you mind terribly if we prayed? For Tabitha? And for you?"

Molly swallowed the lump of frustration and disappointment in her throat. She managed to nod. "Do you want to come in?"

He shook his head quickly. "No. That wouldn't be proper. Or safe. Especially not the way I'm feeling tonight."

Molly's pulse thundered in her ears again. "We could leave the front door open."

He chuckled. "And let in all the bugs?"

She shook her head. "I can't kneel here—not in this dress."

"Did I tell you how lovely you look tonight?"

She grinned. "A few times."

"And how sexy you look in that dress?"

Molly flushed. "No."

He sighed. "Well, let's not ruin your dress or your panty hose. Let's just stand here holding hands as we pray."

So, they bowed their heads, and Mike offered a prayer. He prayed for Tabitha, for Molly, and for himself, that they would all be guided by the Spirit, that they'd all be safe.

And when they both said, "Amen," Mike leaned in for a kiss.

Molly had intended for that first kiss to be mind-blowing, and judging by Mike's response, she succeeded. But one thing was certain—Molly Moonshadow was completely and utterly swept off her feet.

Like phantoms, two white-robed figures floated over the forest. A dense overcast hid the moon and stars, so the passage of the two ghostly figures went unnoticed by all except the night birds. Holding hands, they descended to the forest floor.

They walked toward the light of a bonfire, blazing between the gaps of the trees. Under his white hood, the taller figure wore a ceremonial golden mask. The hood of the shorter figure ballooned around her head, puffed out by a mass of tightly curled golden hair.

As they walked, hand-in-hand, Magnus glanced at his companion. "Perhaps, my dear, you should tie your hair back. Everyone will know what we've been doing."

Beulah held her head high, frowning. "Let them know. Let them all know that I'm your woman. Not them. None of them. Just me." She paused. "I *am* your woman, aren't I?"

"Yes, my dear. Of course."

Beulah sighed. "Oh, it was wonderful tonight! Y'all were magnificent."

Magnus squeezed her hand. "As were you, my dear. Magnificent."

"Making love to you…There's nothing better—the Power flowing through us. Making us one flesh. One spirit." She trembled, and she swore she could feel her hair frizzing all the more at the thought. She sighed again and felt her knees wobble. "Out of this world!"

He squeezed her hand. "Yes, my dear."

They strolled in silence a few steps more. Then Beulah slowed, wanting to hold him back from entering the clearing. "Magnus, we don't need her." She had no doubt Magnus knew precisely who she meant.

"Oh, my dear. We do. I'm so close. So very close. I know I am. She could push us over the top. I'm anxious to try."

Beulah took a few more steps. "But her mom. Why do you have to…"

"We've been over this, my dear. Joey has failed to seduce our Miss Tabitha."

Beulah scowled. *Don't be so certain of that. They haven't done it, yet. Maybe. But he'll have her soon enough. I know he will. He's good, damn him. Damn her.*

Damn them both to hell.

Unaware of Beulah's dark thoughts, Magnus continued, "We need to break her down, get her to cross every line, get her to violate every standard, every value she's lived by her whole life. Only then will she be moldable. Only then will she be truly mine."

Bitch. I hate her.

He squeezed her hand. "Only then will she be truly ours. So, I'm attacking on a different front. In order to get close to the daughter, I need to become close to her mother, to become a part of her life. But the mother's just a tool, a means to an end." He let out a low, sinister chuckle. "And once I get what I need, she'll be completely disposable."

Just a piece of cloth. A sheet, cut up and sewn together. That's all it is.

But to Tabitha, the white thing in her hands felt like more than that. So much more.

And above everything else, it was the hooded white robe which freaked her out.

In the past twenty-four tumultuous hours, she'd experienced highs and lows, twists and turns—as if she'd been riding a roller coaster designed by Caligula and given surreal form by Salvador Dali. She'd seen and done things that had assaulted her core beliefs, shaken her faith, and almost shattered her sense of self.

But at the last, it was the robe which terrified her.

She held the white garment—tinged yellow and orange by the dancing glow of the bonfire in the clearing—held it at arm's length in front of her, staring at it as if the sheet were a burial shroud. It could have been made out of a bed sheet, but even so, it had been cut and sewn with care and craft.

And it looks like it'll fit perfectly, just the right length. Like it was made just for me.

Like they knew for sure I'd be joining them.

She shuddered at the thought.

They knew I was coming.

They want me.

They need me.

And like all human beings, Tabitha needed to be needed, wanted to be wanted.

But if I put on this robe, does that really make me a witch? Do I really want to cross that line?

Oh, she'd crossed lines. She'd lied to her mother, and that still ate at her. She'd kissed her best friend's boyfriend—and the kisses had left her breathless and confused.

But there were also lines she had not crossed. She had stopped Joey when he wanted to go further than passionate kissing.

And she wasn't exactly certain why.

Church standards—what do they even mean anymore?

She hadn't crossed that line. Not yet.

But to Tabitha, the white robe with its deep hood represented a whole new line.

If I put this on, there's no turning back.

No turning back? Now you're just being a drama queen. That's stupid. Crazy. It's just a robe.

But it's so, Pagan. So, not-Mormon.

But am I still Mormon?

Her faith—which Tabitha had always clung to like a lifejacket in a tsunami, had cleaved to all her life—her faith had defined her. She'd walked in absolute certainty her testimony of the gospel of Jesus Christ was as inescapable and as unquestionable as the force of gravity.

But I have defied gravity.

I have flown.

It was my power. Not men's priesthood—woman's power. My power.

"Y'all're supposed to wear the dang thing, not stare at it, ya silly goose."

Tabitha turned her gaze away from the thing in her hands and toward Patsy. Patsy was, of course, already wearing her robe, her face hidden deep in the shadows of the hood. All the other girls of the Circle had already donned their ceremonial garments. They stood or sat around the fire like a congregation of phantoms—assuming phantoms chattered and giggled like a bunch of Mia Maids at their first Girls Camp.

Tabitha balled up the white cloth. "Where's Joey? Isn't he supposed to be here?"

I'm stalling.

Patsy flicked her hand dismissively. The loose robe hid everything, except the hands. "He's off with Mary Sue." She waved vaguely toward a deeper part of the woods. "Joey likes to be all charged up before the ceremony begins."

Tabitha's jaw dropped. "You mean they're?"

Patsy waved both hands and shrugged. "What else? It's not like we ain't *all* done him. At least once." She placed a hand on her hip. "Some of us"—she paused, and the pause left no doubt she included herself—"a whole buncha times. It's no big deal, girl." Then she sighed as her hand came up to caress her other arm. "Although, I gotta admit—Joey's one hell of a lover. And doin' it with a man who can channel the Power? Mm-mm. Ain't nothin' can compare. But it's no big deal."

Stop saying that! A sudden wave of nausea frothed up from Tabitha's stomach, and the forest seemed to spin around her. She took a couple of deep breaths to clear her head and settle her gut.

It is a big deal.

But the memory of Joey's lips, his strong hands, his firm, muscular body pressed against hers as they danced in the air. The warm pulsing of the Power flowing from her into him—through their hands, through their lips.

Even the disgust she felt, knowing Joey had been with each of these girls—including Beulah—and was with Mary Sue at that very moment—couldn't quell the ache in her body. She wanted to be with him. To fly with him. To kiss him.

To more *than kiss him?*

She thought of Joey and Mary Sue, fighting *not* to picture exactly *what* they were doing. And a flame of hatred blazed in her—hatred for Mary Sue—hatred for Joey. And, inextricably churning with the flame of hatred, was a flood of longing.

"Now Beulah," Patsy said, ripping Tabitha out of her whirlwind of conflicting passions. "She's the only one that's been with Magnus."

"Magnus?"

Patsy shrugged twice, paused, then shrugged again as if she were trying to convince herself of something. "I can only *dream* what it's like to be with him. But I bet when it comes down to doin' the dirty, he's no different'n Joey. Maybe not even as good. Still, Beulah's his particular pet."

"But you said—all of you said—*we* were the"—Tabitha could barely bring herself to say the word—"g-goddesses. Magnus serves us." *Worships us.* "The Divine Feminine and the priest and all that. Right?"

Patsy waved her hand again. "Oh, yeah. Course. But Beulah's the only one he's *chosen*, the only one he truly trusts." She leaned in close and whispered in Tabitha's ear. "She's the only one who's seen his face."

Seen his face? Tabitha peered into the other girl's hood. She could see a wisp of hair, but nothing else in the depths. "Because he wears a hood?" *Like us?*

"Because he wears a mask."

"A mask?"

"Sure, a ceremonial mask. It's gold and all."

One of the other girls—as anonymous as the rest in her robe and hood—cried out. "They're coming!"

"Quick!" Patsy said. "Put it on!"

Put it on? Now? But...

Here goes nothing. With only a moment's further hesitation, Tabitha slipped the robe over her head. She wriggled her arms into the long, voluminous sleeves. The bulk of the garment gathered around her waist, above her customary full-length skirt. Tabitha fussed with it, desperately trying to force the white fabric down over the skirt.

With a growl of exasperation, Patsy bent and helped Tabitha yank the white over the black. "Pull up your hood. Now!"

Tabitha obeyed as Patsy finished smoothing Tabitha's robe. "Why the hoods?" Tabitha asked. "Why the mask?"

Patsy stood. "It's the *old* way. The way of the goddess. The way of the Circle. The way it's been since the dawn o' time. 'Sides, we gotta protect Magnus and Joey, protect their identities. Well, not Joey so much. He has to make skin contact, so his hands have to be bare. And, well frankly, there just ain't that many tall black boys in BBR. Joey used to wear a mask—at first—in the early days of the Circle, we all did—but I mean, what's the dang use? But now Magnus. Well, without him and Joey, we can't do nothin'. We own the Power, but we can't— Here they come!"

Hand in hand, a pair of figures entered the clearing. There could be no doubt the shorter figure was, in fact, Beulah, with her hood puffed out like a ball or a spacesuit helmet around her head—puffed out by very frizzy blonde hair. Beulah strutted like a model or a dancer—or a cheerleader. The man beside her, his mask glinting gold in the firelight, strode with a regal dignity—a lion padding into the center of his pride of young lionesses.

The girls of the Circle flocked around him.

Tabitha stood where she was, anxiety and doubt churning like worms in her gut. *What am I doing here? Who is he?*

The sea of robed figures surged around the tall man, like white-capped waves crashing around a lighthouse. Then the sea parted, and Magnus, still holding Beulah's hand, strode toward Tabitha.

The light of the fire reflected off the golden mask. The mask covered his entire face, one solid sheet of gold, smooth, broken only by three horizontal slits—two for the eyes and one for the mouth. Tabitha was reminded of the mask of Iron Man in the old Saturday morning cartoons.

He's like a rock star, and we're his groupies. I thought we were supposed to be the goddesses—in charge, somehow.

Last night, Joey deferred to Beulah, did everything she said.

Tabitha couldn't imagine this Magnus deferring to anyone.

As he approached, his height added to his regal image.

Tabitha was about to take a step back, when Magnus suddenly dropped to his knees before her.

"This is Magnus," Beulah said—as if the man *needed* an introduction. She spoke with a pride and possessiveness which seemed to also say, *And he is mine.* "Magnus, this is our Miss Tabitha."

Still holding Beulah's hand, the High Priest of the Circle bowed his head. "My lady, please accept my humble adoration. Let me worship you, my goddess. Let me serve you all my days. I humbly await your command."

Tabitha was stunned into mute silence.

He raised his head slightly. "My lady?"

Beulah pointed at the kneeling man with her free hand. "Tell him to rise."

Beulah's exaggerated stage whisper startled Tabitha out of her openmouthed staring. "Uh, yeah. Please, uh, please rise."

Magnus stood, towering over her. His head was still slightly bowed. "As you wish, my dear. Thank you." He extended his free right hand. "If I may be so bold as to touch the divine?"

Tabitha stared at the large, powerful hand. For an instant, she almost obeyed her instinct to shake it in typical Mormon fashion. Then it dawned on her what the man was asking.

Gingerly, she took his right hand in her left.

154

His hand enveloped hers, entwining his fingers with hers—an intimate clasp, like a lover's.

Then the Power began to flow. It began as a warm glow in her belly. And Tabitha was certain it could be originating from only one place—her womb. *The source of life.* The warmth radiated outward, filling her, making her skin, her fingers, her toes, even her hair tingle. It flowed through her hand and into his.

Magnus seemed to tremble. "My dear! Forgive me! I did not mean to channel without permission. But your Power! Joey did not exaggerate. Forgive me."

"I told y'all," Beulah said.

Almost unable to catch her breath as if she'd been running laps in gym class while inhaling laughing gas, Tabitha shook her head slightly. "It's…It's okay." *Wow! This feels so good. So, so right.*

"But, my dear." Magnus sounded out of breath as well. "This is only a fraction of what you possess. I am merely dipping my toe in the ocean!"

Only a fraction? This is incredible. And we're not even doing anything yet!

"Let us begin," Magnus said, calming his breathing. "With your permission?"

Before Tabitha had begun her walk from the cottage to the clearing, she had planned to listen to Magnus's voice—to listen for anything familiar—an accent or a pattern of speaking. Magnus sounded totally unfamiliar, without the slightest hint of a Missouri accent—or any accent she could identify.

Who are you? she wondered. The man holding her hand, channeling her Power, was a complete stranger, yet she felt comforted by his presence. *Or is it just that I feel so good?*

The robed figures, who had gathered round them, joined hands and formed a circle. A robed girl grasped Tabitha's free hand. Instantly, she felt Power flow from the hooded girl into her. And once it entered her, she felt it blossom and expand.

Exponentially. Like I'm magnifying the strength of all the other girls down the line.

Tabitha noticed two figures hurrying toward them, white robes flapping. They were holding hands, but the shorter of the two yanked her hand out of the other's and pushed her way into the Circle.

Joey and Mary Sue, Tabitha thought, with a final twinge of jealousy.

Joey held back. He did not join the Circle. He merely stood in the shadows.

Why's he holding back? As she felt the Power flowing through her, she hit upon the answer. *Maybe only one man can wield the Power at the same time?*

Well, good! Serves him right. Too bad Mary Sue gets to join in. And then she felt ashamed of her resentment. And besides, the Power felt so good, she didn't want to concentrate on anger or hate.

Or love.

"Woman is life!" intoned Magnus, raising his voice.

"Woman is life!" echoed the Circle.

"Woman is power!" Magnus's voice seemed to fill the clearing as if amplified by the Power he was drawing from the Circle.

"Woman is power!" cried the Circle as one voice.

All except Tabitha, and she felt the words pulling at her, drawing her, filling her with the desire to accept the adulation, to join in the ritual.

"Woman is magic!" cried Magnus, and he gave Tabitha's hand a gentle squeeze.

"Woman is magic!" And that time, Tabitha joined in the chant. *Magic!*

"Woman is divine!" Magnus chanted, his rich voice just short of a bellow.

"Woman is divine!" The Power surged through the Circle, through Tabitha, lifting her as if on the wave of an ocean—an ocean of warmth and strength and joy.

And then they were flying, soaring into the night sky.

A hundred feet or more they climbed and then halted, like a ring of spectral figures hovering expectantly in the air.

Tabitha saw a flicker of light in the darkness at the center of the Circle.

She heard a collective gasp from the girls.

What? Is this something new?

Slowly the light grew until it became a sphere of light, like a tiny, wraithlike sun shining just for them, illuminating their hooded faces in its magical glow.

"Yes!" roared Magnus. "My dears!" He gave her hand a squeeze so enthusiastic it hurt. "Let there be light!"

And beside her, she felt and heard Magnus laughing with unbounded glee.

"Thank you, my dear!" Magnus knelt on both knees before her. He knelt and held her hand, like a knight before a lady—or a penitent before a priest—or a worshipper before his goddess. "You are magnificent!" He bent his head over her hand as if to kiss it, but merely pressed the gold of the mask over the back of her hand.

Startled by the unexpected warmth of the metal, Tabitha nearly withdrew her hand. *Just his body heat—coming through the mask.*

She shot a furtive glance away from the bowed head of Magnus to the massive beech tree lying on its side at the edge of the clearing. Many of the branches lay broken beneath the unaccustomed weight of the tree. Some of the roots were naked to the night air, twisted, reaching out as if in agony for the nourishment of dirt and moisture that would never be theirs again. The rest of the roots were still entombed in the remains of the great, irregular ball of earth that'd come out of the ground when Magnus had ripped the wooden behemoth from the forest floor. The great pit where the tree had once stood resembled the crater left by an exploded bomb.

Once a majestic woodland prince, probably more than a century old—it had probably been here when White Lettie roamed those woods—the blue beech tree was slowly dying. And nothing could save it.

He just tore it out of the ground. And he laughed as he did it.

He probably would've destroyed more of them. Beulah told him to stop—and he did stop. But...

I did this. At least, I was part of it.

Because of me, that beautiful tree is dead.

The Power still pulsed within her—a low, pleasurable throb. She felt so good. And she felt as if she might vomit.

She turned her gaze back to the hooded head of the mysterious High Priest. "We killed that tree."

Magnus's head bowed lower. He sat down on his feet, then let go of Tabitha's hand. He clasped his hands together and laid them on his knees. It was the same posture Tabitha's mom used when she prayed at home—when she wasn't kneeling at her bedside. "Yes, my dear. Please, forgive me. The Power…it was so— In my joy, I…"

Beulah stepped forward and laid a hand on his shoulder. "It's all right, hon. Y'all just got carried away." She whistled softly. "We all did. It was, oh man, it was out of this world!"

His head bowed even lower. "Praise to thee, my goddess. Thou art merciful." He raised both hands toward Tabitha. "And praise to thee, my goddess, my Lady Tabitha. Thou art merciful and gracious unto me. I thank thee for allowing me to touch the divine."

The intimate, familiar phrasing—the language of prayer—startled Tabitha, making her intensely uncomfortable. To her mind came an image from an old *Star Trek* episode—Captain Kirk being forced to kneel to an old friend who had become extremely powerful. *Pray to me*, he had said.

Tabitha shook her head. "Please, don't, don't pray to me. I'm not…" She didn't know what to say. The Power felt so good. Having friends, here in this little town in the middle of Sticksville. She wanted the friendship, the Power. She craved it. She needed it. It felt wonderful and wrong.

Wonderful and wrong. How can it be both at the same time?

Magnus lowered his hands to his lap. "As you wish, my dear."

Who are you? All she could see of him were his hands. Strong hands—so gentle as he had held hers in the Circle—except when he'd squeezed too hard.

His touch brought pleasure and pain and unbridled joy. And a dying tree—ripped from Mother Earth with merely a thought, and a laugh.

A line from an old Don McLean song came to her mind. *I saw Satan laughing with delight.*

"I need to go home."

"Hey, Tabitha! Wait up!"

Tabitha heard Joey's voice calling after her. She forced herself to walk—not run—from the clearing. As a matter of fact, she was doing her best to appear to stroll casually. She wanted to get away, to escape, but she wasn't going to show her fear.

She didn't even tremble.

I'm an actress. I can do this. Just a little farther.

"Tabitha!"

I don't want to talk to you, Joey Parsons!

She'd removed the white robe. Her hands hadn't even quivered when she handed it back to Patsy. Tabitha felt exceptionally proud of that.

"Tabitha!" He was closer. "Moonshadow!"

When he grabbed her arm, she jumped. *At least I didn't scream.*

"Girl, didn't you hear me?" Rather than pulling her around to face him, he swung around in front of her—blocking her escape. "Where're you going?"

She forced herself to meet his eyes—sort of. He was still wearing his robe, but had pulled the hood back. In the darkness, even with the light of the bonfire, she could distinguish his eyes only by the whites around his dark pupils.

I can look him in the eye without really seeing him. And I know he can't see me.

She managed a vague smile. "I gotta go home. My mom's expecting me."

"Come on." His teeth were a dim white in the black of his face. "It's Saturday night! We're barely getting started!"

"What's next?" She fought to keep the anger—and the fear—out of her voice. "Dancing naked around the fire?"

Joey laughed, but there was a nervous edge to his laugh. "Dancing naked? We don't do that." He paused, and she could see enough of his teeth to discern he was grinning widely. "Not a bad idea, now you mention it."

Tabitha turned away from that grin, risking a glance back toward the clearing. They weren't dancing. They weren't doing much of anything that she could tell,

THE WITCH OF WHITE LADY HOLLOW

other than standing around. Magnus, distinguishable by the golden mask, sat alone at the focal point of an arc of shorter figures. One of the girls—Beulah, Tabitha assumed—approached the High Priest and grasped his hand.

Suddenly Tabitha felt weak, as if someone had pulled the stopper in a sink and all the water was suddenly draining out. *Like touching Lettie's broom...or my grandfather's iron washer.* She thought then of the washer in the pocket of her skirt. She resisted a sudden urge to pat it, to assure herself it was still there.

She felt a tug at her arm. *Joey,* she thought, as if she'd momentarily forgotten his presence.

"You coming back?" he asked.

She turned her face to him. He was still grinning, but that was all she could make out in the dark. She shook her head. "No. I have to go home."

She glanced once more toward the fire. They were all still standing, watching. Even Magnus was standing, facing her.

They're waiting to see what I do, if I'll come back. She shivered.

"You cold, baby?" Joey's grin had faded, and Tabitha imagined a look of concern on his face.

She shook her head. "I have to go."

He tugged at her, and she realized he meant to pull her into his arms. "Let me warm—"

She jerked away, out of his grasp. *You were just having sex with Mary Sue!* "I told you. I have to go home."

"Magnus…"

That's it, isn't it? This is all about Magnus. Magnus and the Power.

She took a step to the side and walked around him, staying out of arm's reach. Then she strode with a deliberate casualness toward the darkness of the trees.

"Can I walk you home?"

She took a couple more steps.

"It's dark. Let me walk you home. Please?"

She stopped and turned.

And nearly screamed with fright.

He was *right* there.

Her eyes were level with his chest.

Tabitha took a deep breath to calm her trembling. "That's really sweet. But I'm okay. Really."

"Baby, what's wrong?" His face was just a shadow framed by the light of the fire. "Was it the tree?"

She hesitated. Then she pivoted and walked into the woods.

He walked beside her, pulling off his robe as he went, but he said nothing. And he made no effort to touch her.

"I think," he said after a minute of silence broken only by the crunch of the leaves beneath their feet, "Magnus was just caught up in the moment. Your Power is out of this world. He didn't mean anything by it."

"You know," she said, "I read a book on witches." Although that was not exactly true. She hadn't exactly *read* it—she *had* spent a nervous half hour in the high school library skimming through a book on modern-day pagans and witches. The oversized book contained a number of black-and-white photos of naked people—many of them overweight or at least what Tabitha thought of as "lumpy"—dancing in woods. Though she had quickly passed over the unflattering and unsettling images, she'd been terrified someone would catch her—catch the Mormon girl—looking at "dirty" pictures.

Witches are supposed to be all about nature, not ripping trees out of the ground.

"Anyway," she said, "the Circle—you're not anything like what I read about."

He chuckled. "No dancing naked?"

She shrugged, and the ghost of a smile played at the corners of her mouth. "Yeah."

"I'd think you'd be relieved." She could almost hear the grin in his voice.

She laughed softly. "Yeah. Well, I guess you're right about that."

"But I bet you'd look *fantastic* naked."

"Stop."

"Seriously—a total fox! Dyno-mite, outta sight!"

She rounded on him then. "Stop it!"

He threw up his hands, dropping the robe. "Hey, it's cool. You're not ready, so—"

"I tell you no, so you go get it on with Mary Sue?"

"You know about that?"

She barked out a bitter laugh and crossed her arms protectively. "Yeah. You weren't exactly discreet." And the words of Suzanne Tulane came to her mind. *Loose lips sink ships, and all that. And nobody has loose lips like a teenage girl.*

He ran a hand through his hair. "It's not like that."

"And before that—before you…before we danced in the gym, there was Beulah. Was there somebody else in between?" She jabbed a finger into his chest. "I'm not gonna just be another whore in your stable, Mister Parsons!"

She wheeled around and stomped off.

"It's not like that!" he called, his voice coming from a distance behind her.

He's not following.

And a part of Tabitha hated herself, because she was disappointed—she wanted him to follow her, to come after her.

"It's just sex!" he yelled. "It doesn't mean anything!"

She spun back and dashed toward him, heedless of the uneven ground. "Stop saying that! It means a lot! It means a lot to me!"

She *felt* the boom more than she heard it. A burst of power exploding from her like a shockwave. She knew what it was now. She recognized it. She couldn't *control* it, couldn't aim it, but it ripped out of her, blasting in all directions at once. She heard wood crack all around her.

And she saw Joey topple backward.

No, she saw him *fly* backward. He hit the forest floor a dozen yards from where he'd stood, landing with a thump, followed by a grunt.

He groaned and uttered what sounded like a particularly foul word.

She stumbled toward him, tripping over a newly fallen tree branch. "Joey! You okay?"

He coughed, then let out a low chuckle as she approached. "Girl, the PB High offensive line has got nothing on you. I feel like I been kicked in the chest by a whole herd of Poplar Bluff Mules. With cleats on." He took a couple of deep breaths and appeared to be patting his body, checking for broken bones.

She stopped just short of where he lay. "You okay?" she repeated. She stopped herself from apologizing. She was sorry, but she wasn't about to admit it.

He shook his head. "Nothing broken. I think." He hissed. "I hope."

She let out a breath she hadn't realized she'd been holding. "Good. I didn't mean to hurt you." That was as close to saying sorry as she wanted to get.

He laughed. The sound was low, but genuine. "Oops. So much for that. But it's okay. I deserved it. I took you for granted."

She stepped closer and extended a hand to help him up.

He waved her hand away. "No. This is all on me." He clambered slowly to his feet without her assistance. "The next time—and I hope there is a next time—I *want* there to be a next time—the next time I touch you, it'll be with your permission. And *only* with your permission."

Tabitha's night vision must've been improving, since she was away from the light of the bonfire—she could see his face well enough to make out an expression of pain and chagrin.

He drew himself to his full height. "I don't expect you to believe me right now, but I'm gonna prove myself to you. I won't touch another girl, except for holding hands in the Circle. I gotta do that for now. I have to learn. But I promise I won't touch another girl any other way. Not Mary Sue, not Patsy, not even Beulah—none of 'em. I'll prove it. I'm yours, and yours alone, if you'll have me."

He paused, and then his head bent down, his dark face hovering over hers.

For a moment, Tabitha tilted her head back in response. Then she stepped back. "I have to go."

She turned and walked as quickly as she dared away from him. Tears leaked from her eyes, and she wasn't entirely certain why. She wasn't certain of anything at that moment.

All she knew was that she was miserable. Miserable and alone.

By the time she reached the ruins of White Lettie's cabin, halfway to home, she was sobbing.

I want my mom. I need to talk to my mom.

"But I can't talk to my mom," she said softly. *I can't tell her about this, about the Power and the Circle. About Joey. Besides, she's out on a date with him.* A bitter laugh escaped her. "I bet she won't be home before midnight."

Tabitha sobbed and dropped down onto one of the rotten logs that were all that remained of the walls of White Lettie's cabin. She wrapped her arms around her knees and wailed like a child—a little girl, lost and alone in the dark woods—rocking back and forth on the rotten log. A soft, quiet, childlike admission passed her quivering lips, words she would never have uttered in front of another living soul.

"I want my mom!"

Then, more quietly, as if not even wanting the trees to hear, "I want my mommy." She let the sobs wash over her, smothering her, cleansing her.

But when the tears were past, she still ached for the comfort of her mother's arms. *Even if I can't talk to her, even if I'm keeping secrets, she'd still hold me. She'd still make me feel safe. Loved. Valued.*

Not just a thing, *a commodity to be used.*

Then, like a match struck and flaring up in the darkness, the realization came to her—*I can be with her right now.*

Slowly, deliberately, she reached into the pocket of her skirt and closed her hand around the iron washer.

"I want my daddy!"

The child wriggled in her arms, squirming, kicking, thrashing like a wild animal. But Molly held on to the little girl, holding her to her chest.

"I know, Tabby-Cat. I know." She tried to keep her voice smooth and calm, keep the tears and the anger and the pain out of it. But it was a struggle with a six-year-old in her arms, and that six-year-old was throwing a fit worthy of a child half her age. "Please, honey. Hold still. You're hurting Mommy."

Small fists pounded on her shoulders. "I hate you! I hate you! You made daddy go away!"

"No, Tabby-Cat. I didn't." Oh yes, I did. I wasn't enough for him. I didn't give him what he wanted. Frigid Bitch of the West.

But I wasn't frigid. I was passionate, loving. But I just couldn't—

"I want my daddy!" The screaming cut off abruptly, as did the violence of the tantrum. Tabitha collapsed as if the fight had gone out of her. As if she had surrendered to her grief and her loss.

And then the little girl began to wail and tremble with wracking sobs. "I want my daddy back."

And Molly held her daughter close, squeezing almost too tightly. Almost. "Oh, honey, I want him too." Heaven help me, but I do. *Still holding the girl close, Molly ran her fingers through Tabitha's long, thick, raven hair, lovingly smoothing the tangles caused by the child's physical outburst. "But he's not coming back, Tabby-Cat. He's not."*

Tabitha snuffled, blowing snot onto Molly's blouse. "Doesn't he want me anymore?"

"Oh, honey, it's not you." It's me. No, it's him. This is all on you, Jerry. *"It's not you. It's me he doesn't want anymore. He doesn't . . ."* No, I'm not. I'm not going to

tell her that. She wouldn't understand. Not now.

She's too young. I have to protect her. Someday I'll explain it.

Or he will.

But not now. Not tonight.

"Was I b-b-bad?" Tabitha's frame shook with a tremendous sob. "Was I a bad girl? And Daddy went away 'cause of me?"

Molly continued stroking Tabitha's hair. "Oh no, honey. You're not bad. You're never bad. Daddy just doesn't want to be with us— with me anymore. It's not you."

"Were you a bad girl, Mommy?"

A bitter laugh forced its way out of Molly's throat. Not bad enough for him. "No, honey. It wasn't me."

"Then why did he go?"

Molly sighed, her chest heaving with smothered anger and pain. "Because, because your daddy decided he wanted something"—someone—"else." A man. He wanted another man. "He decided he couldn't be happy here with me, with us. That's all. It's just you and me now."

"B-but, who will protect me? From the monsters? In my closet? Under my bed? Who will fight the monsters?"

A tear escaped from Molly's eye. She released her hold on Tabitha and gently put a hand on either side of the child's face. "I will, Tabby-Cat. I'll fight the monsters."

Tabitha wiped a grubby fist across her nose, then shook her little head. Her sad face took on an expression of doubt. "But you're a girl. Girls don't fight monsters."

Molly took a deep breath and looked her daughter in the eye. She forced a brave smile. "Mommies do. Mommies fight the monsters. Mommies protect their children. They stand between their children and the monsters in the dark."

Fresh tears fell from Tabitha's eyes. "Really?"

Molly nodded. "Really."

"You stand between the monsters and me?"

"Uh-huh."

The little girl's face grew suddenly very serious—serious as only a child can be—as if she were pondering this, picturing her mother standing between her and something growling in the night. "What if the monster breaks your legs? How you gonna stand up if the monster breaks your legs?"

Molly laughed then. It wasn't a great laugh—not cathartic, nor cleansing—it was just a chuckle. But it was the first time she'd laughed in days. "If the monster breaks my legs, I'll crawl. I'll bite. I'll scratch. Whatever it takes. I will protect my little Tabby-Cat."

The child threw her arms around Molly's neck. "I love you, Mommy."

Molly hugged her back. "I love you too, honey. And I will always protect you. No matter what."

Tabitha released the washer. Leaving it in her pocket, she wrapped her arms around herself. She closed her eyes and rocked back and forth on the rotten log. "I love you too, Mom."

But I still can't tell you about the Circle. But you'll love me anyway. I know that.

Opening her eyes, she stood, stepped over the rotting log, and sat down again, facing the other way. She faced into the ruins of the cabin and ran her eyes over the rotten logs and strewn stones. Her eyes focused on the place where she'd found Lettie's broomstick.

Wish I'd brought the broom. The witch's broom. I could've left it here and picked it up on the way back.

She pictured the broom in her hands, imagined its reassuring weight.

Then I'd have a weapon. To protect myself. From what? Wolves? Bears? The Circle? Magnus?

She remembered the dying tree and shuddered. *No. They—he won't hurt me. They need me. No, not me. They need my Power.*

A part of her was afraid—afraid of what Magnus had done—in her name. A part of her desired to feel the Power surging through her again.

And that desire, that longing, frightened her all the more.

Joey Parsons walked slowly back toward the clearing, carrying his robe rolled up and held gingerly under one arm. He walked slowly, because walking hurt. Breathing hurt. He was pretty sure no bones were broken, but his ribs ached. "Like the whole PB offensive line…twice." *That girl packs a wallop.* He chuckled, then winced in pain. "Like a herd of Poplar Bluff Mules."

Stupidest damn mascot in the world. The Poplar Bluff Mules. Rival schools—for instance, BBR High—got into trouble at games, calling the PBHS teams "the Poplar Bluff Jackasses," but folks kept right on calling the fools that, and the Mules—like their stubborn namesakes—refused to change the stupid name. *They play dirty too. Man, I hate those guys.*

But they've got nothing on Tabitha. He gingerly probed his ribs again. *Man, she's strong!*

A few of the other girls in the Circle could sometimes manifest the Power all by themselves—always when they got angry or upset. But just a gust of air, or maybe knocking over a few chairs. He'd seen Beulah do that once.

But Tabitha… He whistled softly. *Hoo, boy! Sex with that chick's gotta be psychedelic!*

He shook his head. *You keep on dreamin', Hoss. That girl's not gonna. Damn uptight virgin. Wonder if Beulah's up for another round tonight?* A grin curled the edges of his mouth. *She knows how to kiss my bruises and make them all better.*

But Tabitha… Imagine having a girl with that much Power!

Gotta get her back. Convince sweet-and-innocent little Tabitha Moonshadow that ol' Joey Parsons is the real deal. Yeah. That's the ticket.

Maybe I'll convert to Mormonism. That might do it. I get baptized in her church, and I'd get her for sure. Nothing gets a girl hot like a man who'll change for her.

Probably even marry me. Then the two of us, we can get away.

Escape.

He entered the clearing.

Escape from him.

The clearing was deserted, except for Magnus and Beulah. *Guess the party's over.* Both the man and the girl were still clad in their robes. Beulah's hood was thrown back exposing her pretty features and blonde ponytail, but Magnus, of course, wore the golden mask.

Can't take any chances. Can't let anybody see your face.

Magnus and Beulah sat, holding hands like sweethearts, on a log near the dying fire. When Beulah saw Joey, however, she stood. She did not look happy—not happy at all. In a word, she looked…pissed.

Joey groaned softly. *So much for kissing it all better.*

Beulah put her hands on her hips. "Where is she? I thought y'all were gonna go fetch her back."

He shook his head. "I tried. She's going to need some space. It's not my fault."

"No," said Magnus, still in character, still using his "High Priest" voice. "The fault is entirely mine. I went too far…with the tree."

Joey chuckled bitterly. Painfully. "Ya think?"

"But come on, y'all!" Beulah, pointed up to the night sky. "That light!"

The light, of course, was no longer there.

Magnus nodded. "Yes. That was unprecedented. Glorious."

Joey reached the log, and eased himself down, wincing. "Yeah." He grunted with the pain. "How'd you do that?"

Suddenly, Beulah was kneeling before Joey, her hands resting on his knees, her eyes brimming with concern. "Joey! What's wrong, baby?"

Joey grimaced. "She got…upset."

Beulah's pretty face screwed up into a look of disgust. "She hit you?"

He nodded. "In a manner of speaking."

Magnus nodded. "The Power."

Joey chuckled. "O-o-oh, yeah."

Beulah squeezed one of his knees. "Like in Ol' Waddle's classroom?"

Joey shrugged, then winced again. "I wasn't there—in Waddle's room. Nah. This was more like a bomb blast. Broken branches everywhere." He paused. "And me knocked on my black butt, of course."

"Like a bomb," Magnus said, considering. "And it was directionless? She couldn't aim or control it?"

Joey shook his head. "Nope. Shapeless and without form. That's what it looked like to me." Then he muttered, "And felt like."

"Well," Magnus said, "at least there is that—she can lash out, but only in an uncontrolled burst. She can't target anyone. Which is good—we can't have her using her own Power. She still needs one of us to direct it."

Yeah, baby. She still needs a man. She still needs me. "So, tell me about the light, Magnus. How'd you do that?"

"That"—Magnus's body seemed to tremble under his robe with excitement or remembered ecstasy—"was amazing! It was as if, as if I could see everything. Big things, little things. Very little things. Microscopic things. I mean, I'm sure I couldn't really *see* the photons, but…It's similar to when we manipulate the air."

Joey nodded. "Like moving the air around."

Magnus nodded. "Yes. We can't really *see* the air molecules."

"But," Joey said, "we can *feel* them. Sorta."

"Yes," Magnus said, "and I felt the *potential* for light. I just pulled that potential together and—"

"And there was light," Beulah said. "And the light was good."

Magnus nodded vigorously. "Yes! Intuitive manipulation of energy. Makes me wonder what other forms of energy we might master. The possibilities are endless!"

"Yeah," Joey said. "That's really cool."

"And it's not just the big things," Magnus said. "I can control smaller and smaller things. I can—"

"Y'all just hold your horses now," Beulah said. "Ain't none of this gonna work if mighty Miss Moonshadow don't let y'all use her."

Joey noted the bitterness in Beulah's voice when she uttered Tabitha's last name. "So-o-o," he began, "like I said, we need to give her some space—at least for a little bit. You really freaked her out."

Magnus nodded. "Agreed. We shall indeed 'give her some space,' as you say. For a little while." He pointed at Joey. "You continue your efforts to romance her. I'll keep working on the mother. It will be so much the better, so much easier, if she is cooperative. But, in the end, willingly or not, I shall have her."

Joey forced a smile. *Not if I get her first.*

What am I doing here?

Tabitha shut her eyes and attempted to zone out. It wasn't as if it was hard to tune out Sister Blackthorn's high, saccharine voice. Even in the confines of the church's small kitchen, the woman's voice didn't carry well. To Tabitha, it seemed as if the Sunday school teacher practiced speaking at a volume that, while not exactly a whisper, was intended to go unheard and unheeded.

Are you trying to put people to sleep? If so, you're a rousing success. Or perhaps just the opposite of "rousing." Maybe it's all part of a nefarious plot to make church as boring as snot.

A yawn to Tabitha's right seemed to confirm her hypothesis.

Tabitha opened her eyes and glanced around the classroom. *Classroom, my eye!* She forced herself to not sneer at the thought. *Whoever designed this chapel was on drugs, I swear.* The entire contingent of youth in the branch—the four who were in attendance, at least—were meeting in the chapel kitchen. And even that was too small.

The other three kids—two girls and the usually ebullient Buster—sat looking utterly dejected or nearly comatose. Buster always managed to sit next to Tabitha during Sunday school—probably because no one else wanted to—and it was he who had emitted the yawn only moments before. He sat with his head in his hands as drool descended in a long, viscous string from his open mouth toward the linoleum floor.

"So, God saved two of every creature in the Ark," twittered Sister Blackthorn, "because God loves animals." In her early forties, the teacher stood, tall and thin. She wore her long, brown hair straight, bound in a headband right out of the sixties. And the woman never wore makeup.

Or a bra.

Or deodorant.

Probably owns a tie-dyed skirt and refuses to shave her legs, Tabitha thought for the umpteenth time. *Or her pits.*

She sighed inwardly. *Be nice. Different strokes for different folks. And if some old flower-child hippie can make it in this church, maybe there's hope for a confused and budding witch like me.*

Maybe.

Maybe not.

What in the world am I doing here?

Sister Blackthorn smiled as she surveyed her disinterested students. Her teeth were too straight to have been completely natural. *Apparently, her parents, at least, believed in braces.*

"God loves all animals," the teacher repeated. "He loves the birds, and the fish, and the insects…"

What is this? Sunbeams? Are we six-year-olds? Tell me something interesting, please. Something real. Something I can grab ahold of.

Something to give me a reason to stay in the Church.

Please, Heavenly Father. Please give me a reason to stay. I'm not . . . asking for a sign. Not really.

But, are You…art Thou really there? Do You love me? For me? Even as I am? Please?

"And that," said the too-sweet voice, "was why Jesus was a vegetarian."

What?

Tabitha sat up, giving Sister Blackthorn her full attention for the first time. "What did you say?"

The Sunday school teacher, possibly overjoyed at making eye contact with one of her students, beamed. "God loves the animals."

Tabitha shook her head. "No, that last part."

"Jesus was a vegetarian."

"No, He wasn't." Tabitha didn't bother to hide her sneer.

Beside her, Buster snorted, jolting awake. He sat up. Even the other two girls seemed to rouse from their stupors.

Sister Blackthorn folded her arms across her chest protectively. "Of course, He was. Jesus never ate meat. He never would have eaten meat."

Tabitha tried to count to ten.

She made it almost as far as two.

"That's ridiculous. Jesus ate the Passover. He ate *lamb*."

The teacher's smile remained, but it seemed forced, painted onto her cosmetic-free face. "He ate unleavened bread and wine. That's all."

"He ate lamb," Tabitha repeated. "Jehovah commanded the Israelites to eat a lamb at Passover. He commanded animals to be sacrificed, burnt on the altar of the Temple, and eaten."

Sister Blackthorn frowned. "A loving God would never do that." Her voice was louder and had lost its childlike sweetness. "And the Jews—they got it all wrong. The sacrifice was something *man* invented, not God."

Tabitha wasn't backing down. "The whole book of Leviticus is about God giving detailed instructions on how to kill, eat, and burn sheep and bulls and goats and doves. Have you even read the Bible?" She didn't wait for an answer. "Even in Noah's Ark— Noah didn't just take two of every creature. He took seven of some— the *clean* beasts. You know, the ones Noah and his family could eat? And offer as burnt sacrifices?"

The teacher scowled and folded her arms. "A loving God wouldn't do that. He would never do that."

For a moment, Tabitha caught herself. *Keep your temper, girl. Don't want an "incident"—especially here at church. No witchy powers exploding all over the place.* She kept her rising anger in check. "So, you make Jesus into a vegetarian? You remake God in your own image?"

Sister Blackthorn looked as if she might burst into tears. "I'm not—"

"Either God is God or He's not. Either He's real or He's not. He's not just some story you can twist to fit the way you want the world to be."

Any second now, the cabinets are going to start slamming. Keep it together! "And if He is just some story, something you can change when you want, then what's the point?"

Tabitha became suddenly aware of the eyes of the other youth staring at her in mixtures of horror and wonder and perhaps, some admiration.

She took a deep breath, as much to calm herself as to gather courage for a parting shot. But she saw the look of horror and pain in the older woman's eyes, and Tabitha's courage, if that was what it was, crumbled like a sandcastle after a wave.

"I'm sorry," Tabitha said. "But what you're saying. It's not right." Tears of frustration leaked from her eyes. "I don't even know what I'm doing here."

She grabbed her tattered scriptures and her bag, stood, and fled the room and the building.

What am I doing here?

Beulah Martineau held a painted, rapturous smile on her pretty face as her daddy strutted on the stage, only occasionally pausing to lean on his pulpit. The tall man, handsome for his age, wore a pastel blue, three-piece silk suit. Rather than a tie, he wore his wide-lapelled, white silk shirt open, exposing the large gold cross dangling over his forest of blonde chest-hair.

"Praise Jesus!" he bellowed. "Praise You, Almighty Jesus!" Sweat streamed down his face as he pranced, raising one hand to the vaulted ceiling of the chapel, and holding a microphone in the other. He held the microphone against his wide-open mouth like a rock star, shut his eyes as if in a paroxysm of religious ecstasy, and roared, "Jesus! Jesus! Jesus! How I love to shout Your name, Jesus!"

Behind Reverend Billy Martineau, the band played short and timely riffs on electric guitars, saxophone, drums, and cymbals to punctuate the pastor's words.

Spontaneous choruses of "Praise You, Jesus!" and "Amen!" sprouted throughout the cavernous hall like vocal weeds erupting on the pastoral lawn. But such acclamations couldn't compete with the howling of the pastor and the electric twang and amplified thundering of the band.

Beulah clapped along with the congregation and made dutiful and almost-convincing declarations of devotion. She grinned and she cheered and she hooted. She knew the part she had to play.

Yes, she knew it well. And she played it to the hilt.

But inside, she was revolted—utterly grossed-out.

Honestly, Daddy. Sweating like a hog in a silk suit!

She knew darn well pigs didn't sweat, but she liked the expression—having invented it herself.

Like a hog in a silk suit.

The sweatiness was a new thing, a recent addition to the aura of Reverend Billy. Her daddy had seen a black preacher on TV, and the fellow had been sweating like a man picking cotton in the hot sun. And Billy Martineau wasn't about to be outdone by some uppity black pastor on the boob tube. And so, he'd cranked up the stage lights until it had become a sauna up there. Even the band was dripping, the pits of their rayon shirts dark and dank, as if they were a real rock band—not just a bunch of Pentecostal Osmond wanna-bes.

Serves y'all right if y'all get a sunburn. 'Sides, it ain't like they can see all that sweat on the radio.

Pastor Billy was carried live on one AM station, and one week delayed on two more. But radio wasn't where the real money was. Oh no. For serious money in the God business, one needed TV. That was the wave of the future.

And Beulah's daddy was just itching to get into TV.

For years, he'd had ambitions to expand into the wonderful—and highly profitable—world of televangelism, but establishing a television ministry had taken on a new urgency of late.

Ever since your secret stash just up and disappeared. Ain't that right, Daddy? No trace at all, 'less you count that wall-safe-sized hole in the lovely oak paneling of your home office.

"Praise Jesus!" Beulah cried.

Maybe that's God's reward for all that "ministering" you do for the ladies of the congregation—when their husbands are out of town or working late. What y'all think, Daddy? Can I get a amen?

Magnus had required the strength of the entire Circle to pull the metal box out of the wall and then to force it open. But they'd found more than eight hundred thousand dollars of church funds in that safe—church funds too holy to keep in a bank, it seemed.

That night, Reverend Billy had come home, reeking of Mrs. Lacey Thibodeaux's cheap perfume, only to find a black hole where his Judas-funds should've been. And the look on his face had been priceless—a memory Beulah would cherish for as long as she lived.

And shortly after the loss of the embezzled money, an anonymous donation had been made to the BBR High School theatre department.

"Amen!" Beulah cheered with the rest of the congregation. *Just like cheerleading. Just like it.*

Only there's money in this. Money for Magnus and me. So, go on, Daddy! Fleece the suckers!

"Hallelujah!"

She snuck a quick glance at the stranger sitting a few rows back and to her left. Newcomers tended to stick out anyway—even in this sizable congregation—but this guy stood out in a way that just screamed, "Hollywood sleazeball!" He sported a head full of permed, bleached blonde hair, mutton-chop sideburns, a thick mustache, and a forehead which appeared to have been stretched by one too many facelifts. He wore a lime green leisure suit, a gold bracelet which would've been at home on Mr. T, and a ridiculous gold-and-diamond watch that glittered as he raised his hands to join in the religious fervor.

Seems to be enjoying himself.

However, the stranger's enthusiasm was tempered by the way he seemed to be observing the congregation as much as he was the preacher.

TV scout. Looking for the next big thing, the next Billy Graham or Oral Roberts. Gotta be. I wonder if Daddy knows? Probably. That's why he's up there, sweating like a hog. Like a hog in a silk suit.

A rumble at her side shook her out of her thoughts.

Beulah didn't have to hear the massive belch that had exploded from the woman sitting beside her—she had felt it. She didn't bother to look at her mother. And she didn't have to see to know that her mom was drunk. The woman was clapping and praising right along with everyone else…for the most part. Mary Martineau was that kind of alcoholic—functional during the day, usually, when she was expected to be in public, but never quite sober. And Sunday was one of those days when the pastor's wife was expected to be in public.

And reasonably sober. She had passed *reasonable* some time ago, even for a Sunday.

Beulah had arrived a few minutes late for the service, and had slid into the pew next to her mother after the service was well underway. So, Beulah hadn't realized just how bad her mom was that morning.

Until that moment.

*If she's this soused already, she'll be unconscious by tonight. And if she's that far gone…*Beulah's gut clenched. And for a moment, her smile sagged.

Damn. Then she beamed, flashing her perfect teeth, just as if she'd donned a ceremonial mask. "Hallelujah! Praise You, Jesus!"

Sheltering against the trunk of a leafless tree, her sweater wrapped tightly around her, Tabitha watched as Angelica Goldsmith exited the ridiculously small church. The short woman, barely taller than Tabitha, took a few steps toward the parking lot, turning her head left and right, obviously looking for something. Or someone.

Looking for me, probably. Who am I kidding? After that stunt? Of course, she's looking for me.

Briefly, Tabitha thought of making a run for it. But the church grounds weren't extensive, and there was no place to hide.

Except behind a car. Oh, yeah. Crouching behind a car. Now that'd be real dignified.

Besides—I'm not sorry. I'm not.

A light breeze stirred the short woman's long, blonde hair as she continued to scan the parking lot. Then, spotting her quarry, she wrapped her arms around herself to guard against the chilly and overcast September day. She strolled in Tabitha's direction. And to Tabitha's eye, it seemed as if the English teacher's gait was a bit too *casual*.

Like she's creeping up on a wild animal. Well, I'm not going to run away. 'Cause I'm not sorry.

Angelica approached to within a dozen yards, then slowed. She waved. "Hi, Tabitha."

"Hi, Miss Goldsmith." Tabitha grimaced. "Uh, I mean, *Sister* Goldsmith."

The teacher shrugged, grinning. She was pretty, with blue eyes, rosy cheeks, and a disarming, almost pixielike smile. "It gets confusing, doesn't it? Seeing each other at school and at church?" She chuckled and added, "And at play practice."

"Yeah." *Confusing. Good word.* Play practice added a new and complex dimension to any relationship. *We spend half the time pretending to be other people. Well, not Miss Goldsmith. She directs. We pretend.*

The woman pointed at the ground in front of the tree. "Mind if we sit?"

Tabitha shrugged and pursed her lips. Then she nodded and sat on the rough, autumn grass. *At least the leaves have been raked away.*

Miss/Sister Goldsmith sat next to her.

Tabitha plucked up a blade of the faded grass, holding it between her thumb and forefinger. "You heard?"

"Yep."

Even without looking at her, Tabitha knew the woman was smiling. The drama coach always seemed to manage to wear a smile.

"I figured you could use some company." Angelica waited, but Tabitha didn't respond. "I don't suppose you want to talk about it?"

Tabitha shook her head. "Nope."

"Okay." Sister/Miss Goldsmith leaned back on her hands. "You know, nobody here likes me either, except…well, President Roylance, Brother Kilmore, and your mom. She's nice. And smart. And ooh, she's got a sharp tongue on her when people are being stupid. *Especially* when they're being stupid. And you know what? Her command of the English language is impressive! I should know—I'm an English teacher. She can carve these people up using words as sharp and precise as a scholarly scalpel. Even if they don't comprehend every word in her impressive vocabulary, she says those words with such passion and expression, you can't help but get the gist. And she doesn't back down from a fight."

Sister Goldsmith nudged Tabitha with her shoulder. "Reminds me of you." She chuckled. "You're not afraid to stand up and speak your mind."

Tabitha muttered, "Sister Blackthorn said Jesus was a vegetarian." She sighed. "And I got mad."

Angelica Goldsmith laughed and shook her head. "You're kidding! That wa…"

"Yeah."

"Wow." Angelica shook her head again. "Of all the stupid things—and believe me, I've heard some real *nuggets* here—that one is a real gem. And that's what upset you?"

Tabitha shrugged.

"Well, let me talk to President Roylance about that. She shouldn't be teaching the youth, or anyone for that matter, if she's teaching false doctrine."

Tabitha ripped up her blade of grass. "Yeah, well." She snatched up another. "If Jesus is real, we can't just change Him to fit our wacky—" She growled and tore the blade to tiny bits. And seeing the destruction she had wrought on a very small scale, she was reminded of a massive blue beech tree ripped out of the earth. Using the Power.

My Power.

"If?" Angelica Goldsmith gently grasped her hand. "If? *If* Jesus is real? Is this really a question for you?"

"I don't know. I mean, I mean, I know He lived. It's just, I…" Tabitha tilted her head back and closed her eyes. "I don't know what I mean."

What am I doing here?

Tabitha's words hung on the chill air, then dissipated like a puff of smoke in the crisp autumn breeze.

Angelica squeezed her hand. "Can I tell you a secret?"

A grin tugged at the corners of Tabitha's mouth as she glanced at her teacher. "If you want to."

Angelica sighed. "When I was a missionary in Spain, there came a point where I was, well, I was pretty down. I was only three months in-country. My fiancé had Dear-Janed me right before Christmas. He'd broken it off. Right before Christmas. I mentioned that, already, didn't I?"

Tabitha grinned. "Yep." Her grin faded. "That must've sucked."

"Yeah, well," Angelica continued, "on top of that, my companion didn't like me. To be honest, she hated my guts. She was a native Spaniard, and my Spanish still wasn't the greatest. Anyway, she wouldn't talk to me, and when she did, she spoke really fast—on purpose, I was sure—so I couldn't catch what she was saying. We weren't having any success. I swear, we knocked every door in that little town. And nothing. Absolutely nothing. The local men—the Spaniards—were always grabbing my butt as we walked past. And making lewd comments. My Spanish was good enough to catch those words. It was awful. And I was depressed. I questioned why I was even there."

She bowed her head. "I got to the point where I questioned the very existence of God."

Tabitha turned her eyes to the woman's downturned face. "What did you do?"

Angelica Goldsmith raised her head and looked Tabitha in the eye. "Nothing dramatic. I prayed. That's it. I begged Heavenly Father to help me. I begged Him to assure me He was there and He loved me. That's all."

"And did He answer you?"

"Yeah, but not the way I asked." Angelica shrugged. "I guess I wanted a sign. I wanted the Spirit to burn within me again. I'd lost that, you see. But that's not what happened."

"So, how?"

The woman smiled, and tears spilled down her face. "He sent me Paulo." She wiped at her cheeks, smearing her rouge. "It was late December. Christmas had come and gone, and I was really down. And lonely. And it was cold. Really cold. Not snowing. It never snows where we were. Just bitter cold. And the wind!"

She shuddered as if suddenly chilled by the memory. "We'd been out all evening, with no luck at all—nobody let us in. And we were on our way home, back to our apartment. I heard a sound—a wailing sound. I mean, I barely heard it above the howling of the wind. Actually, I shouldn't have been able to hear it. My companion certainly didn't."

A hint of a shadow passed across Angelica's face. "Anyway, I followed the sound. And I found him. He was hiding—no, that's not the right word. He was *sheltering* behind some trashcans in an alley. This little boy. He was six. He wasn't wearing much—just sport pants and a shirt. And he was cold. I mean, he'd stopped shivering. He was in hypothermia."

Angelica paused as if lost in her memories.

"What did you do?" Tabitha prompted.

Angelica squeezed her hand again. "Sorry. Paulo was the cutest little boy. But he was in serious danger then." She sighed. "My companion said we should take him to the police station. But I ignored her. I wrapped him up in my coat, picked him up, and ran for home. I put him in the shower and got him warmed up. Saved his life."

"That's cool."

"Yeah, it was pretty cool. But it wasn't me. I shouldn't have been able to hear him in the wind. I think it was a miracle. But it doesn't end there. My companion called the police on our landlady's phone. And we got Paulo back to his family. They were so grateful, they *listened* to us. We got to teach them the gospel. They all joined the Church. And my companion and I started to get along. I mean, we were never close friends or anything like that, but at least we started talking."

She chuckled. "Turns out, she could speak decent English all along. The stinker.

And more importantly, being led to Paulo changed *me*. I knew God loved him and me. I knew Jesus Christ lives. I found my way back."

"So, what's the secret?"

Angelica shrugged. "I guess it's not really a secret. It's just sacred. I haven't told that story to very many people."

"Why'd you tell me?"

"Because something's going on with you. I mean, you're a great young woman. But you're struggling with your testimony. I can see it."

Tabitha said nothing.

"He's there, Tabitha. He lives. And He loves you. And if you're questioning that; well, then talk to Him. Talk to Heavenly Father, I mean. He's there too. He'll answer your prayers."

Tabitha pondered this. "Will He send me a Paulo?"

Angelica Goldsmith reached over and put her arms around Tabitha. "When you're ready, or when the time is right, He'll send you what you need. Or who you need." She clicked her tongue. "Whom you need. That one always gets me. Some English teacher, huh?"

Tabitha returned the embrace. "You're the best English teacher I know. Well, except maybe my mom."

Angelica patted Tabitha's back. "That's quite a compliment. I'll try to live up to that one."

Tabitha wanted to say, "Thank you," but the words stuck in her throat. She pulled out of the hug. "How do you do it?"

Confusion clouded Angelica's face. "How do I do what?"

Tabitha sighed and looked away. "Put up with all the crap? You said it yourself. Nobody likes us here. And…" *This is it, isn't it?* "Old Brother Chatham and the rest of men in the Church? I mean, what are women for? Sex? Breeding? House slaves? Nobody cares about us, values us in this Church. Unless we get married and have lots of kids. We aren't important." *We aren't goddesses.* "We're not special. I mean, men are in charge. Men have the priesthood. We don't. We don't do anything."

"Is that what's really bothering you? Not just Sister Blackthorn?"

Tabitha shrugged. "I guess. I don't know. I don't know where I fit in."

"Join the club, sister." Angelica pursed her lips. "You know what I want more than anything?"

Tabitha shook her head.

"I want a temple marriage. That's what I want more than anything in this whole world. But there are no men! No good ones, at least. Well, there was Mike Kilmore."

Tabitha groaned. "Oh, not you too."

Angelica sighed, and her lips curled in a wistful smile. "Well, what do you expect? He may be a decade older than I am, but he was perfect."

"Was?"

"Well, you weren't in Sunday school today—adult Sunday school, I mean. He was holding hands with your mom. Seems he's taken."

175

I don't want to talk about Mike Kilmore!

"But," Angelica said, "as to the other question about women and the priesthood? You ever been to the temple to do baptisms for the dead?"

Tabitha nodded slowly. "We used to go every couple of months when we lived in Maryland."

"Can I tell you another story?"

Tabitha resisted the urge to roll her eyes. She grinned instead. One of the reasons Angelica Goldsmith was such a great teacher, like Miss Tulane, was that she told stories. "Sure. Go for it."

"Well, when I was a kid, we lived in Idaho. In Rexburg. Did I ever tell you I'm a twin? I guess not. Well, I have a twin brother. Mark. Anyway, for our twelfth birthday, we really, really wanted to go to the temple to do baptisms for the dead. You have to be twelve, you know."

Tabitha gave her a dubious look. "*That's* what you wanted for your birthday?"

Angelica grinned. "Cross my heart and hope to die. I told you—I really like the temple. It's special to me."

"Okay. So, did you get your wish?"

Angelica grimaced, shook her head, and then nodded. "Half of it."

"What do you mean?"

"Well, we—Mark and I—we had our interviews with the bishop. We were both worthy. We were all set to go. It was going to be the coolest birthday ever. I mean the temple in Idaho Falls was only about half an hour away. We had our appointment at the temple." She counted on her fingers. "Our birthday was on a Tuesday. And we'd made special arrangements with the bishop to get Mark ordained a deacon on Tuesday morning so we could both go. But there was a hitch."

"What happened?"

"The bishop got a really bad case of the stomach flu that morning. He wasn't able to make it." Angelica paused as if waiting for Tabitha to understand something—something unspoken.

But Tabitha had no idea what she was supposed to get. "I don't get it."

"Well, Mark couldn't be ordained unless the bishop was there. Anyway, we were going to miss our appointment at the temple if we didn't leave. And Mark couldn't go."

"Why not?"

Angelica shook her head. "Because he didn't have the priesthood."

"So?"

"Don't you see? Mark couldn't enter the temple. No matter how worthy he was, he couldn't go in. Because he didn't have the priesthood. I could go, because I'm a girl. But he couldn't."

"What are you saying?"

"I'm saying that *boys*—men—need the priesthood. Girls, women don't. The priesthood doesn't make them better than us, it elevates them to the same level as us. Girls are special, just by being girls."

"Goddesses," Tabitha muttered.

"Potentially, yeah. But men are incomplete, insufficient, at least without the priesthood."

"So, you went without him? To the temple, I mean?"

Angelica nodded. "Yeah. It sucked. But he insisted. He knew how much it meant to me. My brother's a really good guy."

"Sounds like it." *Wish there were more like him here.*

Angelica sighed. "I wish there were more like him. Here, especially."

Tabitha laughed. "That's freaky! I was just thinking the same, exact thing!"

Angelica waggled her fingers at Tabitha like a magician conjuring a spell. "I haff you under my power!" she said, doing her best Bela Lugosi. "You vill tink and act only as I command!"

Both of them laughed, the teenager on the cusp of adulthood and the novice teacher, barely a handful of years Tabitha's senior.

"Besides," Angelica said, as the laughter dissipated into the autumn air, "I am your director, your teacher, and your Young Women's advisor. And I hope, your friend."

It was Tabitha's turn to take the woman's hand and squeeze. "I hope so too."

Angelica beamed. "Then it's settled. Friends too. But no hangin' out, except for school and church. Don't want people to think I'm playing favorites." She winked.

Tabitha smiled. *I have a friend. A friend who really cares. A friend who doesn't want to use me.*

"But," Angelica said, "you still have to call me Miss Goldsmith at school and Sister Goldsmith at church—at least in public. Okay?" She winked again. "Even if you mix it up sometimes."

Tabitha nodded, grinning. "That's the way my mama brung me up, Miss Goldsmith."

"What say we go inside, hmm?"

Tabitha hesitated. "Uh, Sister Goldsmith?"

The teacher glanced around, ensuring they were still alone. "Angelica's fine. Here."

"Angelica?"

"Yeah?"

Tell her. Tabitha almost blurted it out, almost told her everything—about the Circle and Magnus and Joey. She tottered on the precipice, ready to leap over the abyss.

Then she stepped back.

"Tabitha? What is it?"

I can't. I just can't. She wouldn't, she can't understand.

But there was something Tabitha needed to know. "Um, about the play."

Angelica chuckled. "I thought it was something important."

"Well, it is."

Angelica sighed and settled her shoulders. "Okay, sock it to me, baby."

Tabitha almost smiled at the Laugh-In reference. Almost. "Eliza." She paused. *Ask it. Just ask it.* "Did I get the part? Did I deserve it? I heard about the big donation. The anonymous—"

Angelica Goldsmith raised a halting hand. "Stop right there."

"But..."

"I know what you're thinking. So, just let me lay it out for you."

But the director pursed her lips, stared straight ahead, her eyes unfocused. And said nothing more.

Oh, no! It was a setup. "Well?" Tabitha nearly choked on the word.

Angelica growled softly, then took a deep breath. "There was a big donation. Huge. And there was a condition attached. *My Fair Lady.* Which, believe me, I was more than delighted to do." She shook her head. "*Guys and Dolls* is just so done. But it's also cheap. But *My Fair Lady*! I... Well, I mean... Wow. You know what I mean?"

Tabitha managed a tiny nod. *But what about me?*

"So," Angelica said, "of course, I said yes. I mean, it was more like, 'Heck, yeah!'" She shook her head and laughed softly. "Dream show. You know what I mean?"

Tabitha nodded again, more urgently. "Yes, but what about?"

"You?" Angelica smiled. "Tabitha, when you got on that stage and introduced yourself, I have to admit—I wasn't impressed. You're so short, and as sympathetic as I am to short people, you seemed, well, a bit awkward and unsure. But then you opened your mouth and sang, 'I could have danced all night.' And I was blown away. I thought to myself, 'How is all that rich, gorgeous, confident sound coming out of that little girl?' Tabitha, you shook the rafters. There was no competition at all."

Angelica winked and poked Tabitha's shoulder. "And your reading!" She chuckled. "Well, you didn't read. You already knew the lines by heart. Accent was spot on—both of them. Trust me. You *earned* that part. I wouldn't have given it to anyone else."

Tears spilled from Tabitha's eyes. "There wasn't...another condition?"

Angelica blinked. She opened her mouth as if to say something, stopped herself, then blinked again. "What do you mean?"

Tabitha wrapped her arms around herself and began to rock back and forth. She swallowed hard. "The donation. Was there a condition...to cast me? Me as Eliza?"

Angelica uttered a sound that was half a groan and half a sigh. She shook her head. "Oh, sweet girl, if there was, I never heard about it. And I wouldn't have done it. That part—it was all yours. You were born to play it. After that audition, I would have cast you as Guinevere, Lady Macbeth, Maria Von Trapp... whomever! I'm just sad I only get you for one year!"

Tabitha threw her arms around Angelica Goldsmith and hugged her, clinging like a rescued child, and wept.

Beulah hugged herself and wept.

At the sound of her bedroom door opening, she curled into a fetal position and quieted her sobbing. But silent or not, tears continued to water the rumpled sheets of her bed. With one hand, she pulled the blanket more tightly around herself. With the other, she quickly and futilely attempted to flatten her puffy hair.

"Y'all did good, baby girl." Her father's voice came from the doorway. "Proud-a you. Praise Jesus, but y'all make me so proud."

Go away. Please. Leave me be.

But she heard his footsteps approaching. "So proud."

Ain't I done enough tonight?

"He was very pleased, I'd say. Liked that cheerleader outfit o' yours."

Beulah felt his weight press down on the edge of the bed. "We're talkin' a six-station contract, baby girl. Six TV stations, carrying' the word o' God. Every Sunday. 'Course, only one'll be live. The rest'll be delayed a week. 'Tape delay,' he called it. My, what wonders the good Lord has wrought. All those souls comin' to Jesus through the miracle of the boob tube. 'A marvelous work and a wonder,' indeed. Praise His holy name."

Beulah felt his strong, heavy hand through the blanket as he rested it on her thigh.

She didn't recoil.

She knew better.

It only gets worse if I flinch.

"So proud-a y'all." He slid his hand down her leg. "'Course, I don't much care for the sharin'. But what you did for that fellow? It sealed the deal. And we do what we must in the Lord's holy callin'. But y'all's mine, baby girl. Mine. The good Lord gave y'all to me. To comfort me."

As he began to slide the blanket up her thigh, Beulah resisted the urge to clutch at the thin covering.

What the hell does it matter? Whore. Slut. Sleep with any boy I want. But when I want. When I choose. That makes a difference, doesn't it?

Not this. Not you, Daddy. Not tonight. Not after you made me… Please! Ain't I done enough?

"Yes, the Lord gave y'all to me. Like the daughters of Lot, preservin' the seed o' their father, when Lot's wife abandoned him and became a pillar o' salt. Y'all know the story, don't y'all, baby girl? Don't y'all?"

Whore. Filthy whore.

"Yes, Daddy. I remember." *I always remember. Every time.*

"Then say it, baby girl. Say the holy words."

And just as she had done so many, many times, she repeated the scripture, her voice as lifeless as the final exhalation of a corpse. "'And the firstborn went in, and lay with her father.'"

As he unbuttoned his silk shirt, the Reverend Billy Martineau bowed his head in prayer. "Amen."

179

"Half a million dollars." The old Marine shoveled a bite of pancakes into his mouth. He chewed vigorously, then swallowed. "That was the size of the endowment. Half a million! Even I didn't suspect it was so much."

Molly set down her mug of fragrant hot chocolate—not that she'd actually consumed any of it—and blinked. *Half a million?* "Five hundred thousand dollars?"

Fergus MacDonald lifted an eyebrow. "Y'all do realize that physics—and therefore mathematics—is my specialty? My field of expertise, as it were? I do know how much half a million is."

It took Molly a second to overcome her own shock enough to comprehend that the old man was teasing her. "I know. It's just." She blew out a long breath. "Who has that kind of money? And why would they spend it on *Tabitha*? To ensnare Tabitha?"

Fergus waved a fork vaguely at the ceiling. "Obviously, Magnus does. He has that kind of money." The Sambo's in Poplar Bluff had become the regular meeting place for Molly and Fergus over the past several weeks. On Mondays at 5:30 sharp—after school and set construction for him, and after school and office hours for her. "Magnus." He growled in his throat, shaking his head. "Whoever the hell he is."

All this time, and we still don't know. Molly reached across the table and laid a hand on the old man's arm. "I know you're trying. And I really appreciate it. I really, really do."

A sad smile slid across his face. He laid a strong, firm hand atop hers, a hand calloused by hard work and by turning the wheels of a wheelchair. "My pleasure, Molly. But I'm sorry I don't have more to report."

"How did you find out the amount?"

He shrugged, scratching absentmindedly at the bump on the top of his right ear. "The same as I always do. I listen. And people tend to ignore my presence." He took a sip of his coffee. "And my intelligence. Ironic, in the case of a physics and chemistry teacher." He winked, though Molly barely noticed.

Who has that kind of money? It always comes back to the money, doesn't it?
"Now, if I were a biology teacher…"
What's he saying? "I'm sorry. Biology teacher?"
He smirked. "Biology. If I taught biology, folks around here would treat me like I was in league with the Devil himself. Nobody would even dare to whisper in my presence. And they'd all be certain I was off my rocker."
Okay, now I know he's teasing me for sure. "Okay, I'll bite. Why's that?"
His face took on a look of bland innocence. "Why, *evolution*, my dear lady. I'd be required to teach evolution, and to the good Pentecostal folks—hell, even the Baptists—in this neck of the woods, that's tantamount to witchcraft. And insanity."
Molly managed a small chuckle, but the joke largely fell flat. "People around here aren't that ignorant."
"Why, Molly, I'm surprised at you. Staunch Mormon lady like you? Defending evolution? With the central role that Adam and Eve play in Mormon theology?"
"Adam and Eve, yes. But that doesn't mean there weren't dinosaurs and so on." *Hold on a second.* "Besides, how do you know about LDS theology? Don't tell me you've been reading up on us—on me?"
For a moment, Fergus appeared mildly irritated. Then his expression morphed into one of guilt. "I'm afraid, Miss Molly, y'all've caught me. You know I attend the Assembly of God—the one in Blue Beech Ridge, not the one in Poplar Bluff."
Molly shook her head. "No, I didn't know." *So?*
"Well, I don't just *attend* there, I also teach Sunday school. Unlike in the Mormon church, Sunday school teachers get paid. It's a pittance, but it supplements the income. I've…" He pushed his plate of half-eaten pancakes away. "I'm afraid that I have, well, I have taught a lesson or two or three or more on the, well, evils, if you will, of Mormonism. I teach what I'm supposed to, but I know a great deal that I don't teach. I have been guilty, as it were, of focusing on unsavory half-truths… and some less-than-half-truths and skipping anything that might present Mormons as Christians. I actually *know* quite a bit."
Molly didn't even try to hide her disappointment. Or her disgust. But she said nothing.
The old man lowered his eyes and seemed to slouch in his wheelchair. "I have, uh, no. I have no excuse. A lie is a lie, and a half-truth is as bad as a lie. I'm sorry."
Molly placed her hands in her lap. She was mildly surprised to realize that she was actually quite angry. "You know what people in this state did to us? Of course, you do."
"Yes, but—"
"Yes, but what? Persecution? Burning homes and crops? Raping women and girls? Murder? Dashing out the brains of infants? All because so-called good Christians didn't like the way we prayed or believed or voted? They spread lies then, and you spread lies now. Calumny and defamation to rationalize the unconscionable. And you—you're a part of it."
"Miss Molly, I'm truly sorry."

Molly rose to her feet. With trembling fingers, she fished a five-dollar bill out of her purse—more than enough for the hot chocolate and a generous tip for Juliette Parsons—and set it on the table. "I need your help, Mr. MacDonald, to protect my daughter. And I am grateful for what you have done in her behalf. But since you have nothing further to report, I think I'll take my leave."

Fergus MacDonald looked up at her with stricken eyes. His lower lip trembled. The old Marine looked as if tears might leak from his eyes. "Forgive me, please. I was wrong—"

"I forgive you." Molly met his gaze, but she was certain there was no hint of forgiveness in her wintry stare or her icy voice. "Let me know if you have anything *useful* to report."

And with that, she turned on her heel and walked slowly and deliberately toward the exit. Furious tears threatened at the corners of her eyes. She opened them wide in an effort to corral and dry the tears before they could run down her face.

Juliette Parsons started toward her, slipping her pad and pen into the pocket of her waitress's apron. "Is everything all right, Molly?" Then, catching the look on Molly's face, she stepped close and lowered her voice. "You okay?"

Molly's smile was, she was sure, unconvincing, especially coupled with the tears that had just spilled from her eyes. "I'm fine."

Juliette put a hand on Molly's arm. "He doesn't mean it, you know." She glanced away toward Fergus. "And even if he does, he's harmless. I'm just so glad, so grateful he's found a friend."

Molly's false smile twitched, flickering between a tight-lipped grin and a quivering scowl. "Yes, well…"

"He doesn't have any other friends. He comes here alone. Almost every night. But he's a good man. A bona fide war hero. A good teacher. He's helping my Joey get a scholarship. An *academic* scholarship, not just athletic—"

Molly put a hand on Juliette's arm. "I know." Her smile eased, becoming less forced. "I know he is, but even friends can disappoint sometimes."

Juliette searched Molly's eyes. "But you'll be back, won't you? Next week?"

Molly shrugged. "We'll see." She gave Juliette a brief but warm hug. "You take care now."

And Molly Moonshadow walked out of Sambo's for the last time.

By the time Molly arrived home, her tears and her anger were spent and dry.

And Mike Kilmore was already waiting. He slouched like a too-casual sentry against the door of his car.

And he was a welcome sight.

As she slowed her Chevy to a stop, he detached himself from his own car, a decade-old Mustang. He was at her car door before she could even think of opening it, and he was grinning like Robert Redford on a red carpet. "I've got something."

He gave her a hand and helped her out of the car, then closed the door behind her. He pulled her into his strong arms and kissed her. She threw her arms around his neck and held him tight. *I hope this is for real. I really, really do.*

He ended the kiss before she did. "Hello, by the way."

A little breathless, she smiled up at him. "Hello."

"I could do that all day."

I couldn't. You are driving me crazy, Mr. Kilmore. "Me too."

"Ooh, woman." He shook his head, and his smile seemed to take on a wistful quality. "You have no idea what you do to me."

Still smiling, Molly bit her lip. *If you asked me, you know, I'd say yes. To marriage, that is. That's what I meant. Marriage.* "I think I have an inkling." *Temple marriage. That's what I meant.*

He gazed into her eyes and opened his mouth, hesitated, then said, "I have something. About Tabitha."

"Want to come inside? I've got soda in the fridge."

His grin tightened, and he lifted his eyebrows. He took a deep breath, held it, then let it out in a sigh. "Yes, I do want to come inside." Then he shook his head sharply. "And I'm not going to."

She raised a quizzical eyebrow. "Why not?"

"Because, Molly, being out here alone with you in the woods—sorta out in the open… Well, that's bad enough. I will not be alone with you behind closed doors. I couldn't be responsible for my behavior."

She shivered. *Then don't be.* "I understand." She hugged him close, lifted her lips to his ear. "I really do." *And thank you, Mike Kilmore, for being a true gentleman. One of the few. Dang it.*

"So," she said, pulling out of the embrace. "What do you have?"

He grinned, and Molly felt as if her knees would give way.

"Wanna sit?" He indicated the hood of his car. "I wiped it off special. And the engine's still warm."

Molly turned her gaze toward the Mustang. *The man even has a sexy car.* "Sure."

He extended two strong hands toward her waist. "May I?"

She nodded, grinning widely. *I'd never get tired of your chivalrous ways, sir. Never.*

He gripped her gently but firmly about the waist, and she gripped him by the shoulders. He lifted her as if she were a teenage girl at a sock hop and not a matriarch tempting forty. He set her on the hood—which did indeed appear to have been freshly wiped in the front—then sat down beside her. "Okay, here's what I have." He held her hand, intertwining their fingers. "Realize I have to move cautiously, because if a crime has been committed, I have to make sure the evidence is, well, by-the-book. But I'm closer to finding out where the money came from."

"Half a million dollars," Molly muttered.

He looked at her in mild surprise. "Your other source?"

Molly nodded, feeling a twinge of anger and hurt at the thought that Fergus

MacDonald now engendered.

Molly shrugged. "He doesn't know where the money came from."

His face brightened a bit. "Oh, well, I can't say as I do either, exactly, but I know it came through a law firm—Perkins and Marsh."

He paused as if expecting Molly to recognize the name. When she said nothing, he continued, "Same one as handles—or used to handle—all the affairs of the Thibodeaux family, before the Thibodeauxs went broke. Before Bradley Thibodeaux came of age, inherited the family fortune, and up and disappeared with it all. The Thibodeauxs—the ones with the name, at least—were Perkins and Marsh's biggest client before that. Those shysters got the family outta a mess of scrapes, I can tell ya. I don't have quite enough to go for a warrant on money laundering. I don't think it's *that* anyway. But I did kinda *imply* I might be investigating something like that. Anyway, old Mr. Marsh—he handled the whole transaction—with the school, I mean. And when I tried to lean on him a bit, he acted as nervous as a long-tailed cat in a roomful of rocking chairs. I got the distinct impression he was scared."

"Scared?"

"Yeah." Mike scratched at his five-o'clock shadow. "So, I mentioned that name, Magnus, to him. I swear he about dropped a load in his, uh, I mean it frightened him pretty badly."

In spite of the gravity of the situation, Molly had to suppress a smile. Mike always seemed to catch himself halfway through some crude expression or other. *You're so stinking cute, Mike Kilmore.* "Did he say anything else?"

"No, except to say over and over again how he hadn't told anyone. How he *wouldn't* tell anyone. Ever. Take it to his grave, he said."

"So, what does that mean?"

A sudden gust of wind stirred the fallen beech leaves, and Molly shivered—not entirely with the autumnal air.

Mike put his arm around her. "It means whether he's met this Magnus character face-to-face or not, Magnus has done something to him or his family. It means this Magnus is dangerous."

He chuckled low in his throat. "And the way he looked at me? Well, it's like he was thinking like I could be this Magnus guy. Imagine that!"

Molly stiffened. *Magnus? Mike?* "Why would he think that?" *No. You can't be. You can't.*

Mike shrugged and wrinkled his nose and brow. "Beats the snot outta me." He scratched at whiskers again. "Maybe he's never seen Magnus or never seen his *face*." He paused. "Maybe it's because I'm part Thibodeaux and all. I gotta say, though, there're times I wish I could put the fear of well, *me* into some of the crooks around here. It'd make my job a heck-of-a-lot easier." He grinned. "I mean, I try to be a nice guy, but there're some folks I'd really like to scare the piss outta."

She snuggled closer to him. "You know, I *can* picture you as the scary, Clint Eastwood-type. But you, you're part Thibodeaux?"

"Yeah. I told y'all this before."

"No, you haven't."

"Well, I got the ear." He pointed to the bump on his right ear. "It's a Thibodeaux trait."

Molly nodded. "Oh, that. You said half the town has Thibodeaux blood, because of old Elias Thibodeaux being such a womanizer." *Seducing and raping. Like poor White Lettie.*

"Yeah, but it's mostly the men that have the bump. Not many women, and when they do, it's hardly noticeable." He squeezed her shoulder, pressing her to him. "Anyway, how's the play going?"

Molly shrugged. "To hear Tabitha tell it, the play is one step away from being a complete and utter disaster. Which means everyone is working really hard. And she's nervous. And it'll probably be great."

"Good. I'll bet she's just amazing. That young lady is quite a powerhouse, I hear."

Something about the way he said "powerhouse" pricked Molly's ears. *It always comes back to Tabitha.* She felt the slightest twinge of jealousy. *Well, I did ask him to take an interest in her. But he chose me.*

And this is all about protecting Tabitha. Right?

He squeezed her hand and her shoulder. "Who's she dating?"

Molly blinked. Dating? "Nobody. She's too focused on the show. And school." *Why?*

"There's a rumor going 'round 'bout her and Joey Parsons."

Molly pulled away and looked at him askance. "Joey?"

He shrugged and wrinkled his nose again. "Joey's a good kid. Stays out of trouble, but he has a *reputation* with the girls."

Molly nodded. *Is she seeing Joey? She goes to those wienie roasts on Saturday nights sometimes. Is Joey part of those?* "She told me about that. And she used to accept rides home with him, but not lately. Not for several weeks."

"Okay." He scratched at his cheek again.

He does that when he's trying to work something out in his head. What's he thinking? "Why? Tabitha says she refuses to date anyone who's not LDS."

"Did you know he's taking the missionary discussions?"

Molly's jaw dropped. "J-Joey?"

Mike nodded, his expression serious. "Yeah."

"I haven't seen him at church." *There's no way you could miss a tall black kid at church.*

Mike nodded again. "Nope. Not yet. Makes me wonder, though. Is he taking the lessons because he's really investigating the Church? Or is he just doing it for Tabitha?"

"I thought he was dating another girl." *Beulah Martineau.*

He scratched again. "You know, that's what I heard too, though not going steady, for sure—given his reputation. And hers. But word is, he's not rooting around like he used to. I mean, he used to be like a rooster in a hen yard, chasin' every piece of…"

He caught himself. "Anyway. Could be he's serious."

Joey? Get baptized? He can now, of course. Well, he could've anyway, but now he can receive the priesthood too, go to the temple. "Well, that'd be a good thing, wouldn't it?" *Marry Tabitha. In the temple.*

Scratching again. "Yeah. If he's serious. I hope—for both their sakes—he is."

They sat in silence as the gray shadows of twilight blackened into night.

"This is gorgeous!" Tabitha fought the urge to turn about as she gazed in wonder at her reflection in the full-length mirror. The ball gown, all done in white, empire-waisted and straight, with strings of fake pearls and a great satin bow at the back, was breathtaking. "It's better than anything anybody wore to homecoming." Even standing on the stool in the backstage corner which Miss Tulane used as a costume shop—curtained off for privacy, of course—Tabitha could see her entire reflection in the mirror. Her long, raven hair had been pulled up and temporarily secured atop her head with a pair of metal hairclips. "I can't believe this is *me*. I can't wait to see it with the wig and tiara and all. And the jewelry! I mean, I know it's all fake, but it looks good enough! Can I try it all on? The whole thing?"

"Not today," Miss Tulane said in a slightly impatient sing-song. "We're just pinning the hem. And if you don't hold still, Tabitha, I'm going to mess it up."

Tabitha realized that, try though she might, she had not been able to contain a bounce of excitement. "Sorry."

"Besides," said the history teacher, "I thought you didn't go to homecoming."

Rub it in, why don't you? "No." Tabitha successfully managed to suppress a sigh. "I didn't."

"But you were asked, weren't you?"

"Yeah."

"So, why didn't you go? I heard both Scott *and* Jason asked you." She giggled—a surprisingly girlish sound coming from an adult woman. "Heard there was a fight about it. Jason got a black eye, and Scott got some loose teeth."

Scott and Jason were both in the play, cast as Colonel Pickering and Alfred P. Doolittle, and as such, spent a significant amount of time with Tabitha on set. She'd heard about the fight, but hadn't been able to bring herself to concede she could've been the rumored cause.

From the stage, Tabitha could hear Jason singing "With a Little Bit of Luck" in a decent cockney. "…goodness at ya," he crowed. "…with a lit'l bit o' luck…" He was surprisingly good as Eliza's shady father.

"Yeah," Tabitha said. "I heard about the fight. I hope you don't think I *wanted* anything like that, especially—"

"Of course not." Miss Tulane had worked her way around to Tabitha's left side. Pausing in her work, she looked up at Tabitha with a dreamy expression. "But how romantic! To have boys fighting over you!"

She sighed and went back to pinning up the hem of the gown. "When I was your age, I dreamed about boys fighting over me. I dreamed about being asked to homecoming and prom. Wearing an exquisite ball gown. Looking so pretty!" She sighed deeply, then shrugged. "I was never even asked out on a date 'til I was in college. But you turned both boys down."

"Yeah. I really couldn't accept. I can only date..."

"Mormons." Miss Tulane did not look up. "Yes, I know. Is that your mother's rule or your own?"

"It's my rule."

"Is your religion that important to you?"

Tabitha gritted her teeth. *I wish I knew!* "I…Yes. Well, at least the standards—the *morality* standards of my church are. Important, that is. To me."

"And the good, God-fearin' Pentecostal boys 'round here don't have the same standards?" The woman's tone had taken on a mocking and uncharacteristically southern quality.

Not that I've seen. Even the church-going set all seem to be doing stuff. "I'm trying to be careful." Angelica Goldsmith's words came to mind. *I want a temple marriage. More than anything.* "I want a temple marriage, an eternal marriage. I can't have that unless I marry a Mormon man. A good Mormon man." *Like Mike Kilmore. Not like my dad.*

Or Joey.

"I see." Miss Tulane looked up at Tabitha. A sad smile crept onto her pretty face. "Good for you, honey. Still, it must have been nice to be *asked* to homecoming. Even if you didn't well, *couldn't* go."

"I went to homecoming and prom last year. In my last school." *With Tony.* Tabitha lifted her face to trap the tears which suddenly threatened at the corners of her eyes.

"With a Mormon boy?"

Tabitha shook her head, blinking furiously. "Nope. It was fun—the dance was—but later on, thing's got too serious. Well, he was the reason I swore off non-Mormons."

"He didn't hurt you, did he?"

"He tried." She looked down and shook her head quickly, realizing how that sounded. "Not hurt me. Just tried something. I said, no. I slapped him. And that…" She swallowed the lump which suddenly swelled in her throat. "That was the end of it."

Miss Tulane bent her head, nodded, and returned to her work. "I'm sorry."

"Me too."

"Well, at least you got to go to homecoming once. And prom. So, what did you wear?"

Something about Miss Tulane's voice pricked at Tabitha. The pretty woman's tone had been wistful, even sad.

"I wore blue. You never went to homecoming or prom? Or even a date?" *Not 'til college. That's what she said.*

Miss Tulane stood, apparently having finished with the last pin. Her blue eyes—surrounded, as always, with just a bit too much makeup—were only a few inches lower than Tabitha's, even with Tabitha up on the stool. The woman's smile was tight. "No," she said, her head shaking slightly, more like a tremor than a denial. "I never had that opportunity. Oh, I dated lots of men in college. But high school was a total waste."

Tabitha stared at her. "But you're so pretty! And—and you're so nice! Nobody ever even asked you?"

Miss Tulane smiled that tight-lipped smile again, but there was a hint of softness in her eyes. "You're sweet." She shrugged, setting her pin cushion and thimble on the sewing table. "Let's just say I was a late bloomer." She extended her right hand toward Tabitha to help her down from the stool. "Careful, now. Don't want to rip out those pins."

Once Tabitha was safely on the floor, Miss Tulane said, "Turn around, please. Let's get this off you."

Tabitha turned her back to the teacher and puzzled over her words.

As Miss Tulane unfastened the hook above the zipper and began unzipping Tabitha's gown, she bent toward Tabitha's ear. "I'm trying to be patient, but it's been, you know, several weeks."

What?

And then Tabitha remembered. Of course, she remembered. This was the very conversation she dreaded every time she and Miss Tulane were alone. As much as Tabitha liked her teacher, she avoided talking to the woman after class or at rehearsal. Miss Tulane didn't bring it up every time—in fact, she hadn't for weeks—and Tabitha had begun to cherish the false hope the subject might not come up again.

The Circle.

"I, uh…" Tabitha wasn't ready to discuss her feelings—with Miss Tulane or anyone—about the Circle, the Power, Magnus. Or Joey. "I only started going back just recently."

"I know."

Tabitha stared at the woman openmouthed. "You do?"

The teacher looked around quickly, as if she were checking for prying eyes and listening ears. She leaned in close to Tabitha and whispered, "I have to confess something. I've been spying on you. The Circle, I mean. Not you personally." She glanced around again. Then she locked eyes with Tabitha, and there was an intense hunger in her gaze—so intense, it was almost frightening.

Tabitha had seen that look before.

Jack Palance. Bela Lugosi. Dracula.

Miss Tulane seemed to tremble with her need. "I saw what happened that night—the night after we talked, the first night you were there with Magnus. It was *amazing*! And I want it! I want to experience it all. The Divine Feminine. The magic—the true power of womanhood. All of it! What you can do—Tabitha, why would you turn your back on that, even for a little while?"

"I'm," *Scared. Freaked-out.* "It's complicated." Tabitha stepped out of the gown and backed away from Miss Tulane and her unsettling, ravenous stare.

"Might the complications have something to do with a certain star quarterback?"

I don't want to talk about this! "It's not that. I mean, Joey's part of it, but…" *You were there. You saw the tree. And Joey.*

"I notice you don't stand next to Joey or Magnus anymore, not like you did on that night. You stand on the opposite end of the Circle."

As far away from Joey or Magnus as I can. It doesn't feel as good there, but—

The redhead bent and picked up the gown from the floor. "I assume that's where the less-powerful girls usually stand." She stood and looked Tabitha in the eye. And the hunger blazed afresh in her eyes. "But you're not less powerful, are you? From what I gather, you are by far the most powerful of the entire Circle. By far. That's why they want you so badly."

Tabitha bowed her head, avoiding Miss Tulane's eyes.

Yeah. They want me. They want to use me. So why do I keep going back?

Because it feels so good, and it's nice to be wanted. Tabitha sighed audibly. *Nobody wants me at Church. Except Angelica, maybe.*

"What's that?" Miss Tulane's words snapped Tabitha out of her thoughts.

Tabitha froze. *Holy crap! Did I say that aloud?*

"Did you say," the teacher seemed to be rolling the words around in her head. "Nobody wants you at your church? Except Angelica?"

Oh, crap! I did say it aloud! "I, uh don't exactly fit in. Angelica, Miss Goldsmith, she's nice to me, but almost nobody else is."

"Is Angelica part of the Circle? She's not, is she? I haven't seen her there."

Tabitha shook her head quickly. "Oh, no."

"She makes no secret of the fact she's a Mormon. Neither one of you do, of course." The woman smiled, but there was no warmth in her eyes. Only the hunger. "I admire your courage."

"Uh, thanks?"

"But I don't understand. Why wouldn't you embrace your womanhood completely? Why hesitate when it comes to the Power, the feminine magic? I want it, Tabitha. I want it all! I want you to introduce me, to bring me in."

Tabitha averted her eyes again, but she nodded. "Okay. I'll talk to Beulah. She seems to be the"—she searched for the right word—"gateway to Magnus."

"Tonight?"

Tabitha nodded. This time she met the woman's eyes.

Miss Tulane smiled. And though the hunger still burned, her eyes softened a bit. "Thank you. You have no idea how much this means to me."

"You know, not *every* woman," Tabitha began, "well, every woman has the Power to some extent—at least that's what they say—but not every woman is strong with it."

Miss Tulane nodded quickly, her long, wavy auburn hair bouncing. "Yes, but I want to try. I *have* to try."

"Okay." Tabitha shrugged. She could hear Jason belting out the final line of his song, loud enough to be heard above the rest of the ensemble. "I, uh, should probably get back to the rehearsal. I think they've been through that number at least twice."

The woman nodded, brushing back her hair as she leaned over the table. She pulled her hair behind her right ear.

Tabitha noticed a thin, but easily detectable scar on the top of the woman's ear. *What happened to her ear?*

"What did you say?" Miss Tulane straightened up abruptly. She hastily brushed her hair back over her ear.

Did I say it aloud? Again? "I—I'm sorry. Your ear. It looks like you have a scar." *Why do I keep doing that?*

"It's nothing. A childhood accident."

But from the way the woman was acting, it didn't seem as if the scar was nothing. *She's hiding it. Why?*

Then it hit her. *She's a Thibodeaux! She had the bump removed, but she's a Thibodeaux. And she doesn't want anyone to know.*

She's not supposed to be from around here. But she must be.

Miss Tulane began to gather up her sewing tools and put them into their case. "I'll finish the hem at home." Her hands trembled slightly. She reached for the pin cushion and thimble.

The thimble fell to the floor and rolled under the table.

"I'll get it," Tabitha said. She squatted down, pulling her long black skirt under her knees so she could see the floor clearly.

"Thanks," Miss Tulane said. "It's an antique. It belonged to my grandmother. And my mother."

Tabitha noted the woman's tone when she said the word "mother." The word was devoid of affection. Disgust. Loathing. Not affection.

As Tabitha fished under the table, the woman continued. "It's magnetic. For picking up needles and pins from between the floorboards."

"Magnetic, huh?" Tabitha caught sight of it. "There it is." Her fingers closed around the thimble.

As the weakness overwhelmed her, she managed to think, *magnetic. Iron.*

And the world went white.

"Y'all are such a disappointment, boy. You're a damn disgrace!"

She glared at her son with a disgust and contempt which went beyond her power to express in mere words. Bradley just stood there weeping.

Eighteen years old and still bawlin' like a damn baby, she thought. Like a girl. Well, any wonder?

Tears streamed down the boy's face, over the reddening cheek—red from where she'd slapped him. "Why, Mama? Why can't you even try to understand? To understand me? I can't help how I feel."

"God forbid I should ever—"

Bradley wrung his hands. "God? What's God got to do with it?" He straightened, and fury burned in his blue eyes. "What do y'all know about God?"

"How dare you?" She lifted her hand to strike him again.

But Bradley stood tall, not backing down. "Y'all go to church and y'all clap and sing and shout, 'Hallelujah!' and 'Amen!' But y'all don't mean it. Dad catted around after every pretty woman in town afore he died, and y'all didn't do nothin'. Y'all knew, but y'all didn't do nothin'. Hell, I heard y'all, Mama, yourself, even been foolin' 'round with Henry the driver. And afore him... what was the gardener's name? Or is it both of 'em together? I may be different, but at least I ain't a slut like you, Mama. What the hell do y'all know about God?"

She felt the blood rising to her cheeks afresh. How dare he talk about that? How'd he even know anyway? *"You're a lyin' bag of—"*

Bradley's bitter laughter cut her short. "Hell, Mama, the only way I know I'm a Thibodeaux and not the bastard son of one of the help is this damn bump!" He pointed to his ear, then grasped a handful of his too-long red hair. "And this!"

She slapped him again. Hard. "I wish I never bore ya, ya damn pervert! Ya damn sissy!"

He put a hand to his face, directly over where she'd struck him. "Well, now y'all can pretend y'all never did." His voice was as cold as a January frost. "On account of I'll be gone. Y'all ain't never gonna see Bradley Thibodeaux again."

He spun on his heel and grabbed the doorknob. Then he stopped, turned, and glared at her. "Y'all will never see Bradley Thibodeaux again. And y'all will never see a penny of his money. My money, Mama. It's all mine. I signed the papers afore I came here. The stocks, the bonds, the businesses, the real estate. Hell, even this house. It's all mine. And I'm gonna use it—every last penny if I have to. All the Thibodeaux money. I'm gonna use it to be me! To be how I want. To be who I am!"

He turned and walked out, slamming the door behind himself.

She stood, rooted to the mahogany floor. The money? The house? *"Bradley? Bradley!"* She ran to the door, flung it open.

Her son walked swiftly away, his hands to his face as if he was wiping furiously at his tears.

"Bradley! Honey!" she cried. "I'm sorry, honey! Come back! I'll... We'll figure this out. Together! We'll do whatever y'all want. Whatever y'all need. Y'all can be whatever y'all wanna be! Bradley!" She ran after him.

But he ran as well. He outpaced her and jumped into his car, started the engine, and drove away, engine roaring and tires screeching on the semicircular driveway.

And he was gone.

And the horrid truth slammed into her, driving her to her knees on the lawn.

It was all gone. Her son. The money. The house.

All gone. She had nothing left in the world. Except pain.

It started in her left arm. Then she felt as if a claw had reached into her chest and was squeezing, crushing her heart. The world went white and—

191

Something dropped from her hand. *The thimble. Magnetic. Iron.*

"Tabitha!" Someone calling her name. Shaking her. "Tabitha! Wake up!"

Tabitha's chest hurt. Or did it? She couldn't remember.

The vision.

She opened her eyes. They refused to focus for a moment. And then she saw a face—a familiar face. Blue eyes, red hair.

Bradley?

The teacher's eyes went wide in horror. "What did you say?"

Not again! "I'm, I'm sorry. I didn't mean it." *The thimble belonged to the mother. Last woman to own it. Bradley Thibodeaux's mother. Last woman.*

Not Suzanne Tulane.

Tabitha shook her head vehemently. "Don't go anywhere near the Circle. Please don't. They'll know. Magnus will know."

Not Suzanne. Bradley.

Suzanne began to tremble, breathing heavily, head shaking. "Bradley's gone. There is no Bradley. There never was. I'm Suzanne now. Suzanne. Suzanne!"

21

"Eli-i-i-za! You're wanted on sta-age!" a voice called from the other side of the black privacy curtain—Billy Hammond, a.k.a. Professor Henry Higgins, using his on-stage accent. "Tabitha! Are you in there, Eliza?"

Tabitha, still lying on the floor, where she'd collapsed during her vision, stared up into the wide eyes of the person bending over her—the person Tabitha had known as Suzanne Tulane. *Not a woman? A man? Bradley Thibodeaux?*

"Tabitha? Y'all okay in there?" Billy had dropped the accent.

Say something! "Uh," Her voice caught in her throat. "Y-yeah." She cleared her throat. "Just a sec!"

"Okay. Hurry up."

"Be right there!"

Tears fell from Suzanne's eyes and onto Tabitha's chest. The person—Tabitha was unable to think of her teacher as either a woman or a man at that moment—mouthed a word over and over. It took Tabitha a moment to understand. "Please! Please! Please!"

Tabitha shook her head, then nodded, then shook it again. I *don't know what to think! I don't know what to do.*

"I won't…" Tabitha began, whispering. "I won't tell. Anyone. It's your secret. Your secret."

"I'm Suzanne. Suzanne." The hissed words came across as a plea rather than an affirmation.

Tabitha took a deep breath, then held it, as if to clear her head. Then she let it out. And she nodded. "Okay." *I'll call you that.* Another breath. "I gotta go."

She scrambled to her feet, almost tripping over her long skirt as she gathered it around her legs.

From behind her, she heard, "Thank you!"

Okay. But just please, please, please stay away from the Circle!

Angelica Goldsmith was *not* happy. "Honestly, people. We open next Thursday night. Eight more rehearsals. And that's it." Sitting on the edge of the stage, she shook her head as she surveyed the cast and crew seated in the front row of theatre seats.

Suzanne Tulane was notably absent. Tabitha hadn't seen the teacher leave, but she also hadn't seen Suzanne since the incident with the iron thimble and its unnerving revelation earlier that evening.

The wonderfully elaborate set, incredibly detailed and technically sophisticated for a mere high school production, rose behind the diminutive director. "We were better on Saturday, folks. It's like we were just going through the motions tonight. And not very well."

She fixed her eyes on Tabitha.

Tabitha swallowed hard. *Here it comes.*

"Tabitha, you flubbed your lines. You. Flubbed. Your. Lines." She threw up her hands, and Tabitha nodded, scowling. "You had this memorized, you were off book at the auditions. But tonight… Listen, if you're off, kid, then everybody is off. I mean, everybody has a bad night once in a while, but you're the *star*. You can't have bad nights. Do I make myself clear?"

Tabitha nodded slowly and deliberately.

I really let you down. I let everybody down.

But Miss Tulane or Bradley Thibodeaux or whatever… whoever she or he is. How am I supposed to handle that?

Tabitha felt as if she'd been punched in the stomach and the wind taken out of her, her wrists slit open and bled dry.

Angelica clambered to her feet on the stage so that she towered above them all. "This is not acceptable, people." She shook her head again. "I don't know what's wrong. I know you all have drama in your lives. School. Family. Friends. Boyfriends. Girlfriends. Work. Well, guess what? It doesn't matter." She pointed to the back of the theatre. "When you walk through that door, you put all of that aside. You lock it away in a box. And then you become something *magical*. You become actors and actresses. You become other people with other problems and other lives. It's magic. But, no, it isn't really magic. It isn't all talent, either. It's *hard* work. You cannot let down. Not for a moment."

Her stern expression morphed into a playful grin. "You know"—she pointed with a finger for emphasis at no one in particular—"there's this great scene in *Star Trek* where—"

Beside her, Beulah leaned toward Tabitha and whispered, "And here it comes. I swear she's got a *Star Trek* quote for every—"

"Excuse me!" The grin had vanished from Angelica's face as if zapped off by a phaser. "I was talking."

Duly chastised, Beulah nodded meekly and silently.

"As I was saying," Angelica began again with just a ghost of the former grin, "and yes, indeed, there is a *Star Trek* quote for every occasion." The impish grin blossomed again. "There is a scene from 'The Naked Time' in Season One, where Mr. Spock has been infected with a virus which strips him of all control over his emotions. He's alone, and he's *weeping*. Imagine—the emotionless, always-in-control Mr. Spock bawling his eyes out. And he repeats, 'I am an officer! I am in control of my emotions!'"

She scanned the students seated before her. "Well, who is in control of you and your emotions? When you walk on that stage, you must *become* Higgins and Pickering, and Mrs. Pierce and Alfred P. Doolittle." And she looked directly, pointedly at Tabitha. "And Eliza. Whatever happens off this stage, once you are back on stage, you are in control. But you are in control as your character. Don't do anything your character wouldn't do. You be in control. You have power over yourself and over the audience. You are in control. Nobody else. Don't surrender that control, that power to anyone else."

Control? What control? And power?

I can't even control my own Power. A man has to control it for me. Joey or Magnus. I am not in control. They are. And I'm letting them use it use me. They can't take it without my consent, right?

I'm like Eliza, surrendering at the end to Higgins. But she loves him. That's different. Is it?

Do I love Joey?

"Okay," Angelica said. "Lecture's over. Tomorrow has got to be better. Full run-through. Straight through, no breaks. So, go home. Get some sleep. Do your homework." She paused, then winked at them. "On second thought, do your homework first."

"Y'all need a ride home?" Beulah asked. "I thought"—she lowered her voice to a loud whisper—"with you coming back and all to the Circle, I mean. Maybe y'all'd want a ride again. It's been a while."

Tabitha grimaced sheepishly. "Yeah. Sorry about that. But my mom's here, waiting for me. Tomorrow night?"

Beulah's smile lit up her face. "You're on! Tomorrow night." She patted Tabitha on the knee. "See y'all tomorrow mornin', bright-eyed and bushy-tailed! And sexy. Don't forget sexy. Gotta make all the boys and men sweat!" And then she was gone.

Tabitha sighed. She wasn't at all sure she wanted to ride alone with Beulah just yet. *In for a penny, in for a pound, as they used to say.*

She looked up, only to see Angelica Goldsmith standing over her. Tabitha started. Then she glanced hurriedly around and realized all the other kids had left. And Angelica was looking down at her. If the director's expression had been stern or even angry, Tabitha could've handled it. But Tabitha found only disappointment written on the woman's face.

Angelica lifted an eyebrow. "You know, that speech was mostly directed at you."

"Yeah," Tabitha muttered, "I know." *Everybody knew.*

Angelica's expression softened, and she took the seat beside Tabitha. "You started off brilliant tonight. You had a rough patch a few weeks back, but lately, you've been as great as ever. But then you went back for your fitting, and when you came out."

Tabitha stared at her knees. "I sucked."

Angelica chuckled. "You weren't that bad. You were just not all with us. And you and Billy, you're the whole show practically." She leaned in and whispered, "But don't you ever breathe a word of that to the rest of the cast." She gave Tabitha's shoulder a playful nudge.

Tabitha tried to force a smile, but it died midway between her brain and the neurons in her face, cut off by the confusion roiling inside her.

"Want to talk about it?"

I can't.

"Did something happen in there? With Miss Tulane?"

It's not my secret. Not my secret.

"You know," said Angelica. "She's seemed preoccupied lately. Miss Tulane, I mean. Did she say anything to you?"

Tabitha shook her head. She didn't say anything. *It was her mother. His mother. I don't know how to deal with this. What am I supposed to do?* It felt like that was the only question Tabitha could ask herself these days. *What do I do?*

"Okay," said Angelica, placing a hand on Tabitha's shoulder. "If you want to talk, I'll listen. You can call, come to my classroom, anything. Okay?"

Tabitha nodded. A tear escaped her eye. She wiped it away hastily.

"And if you simply need a shoulder to cry on, I'm good at that too." She paused. "And we're about the same height, so it works out."

Tabitha turned and threw her arms around the other woman. And she sobbed.

Angelica Goldsmith held her and didn't say a word.

After a minute or so, Tabitha regained control. "Thanks. For everything."

"I didn't do anything."

But Tabitha could hear the knowing smile in the woman's voice. "Yeah," she whispered, "you did."

Tabitha pulled out of the embrace. "I have to go. My mom's gonna be worried." She gathered her book bag and walked quickly up the theatre aisle.

"Bye!" the director called. "See you in class tomorrow!"

When Tabitha reached the lobby, however, her mother wasn't there.

But Joey was.

He stood there, clad in flared slacks and a disco shirt which exposed his muscular chest almost down to his navel. All he would've needed to complete the look would've been platform shoes.

And the look was hot.

He smiled his big, charming, knee-weakening smile. "Hey, you."

Tabitha lowered her head slightly, but kept her eyes on him, gazing through the protection of her eyebrows. "Hi."

"Can we talk?"

She shrugged. "My mom's gonna be here any second." *I can't talk to you. When I talk to you, my mind gets all jumbled. And right now, I've got enough to think about.*

"Yeah, well, she's not out there yet. Or she wasn't a minute ago. I mean, we've barely said two words to each other since that night. And I want...I *need* to talk to you. Tabitha, I..."

Don't say you love me! Don't say it. I can't handle it right now!

"Look, Tabitha, I have some questions."

She raised her head and looked at him directly. "Questions?"

His smile morphed into a lopsided grin. Which made him all the more charming. "Yeah, I do." He reached into his back pocket and pulled out a book. A very familiar-looking, blue-and-white book with a large gold statue on the cover.

"*The Book of Mormon?* You're reading it?"

"You know," he said, "you're so dang cute with your mouth all hanging open like that."

Tabitha snapped her jaw shut. Then she said, "You're reading it?"

He winked. "I can read, you know. But, yeah."

"What...what do you think?"

He nodded, and his expression became serious. "It's interesting. I got bogged down in all the Isaiah stuff in the second book—you know, Second Nephi, I think it was—but it's really interesting now. I just have some questions. Can I ask you about it?"

Tabitha felt as if the slightest puff of air would have knocked her down. *Joey? Reading The Book of Mormon?* She couldn't wrap her brain around the idea.

"The whole blacks-and-the-priesthood thing," he said, "it bothered me for a while. It bothered me a lot. But, well, the missionaries explained all that. And that's all in the past, anyway. And I'm all about *now*. But I have other questions, and I thought maybe you could—".

"You're meeting with the missionaries?"

He chuckled. "Yeah. They're pretty cool. But can we—you and I—talk about some of this stuff?"

Tabitha nodded. And she realized she was grinning. Like an idiot. And she didn't care. "Yeah. But not right now. My mom—she'll..."

"Okay, that's cool. Maybe tomorrow? Lunch?"

"Sure!" She immediately regretted the enthusiasm in her voice. *Don't want to give him the wrong idea, right?*

"Great!" He looked down the hall to the outer doors. "I think that's your mom." Tabitha followed his gaze and spied two headlights through the glass panel at the left of the doors. She was no connoisseur of cars, but she would've bet money those were the headlights of a Chevy Impala. "Probably."

"May I escort you to your carriage, my fair lady?" He offered his arm and grinned. His white teeth gleamed in his handsome, dark face. "No pun intended."

She nodded, grinning, and slipped her hand into his elbow. And of course, she had to reach up higher than normal, making her very conscious of the contrast of her short stature versus his great height. But his stature also made her feel a warmth—an unfamiliar yet very welcome feeling of safety and security.

"May I carry your books, milady?"

In for a penny. She shrugged and slipped the bag off her shoulder.

When their hands met, he trembled slightly. "Shoot, girl! You are so *powerful*."

The Power. It always comes back to the Power. Is that why he's reading The Book of Mormon? To get closer to me? To make me love him?

Tabitha still held his arm, though not as tightly. And she pulled slightly away. "That's how you test for the Power, isn't it?"

His arm stiffened a bit.

He knows he's on shaky ground now. Always comes back to the Power.

"Yeah," he said with a lightness to his tone which sounded slightly forced. "Yeah. It's like an electric tingle. With you, it's almost like sticking your finger in a light socket. I mean, it feels good and all, but it's a jolt if you're not ready for it. And with you, it seems like I'm never quite ready for the way you make me feel." He paused. "And you can take that any way you choose."

Tabitha's smile was genuine. But her feelings about Joey were so chaotic and confused. And she had other concerns on her mind. "Do you test all the girls at school?"

"Yeah. Pretty much. At least all the *pretty* ones."

"How about the teachers?"

"When I can. It's not always possible. Or desirable." He chuckled again. "I've never tested Ol' Waddle, for instance."

"Gross!" The image of Mrs. Wardle holding hands with Tabitha in the Circle was both ridiculous and sickening.

"Yeah." He made a face of extreme disgust. "That's what I thought too."

"How about Miss Goldsmith?"

"Yeah, I tested her, but, well, she's about as strong as most women—which means, not much. I mean, all women have it. Some."

Tabitha nodded. "Yeah. So, I've been told."

"Even your mom. And she was maybe a little bit stronger than average, but not much. I mean, if it's genetic, you didn't get it from your mom."

Does that mean I got it from my dad? Her gut clenched at the thought. "*Is* it genetic?"

He shrugged. "Beats the snot out of me. We only discovered what it was a year ago. Magnus and I, we don't know enough yet. We're still learning along with all of you."

Only a year ago? She swallowed. "What about the other teachers? Whom have you tested?"

"Most of them. Most of the pretty ones, at least."

Most. "Most? Not all?"

"Yeah, I have to have an opportunity. I mean, I can't just walk up to a pretty teacher and just shake her hand, can I?"

Tabitha was fairly certain her own unamused chuckle did not sound forced. "I bet." *You're an actress. You can do this.* "What about Mrs. Hargrove? Miss Tulane?" *Those are my teachers. No red flags there. I hope.*

"Hargrove is a little stronger than average. Not enough to recruit. Or to keep an eye on. Tulane? No opportunity so far. I'd like to, though. She's a fox!"

Not yet. Hasn't tested her—him yet.

He shrugged again. "Not sure how we'd go about recruiting a teacher, though. And unless a woman was really strong—not Tabitha-Moonshadow strong, ya dig—but strong, I'm not sure we'd bother. The bigger the Circle, the more chance someone will follow one of us, find us out. No offense, but teenage girls aren't the best at keeping secrets, if you know what I mean."

Already happened.

She shook her head. "Nope."

They had reached the exit at the end of the hallway. Tabitha let go of his arm with a small pang of regret.

Joey handed her the book bag, then opened one of the doors. "Your carriage awaits, milady."

He did not lean down for a goodbye kiss.

As messed up as Tabitha's feelings were when it came to Joey Parsons, she felt a pang of regret. They'd kissed only on that one occasion, but the memory still sent a tingle through her. "Good night, Joey."

"See you tomorrow. At lunch?" He pointed at her with both index fingers. "I'm holding you to that."

For the briefest moment, Tabitha couldn't remember what he was talking about. *Lunch?*

Then, of course, she remembered. *The Book of Mormon.*

Warmth flooded her from head to foot. "You bet."

He bent, but rather than leaning toward her face and her lips, he took her hand and pressed his lips to it.

And she felt the tingle, the unmistakable, delicious, delirious warmth of the Power flowing through her—flowing through her and into him. She felt dizzy and almost consumed by a sudden urge to throw her arms around his neck.

Is he just reading it to impress me? If he is, do I care?

She pulled her hand gently out of his, deliberately severing herself from his channeling of her Power.

At least I can think more clearly now. Dang it.

She favored him with a smile. "'Night."

She turned and walked out the door into the glare of the Chevy's headlights. She shielded her eyes, not daring to glance back to see whether Joey was following or not.

No way Mom couldn't see us walking arm-in-arm. Or him kissing my hand.

Her hand—her whole body—still tingled at the thought, at the memory of the joy of Power flowing through her.

Then it hit her.

He was channeling without my permission.

But I enjoyed it.

Yes, but he didn't ask. He just took it.

But I enjoyed it.

And Tabitha wasn't sure which terrified her more.

She stepped around the side of the car to the passenger door.

This isn't our car!

It was a Mustang. There couldn't be two such cars in all of Butler County.

Mike Kilmore's car.

Is he here to pick me up? Alone?

Where's Mom?

Real terror seized her like ice water poured down her spine. "Is my mom okay?"

"I'm right here, honey." The voice came from the open passenger-side window.

"Mom?"

"Sorry," said her mom, leaning out the window. "We got to talking and just lost track of the time."

Tabitha's heart thundered as adrenaline coursed through her veins. "I thought…" She took a few shuddering breaths.

"I'm sorry, honey. And I'm sorry we're late."

Molly opened the only passenger-side door, and the car's dome light came on. "You wanna sit in the back or squish up here with us?"

Even as night-blinded as Tabitha was, in the dim illumination of the interior car light, she could see her mother's lipstick was smudged.

Talking? Yeah, I'll bet. Sit up front with the two lovebirds?

"I'll take the back."

Before she could make a move, the muscular form of Mike Kilmore, illuminated and outlined in the ghostly glow of the car lights, was out of the Mustang on his side. He pulled his seat forward. "Come in on my side. That way we won't make your mom have to get out."

Tabitha nodded, not sure if he could see the movement of her head and not caring. She looked toward the door of the school theatre.

Joey was standing in front of the building. He waved at her, then bent and waved at her mom. "Hi, Miss Moonshadow!" His greeting was bright and cheerful. And charming as ever.

"Hello, Joey," her mom replied. Her voice carried no warmth, but it wasn't overtly hostile either.

Would she be okay with me dating Joey? Would I be okay with me dating Joey? He's not LDS.

But he could be. Someday.

Joey straightened and nodded at Mike Kilmore and Mike Kilmore nodded back.

Something about the wordless exchange between the two males struck Tabitha as odd—formal, and yet familiar—as if the two knew each other well, but maintained a distinction of rank.

Of course, they know each other. Brother Kilmore questioned Joey at our house. And at school.

As she approached the open driver-side door, Mike Kilmore extended his hand in greeting. "Hey, Miss Tabitha. I hope you don't mind me taggin' along tonight. Your mom and I got to talkin' and—"

"Yeah, I heard." She thought about ignoring his hand, but then thought better of such a slight.

I want Mom to be happy, don't I? Even if it is with him.

She accepted the proffered hand.

As his strong, rough hand enveloped hers, his hand twitched. "Every dang time! I swear, young lady. Y'all have an *electric* handshake."

Tabitha stared up into Brother Kilmore's dimly lit face—his ruggedly handsome face, lit from below and cast with eerie shadows. At that moment, in that light, his was the visage of a ghoul or a vampire.

Jack Palance. Dracula. Sucking the life out of everything. Taking...

And Tabitha was certain she'd felt that calloused, powerful hand before. In White Lady Hollow. In the clearing.

In the Circle.

Magnus.

"Mom, can we talk?" Her daughter leaned against Molly's bedroom doorframe. And judging from Tabitha's expression, she seemed especially troubled. Her eyes were downcast, her mouth pulled into a thoughtful frown.

"Sure, Tabby-Cat. Of course." *Maybe this is it. Maybe she's ready to tell me what she's been hiding these last couple of months. Maybe she knows something that'll lead us to Magnus. To the faceless boogeyman who haunts my dreams.*

Tabitha nodded, but kept her eyes averted. She'd kept an almost complete silence during the ride home, even though both Mike and Molly had tried to engage her in conversation. And whenever Molly had turned around to look at her daughter, Tabitha had kept her head bowed. For a while, Molly had assumed Tabitha's reticence was due to Mike's presence, the fact that they'd been late, or the fact that Molly and Mike had quite obviously been making out. Any or all three of those causes could've fueled Tabitha's silence and her disinclination to engage in conversation. However, as the ride home progressed, Molly had gotten the distinct feeling that Tabitha was watching one or both of them—watching intently, if surreptitiously.

Molly got up from her makeup table—she refused to think of it as a vanity— where she'd been going through her nightly ritual of removing her face. She'd noticed, with some mortification, that her lipstick had been smudged—another obvious sign of her earlier amorous activity.

I've got nothing to be ashamed of, she'd thought at the time. We didn't do anything bad or cross any lines.

That last thought had come with only the slightest twinge of regret. Mike Kilmore had awoken feelings in her she'd thought long dead and buried, and those feelings and desires had returned with an intensity she'd never felt before, even when she'd been married to Jerry—and blissfully ignorant of her ex-husband's true nature.

Molly sat on the edge of her bed and patted the spot beside her.

Tabitha, however, didn't move from the doorway.

This must be serious. Better move to neutral ground. "How about I make us some hot chocolate? Perfect for a night like tonight."

After a slight hesitation, Tabitha looked up and smiled. "That'd be cool." Then her grin widened, and there was a mischievous twinkle in Tabitha's eyes. "Not the chocolate. Let's keep that hot." Tabitha straightened, turned, and walked toward the kitchen.

Molly got up and followed her daughter out of the bedroom. "You know, if it weren't so late on a weeknight—and the weather were cooperating—I'd have called a SNORBS, but I'm sure the A&W is closed."

Tabitha chuckled softly. "I was just thinking the same thing."

Molly sighed. "But it's not a perfect world."

Tabitha sat at the table, slumping into a chair. "Nope."

Molly peeked out the window near the front door. In the yellow gleam of the porch light, she could see a nasty mix of rain and wet snow obscuring the night outside their cottage. "Still yucky outside. Have you seen this? It's gotten worse."

Tabitha didn't reply.

Not in the mood to discuss the weather, I guess. "Good thing we got home before all this started." *Glad Mike made it home safe too.*

Warmth spread through her at the memory of his brief phone call, letting her know he'd made it home in spite of the sudden November storm.

Good night, handsome.

Molly pushed aside the warmth and tingle that thoughts of Mike always invoked. She left the window with its scene of wintry sogginess. Entering the kitchen, she went about retrieving the necessary ingredients—milk, cocoa, sugar, salt, vanilla— water she'd get from the sink. *Should've picked up some marshmallows. Oh, well.*

There was just something comforting about the ritual of making hot chocolate on a stormy night. A howling wind with lightning and thunder would've made it perfect—that and a scary movie on the TV—but as she had already observed, it wasn't a perfect world.

The soft clatter of Molly's activity in the kitchen filled the awkward silence. *Let Tabitha compose her thoughts in privacy.*

Molly gathered a spatula, a small pan, measuring spoons, and a fork. She measured the dry ingredients into the pan, mixed them with a fork, then measured and stirred in the water. She put the pan on the stove to heat. As she stirred, she fought the urge to ask her daughter what was on her mind. *Leave her alone. She'll talk when she's ready. Be patient.*

"Mom…"

Molly waited, stirring as if she had all the time in the world, but Tabitha said no more. "Yes, honey?"

Still nothing. Just as Molly opened her mouth to prompt her daughter once more, Tabitha said. "You really had no clue Dad was gay? I mean, until the night he announced it and walked out?"

What in the world? Where did that come from? Molly swallowed the lump that had suddenly taken up residence in her throat. "No, I didn't. Maybe there were clues or signs or something, but I never saw them. I wasn't looking for them, I guess. And even looking back, I don't see anything." Anger and disgust erupted in her—sudden, unexpected, and frothing like a boiling stew of rot and filth—rage and contempt for Jerry.

And for herself.

Molly closed her eyes and shoved the anger down, attempting to bury it, at least for the moment. She opened her eyes again, added the milk, then stirred once more. "Why do you ask?"

"How can you trust *anyone*?" There was a note of anger mingled with despair in Tabitha's voice. "How do you know what they're really like? On the inside? I mean, it's like Shakespeare said—'All the world's a stage. And all the men and women merely players.' Everyone's acting. Only, it's like everyone's wearing a mask. How do you know what's really *behind* the mask?"

Wow. Molly tested the chocolate. Hot enough. She turned off the burner and removed the pan. She added the vanilla. She was stalling, she knew, attempting to ensure her voice was calm, casual—not reflecting the turmoil swirling inside her. "Are we talking about anyone in particular?"

When Tabitha didn't answer immediately, Molly poured the chocolate into two mugs. She spilled a little on the Formica, but ignored it. *Whom is she talking about?* She carried the mugs, steaming with the inviting, comforting aroma of the magical brew, the alchemy of cocoa, vanilla, sugar, and milk, to the dining table. She set both mugs down, then sat. Molly pushed one mug toward her daughter. "Here, honey."

Accepting the mug, Tabitha muttered, "Thanks."

"Tabby-Cat," Molly began gently, still struggling against the ugly emotions fighting to escape her lips. "Are we talking about anyone in particular?"

Tabitha took a cautious sip from her mug. "Maybe." She grimaced. "Yeah, of course, but I really can't talk about it...about who."

Molly had to force herself to refrain from correcting Tabitha's grammar. *About "whom."*

Stop it. Shakespeare wasn't talking about masks. Cut it out, Professor Moonshadow. Now is not the time.

Instead, Molly said, "Okay."

"I mean, it's not my secret to tell. So, I can't..." Her voice trailed off.

"So, you found out somebody's secret?"

Tabitha nodded, staring into her mug.

Masks. She mentioned masks. "But you weren't supposed to find out?"

Eyes still downcast, Tabitha slowly shook her head.

"And what you found out upset you." It wasn't a question. "You saw behind the mask, so to speak."

"Yeah." Tabitha said the word slowly. "I wish...I *really* wish I didn't know."

"I'm sorry, honey." Molly drew a deep breath. "But sometimes"—*Like with Jerry*—"isn't it better to know the truth? Even if the truth hurts? A lot?"

"It sucks."

All the pain and anger and loathing welled up in Molly afresh. However, almost miraculously, she managed to keep her voice steady. "Yes, it does." *It sucks, indeed.*

"Do you wish you'd known about Dad? Before he told you, before he demanded all those *disgusting* things?"

Molly felt the blood rush to her cheeks. "He, uh, only demanded those things at the end. The night he left. I really didn't know."

"And if you had?"

"If I had," Molly exhaled slowly. "I would've taken you and walked out." Molly took a sip from her mug. "And at least then it would've been my decision. I would have chosen. Not some…" She searched for an appropriate word—one she could say aloud, at least, in front of her daughter. "*Selfish* man. He took away everything. My love." *My virginity.* "My security. My peace. My eternal marriage." She put a hand on Tabitha's arm. "The only thing he didn't take away from me was you."

Tabitha glanced up at her, and the ghost of a melancholy smile floated across her face. And vanished.

"So," Molly said, slowly withdrawing her hand, "what's going on?"

Tabitha shook her head again. "I told you—I can't tell you. It's not—"

"I know. It's not your secret. So, don't tell me the secret."

"Thanks." Tabitha looked up and gave Molly another sad smile. "Thanks, Mom."

"Instead, how about telling me how you feel?"

Tabitha averted her eyes and sighed. "Betrayed, I guess. Confused." She paused, and when she spoke again, her voice was a whisper. "Scared."

I'm scared too, honey. "What scares you? Can you tell me that much?"

Tabitha shrugged. "It's just that I don't know who I can trust anymore."

"Can you trust me?"

Tabitha nodded slowly. "But I can't talk about it." She grimaced and laid her face on her outstretched arms. "It's not my secret!"

Molly set a hand softly atop her daughter's head. She lightly stroked Tabitha's raven hair. "Tabby-Cat, is one of your friends in trouble?" *Are you in trouble?* "If someone needs help—"

"Nobody's pregnant, Mom." Anger and impatience were thick in her tone. But she paused, and when she spoke again, her voice was calmer. "It's not that."

Molly realized she'd stopped stroking Tabitha's hair. She began again. "Okay, honey. It's just, well, I worry. I'm your mother. It's part of the job."

"I know. Sorry." "I love you, Tabby-Cat. My beautiful, talented, smart, wonderful girl."

Tabitha said nothing, and Molly's heart ached. *I wish I knew how to help you. I wish I could take your pain, take it inside myself, and carry it for you. I wish I knew where the danger was coming from, who Magnus is. And why he wants you, why he's gone to such great lengths to trap you.*

Tabitha lifted her head. She put her arms around Molly.

Molly held her daughter close. She had expected Tabitha to be weeping, but as far as she could tell, Tabitha was not crying. The two of them simply held each other and allowed the warmth of sympathy and love to envelope them like the comfort of a cozy blanket.

"Mom?" Tabitha whispered.

"Yes, honey?"

"Be careful."

Molly was completely caught by surprise. "What? Me?" She tensed.

Tabitha nodded slowly, her head still on Molly's shoulder. "Yeah."

"Why me? Careful how?"

"I'm worried about you."

Molly grinned. "Well, I'm not pregnant either."

Tabitha chuckled then. It wasn't much of a chuckle, but it helped ease Molly's tension.

Tabitha nodded again. "Good." Then she sighed. "It's not that. I just don't want you to get hurt again."

"Are you talking about Mike?"

Tabitha shrugged. "Just be careful, okay?"

Molly held her daughter more tightly. *I'm trying. Heaven knows I'm trying.* "Okay."

"Go slow."

Me? She's telling me to go slow? "I'll try."

"Do you love him?"

Hopelessly. Madly. "Maybe."

"But what do you really know about him? I mean, what if he's, you know, wearing a mask?"

Where did that come from? Mike? Does she know something bad about Mike? Is there something bad? Something he's hiding?

But he's so good. He's such a good guy.

But I thought the same thing about Jerry. And I didn't really know Jerry. Not at all. How can I be sure I know the real Mike Kilmore?

Molly patted her daughter's back. "Okay. I'll be careful." *I'll try. No, I will. Not just for my sake and Mike's, but for yours, my precious girl.*

THUMP-THUMP-THUMP-THUMP!

Mother and daughter shrieked at the sudden pounding, a loud knocking at the door. Jerking out of each other's arms, both leapt to their feet. Molly scrambled to the kitchen drawer, withdrew the gun, and thumbed off the safety.

THUMP-THUMP-THUMP!

She went to the door, weapon in hand, trigger finger pointed down the barrel. "Who is it?" she demanded.

Tabitha appeared at her side. The girl held White Lettie's broom in both her hands. Tabitha wielded the heavy broomstick like a staff—like a weapon.

Molly motioned for Tabitha to get back, out of danger. But the girl refused, her face grim and determined.

206

"Who is it?" Molly demanded again.

"Molly? Molly? Is that you?"

The voice sounded horribly familiar—a voice Molly had hoped she'd never hear again.

Jerry? Here? No!

"Go away," she shouted. "It's late." *What is he doing here?*

"Molly, it's Jerry. I know it's late. B-but—"

"Go away!"

"Come on, Molly! It's f-freezing out here. I've been searching and searching for this place. Got lost! The top on my car is busted. I've been d-driving around in this crap for over an hour. Come on! Open up, will ya?"

"Dad?" Tabitha said. "What's he doing here? He can't come here! Make him go away!"

Molly could hear the panic and terror in her daughter's voice. *You're not getting to Tabitha, Jerry. We're here because of you!* "Go away, Jerry!" Molly yelled. "I'm armed. I have a gun. You can't just drop in here unannounced, uninvited." *And I would never invite you. Never!* "Go away! Now! Leave us alone!"

"Molly, I j-j-just want to t-talk. Listen, I left Randy. I kicked him out. I'm trying to change, Molly. It's so c-cold!"

"Go away. Get out of here. Go back to D.C.. We don't want you here!"

Silence for a moment. "Look, I'm coming to the window. D-d-don't sh-shoot, okay?"

"No!" Tabitha's voice. "Go away, Dad! We don't want you here! You can't be here!"

Molly watched the window with trepidation, but Jerry didn't appear there.

"Tabitha?" Jerry called through the door. "Is that you?"

Tabitha said nothing in response.

"I'm coming to the window," Jerry said. "Don't shoot. Please, d-don't shoot. I just want t-to talk."

And then he was there, casting a long, distorted shadow on the curtains. From that angle, the shadow wasn't man-shaped—just a void of darkness against the yellow glow of the porch light. "Tabitha, look, I'm s-sorry. I know I was awful this summer. I'm so s-sorry. I should have prot-t-tected you. And I didn't. P-please. I just want another chance. A ch-chance to get to know you b-better." A pause. "It's so c-cold! Look, I want to have a relationship—a real father-daughter relationship— before you walk out of my life c-completely. I love you, Tabitha."

"Go away, Dad!" Tabitha cried. "I *hate* you! You're sick! Disgusting! You let Randy… Just go *away*!"

"Tabitha, honey—" he began.

"Don't call me that! I hate!"

BOOM!

The house rattled as if shaken by an explosion.

Tabitha shrieked.

And Jerry's shadow was gone.

"What was that?" Molly checked her finger on the gun. For a second, she thought she'd fired the weapon. In that small space, the noise of a gunshot would have been deafening.

I didn't shoot. What was that? A sonic boom? A jet?

Tabitha tore past Molly, still clutching the broom in one hand. Tabitha unlocked the front door and yanked it open.

"Tabitha!" Molly cried. "No!"

But Tabitha was already out the door.

Molly followed on bare feet, into the freezing rain and onto the dusty driveway— now turned to mud.

And she still held the gun.

Tabitha was kneeling over Jerry's prostrate form.

"Tabitha," Molly said, her voice preternaturally calm, in spite of the thundering of her heart. "Get back." Molly aimed the gun at Jerry, but kept her index finger straight down the barrel. She circled around to get a clear shot, if necessary, at the man who had destroyed her life, destroyed her family.

I swear, Jerry, if you make a move…

"I'm sorry," Tabitha was saying. "I didn't mean to."

Jerry's face was cast in shadow. "I'm okay," he said. "H-help me up." He raised a hand toward Tabitha.

"Tabitha," Molly repeated, getting closer. "Back away. Now."

Tabitha stood and took a step backward.

Jerry's hand shot out, going low, grabbing Tabitha by the ankle.

Tabitha cried out. She stumbled, but managed to stay upright.

"Yes!" Jerry shouted. "I knew it!" He sat up, still clutching Tabitha's leg.

Molly moved her finger to the trigger. "Let her go, or I'll—"

Jerry jerked his left hand in Molly's direction.

Something slammed against Molly's chest. Her finger jerked. A flash of fire and thunder as the gun went off, the shot going wild. Molly fell backward, slamming into the muddy ground. The wind exploded out of her lungs.

She struggled for breath, fought to pull in air with a diaphragm paralyzed by the impact. Her head spun.

"No!" Tabitha's voice. Screaming. Terrified.

Tabitha!

Molly fought through the lights flashing and swirling in front of her eyes like blazing fireflies.

She sucked in a lungful of air.

One ragged breath. Two.

Her chest felt as if she'd been struck with a baseball bat, but she sat up, and pointed the gun at Jerry.

But her hand was empty. The gun was gone.

Molly struggled to her knees. *I'm coming!*

As her vision cleared, she saw two figures—Tabitha and Jerry. Tabitha swung the broom at her father, swung it back and forth.

Jerry, clutching his right arm to his chest, backed away from the girl, holding his left arm up defensively.

"Go away!" Tabitha screamed, punctuating her command with another swing of the broom. "Get out of here!"

Jerry stumbled backward. His right forearm was bent in the middle at an unnatural angle.

"Leave us alone!" Tabitha swung the broom handle again.

Jerry lurched away, out of reach of the weapon. He stumbled backward, toward his car, fishing awkwardly in the right pocket of his pants with his left hand.

A stream of curses spewed from his mouth like a verbal fountain of raw sewage.

"Get out of here!" Tabitha yelled. "Never touch my mother again. Do you hear me? Never touch her again."

Touch me? Did he throw a rock at me? Is that what happened?

"And never, never touch me again." Tabitha's voice was still loud enough to carry through the falling rain and snow, but it was calm. Calm and unmistakably lethal. "I will kill you. Do you hear me? I will kill you."

"I'm going, damn it!" Jerry sputtered, still struggling in this pocket. "Just let me get my damn car keys!"

The pocket ripped, and Jerry pulled something—a key ring—from the ruins of his slacks.

He turned and clambered into his car, a convertible of some kind—with the roof down. After a long moment and frantic movements within the car—and a lot more swearing—he got the car started. The headlights flooded the night with harsh light, forcing Molly to shield her eyes. The convertible backed up, turned, then, tires spinning on the muddy driveway, careened away, barely missing their old Impala.

Molly sat at the dining table, cleaning and oiling the gun, just as her dad had shown her. The act of cleaning the weapon gave her something to do with her hands while she strove to calm her jumbled thoughts.

Could have killed him. Could've hit Tabitha. But I still wish I'd shot the bastard. No, I don't. I couldn't live with—

I would have, though. I would've killed him to protect my little girl. God forgive me, but I would've shot him.

They'd found Molly's gun, searching by flashlight. The weapon had lain in the mud, a dozen feet from where Molly had been knocked to the ground. Molly had insisted on locating the gun, on not leaving it in the mud, on not leaving the two of them defenseless through the night.

I would have killed him. Without shedding a tear.

But she *had* wept, the whole time they were searching—not that anyone could've

THE WITCH OF WHITE LADY HOLLOW ~

seen her tears in the freezing rain.

The weapon was finally clean. However, Molly continued to wipe it down.

Tabitha stood by the front window, running her finger over the glass. She'd examined the glass a number of times since they'd come in, after they'd both taken warm showers and gotten dressed in clean nightgowns and warm socks.

Not that either of them expected to get to sleep that night.

Molly had almost called Mike Kilmore. Almost. But Tabitha's talk of masks had sown just the tiniest seed of doubt. *I'll call him first thing in the morning. Jerry won't dare come back here. Not tonight. He'll be in the emergency room.*

"Are you sure you're okay?" Tabitha asked, her back still to Molly.

Molly gazed at her daughter with a touch of amazement and more than just a touch of pride. *She fought him off with that old broomstick. My little girl fought him off.*

Damn you, Jerry. Why can't you just leave us alone?

She shook her head, shaking off the anger, like a dog shaking off water.

My little girl.

"Mom?"

What was the question? Oh, yeah. "Yes, Tabby-Cat. I checked. No bruises. Except to my pride. I can't figure out what he threw at me, though. I looked around for a rock or something, but…"

Tabitha shrugged. "And the window didn't break."

The window? What an odd thing to say. "Why would the window break?" Then it came to her. "The sonic boom. I guess we're lucky. It sure knocked Jerry on his butt." She allowed herself a small, wicked grin. *Mike's rubbing off on me.*

Maybe I'll call him. But that'd wake him up. And he'd come over. And hold me.

She blew out her cheeks.

It'd be okay. Tabitha can chaperone. No. I'll call him tomorrow. First thing.

Molly grinned wickedly again. "Knocked him on his butt."

Tabitha chuckled, and there was an element of wicked delight in there as well. "Yep. Sure did. Right on his butt. And the window didn't break. Like it was mostly directed just at him. Cool."

"Maybe," Molly said, considering, "being outside, he was more affected by the jet or meteor or whatever it was."

Tabitha shrugged again. "I guess it worked out just right."

Molly made one last pass around the gun with the oil rag. "Yeah, and you sure did a number on his arm." She grinned as she got up and put the gun back in the drawer.

"After what he did? I'm glad." She paused. "Not really, I guess, but… He could've killed you, Mom."

Molly joined Tabitha at the window and put an arm around the girl's shoulders. *And I could've killed him.* "But he didn't. I can't believe the gall. The unmitigated *gall* of the man, coming out here. Who does he think he's fooling?" She twisted her face and said in a low-pitched, nasally voice, "'I'm trying to change.'" She sounded nothing like Jerry, of course, but it made her feel better to mock him.

A little better.

Tabitha shook her head, staring out the window. Her mouth was drawn in a grim, determined line. "He's not fooling me, that's for sure."

"I wonder what he really wants? Just to mess with our heads? Inflict more pain?"

"I know exactly what he wants," Tabitha said. "Me."

"But why?"

Tabitha scowled. "But he's not going to get me. Not if we can help it."

"I'm going to protect you, Tabby-Cat." *Even if I did a terrible job tonight. But my little girl and her witch's broom can really kick butt!*

"We'll protect each other." Tabitha turned toward Molly. Shadows hid the girl's eyes. A trick of the light, perhaps, but those eyes appeared to Molly as if they were tiny points of light sunken in twin caverns of darkness. "Don't worry, Mom." The coldness of Tabitha's voice, the absolute lack of emotion, seized Molly's heart like a claw of ice.

"Dad won't hurt us ever again."

It wasn't as if Tabitha particularly *wanted* to go to Miss Tulane's class that morning—she really didn't want to face the history teacher—but Tabitha was late.

And Tabitha hated being late.

To her, being late was the same as breaking a promise. And if there was one thing her father had taught her—unintentionally, and only by his negative example—it was that keeping a promise—or a covenant—was important.

It was sacred.

Tabitha had already picked up her tardiness hall pass from the office—over the objection of the school secretary. The bespectacled, older woman with bottle-blonde hair, too-red lipstick, violet eyeshadow, fake eyelashes, and heavy, musky perfume had said, "It's only five minutes, young lady. Just go on to class, already."

But Tabitha had insisted. She was late, and she carried her hall-pass like a badge of penance—like a scarlet letter.

And so, she jogged down the hallway, her long, blue skirt gathered in her left hand. *Show some leg or be even later.*

Miss Tulane probably won't even be there, not after last night. It'll be some substitute.

During the long night in which neither Tabitha nor her mom had slept for more than a cumulative hour or two, Tabitha had finally decided on just how to refer to Bradley Thibodeaux—in her mind, at least. In public, of course, she'd refer to the history teacher as she always had.

Not my secret to tell.

But in her mind, to evade gender-specific references, she would think of the person she knew as Miss Tulane as simply that—"Miss Tulane." *It's just like when somebody has their name legally changed. I bet that's exactly what Bradley Thibodeaux did. So, I call that person by the new legal name.*

At first, it had felt awkward and stilted—*It's going to be weird being in Miss Tulane's class. I wonder how Miss Tulane will treat me in Miss Tulane's class?*

THE WITCH OF WHITE LADY HOLLOW

Will Miss Tulane treat me like I'm Miss Tulane's enemy now?—but it felt more comfortable than using pronouns which felt dishonest.

And Tabitha despised dishonesty, lies, and the masks people wore that concealed their true selves.

I'm lying to Mom. But I'm doing it to protect her. You keep telling yourself that, Tabby-Cat.

The last thought had come in her mother's voice, and it frightened and sickened her.

Just before Tabitha reached Miss Tulane's classroom, she let go of her skirt and slowed. She was still out of breath—but at least she was modest—when she stepped through the open door.

Miss Tulane won't even be there.

But indeed, Miss Tulane was there, teaching and smiling with the customary exuberance. The teacher wore a blue dress, black nylons, and matching blue heels. The hair and makeup were impeccable, if a little too fancy for school.

Just like normal.

Even in her mild shock at finding Miss Tulane in attendance, Tabitha noticed two things about the teacher's appearance that were *abnormal*—the shortness of the skirt and depth of the neckline. Miss Tulane's legs and cleavage were on display, and that display bordered on being inappropriate for school. Perhaps, wildly inappropriate.

Miss Tulane was sending—no—*screaming* a message. *And that message was, I'm a woman!*

"I'm glad you made it, dear," the teacher said in that rich, practiced alto. "We're talking about the women's suffrage movement. You won't want to miss it."

Miss Tulane looked at Tabitha with that wide, pretty smile—looked at her, but didn't exactly meet Tabitha's eyes. "Take your seat, please."

Tabitha complied. She opened a notebook and prepared to take notes.

Miss Tulane continued, "Wyoming was the first state to grant women the right to vote."

Tabitha glanced around the room. It seemed as if the eyes of every boy in the class were glued to Miss Tulane, gawking at the teacher. More than a few adolescent male faces wore lascivious grins as they stared.

Is that drool?

Tabitha's quick breakfast of corn flakes suddenly sat uneasily in her stomach.

"However," said Miss Tulane, "I'll bet most of you would never guess what U.S. territory granted the vote to women just a year later." When nobody raised their hands, the teacher said, "But I'd bet good money, if I were a betting woman, that *one* of you does." Miss Tulane paused, then raised an eyebrow. "Tabitha?"

Tabitha looked up at Miss Tulane, and although the teacher was obviously looking back at her, from Tabitha's perspective, Miss Tulane, once again, avoided Tabitha's eyes.

Tabitha took a deep breath. She actually *did* know that one. Or was pretty sure at least. "Utah?"

Miss Tulane's smile widened in delight. "Yes! You see, it was thought that by giving women the vote in Utah, those women would vote *against* Mormon polygamy. But guess what? Women voted overwhelmingly in favor of polygamy!" A frown replaced the smile. "So, what do you think happened? When women didn't vote the way the government wanted, guess what? Congress took it away! How about that, ladies? Vote the way the men want, or they'll take the vote away. Now tell me, is that right?" The teacher's head shook. "No. It stinks! By show of hands—just the girls, now—who agrees with me?" Miss Tulane raised a hand with an expensive diamond bracelet around the wrist.

The hands of every girl went up. Some had shot up enthusiastically. A few had put their hands up more slowly—in particular, a couple of freshman girls who'd openly made nasty remarks about Mormons in the past—out of Tabitha's sight, but not out of earshot.

"Okay, boys," said Miss Tulane. "How many of you think it stinks? Raise your hands."

The male hands shot up with unanimous enthusiasm. One boy, Jay Ellis, lifted both hands. "Votes for women! And here's to lots of wives!"

Most of the boys sniggered. So did a few of the girls.

"Male chauvinist pig!" snapped one girl.

"Dang right!" said Jay with a leer at the teacher.

Miss Tulane laughed and clapped once. "Okay, that's enough." The teacher smiled. "So, you see, women's rights, our value as people shouldn't be dependent on what men…"

You're talking about women's rights and our value as people, but you're dressed like that? Don't you see how the boys are looking at you?

Well, yeah. Of course, you do.

As Tabitha crossed the open space between buildings on her way to second-period calculus, still pondering her confused, turbulent thoughts about Miss Tulane, she spied Beulah's car sitting in the temporary parking spot in front of the office. And inside the car, sat Beulah. Tabitha waved. However, Beulah didn't wave back.

She's late too. Gotta check in at the office. Beulah's not as concerned about tardiness as some people, but missing all of first period?

Maybe she's sick. Ooh, that wouldn't be good. Especially with the show next week.

I should check on her. Tabitha glanced at her watch. Still time to get to class. She gathered her skirt and trotted over to Beulah's car.

As Tabitha approached, she noticed two things—Beulah's hair was puffy, and the blonde was crying.

Should I?

Tabitha didn't want to hear about whatever sexual escapade Beulah had

214

recently—very recently, judging by the still-fluffy ponytail—been engaged in, but Beulah had been there for Tabitha enough times…

Tabitha tapped on the window.

Beulah's head shot up. She stared at Tabitha with eyes rimmed by smeared mascara and eyeliner. And the expression on her face bespoke terror. "Tabitha?"

"Are you okay?" Tabitha ventured. *Of courses she's not okay! Isn't it obvious?*

Beulah shook her head. "Please!" She hid her hands in her face. "Don't look at me!"

She's never been ashamed of frizzy hair and what that means. Tabitha had seen Beulah arrive at school with frizzy hair before. She'd even seen Beulah sporting a fluffed-out ponytail between classes or after lunch. Although, how Beulah found the time had always been a mystery to Tabitha.

But Tabitha had never seen her friend weeping. And appearing in public with her makeup such a mess? Maybe lipstick a little mussed, but mascara? Never.

Tabitha stepped around to the passenger-side door, and finding it unlocked, slipped into the seat. "What happened?"

"Just—just go away. Please."

Whatever happened, she didn't even take a moment to clean herself up.

Once Tabitha had managed a better look at Beulah, it was obvious the girl had gotten dressed in an extreme hurry. The bright orange of her top didn't match the pink of her pants. Even her socks were mismatched. And that wasn't like Beulah at all.

If her clothes are like this, that means she just threw them on at home.

"Please," Beulah whispered. "I just need a minute. I'll get myself together. Then I'll go in. You can go on ahead."

Sex. At home.

No.

I knew something was wrong at home. Something wrong. For a long time. But not this.

"Was it"—Tabitha could barely force the words out—"your dad?"

Beulah's face transformed from shock and terror, to rage. "That—that's *sick*! How could you even suggest…" A howl of rage burst from her. She swung a fist at Tabitha. In the confines of the car and given the angle, the blow missed. "Get out! Leave me alone!"

Tabitha opened the door and quickly climbed out of the car. But even as she retreated, she said, "It's not your fault, you know. It's *his* fault. *All* of it. You had no choice."

"Sick whore! Filthy slut!" She bowed her head, and her body was wracked with sobs. "Sick. Whore."

Tabitha stopped herself just as she was about to shut the door.

Then she slid back into the seat. Awkwardly, tentatively, she put her arms around the sobbing, trembling girl.

Beulah flinched, but made no move to push Tabitha away.

Tabitha said nothing more. She just held Beulah until her friend's tears were spent, until Beulah had regained a measure of calm.

But there was no calm, no peace in Tabitha. Rage grew, pulsing inside her like poison coursing through her veins. She felt like a cobra, tensed, coiled, and ready to spit venom on the world of men. But she knew she must keep the rage in check, lest she blow the doors off Beulah's car or break the windows.

First my dad. Now hers. Sick. Monsters.

I hate them. I hate them all.

Just dads? Or all men?

No. Not all.

I need one, at least.

"So-o-o"—Joey gave Tabitha a conspiratorial wink—"what was it you couldn't tell me in physics class?" They stood alone on the fifty-yard line of the school football field. The gloomy clouds portended rain or even snow. "You wanna talk about your Book of Mormon out here? It's chilly, babe. Why not in the cafeteria? You don't want people to hear us or something?"

As soon as Mr. MacDonald's fourth-period class had concluded, Tabitha had dragged Joey by the hand to the deserted gridiron. Her handclasp hadn't contained an ounce of affection or even friendliness. It had been insistent, commanding. Angry.

She released his hand and stared up at him. "I need your help." The coolness of her voice belied the lava seething inside her. *Keep it under control.*

At least out here, there'll be no doors to slam.

Joey beamed at her, and under other circumstances—under normal circumstances, or anything even *approaching* normal—that bright smile would've made her pulse race.

Her pulse *was* racing, but that had nothing to do with Joey's charm.

He tipped his head as if in deference. "How may I serve you, my goddess?"

I wish you'd stop calling me that. I don't know what I am, but right now I don't feel like a goddess. "I've got something to tell you. Something awful. But you can't tell anyone. No one else. Do you understand me?"

His smile faltered, then creased into a serious frown. "Yeah. Sure."

"I need you to promise me."

He nodded. "Yeah. I promise."

She hesitated, looking up at him. He towered above her, like a mighty, sheltering tree.

Like the tree Magnus had ripped from the ground. Using her power.

I promised Beulah. But I have to trust him. I need him. I can't do this without him.

Do what exactly? What am I prepared to do?

But in her heart, she knew exactly what she intended to do. She'd begun formulating what she would do as she sat in Beulah's car, comforting her best friend. She had finalized her plan in the ladies' room as she'd helped Beulah clean herself up.

And so, she jumped in. "Beulah's father. He's molesting her forcing her to have sex. With him. *Raping* her."

"Her... dad?" Joey's eyes were wide and white in his dark face. His lip quivered as he dropped his voice to a whisper. "The Reverend?"

The whisper was unnecessary. Not a soul was within earshot.

Calling that devil "Reverend." What a sick joke. Tabitha nodded grimly. *But so is calling him "dad."*

Joey swore. He turned his head away and swore again. "You sure?"

Tabitha nodded again.

"How can you be sure? She...she told you?"

Tabitha shook her head. "No. I found out on my own." The image of her friend— weeping, disheveled, destroyed—filled Tabitha's mind. She shut her eyes as if she could somehow blot out the picture. *I'm sorry, Beulah. But I need his help.* "I can't tell you more. I shouldn't have told you this much. I promised Beulah, but... But I need your help."

Joey shook his head. Disgust and horror fought for control of his face. "Does she... Is she? Does she want...en—enjoy?"

Tabitha pressed her lips together in a straight, determined line. Her molten rage had risen almost to the brink of eruption. "Does it matter? He's her father. Her *dad*. He's supposed to *protect* her, not not hurt her—not use her like a whore. And no. No. No way. I saw her. She was so messed up. You should've seen her." She shuddered, shaking her head in violent, vehement denial. "No. Nobody should see her like that. You have no idea."

Joey gulped and looked as if he might be sick. "Poor Beulah. Poor, sweet..." His face twisted in rage. "That sick bastard!"

Tabitha nodded, closed her eyes, and took a deep breath, shoving the magma back down into the volcano. "Yeah."

"I'll kill him. I will. I'll *kill* the bastard!" A tear fell down his cheek. "Poor Beulah. Poor baby." He swiped furiously at his suddenly wet face. "I'm gonna kill him!"

"No." Tabitha forced her voice to be even, calm, almost robotic. "Killing him would be too easy—and too good for that beast."

"Kill that sick son of a—"

Tabitha gripped his arm, cutting him off. "I have a better idea." She bared her teeth in a savage grin. "A *much* better idea. Will you help me?"

He hesitated, then nodded slowly. "Yeah. I'm in. All the way in."

Abruptly her rage cooled. It was no longer a volcano on the edge of eruption, just a pot simmering on a stove. Still boiling, but in control.

She had decided.

She had an ally. A partner.

THE WITCH OF WHITE LADY HOLLOW

And a plan.

A plan which should have terrified her.

She gripped his hand, firmly, but without anger. She felt the Power flow from her and into Joey.

He knew what she needed from him.

"Just to be clear," she said, "we do things my way. *Exactly* my way."

He nodded in grim agreement. "Command me."

"Take us to the *Reverend's* church. Stay low and keep to the woods so no one will see."

"As you wish, goddess."

As they rose off the ground and the sweetness of the Power surged through her, Tabitha said, "I'm not a goddess."

With Joey siphoning off, controlling her power, Tabitha could at last embrace her rage.

"I'm a witch."

The Reverend Billy Martineau rocked out, filled with the joy of the Holy Spirit. "Jesus is just alright with me!" The Doobie Brothers 8-track blasted from the chapel's spare-no-expense sound system, and Billy gyrated on the stage, stomping, clapping, and howling along with the raucous music. "Jesus is just alright, oh yeah!"

Billy could *sing*, of course. He could sing well. He could sing *pretty*. He could, and frequently did, bring the dear, sweet ladies of his congregation to tears with "When I Survey the Wondrous Cross" or "How Great Thou Art," wringing rapturous sobs from their souls with his God-given talent. But this—this was not a song for *singing*. This was a song which made him feel like howling at the top of his powerful lungs, howling like a wolf at the moon.

Like a wolf among sweet, tender, defenseless lambs.

"Jesus is just alright with me!" He shimmied his hips like Elvis. How Billy would've loved to be a rock star like Elvis Presley, but being a pastor was much easier. A pastor didn't have to travel, he had a captive audience that worshiped and adored him. And besides, with his full head of perfectly coifed blonde hair and movie-star good looks, the Reverend Billy would've bet good money he got as many women as ol' Elvis the Pelvis. Being a man of God was just alright with Billy Martineau. "Jesus is just alright!"

He pounded both fists on the great oak pulpit, overlaid with polished cherry wood. Atop the pulpit, a gold-plated steel crucifix—a foot tall if it was an inch—trembled.

Billy strutted and pranced over to the drums and dropped down on the drummer's stool. In the absence of any drumsticks, he pantomimed pounding on the snares and symbols, thumping out an actual bass beat with the pedal of the bass drum.

The chorus repeated as the song began to fade out. "Amen!" the Reverend roared. "I gotta use that one for sure tomorrow night." *No broadcast on Wednesday nights—no royalties to pay to the Doobie Brothers.*

Suckers!

The band probably can't learn the song by tomorrow, so we'll just play the tape.
The next song, "White Sun," began to play.

Billy groaned. *Not that one!* "Marty, that's enough," he said into his microphone, shading his eyes against the bright stage lights with one sweaty hand. "Shut it off."

The music cut off abruptly as the unseen sound engineer, Marty, pulled the 8-track cassette. "You got it, boss. You know, we'd get better sound out of an LP." The voice blasting over the sound system filled the cavernous chapel.

"Y'all got an LP of that one?"

"No, boss."

"Can y'all get one before tomorrow night?"

"Probably not, boss."

Billy smiled, having won the argument. "Then the 8-track'll have to do, I reckon. 'Sides, I wanna take this one with me in the car." Which was, of course, the real reason. How Billy loved blastin' an 8-track in his T-Bird! Made him feel like Burt Reynolds in *Smokey and the Bandit.*

"Hey," said the disembodied voice. "I gotta make a phone call. Can I take ten?"

Reverend Billy waved in the direction of the sound booth at the back, near the roof of the spacious sanctuary. "Go on, Marty. Take your break." *Smoke one for me, young fella.* And, yessir, Billy wanted a toke! But his dope-smoking days, along with his youth, were gone. A pastor couldn't indulge in such diversions as weed. At least, not so folks could see. Or smell. "Y'all just put on something else for me."

"What do you want?"

Billy gave an exaggerated shrug—a stage shrug. "Surprise me. But make it something that *kicks*—that really *yanks* the Holy Spirit down from Heaven."

"You got it, Reverend."

And the rock-and-roll screams of KISS filled the sacred space. The 8-track, another of the Reverend's favorites, started mid-track with "Shout it! Shout it! Shout it out loud!"

"Praise Jesus!" shouted the Reverend in a near paroxysm of sacred joy. *Tomorrow night is gonna rock!*

What's the blessed sermon about? The evils of fornication? Weed? Or is it some other foolish thing?

Who cares? Just make it up as I go. Them's the best sermons.

'Sides, I feel like shouting my joy to the Lord!

The first payment from the TV broadcasts of *Reverend Billy's House of Prayer* had just come in. The first check for two hundred grand had cleared the bank, and the off-the-books payment of twice that much was hidden in the new, larger, and heavier wall safe. *Let's see them sons of bitches haul that one away.* Yes, the good reverend did indeed feel like celebrating.

And of course, he'd started the celebration off with a round of Holy Love that morning. Oh, his Baby Girl had been sweet! He never came to her—or "went in unto her," as the Good Book said—in the mornings. But that morning, he'd felt the divine need, and Mary was still too drunk, as usual, from the night before to minister unto him in the way the Lord demanded.

So, instead, he'd cheerfully taken his little blonde, blue-eyed gift-from-God as was his divine right. And that morning, she'd let loose with an unexpected flood of tears. Perhaps it was because she wasn't expecting him or perhaps it was simply that her bottom was still raw and bleeding from the hiding he'd given her the night before. She'd come home a couple hours late, her hair all poofed-out like some nigger whore. And he knew what the poofy hair meant—it meant she was desperately in need of correction and repentance for the sin of fornication. As the scripture said, "Spare the rod"—or in this case, the belt, buckle and all—"and spoil the child."

She hadn't bawled like that, not in the act of Holy Love, at least, since she'd been eleven and barely ripening—since the night he'd first claimed her as his own. And, oh, her tears made it all the sweeter! *Maybe we should always start out with a good strapping. After all, a little humiliation is good for the wayward soul.*

He smiled beatifically. "Praise Jesus."

KISS howled, "Shout it out loud!"

He raised his fists toward heaven. "GOD! IS! GOOD!"

The song faded, replaced with the much quieter, much tenderer "Beth."

Deflated, the Reverend Billy sighed at the ballad, but he wasn't about to make the trek up to the sound booth to change it. *Might as well run through the sermon at least once.* He snapped his fingers! J*esus's grace! That's it. Grace is always a crowd pleaser.*

Folks just love to be told that Jesus will save 'em in the end, no matter what they do. It comforts 'em, poor sinners, knowin' they can go on sinnin' and Jesus will save 'em, so long as they believe.

Now, where was I?

He smiled. *Oh, yeah.*

"For God may beat us with a few stripes," He pantomimed the action of whipping. *Just like I whipped Beulah's lovely behind last night.* "Yes, indeed He may! He may beat us with a few stripes, for we have all—every last one of us—we have all sinned. But if you have been sa-a-ave-duh"—he paused for effect—"yes, if you have been saved, as I have, by the Grace of Lord Jesus, and as so many of you have…Praise Jesus! Can I get a amen?"

He paused again, raising his hands as if the empty hall were filled with rapturous worshippers shouting, "Amen!"

The music cut off. *Marty's back. Sooner than I thought he'd be.* That suited the Reverend just fine. *Always better with an audience. Even an audience of one.*

"Yes," Billy continued, raising his voice because he had someone to preach to. Even without a microphone, he could make his voice carry with the near-perfect—and costly—acoustics of the sanctuary. "Yes, my brothers and sisters, if you have been *saved*, you will be caught up to meet Him in the glorious Rapture! Caught up, I say! Caught up in the air to mee-ee-ee-ee-EE-EE!"

Billy screamed as he was lifted up into the air. He floated, suspended as if by an

221

unseen hand, a dozen feet below the vaulted ceiling of the sanctuary. The massive speakers of the sound system hung from the ceiling, suspended by cables, below him.

He flailed his arms and legs and wriggled like a worm impaled on a fishhook. His body tilted slightly head-downward as if he were about to slide headfirst down an invisible playground slide. Down to the stage. A hundred feet below.

His screams trailed off, but his breathing remained rapid and shallow, the rapid thundering of his heartbeat, pounding in his ears.

Though Billy was still hyperventilating, the expression of horror on his face was replaced by a manic smile. "This is it! The Rapture!" He twisted his body, attempting to right himself, to turn himself toward the heavens. "I'm ready, Lord Jesus! Take me to Thy bosom!" His efforts were in vain, however. He was still pointed toward the ground. His smile faltered as the blood pooled in his face. "Let me see Thy glorious Face, Lord Jesus! I praise Your holy name! Jesus! Je—"

"You think you know Jesus?" The voice was everywhere, echoing through the vast emptiness of the chapel. "You think you know God? That you know *anything* about Him?"

The omnipresent voice sounded British and unmistakably female. And it was definitely pissed.

"God?" Billy forced his smile to return. "You're a-a-a woman?"

Laughter filled the chamber, echoing and reverberating off the walls, the ceiling. "You think I'm God? Tell me, *Reverend*, is your theology so malleable that you'll believe anything? Anything that gets you what you want?"

Billy swallowed. "Yea, Lord, I will believe anything You say."

Another laugh, shorter and devoid of mirth. "I'm not God. And trust me, Billy, you don't want to meet God. You would rather the mountains fall upon you and hide you from the Presence of God."

Sweat dripped down the Reverend Billy's face, slipping from his forehead and into the abyss below. He looked about wildly, desperately seeking escape. Or the source of the voice. "Lord"—he tried to swallow, but the lump in his throat felt as big as a baseball—"Lord L-Lucifer?"

And there was silence in the heavens for the space of several seconds.

The voice spoke again. "Tell me, Reverend, if I told you I was the Devil, would you switch allegiances so quickly?"

Billy hesitated for only a moment before nodding his head vigorously. With the blood pressing on his face and brain, the act of nodding was painful. But he didn't care. "Yes! Lord Lucifer! Let me do thy bidding!"

Another laugh, longer that time, cold and cruel. "Oh, Billy, Billy, Billy. You have been doing Satan's bidding for a very long time. But no, Billy, I'm not the Devil. I'm just someone who *despises* evil men. And you, Billy, are an evil man. As wicked and sick and evil as they come."

Billy felt his lunch of chicken enchiladas churning in his stomach, fighting its way down toward his throat. "No-no-no! I'm a *good* man. I *save* people!"

"Oh, so now you're back on the side of the angels, Billy? You're switching sides so fast it's like watching a theological tennis match. Now, you save people? I thought only God could save us."

"I-I didn't mean it like that."

Another quick laugh. "Oh, yes you did. You see, Billy, it's all about *you*—you and only you. You live for the worship. You get these people to worship *you*, like some idol in a gold lamé jumpsuit. And when they do, how do you repay their adulation? You *steal* from them. You bilk them out of their money to pay for your cars, your clothes, your jewelry, your mansion, this false temple to the blessed name of the Reverend Billy Martineau."

"N-no! That ain't right! I—"

"But that's not all, is it, Billy? No. You seduce their wives and their daughters. Then when you get them pregnant, you pay for your victims to abort their babies. And if they don't want to go have an abortion, you bully them. You threaten them. Tell me, Billy—how many babies have you murdered to cover your sins? How many innocent children have you murdered? Like wicked King Herod?"

Billy shook his head, but his head hurt something awful. His face felt as if it might explode, his eyes as if they might burst from their sockets. "I ain't murdered no babies. I ain't done nothin' like that!"

"Liar." The word was spoken calmly in that feminine, British accent.

"I ain't—"

And Billy fell.

The stage rushed up at him. He didn't even have time to scream.

He stopped. Just above the floor.

Stunned and trembling, as if he'd forgotten to breathe, he sucked a lungful of air.

He hung there, his face just a couple of feet above the stage floor. Billy reached down and clawed desperately at the carpet. But his fingers could find nothing to grab hold of.

"Don't lie to me, Billy. Whatever else you do in these final moments you have left, don't lie. It will be so much worse for you if you lie."

"I'm sorry!"

"I don't believe you."

He was yanked upward again. He stopped abruptly, suspended above the stage once more.

"How many babies have you murdered?"

"I—" Billy's stomach emptied itself, the half-digested chicken enchiladas streaming out into the void below Billy's mouth.

"How lovely," said the voice. Somehow, the British accent gave the sarcasm an extra bite. "How many, Billy?"

"I—I don't know." His hands flew up and out. "Don't drop me! Please! I really don't know. Twenty, maybe. Thirty. I don't know!"

"Name them. Name the women and girls. Name your victims."

And Billy did. Blubbering, with tears raining from his eyes and snot stringing from his nose, he named them all. He named a few twice, sometimes because he'd impregnated them twice and sometimes simply because he was terrified. Mostly, however, he stumbled over the names of women and girls who had been more forced than seduced. And in spite of his fear, he tallied them in his mind.

"Well done, Billy. We're finally getting somewhere. I suspect this is the first time you've spoken honestly in quite a while. I counted forty-four. Does that sound right, Billy?"

Billy nodded. And vomited again.

"Forty-four innocents murdered to cover your sins. You know what they do to those babies? They shred them. They rip them apart while they're still alive. Yes, Billy, you've been doing Satan's bidding for a very long time. Isn't that right, Billy?" The voice paused, then repeated in a much sterner tone, "Isn't that right?"

"Yes!" Billy sobbed.

"And that doesn't count all the women and girls who didn't get abortions—the ones you just seduced or raped. Name them. And if you raped them, say so."

So, Billy named them. All of them. He remembered them all. And after the names of so many—too many—he said the word: raped.

"Well, Billy, you're a regular Elias Thibodeaux. Bet you have the legendary Thibodeaux blood in you. Bad blood. Bad men. Evil, wicked men. Are you a wicked man, Billy?"

"Yes!"

"Say it."

"I'm a wicked man."

"But that isn't all, is it, Billy?"

"I—I d-don't know what y'all're—"

His body rotated, seemingly of its own accord, until he was upright. He drifted, high in the air, to the right and forward.

"Look down, Billy."

He complied. He was directly over the huge oaken pulpit.

Or more precisely, he was directly over the gold-plated steel crucifix at the front.

Billy's legs were forced apart as if by strong, invisible hands. And into his confused, terrified mind came an image—himself, years ago, forcing apart the legs of a frightened, resisting woman, Sally Griggs, the young, pretty, brunette wife of his sound tech, Marty. As far as Billy knew, she never told Marty. Sally took her own life some months later, taking her secrets and her shame to the grave.

"If I drop you now, Billy," said the voice, "you'll be impaled on that gaudy cross, won't you? You'll likely survive, but your precious and prolific manhood—if it can be called such—will be crushed, severed, destroyed."

"No! No! Please!"

"Tell me what else you've done. To your own child?" The pitch of the voice rose in anger. "To your precious daughter, entrusted to you by God? To your own little girl, whom you should have protected?"

"I—I—"

"Say it! Say it, or I'll drop you, and you can say goodbye to your—"

"I slept with her!"

"You mean you raped her!"

"Yes!"

"Say it!"

"I RAPED HER!"

"And how old was she when you started this?"

"Eleven!"

Billy fell, screaming, legs open, toward the cross.

"NO!" shouted the voice.

And Billy stopped, mere inches from castration and emasculation.

He hung there sobbing, blubbering, unable to move his legs.

But the voice was silent.

Billy felt warmth spread from his crotch and down his leg. For one terrifying moment, he thought it was blood. When he saw the urine streaming past his sock and shoe to the floor, he was actually relieved. "Thank you! Thank you! I—I'm s-s-so sorry."

"All right, Billy. I'll give you a chance. Just one chance to escape intact. Are you listening?"

"Yes! Anything! I'll do anything!"

"You're going to leave Blue Beech Ridge. Forever. You will leave the state and never return. You will not go home. You will not go to the bank. You will not pass 'GO' and you will not collect two hundred dollars. You will not attempt to contact Beulah or your wife. Ever. You will not touch them or pollute them or violate them anymore. Do you understand?"

Billy nodded. "Yes! Yes! I understand. I promise."

"Your promises are worthless. Promises are sacred. They should be kept. But you, you are a lying, worthless, waste of skin. Take your car and run away. And never come back. Because, if you do…"

Billy rose into the air. He hung just out of reach of the vaulted ceiling. Then he fell. Screaming.

And landed on the carpet of the stage, face-down in his vomit.

"Go! Run away and don't look back."

Billy, wobbling on his feet, a urine-soaked sock squishing wetly in his alligator shoe, ran from the chapel.

Hide in the woods. Come back tonight. The money in the safe.

When he reached his car—a cherry red T-Bird sporting a bumper sticker that read, "WARNING: In case of Rapture, this car will be unmanned!"—Billy fumbled for his keys. He dropped them to the parking lot pavement inside the brightly painted yellow lines of his reserved parking space. With a gurgling sob, he bent and picked up his keys. *Take Beulah with me. She'll come. Make her.* His hands trembled, and snot bubbled from his nose as he forced the key into the door lock.

Wire for the money in the bank.

He felt something press against the back of his head—something hard.

He froze.

"Put your hands in the air," said a calm voice, "and turn around slowly."

Scared as he was, Billy felt relief that the voice was masculine. He raised his hands, turned around, and beheld a familiar face. "M-Marty?" After the shock of recognition, Billy could focus on only one thing—the gun barrel pointed at his face. The scent of gun oil, pot smoke, urine, and vomit filled his nostrils.

Marty extended a hand. "Give me the keys. Slowly."

And slowly, Billy complied.

The sound technician led the Reverend at gunpoint to the back of the car.

"Listen, Marty, I—"

"I'm done listening to you. I heard what you said in there. So, keep your trap shut."

Marty opened the trunk, reached in, and grabbed the tire iron. "Get in."

"It was witchcraft! That's what it was. She *made* me say those—those lies. It's not my fault!"

He glanced at Marty, and the sound tech was smiling, a rictus grin, full of teeth. His eyes were red and devoid of humor. "You know," Marty began, "I knew something had happened. I knew somebody had hurt her. My Sally... She never told me. Never breathed a word. She just checked out. And then she took those pills. I found her, you know. She was already cold. Cold and pale. Her eyes all milky. She was pregnant, they told me. A baby girl. Only now I know it probably wasn't mine. We'd been trying for years and..."

Marty's smile twisted into a scowl of rage. "I came to you! For counsel! For comfort! You hugged me. Told me she was a troubled soul. You sick son of a bitch."

"It was witchcraft! Y'all saw!"

"Yeah. I saw. And I heard. Don't care about the how, 'cause now I know the truth. Now, get in."

"Why should I?" Billy was blubbering again. "Just gonna kill me anyway."

Marty's rictus smile returned. He pointed the gun at Billy's groin. "Get in now, or I shoot you in the nuts. You'll probably die eventually, but you won't die quick and merciful. And trust me, Reverend, you don't deserve mercy."

For one mad moment, Billy thought of making a run for it. But Billy Martineau was a coward of the yellowest stripe.

Wait 'til he ain't lookin'. Kick out the back seat. He got in the trunk. *Wait for my chance.*

"Lay on your back."

Billy complied.

"You stink, Reverend. Pissed yourself, did ya?" Marty raised the tire iron.

Billy sucked in a terrified gasp. He held up his hands to protect his head.

But Marty wasn't aiming for Billy's head.

Marty swung the iron down and shattered Billy's right kneecap.

Blinding pain filled Billy's world. He opened his mouth to scream, but the scream died in his throat when his left kneecap shattered as well.

Pain blossomed in his left arm, then his right.

A rag was shoved into his mouth before he could give voice to his agony. The cloth tasted of motor oil and brake dust.

From far, far away, Billy heard a voice. Some part of his brain recognized the voice as Marty's. "That's just being practical, so you can't escape. But don't worry, Reverend. I'm not going to kill you just yet. Oh, no. I want you to suffer, suffer for a long time. For the rest of your life actually—however long that's gonna be. But it won't be near as long as my Sally suffered. And where we're going, nobody'll ever find your body. I know a fella that's got hounds. And he keeps them hungry. Won't be nothing left of ya. But before I close the trunk, and we get on our way, I have a gift for you. A gift from Sally."

Something about those last words brought Billy back to full awareness. He watched through a haze of agony and horror as the tire iron came down one more time. And Billy knew exactly what the target would be. He flailed his broken arms and tried to close his ruined knees. But he was too slow. The iron caught Billy squarely in his groin. Crushing. Obliterating.

Agony consumed his mind, turning the world white. Two more blows followed the first, until finally, mercy—of a kind—came to the Reverend Billy Martineau as his mind shut down, sending him, *temporarily*, into insensate oblivion.

The empty parking spot behind the church sported a sign which read, "RESERVED for the REVEREND BILLY MARTINEAU."

Tabitha scanned the parking lot. She didn't know what the pastor's car looked like, but she suspected it wasn't the aging Ford parked nearby.

Joey still held her hand, and she could feel the gentle, tingly flow of the Power as it moved into him. To Tabitha, it felt as if her body was a powerful engine purring at idle. Joey was not *doing* anything with the Power, but he was ready to channel at a moment's notice.

He squeezed her hand. "Do you think it worked?"

Tabitha shrugged. "Well, his car is gone." *I can't believe we just did that.*

"But he could come back."

"If he does"—Tabitha took a deep breath—"we'll have to be more persuasive." *Go away, you sick fraud. Go away and leave Beulah alone.*

"Hell, yes." Joey growled low in his throat. "You should have let me castrate the son of a—"

"No! We do this my way or not at all. We did enough." *I hope.* "You cannot use my Power...*my* Power to hurt people."

At least we didn't actually hurt him. Or kill him. I couldn't live with that. Not even that creep. I should be shaking. How come I'm not trembling?

Joey grasped her shoulder with his free hand, forcing her to face him. "But what he did to Beulah! And all those other women. Girls." He trembled, and a sob burst from him. "And those b-babies! I didn't know they"—he gulped—"shred them up...alive." A murderous rage twisted his handsome face. "I wanna kill him. It's not enough! I wanna kill him a-a-and every last one of those bastards who shred up babies! It's not enough to just scare them!"

"What we did was enough! At least for now." She reached up and laid a hand on Joey's cheek. His skin was rough, sandpapery with midday stubble, and wet with his tears. "At least for him. I don't think he'll be back."

Joey searched her eyes. "He better not. Because, if he does come back, I swear I'll do it myself. I'll cut his damn nuts off and feed them to him."

He deserves it. "Come on. Let's get back to school." *He deserves that and worse. But I can't do that. What we did just now, in there was bad enough.*

Joey nodded. They rose into the air, a few feet above the ground—low enough to fly quickly, but lower than the tops of the trees, low enough to stay out of sight. In moments, they were speeding through the woods which separated the church and the school.

It won't come out. Beulah won't be humiliated. And she'll be safe from her father. Sick, rotten, miserable excuse for a dad. Her rapist.

For a minute which seemed like an eon, the two of them were silent, each lost in his or her own thoughts.

But Tabitha didn't like where her thoughts were going. She felt darkness gnawing at her soul. *Think of something else.*

But she couldn't. All her thoughts ran toward the darkness, toward the pit. *What I did was incredible. It was terrifying. The Power… That's it. Focus on the Power.*

Tabitha broke the silence. "How do you do it?"

Joey glanced at her quickly. "What?"

"Channel the Power? How do you make something or someone do what you want?"

"Oh, that." He shrugged slightly. "I look at my target. I have to see it. Line of sight, you know. Then I just think about moving it."

"That's it?"

"Well, for the simple stuff. The heavier it is, the more I have to concentrate. Or sometimes, the smaller or more delicate the task, the harder I have to focus. Making the air move or amplifying sound, that takes practice. I have to imagine the air itself moving or forming a cone—even though I can't see it. It's hard to explain. Just takes practice. But Magnus can make lights appear. Well, he can if you're in the Circle. I have no idea how he does that. Maybe he's manipulating photons or something. I don't know."

Tabitha nodded. "Maybe. Better put us down behind the stadium. So, nobody can see."

"Good idea." He paused. "I'm sorry. I just lost it back there."

She squeezed his hand. "I understand. I really do."

They settled to earth just inside the woods. Tabitha could see the stadium.

"We'd better get to class," she said. "Sorry about lunch. I bet you're starving."

"I'm fine." But he didn't look fine. He looked angry and distant. He let go of her hand abruptly, almost as if her touch was something disgusting.

A surge of rage washed over her body, but then the wave broke. *It's like when he's channeling my Power, he siphons off some of my anger too. Does that mean he's feeling my anger?*

He locked eyes with her, and a barely controlled rage smoldered in his gaze. "How do you know all that stuff about he babies? I mean, 'cause my great-aunt says they're promoting—no, pushing abortion in black neighborhoods—even some of the black churches, even some of the *pastors*, up in St. Louis. How do you know about what they do in those abortion places?"

Tabitha suddenly felt like she wanted to vomit. "I know because that's what my"—she almost gagged on the next word— *"father* does."

"What?" The shock and pain were starkly visible in his eyes.

"He doesn't do the abortions. He schedules them. He's an administrator in a clinic. That's basically all they do there—kill babies."

"Your dad?"

Don't call him that. I don't want him. I hate him. She swallowed the lump of acid which wanted to force its way up and out of her throat. "Yeah. He jokes about it. And he jokes about targeting black neighborhoods."

"Your dad," he growled through clenched teeth, "is one sick bastard."

Tabitha nodded curtly. "Evil."

"Yeah. That's the word."

Tabitha scurried toward fifth-period choir, ignoring the press of other students likewise on their individual journeys through the halls of BBR High. Tabitha's mind was a distracted muddle of anger and revulsion—at the unholy Reverend Billy, at her own father and at herself.

I didn't hurt him. I didn't. I just scared the pee out of him. I had to. I had to stop him from hurting Beulah. Never again.

But what if he comes back? Tabitha swallowed and felt herself stand a little straighter. *Then I'll do it again. Scare him even worse the next time.*

But she wasn't sure she could do that again—that or anything like it. Using her Power—wherever the Power came from—to hurt another human being, even one as despicable as Billy Martineau, made her feel dirty.

Like squishing a worm on the sidewalk after a rainstorm. Whenever it rained, Tabitha scrupulously avoided stepping on the bloated, stranded earthworms. Or tried to. Sometimes, try as she might, she would flatten—or worse—partially flatten one of the poor, disgusting creatures. And then she'd feel awful. Worse than awful.

But spiders? Tabitha had no qualms about crushing a spider under her heel.

Spiders deserve it. They crouch in wait until some helpless creature gets trapped in their webs. Then they drink its blood.

That's it. Billy was a spider.

Was? Why am I thinking of him in the past tense? Joey and I didn't...

Joey! I wish I didn't have to involve him.

Tabitha stopped dead in the middle of the hallway.

"Hey, watch it!" A boy's voice. From behind her.

Tabitha muttered, "Sorry," but her response had been automatic. The fact that she'd almost caused a collision or that she was standing stock-still in the middle of a rushing throng of teenagers barely registered on her.

He didn't kiss me goodbye.

She could picture Joey's face when they'd parted in the woods behind the football field. His expression had been cold, almost unreadable.

And he hadn't bent down to kiss her. At the time, tenderness had been the furthest thing from her own mind.

All this anger…

The bell rang, snapping her back to the present.

She realized with a start that the hallway was deserted. She was alone.

And she was weeping.

"Miss Moonshadow?"

She spun around, dashing her tears away.

Vice-principal Hardin strode toward her from the far end of the hallway. He adjusted his glasses as if squinting at her. "Miss Moonshadow? Yes. I thought that was you."

Tabitha didn't much care for the man, due to his handling of the incident with Ol' Waddle, but he was, after all, the vice-principal. *Be nice. 'Cause, I'm late. Again.* She forced a smile and assumed a calm she didn't feel. *Gotta hold it together. I'm an actress.*

"And here I thought I was being so sneaky, blending in among the natives. What gave me away?" She made a sweeping, dramatic gesture at her long skirt. "My unique fashion-sense?"

Hardin actually smiled. A little. "You do tend to stick out a bit."

Tabitha curtsied. Then she shrugged and pointed at the choir room door, barely a dozen yards away. "Sorry. I'm late. Just daydreaming, I gue—"

He waved dismissively. "That's no nevermind right now." He paused. "You've been crying?"

Tabitha hastily retrieved a makeup compact from her bag, flipped it open, and looked at herself in the mirror. Her gasp—at the sight of mascara running in rivulets like black blood from her red eyes—was followed quickly by a growl of frustration. She dug furiously in her bag for a tissue, then swiped savagely at her ruined makeup.

"My dear"—there was genuine concern in the man's voice—"whatever is the matter?"

"Nothing. Really. I'm…" *It's hopeless. Just making it worse!* "I just need a minute to…" Tabitha gestured to her face.

"Of course." He pointed at the ladies' room a few yards behind him. "Y'all just take a moment to collect yourself." As Tabitha scurried past him, the man inclined his head in a slight bow. "I'll wait right out here."

He's going to wait? Am I in trouble?

Standing in front of the restroom mirror, staring blindly at her mascara-streaked reflection, Tabitha froze in a moment of gut-clenching, adrenaline-pumping terror. *He knows! He knows what I did! Beulah's dad is back. He drove straight to the school, and he told everyone!*

She closed her eyes. *No. Stop it!* She took a deep breath, held it briefly, then exhaled. *He's gone. Nobody saw us.*

She quickly wiped away the smeared and streaked makeup. Took another deep breath and stared at herself in the mirror. *I'm an actress. I can do this.*

Her hands barely trembled as she touched up her mascara and eyeliner. She didn't wear heavy eye shadow—not like most of the girls—but she had to blend the edges of her eye shadow a bit.

They don't know. Her eyes narrowed as a flush of anger washed over her again. *The Reverend Billy Martineau is already in Arkansas by now. The sick coward.*

She drew another deep, calming breath and tucked her makeup back in her bag. *They don't know. Nobody knows.*

Vice-principal Hardin stood in the middle of the hall, facing politely away from the ladies' room. Whatever else the man was, Tabitha suspected he would not be caught dead staring at the door of the ladies' room.

But he must've been listening for the door, because he instantly turned around. He nodded in approval at Tabitha's hasty cosmetic triage. "Miss Moonshadow, if you'll come with me?" He pointed back down the hall, away from the safety of the choir room—in the direction of the office.

Tabitha hesitated for an instant, then turned and walked in the direction indicated. Out of the corner of her eye, she could see Hardin following. "Am I in some sort of trouble?"

He chuckled. "Should you be? You got a guilty conscience?"

Tabitha flushed, half in embarrassment, half in irritation. "No, sir."

He laughed a bit louder. "Well, if y'all're in trouble, it's not with me. Or the school. There's just someone who wants a word with you."

Tabitha's heart almost stuttered. "Someone?" *The police? If it's Brother Kilmore... If he really is Magnus, maybe he does know what we did. Maybe Joey told him.*

"You know, Miss Moonshadow, I'm very much looking forward to the show." *The play?* "You are?"

"It's one of my wife's favorites. I'm kinda partial to it, myself. And I'm hearing tremendous things. *Tremendous* things. 'Specially about your performance, young lady. You know, BBR High hasn't ever done anything of this caliber before. And the budget! But I hear y'all are really doin' us proud."

Why is he being so chatty? I'm so scared I'm ready to wet myself, and he's just going on.

He laughed softly. "Listen to me just going on. But it really is an exciting thing. Do you know both performances are sold out completely? Have been for weeks. We're adding folding chairs at the back and along the sides. Just don't tell the fire chief. Maybe we'll add a matinee. Well, our Miss Goldsmith certainly is doin' a fine job, a fine job, 'specially for such a young teacher. Just between you and me—but what with that *incident* on the first day of school and all, I'm sure you'll understand—the school board was more than a little concerned about hiring…well, a

Mormon teacher. But pretty is as pretty does, as the sayin' goes. Well, here we are." He indicated the open front doors of the school offices and his own office beyond. "You go on in. Y'all can talk in my office. In private. I'll wait out here. Holler if y'all need anything."

It's not the cops. It can't be. He wouldn't be talking like this. He wouldn't be so cheerful.

"Who is…" Tabitha asked, but as she turned her head toward Mr. Hardin, he had already turned his back on her. *Who wants to talk to me?*

She froze, rooted to the spot. *It's him! It's Reverend Billy!*

Clenching hands suddenly slick with sweat, she took one tremulous step toward the open office door. The door seemed to grow larger, looming like the open maw of a ravenous beast.

It can't be him. We scared him off. He puked. Peed his pants. It can't be him. He'd never make it back to the school so soon.

She took another step, then another, shaking like a last dying leaf clinging to a bare branch in an autumn wind.

She crossed the threshold. A desk with a chair, a guest chair, framed photographs and certificates covered the relative sterility of the office. But these barely registered on her. There was no one else in the room. Not a living soul. *Who is it?*

Behind her, the door closed.

She jumped, then whirled about, smacking her bag against the guest chair.

"Hello, honey."

Dad?

He wore a navy-blue overcoat. The right sleeve hung empty at his side. His right hand, encased in a bright-white plaster cast so only the ends of a thumb and four fingers were visible, peeked out from under the coat. Tabitha could just see the end of a sling holding his right arm across his chest. The virgin whiteness of the plaster testified to the newness of his injury. But if he was suffering any pain from the break, he didn't show it. He bared his teeth in a wide grin—feral and hungry.

And he stood between Tabitha and the closed door.

Tabitha glanced around quickly, desperately seeking a route of escape, but other than the pane of glass in the door, the vice-principal's office had no windows.

Trapped.

She swallowed hard and dried her sweaty palms on her skirt. She gripped the strap of her bag tightly. "What are you doing here?" She backed away, maneuvering to place the desk between herself and the man who'd returned to upset and invade her life. She shrank against the back wall as if she might fade into it.

Her father cocked his head and stared at her. "I told you last night. I want to get to know you. *Really* get to know you. To have a relationship with my daugh—"

"Bull. Crap." She enunciated each word separately. The blatant lie infuriated Tabitha, and her anger almost subsumed her fear. Almost.

He shook his head, smiling sadly. "Listen, honey…"

"Don't call me that!"

He appeared genuinely puzzled. "What?" He blinked stupidly.

"Don't you ever call me that. My mother calls me Honey. My *mom*. She raised me, took care of me. She was *there*! Not like *you*." She imbued the word "you" with all the hatred and loathing and disgust she felt for the creature in front of her.

He nodded slowly. "Fair enough." Although he blocked the exit, he made no move to close the gap between them. "I wasn't there for you. I abandoned you and your mother. That was wrong. I'm sorry."

"Bull. Crap. I don't believe you. You can take your fake apology and your lies and your misogyny and just go away. Leave us alone."

He shrugged. "I can't do that, hon— I'm trying to change. I…want to make up for—"

"You can't! You can't make up for the years of—of… And Randy! I was so afraid. The whole time I was with you! You can't make up for that!"

He lifted his injured arm slightly, winced. "Randy's gone. I threw him out. He's a pig. I can't forgive him for how he treated—"

"You let him! You laughed at me. Told me to *deal* with it! I had to sleep in the bathroom! He said he was going to 'make a real woman out of me.' And you didn't even care!"

"I was wrong. I'm sorry. I—"

"Stop saying that! I don't believe you. You sick, perverted—"

"Tabitha, I can't help what I am. It's not my fault. God made me—"

"Bullcrap." Tabitha straightened up, no longer leaning against the wall. "All you sick creeps invoke God. 'God made me do it.' That's no better than 'The devil made me do it.' Well, God did not make you abandon your family. God did not make you treat women like garbage. God did not make you do anything. That was all *you*!"

His expression hardened, lines appearing at the corners of his eyes and mouth. "Your mother and I—"

"Don't you dare talk about her!"

He laughed softly, low and bitter. "I can only *imagine* the things she's told you. You've only heard her side of the story."

It was Tabitha's turn to laugh. "Oh, she never told me. But I know *all* the things you said. All the things you did." Tabitha gripped her skirt with her right hand, her fist encircling the outside of her pocket—the pocket containing her mother's iron washer. "I know everything. You see, dear, old, nasty father of mine, I've *seen* it all."

A puzzled look crossed his face. "How would you? How could you possibly know…"

Masking her fear, she let the anger rise to the surface. She bared her teeth and emitted an evil chuckle. "I'm a *witch*. Or haven't you heard? I know every last nasty, despicable thing you did to her. You sick bastard. You had no right to treat her—or *any* woman—that way."

He scowled then, and disgust was written plainly in the twist of his lips. "I never laid a hand on her. Not once."

"You tried to *kill* her last night!"

234

"She pointed a gun at me!" Anger smoldered in his eyes. "And besides, I didn't touch her. And you know it."

"No, you didn't touch her." Tabitha took a step forward, still keeping the desk between them. "But you touched me, didn't you?" She clenched her teeth and growled, "I know why you're here. And I know what you really want."

"Honey, I don't know what—"

"Bullcrap! Do you even know *how* to tell the truth?"

"It's not like that, Tabitha, honey."

"I told you not to call me that!"

He held up his left hand in a placating gesture. "Okay. Look. I'm sorry."

Tabitha narrowed her eyes and grinned like a wolf confronting a cornered rabbit. "I broke your arm. *I* did that."

He looked down at his broken limb and wiggled the fingers of his right hand as they protruded from the end of the cast. The movement appeared to cause him pain, and he hissed. "That was an accident."

A chuckle growled low in Tabitha's throat. "Yeah. Right."

"Okay. Fine." He sneered at her. "But you can't wield it. Not on your own."

Tabitha's feral grin widened. "Are you sure of that? You hurt my mother. So, I. Hurt. You." *But he's right. It was an accident. I couldn't duplicate it, not intentionally.*

He shook his head. "You need a man." He straightened as if pride added a foot to his stature. "A *special* man. One in a million."

Tabitha sneered back at him. "Like you?"

"Like me." He sidestepped to his left as if to move around the desk. To get to her. To touch her.

To steal her Power.

Tabitha took a step to the left, echoing his movement and keeping the desk between them, staying out of his reach. "You're not a man. A man—a real man— keeps his promises, his covenants. And he doesn't treat women like things to be used and then thrown away."

He took another step to the left, and she countered with a step of her own.

"I told you," he said through gritted teeth, obviously struggling to keep his anger under control, "I'm trying to change. I've learned a new appreciation for women."

She coughed up a bitter laugh. "You mean a new way to use us. To use *me*."

He took another step. She countered.

He said, "We complement each other. A man—a *special* man—and a *special* woman working together—"

"You will *never* have it." She shook her head decisively. "It's not yours. It's mine. And I will never let you touch it or me again."

Naked anger twisted his features. "You little bitch!" He lunged across the desk at her, his left hand extended, grasping like a vulture's claw.

"No!" The word exploded from her lips.

BOOM!

Her father flipped backward, like a drunken acrobat attempting a backward handspring. Face-first and inverted, he slammed into the office wall. Framed pictures and certificates shattered and crashed to the floor.

Tabitha heard a sickening crunch.

Her father screamed.

Ignoring her fear and loathing, Tabitha scrambled around the desk which, in spite of her rage-fueled outburst of the Power, hadn't budged. Not even a single paper or paperclip had been disturbed. When she saw her father, she stopped—well out of his reach, but she needn't have bothered to keep a safe distance.

Her father lay, crumpled on the floor. He clutched at his good left arm with the fingers of his newly plastered right hand. But his good left arm was "good" no longer. It bent crazily a couple inches short of the wrist.

Jerry screamed again. He looked at her, pain and terror and hatred in his eyes. "Bitch! Little bitch!"

The door of the office burst open. Vice-principal Hardin stood in the door, flanked by two school secretaries. Their eyes were wide with shock, and Mr. Hardin's glasses were askew. "What the hell?" he cried.

"He—he—" Tabitha wrung her hands. "He hit the wall!"

"Little bitch attacked me! She hit me with…" Jerry flung his gaze around the room.

He needs an explanation! He can't tell them the truth.

"She hit me with—"

Tabitha cut him off. "He lunged at me. Across the desk. He hit the wall. Hard."

The vice-principal nodded curtly. "Call an ambulance." When neither secretary moved, he shouted, "Now!"

Both women scrambled out of view.

Mr. Hardin knelt beside Jerry, but his hard eyes stared at Tabitha. "Is that what happened?"

"She attacked me!" Jerry shouted. "Little bitch."

While he let fly with a loud string of profanity, Tabitha muttered something about "noncustodial parent" and "no unannounced visits." Then she finished with, "He tried to grab me. And he fell. I didn't touch him."

Hardin nodded, curtly. "Get on to class. I'll let you know what happens. Go on."

Tabitha fled the room.

Once in the hall, she gathered her skirt and sprinted toward the relative safety of the choir room.

I did that. I broke his arm. I broke both his arms. I didn't mean to.

Did I?

Halfway down the hall, she slowed as she fought for control of the maelstrom of emotions.

He can't use me now. He can't touch me. A hysterical laugh escaped her. *I didn't mean to hurt him. I didn't!*

Another of her father's distant howls echoed down the hall, splitting and multiplying, chasing her like a psychotic lynch mob. Doors of various classrooms opened, and curious students and teachers alike peered out.

Mrs. Wardle emerged from her classroom and peered out with wide, cow eyes from behind her spectacles. However, upon spying Tabitha, she disappeared back inside and shut the door.

She thinks I'm a monster. I did that. Me. I hurt Dad. I broke both his arms with my Power.

What have I become?

Tabitha felt her gorge rise. She stumbled into the nearby ladies' room and barely made it to the sink before being violently sick.

"I told you before, Señor Boyardee, this here town just ain't big enough for the both of us." Tabitha stared intently at the bullet-ridden, corroded remains of the ravioli can. The can so ominously addressed perched alone upon a rock in front of the ruins of White Lettie's cabin in the Hollow. Months ago, Tabitha had aimed her mother's gun at the same tin menace as it had perched upon the same rock. On that day, Tabitha had eventually proven herself an adequate amateur markswoman—at least against empty metal containers. At the present moment, however, she felt as if she couldn't hit the broadside of a barn.

Maybe if I actually had a gun.

She tried pointing her index finger at the can and raising her thumb, in imitation of a firearm, but quickly abandoned the idea.

No. I've got to know if I can control it. By myself. Even if just a little.

I don't need him. I can do it by myself.

Softly she sang, "If they can do without you, ducky, so can I!" Only she wasn't Eliza Doolittle declaring her independence from Henry Higgins.

By myself. Without a man.

She had stared at the can for nearly a quarter of an hour. She had focused with all her might on her target.

But the can stubbornly refused to show any sign of movement, even so much as a rusty wobble.

Come on. Think it through. Maybe I can't move it like Joey does—just focusing on it and imagining it doing what I want.

It's only worked in the past when I was angry. Or scared. But I'm not angry, now. I'm just frustrated.

She rolled her head around as she'd been taught to do in choir class, trying to ease the tension in her neck.

Only when I'm angry. So, get angry about something.

There were plenty of things for her to be angry about—her father, Reverend

Billy, the possibility her mom might be dating Magnus, Problem #3 in her calculus homework that had taken nearly half an hour to solve.

But anger wouldn't come. No anger—only guilt and doubt in abundance.

I broke both his arms. I didn't mean to, but I couldn't control myself. I couldn't *control my Power.*

And I hurt him.

I could've killed him. It's not like I struck at his arm—I didn't. I struck at him. And he flipped backward, head over heels. The broken arm was just a coincidence. Right?

She knelt upon the moldering carpet of fallen leaves that covered the floor of the Hollow. She was alone in the woods with her thoughts, her doubts, and a rusted pasta can which stubbornly defied her efforts to move. In her mind, she pictured a young Joseph Smith kneeling in a wood far away, more than a century and a half before. He had knelt with his questions. And he had received an answer.

She glanced around to be absolutely certain of her solitude. And then she bowed her head.

Heavenly Father, I don't know what I'm doing. I don't even know who I am anymore. I don't know what I believe. Are You there?

She breathed out a low growl of frustration.

Sorry. Art Thou there? Dost Thou care about me? About my mom? She believes in You—in Thee.

I used to, unquestionably. Now, I just don't know.

Do we even matter? I mean, women—do we even matter? Where do we even fit in the Church?

We can't do anything. It's like, "Look after the kids. Be a good homemaker, a good wife. Look pretty. Be modest. Don't ask any hard questions—just sit down and shut up." Where do we fit, huh?

Where do I fit?

Do You…Dost Thou love me?

She paused, just breathing, drinking in the crisp autumn air, the scent of the decaying loam.

I'm supposed to listen. Listen for an answer.

Tabitha searched her feelings, searched her heart. And felt nothing—no feeling of peace, no burning, no whispering of the Spirit. Nothing.

An owl hooted.

Is that supposed to be my answer?

Silence, except for the rustling of a few bare branches.

I can do all these things. With Joey. Or Magnus. They don't even hold the priesthood. They don't hold Your… Thy power or authority. They don't.

Unless Magnus is Mike Kilmore.

Is he?

Silence.

Please! Answer me. Please!

She whispered, "Please. I'm so scared. I could've killed him…my da— my father."

Does this power come from Thee or from somewhere… someone else?

Even in her mind, she couldn't bring herself to voice her fear—the fear as to from whom the Power might emanate.

I didn't mean to hurt him. I'm sorry. I mean, I don't want him around. I don't want him to hurt me, to hurt Mom, but… I'm sorry.

Her praying stalled. She didn't conclude the prayer. It merely faded away as if she'd just run out of words.

Tabitha reached beside her and wrapped her hand around Lettie's broom. The heavy broom lay on the leaves. Tabitha had decided to bring the broom with her to the Hollow.

She didn't know why she'd brought it, at least not consciously. Perhaps as a weapon. Perhaps as a talisman—a symbol of what she was becoming, whatever that might be.

She rose to her feet, held the broom in both hands in front of her. She held it in an uncertain attitude as if she couldn't decide whether to sweep the floor or strike at imagined enemies.

Am I really a witch? What does that even mean? "Thou shalt not suffer a witch to live." Isn't that what the scripture says? Why? Because witches are evil?

The lines of her face creased in a frown. *Or is that just a way for patriarchy to suppress the natural power of women? We have more power than men, so kill us? Is that it? Is that it? Burn us before we can threaten their authority?*

She had found her rage.

She let it build, nursed it, squeezed it in her gut, ground it with her teeth.

And she turned it on the unsuspecting can.

BOOM! CRACK!

The can and the heavy stone upon which it sat exploded.

Wow. I mean, wow. I did it.

Breathing rapidly, Tabitha took several trembling steps forward to examine the blast crater, for crater it was. It extended back a few yards in a roughly conical shape. She could see chunks of rock, the remnants of the stone, scattered toward the ruin of White Lettie's cabin. Some of the rocks had dug furrows in the ground to mark the violence of their trajectory.

The can was nowhere to be seen.

But the devastation didn't stop there. Beyond the blast cone, an old blue beech tree had broken, its thick trunk snapped a few feet above its roots, the rest of the tree having fallen to the earth.

I can't believe I did that.

But something felt *off* about the destruction.

No burning smell. No smoke. No charring. Okay, so no heat. Just the Power. Just raw kinetic force. Raw. Force. Raw. Unfocused.

She shook her head violently. *I can't control it. Not like Joey. With him, it's precise. Like a laser beam. With me, it's like a grenade. A bomb.*

I'm a bomb.

She swallowed hard. *What if that had been a person? What if—*

"Tabitha!"

The cry had come from off in the woods to her right.

From the direction of home.

"Tabitha!" Her mom's voice, frightened, panicked.

Tabitha gazed in horror at the destruction she'd caused. *I can't let Mom see this!*

She gathered her long skirt and dashed out of the Hollow and into the woods, toward her mother's cries.

"Mom?"

Molly could see her daughter striding quickly through the woods toward her. "Tabitha!" Molly increased her own pace. "Are you"—Molly gulped down air as she stumbled forward—"all right?"

Tabitha waved. "I'm okay!" The girl seemed out of breath, almost as winded as Molly. Almost.

She's okay!

Tabitha was carrying the old broomstick they'd found in the Hollow. *Why's she got that thing? Never mind. I found her. She's okay!*

Ignoring the aching stitch in her side, Molly collided with her daughter and enveloped Tabitha in her arms. "I was s-so worried!" She could feel her heart thundering in her chest as she held her daughter close. "So scared!"

Tabitha managed to ease herself out of Molly's grasp. "I'm okay, Mom."

Molly put a hand on each of her daughter's shoulders and examined Tabitha's face. "Are you sure?"

Tabitha chuckled and shrugged. "Why wouldn't I be?" Then her face grew serious. "You *heard* that, didn't you?"

Molly nodded. "That big noise? What *was* it?"

"A tree broke. In the Hollow. By White Lettie's old cabin. It was the freakiest thing."

"And you saw it?"

Tabitha hesitated for just a moment, then shook her head. "No, but I heard it. I was right there. I mean, right there. Not under it or anything. But I saw it afterward." She raised her eyebrows and shrugged. "Freaky."

"I'm just glad you're safe."

Tabitha wrinkled her brow. "Is that why you're here? The noise?"

Molly shook her head, then pulled her daughter into her arms once more. "No. I heard about what happened at school." She felt Tabitha tense up. "With your dad."

Most of the girl's tension seemed to melt away. "You know about that?"

"Of course, I do! I went right over to the school as soon as I heard. You'd already left, so I went home. Then I came here."

"Who told you? Vice-principal Hardin?"

"Actually, it was Fergus MacDonald."

Tabitha pulled back and gazed at Molly with a quizzical expression. "Mr. MacDonald? My teacher?"

Molly nodded. *It should have been the principal. They should have called me right away, but Fergus beat them to the punch. He's still looking out for Tabitha, even after I told him off.*

Bless him. "But you're okay? You're not hurt?" *Jerry didn't hurt you?* She ran her hands down Tabitha's arms, checking for broken bones.

Tabitha nodded quickly. "Yeah. I'm fine." She let out a shuddering sigh. "Dad's not."

Molly swallowed the sudden flare of anger and revulsion she felt. "He had no right! Going to the school like that. Trying to get to you directly. The nerve of that creep!" *And I'm not buying that whole I-just-want-a-relationship-with-my-daughter crap.*

Maybe Fergus has a point. Even if it is a long shot.

"Honey, listen to me." Molly fixed her daughter with her eyes. "Until further notice, I don't want you to be alone."

"What?"

"I mean it. I'm worried about what Jerry—what your dad might do." *And if not him...*

"I don't think—"

"Promise me. Stay with me. Or with friends. Just don't be alone. Promise."

Tabitha nodded slowly. "Okay. I promise."

Molly managed a weak smile. "Come on. Let's get you home. And fed. And on to rehearsal."

They turned and headed toward the cottage. "It's getting late," Molly said. "I don't have anything fixed. Of *course*, I don't have anything fixed. I never do anymore."

"I usually just scrounge something up on rehearsal nights."

"I know. It's just that, I feel like I'm letting you down, honey." *I almost never see you on rehearsal nights. Not 'til you get home late.* "I feel like I'm not there for you enough."

"Oh, Mom..." Tabitha slowed.

Molly turned and looked at her precious girl.

Tabitha was crying.

"Honey, what is it?"

Tabitha threw her arms around Molly's neck. The broom, still in Tabitha's hand, bounced off Molly's backside. "Oh, Mom! You have *always* been there for me!"

Molly held her daughter close. Tears welled in Molly's eyes and spilled down her cheeks. "Always." *You're my baby. My little girl.* "Tabby-Cat?"

"Yeah?"

What's going on? What aren't you telling me? "You know, if there's something going on you know you can tell me, right? No matter what it is."

Tabitha squeezed her neck. "I love you, Mom."

That's not an answer. What is it? What are you holding back? "I love you too, honey."

Tabitha pulled herself free from the embrace and smiled through her tears. "Gotta get going."

Mother and daughter resumed their homeward walk. The silence was broken only by the muffled crunch of leaves under their feet.

What happened with your dad, Tabby-Cat? Please tell me. But Tabitha almost never talked about her encounters with Jerry.

She's okay. Physically. "I've got a Salisbury steak TV dinner, but that'd take too long. How does a can of ravioli sound?" P*athetic. We're keeping Chef Boyardee in business all by ourselves.*

Tabitha chuckled. She moved the broomstick to her other hand, then clasped Molly's hand. "Ravioli sounds perfect."

Tabitha was long gone, having been picked up by Beulah as usual. Her empty bowl, long bereft of the half-can's worth of ravioli and now filled with water, sat in the sink. The other half of the ready-made pasta was in the fridge, safely ensconced in a second bowl under Saran-wrap. Molly hadn't eaten. She had dinner plans with Mike Kilmore.

And Mike was late.

And Mike was late.

Molly let the curtain drop back into place and stepped away from the cottage window. *I need you, Mike. I need to talk to somebody.*

No, I need to talk to you, Mike.

It wasn't as if Mike hadn't been late occasionally. He was a cop, after all. Not always an eight-to-five job.

She checked her watch. *Only ten minutes. He'll be here.*

And besides, it wasn't as if she had nobody to talk to, not anymore.

When she'd answered her office phone that afternoon and recognized Fergus MacDonald's voice, she'd almost hung up. But Fergus had been quick and to-the-point. "Molly, there's been an incident with Tabitha at school. She's okay, unharmed, but—"

And so, Molly had not hung up, and she and Fergus had talked.

The conversation had necessarily been brief, because Molly had been desperate to get to Tabitha. But the distance, the tension between Molly and Fergus had evaporated, to be replaced by the mutual concern they both felt for Molly's daughter.

Thank you, Fergus.

It felt good to have her ally back. And her friend.

Almost as an afterthought, before Molly had hung up, the old man had said, "I've been wondering…now this is just a thought, but do y'all suppose Mr. Harris, Tabitha's father, might actually be—" He'd left the name unspoken. They never said the name where it could be overheard—or wiretapped. *Magnus.* "I mean, I don't know if he has the type of money we're talking about, but he could've engaged an agent here. Perhaps a law firm?"

At the time, it'd seemed like a ridiculous idea. *Jerry is Magnus?* But two things had nagged at her. The first being that Jerry seemed obsessed with Tabitha, and the second that Jerry did have a bit of money. How much, Molly didn't know. She'd never known, not that it'd been important. Not until that moment.

And here Jerry is in town, just as the play, the trap Magnus has laid for Tabitha, is about to come to an end. After the show, Magnus might not have any hold on Tabitha, any way to keep her in Blue Beech Ridge. So, it makes sense he'd make his move soon.

Or now.

Molly peeked out the window again. *Where are you, Mike?*

As if on cue, Mike's Mustang rolled into view.

Molly's pulse pounded like timpani in her ears.

Her palms were suddenly so sweaty, she could barely turn the frontdoor knob. And she nearly dropped her keys as she locked the door from the outside.

She turned around and there he was.

A moment later and she was in his strong arms, and he was kissing her, and she didn't care that her knees suddenly refused to support her.

Mike will catch me if I fall.

Several breathless moments later, he pulled his lips from hers and placed them near her ear. "You're okay?"

She nodded. Weakly. "I am now." She clung to him. *Don't ever let me go.*

"And Tabitha's okay?"

She nodded again. "At rehearsal. I told her to stay with others. Not be alone."

"Good." He kissed her again, long and hard. Then he smiled. "Hey, pretty lady. Have I told you how much I love you lately?"

She grinned back. "In a manner of speaking. Or of *not* speaking." *There is one question you could ask. And I'm ready, so ready to answer.*

"Sorry I'm late."

Doesn't matter now. You're here. "I'm sure you had your reasons."

He nodded, and the smile faded. "Yep. Tell y'all 'bout it on the way." He pulled out of the embrace and offered her his arm. "We better go. That old line at Ponderosa can get mighty long right 'bout now."

"Ponderosa? Again?" She breathed out an exaggeratedly dramatic sigh. But the truth was, she had a soft spot in her heart for Ponderosa. It'd been the site of their first date. "You're going to make me fat."

Mike's eyebrows rose, and his eyes widened in mock horror. "You? Fat? Woman, if that ever happened, y'all'd *still* be the sexiest woman alive!"

Bare trees arched skeletal fingers over the darkened road. The chill air felt heavy, as if threatening snow, but the clouds were patchy. The moon shone with a spectral light through the gaps. Mike waited until they got to the highway before recounting the events that had detained him. "I had myself a little chat with Mr. Gerald Harris."

Molly glanced over at Mike, his profile illuminated by the ghostly glow of the instrument panel. The thought of those two men facing each other—the man who had betrayed her and the man who seemed as if he'd die for her—sent a shiver of unease down her spine. "You did?"

"Yes, I did." He shrugged his shoulders slightly, then squeezed her hand. "Could've sent a deputy. Normally, incidents at the school don't warrant my direct attention, but when I found out Tabitha was involved—"

"Did you talk to her?" *She didn't mention anything about that.*

He shook his head. "Naw. Wasn't necessary. 'Sides, she'd already left school at that point. I was more interested in having a chat with the man who hurt you." He wrinkled his nose as if he'd caught a whiff of something particularly malodorous. "No. 'Man' is too good a word for that piece of, uh, garbage."

Another shudder ripped through her. She squeezed Mike's hand back. "Did you…" A series of indistinct but savage images flashed through her head—all of them involving Mike beating the living tar out of her ex-husband. H*e hurt my baby. And he could be Magnus.* "What happened?"

Mike chuckled softly, and Molly could detect an undercurrent of anger in that soft, wolfish sound. "You were gonna ask if I kicked his you-know-what. Well, I didn't. I wanted to." He paused as if attempting to suppress and control dark emotions. "I deal with a lot of rotten, messed-up people in my line of work. I can approach them with professionalism, even courtesy. But when it's someone who has hurt someone I love…" He squeezed her hand again, harder that time. "And I love that little girl of yours—not the same as I feel for you, of course—but I love her like my own kin. I know I won't ever get the chance to really be her daddy, but, well, she's important to me."

Molly nodded and looked away. "She's important to me too." But for reasons Molly couldn't quite put into words, she found Mike's words unsettling.

"Anyway, I caught up with him at the hospital." He chuckled again. "Broke both his dang arms! How clumsy do ya gotta be?"

Molly fought down a brief thrill of savage glee. "Yeah."

"He says Tabitha attacked him, says *Tabitha* broke his arms. And I told him, 'That little thing?' Got the better o' y'all? I'm havin' a real hard time believin' that, Mr. Harris. I just can't picture it in my head. Now, how exactly did she do that?' He said she shoved the desk at him, knocked him down. To which I replied, 'Let's just suppose that's true for a moment. That's a big, heavy desk. And y'all're trying to tell me a short, petite, little girl got the drop on y'all, shoved that desk so hard and so fast it took y'all by surprise and broke your arm?' Well, he stuck with that explanation. So, I said, 'The only way that's humanly possible is with adrenaline. I've seen people perform amazing feats of strength with adrenaline. But you know what? That means she had to have been scared out of her freaking mind. Now tell me, Mr. Harris, what in the world did y'all do to your own daughter to scare her that badly?' He didn't like that."

Molly shook her head. "I bet he didn't."

"Anyway, I told him he was facing a number of charges, including custodial interference and assault. At that point, he wanted to lawyer up. Says he has an attorney *in town*."

Molly gasped. "He does?" *Fergus said he might be working with a lawyer here. Could Fergus be right? Could Jerry be Magnus? Or at least in league with him?*

"Yeah. I thought it was pretty strange myself, but it makes sense if he's been planning this thing for a while. He'd need an agent here." Mike shrugged again. "So, I told him I'd be happy to put him in county lockup while we fetched his attorney, but I also told him he could just leave town, and we could let the matter rest. 'Leave Butler County and don't come back. Leave your daughter and ex-wife alone, and y'all can leave as soon as the doctors are done with you.'"

"What did he say to that?"

He shrugged. "It took some persuading, but I can be persuasive if I want to. Let the ol' Kilmore charm do its magic."

"You said you didn't…"

He laughed at that, glanced at Molly's face, then laughed again. "No, I didn't. I told you, I just *talked* to him. Honestly, Molly. I didn't lay a hand on him. Scout's honor." He lifted his hand, arranging his fingers and thumb into the Boy Scout sign.

Molly gave him a weak smile. "Okay." *Almost wish you had. Almost.*

"So, in the end," Mike continued, "he saw it my way. He's leaving tonight. Probably already gone. Soon as he and his *friend* check out of their motel."

Randy.

I knew it. So much for trying to change. "So, he wasn't alone?"

Mike waggled his lower jaw as if trying to dislodge something distasteful. "Nope. Some *fella* named Randy. I didn't bother questioning him, other than to confirm he would drive and ensure Mr. Harris got safely back to Maryland. Out of my county, out of my state, and"—he squeezed Molly's hand gently—"out of your lives. Out of *our* lives."

Please, God. Let it be so. "Mike?"

"I'm right here, darlin'."

"My, uh, source suggested Jerry might be Magnus." Molly watched Mike's face, looking for a reaction.

"He did, huh? Well, now that's interesting."

"You said he's got a lawyer in Blue Beech Ridge. He could've orchestrated this whole thing through the lawyer."

Mike nodded, scowling. "Perkins and Marsh. Should've put two and two together. I'll have to pay Mr. Marsh another visit."

"So, you think it's possible?"

"Possible? Sure. How likely? I don't know. But the fact that he had a lawyer before he even arrived, and its Marsh. I had assumed it was just 'cause of the custody thing." He glanced at Molly. "Does Mr. Harris have that kind of money?"

It was Molly's turn to shrug. "I don't know for sure. I know he's really good at keeping his money hidden. I never wanted a dime of his money, not even the court-ordered child support."

Mike growled. "So, it'd be in his best interest to keep any assets hidden. The creep."

"I suppose he might have some money. He does have some well-to-do relatives, but I haven't kept up with that."

"Tabitha's father as Magnus, huh? I never would've suspected, but, well, he showed today he sure as heck wants her for something."

"I just hope he's gone." *Please, Jerry! Just go away. Leave us alone!*

Mike scowled. "If he comes back, I really will, uh, that is, I'll throw the book at him."

"If he just stays away, that'd be enough."

"Molly, I swear I'll protect you and Tabitha. I promise." He paused. "I love you. And I won't let anything happen to you."

"I love you too." *And more importantly, I trust you.*

"And, Molly, if it came to it, I would lay down my life for you. And for her."
You know something, Mike Kilmore, I believe you would.

By the time they managed to sit down to dinner at Ponderosa, Mike with his T-bone and Molly with her New York strip, their mood had lightened. Molly was out on a date with the man she loved, and thoughts of Jerry and the events of the afternoon and the night before had evaporated like a bad dream. Jerry was gone, and Molly dared to hope the threat of Magnus might be gone with him.

Mike had taken her back to the site of their first date. And even if it wasn't the most romantic location in the world, it had romantic overtones for her. They laughed and joked and frequently reached across the table to hold hands.

And Mike couldn't keep his eyes off her.

Not that Molly could keep her eyes off him with his handsome, strong face, and twinkling blue eyes.

About the time they were finished with their cheesecakes, Mike said, "I didn't tell you the real reason I was late."

Molly gave him a tight-lipped, perplexed smile. "Okay. Something else unpleasant?"

He shrugged. "Could be. Depends. You might think so. Anyway, I had to make a stop to pick something up."

Mike slid out of the booth and took the two steps toward Molly's side of the table. He knelt and presented a startled Molly with a diamond ring. "Molly

Moonshadow, would you do me the very great honor of—"

In a most unladylike fashion, Molly launched herself out of the booth, nearly bowling him over, crying, laughing, and smothering his face with kisses.

And somewhere in the midst of all the joyous confusion that followed, with cheering restaurant staff and patrons looking on, Mike managed to finish his question, and Molly replied with many repetitions of "Yes!"

Later, when they parted at her doorstep, after a long, lingering, tender goodbye kiss that left her aching for more, longing for the night when "goodbye" would be "good night," Molly sat alone, curled up on her living room sofa. Dressed for bed in a warm nightgown and wrapped in her bathrobe, she sipped a cup of hot chocolate. The hot, soothing liquid warmed her.

She'd thought about lighting a fire in the fireplace, but that had seemed like just too much work. No, the hot chocolate was enough—that and the warm glow of her thoughts.

She sighed contentedly, then looked at the mantle clock. *Tabitha'll be home soon. Should I tell her tonight?*

Tabby-Cat, honey, you're going to have a new daddy.

She shook her head and frowned. *Nope. That won't do.*

Honey, you know that hunky, handsome Brother Kilmore? You know, the one you used to have a crush on...maybe still have a crush on...

A groan escaped her lips. *No good.*

I have to tell her. Maybe it can wait for a few days, but I have to.

And it'll be okay. She'll understand. She'll be happy for me.

She took another sip. Then she imagined her daughter sitting beside her on the sofa. Molly cleared her throat. "Honey, Mike proposed. We're"—she felt a lump in her throat and a joyful tear sliding down her cheek—"engaged. We're going to be married. In the temple. Probably the D.C. Temple. I love him. And he loves me. And he's not like your father. He's kind and he's loving and he's...perfect. And he would never, never betray me."

"Come to me." Magnus said into the phone. "I need you."

"It's a school night." Beulah sounded exhausted. "And it's been a...a bad day. And daddy's not home yet. He's real late. If he comes home and I'm not here. After we were together last night, you and me, and I came home late. He walloped me last night. He whipped me so hard, I..." Her voice trailed off.

Here it is again. She wants me to take retribution, to punish him. Perhaps even kill him. But he just got a whole lot more money. And I want it.

And right now, I want...

"I need you," he said again. *Not precisely true. I just need a woman. Hell, any woman would do right now. I'd even settle for Molly Moonshadow, but she's not an option, yet.*

"Please," Beulah said. "Not tonight. Please? I'm so tired. And I hurt so—"

Magnus gritted his teeth. "Yes, my dear. I understand. Get your rest. Tomorrow night, perhaps?"

"I—I don't know. Sure. I guess so. I'll be over. Soon as I drop Tabitha off after rehearsal. I love you. I'm your woman, right? Tell me I'm your woman? Your one and only?"

Magnus rolled his eyes. *So damn needy.* "Yes, my dear. You are the only woman for me. Now rest up."

He hung up. *Little bitch.*

He let out a long sigh. *So much for that. Still, things are going well, according to plan. The trap is closing. Soon, one way or another, I will have her. I'll have Tabitha. Then I won't need anyone else.*

He smiled. *Yes, all things considered, it's been a good day. Molly trusts me.* "Stupid bitch trusts me completely," he said aloud.

Yes, indeed. A very good day.

"What y'all got there?" Patsy pointed at the broom in Tabitha's hand.

"It's, um, just an old-fashioned broom." Tabitha knew that wasn't the answer Patsy was looking for, but suddenly, as other white-robed girls of the Circle gathered around them, Tabitha felt a reluctance to talk about it. She'd brought the broom to the weekly bonfire intentionally, of course—she'd even started bringing it to rehearsals—but suddenly she regretted it.

"A broom. I can see that much." Patsy's voice held just a touch of irritation. "So, where'd y'all get it? Is it an antique? It looks *old*."

"I found it. In the woods." *Stick to the truth, but I don't have to tell them everything.* "I think it's pretty old."

Cassie came closer to get a better look. She reached out a hand to touch the handle. Tabitha fought the urge the yank the broom out of her reach.

"Feels like y'all've oiled it. Linseed oil? That's what my mama puts on her antiques."

Tabitha shrugged. "I think. Old English furniture polish, whatever that is."

"It's big," said Cassie. "Almost too big for a broom."

That's because it's really a weapon. Or it started out that way.

"Can I hold it?" Patsy asked.

No! Mine!

Don't be such a baby. You brought it. Of course, you wanted them to see it. Trembling only slightly, Tabitha handed the broom to the redhead. "Careful. It's heavy."

Patsy nearly dropped it, though she held the broom with both hands. She grinned widely. "Sure is! This ain't just wood. What's it got in it?" She turned the stick so she could examine the exposed end. She put her hand toward the tip.

"Be careful!" Tabitha said, thrusting out a cautionary hand. "It's got an iron core, I think." *If Patsy collapses with a vision…*

Tabitha realized with a start that this, of course, was the reason she was reluctant to share the broom. The visions, and White Lettie, were hers. Not Patsy's. It was personal. Private.

Mine.

"Don't touch the tip," she said. *Please.* "It'll rust."

Patsy's grin widened, she winked. "Oh, you mean like this?" She placed her thumb onto the iron tip.

And continued to stand perfectly upright, still grinning wickedly.

Nothing. She's not seeing anything.

Relief washed over Tabitha like an ocean wave. The secret was still hers and hers alone.

Mine.

"Don't y'all know 'bout iron?" said Cassie. She showed them all a mischievous grin. In the light of the fire, her expression reminded Tabitha of a girl telling ghost stories round a campfire. "Iron's what was used to bind witches. In the Middle Ages. They'd make shackles and chains and stuff like that so a witch couldn't use her power. All of iron."

"I don't *feel* any different," Patsy said, her thumb still firmly in contact with the iron.

"Maybe you ain't strong enough," quipped Cassie. She snatched the broom out of Patsy's hands and returned it to Tabitha. "You're strong, Tabitha. Strongest yet. Does it bind y'all?"

"Me?" Tabitha could never be sure if "y'all" was collective or singular. In this case, she was fairly certain Cassie was addressing her personally. *I feel weak when I touch iron, but that's just the visions. Right?* "I don't think so."

"Why'd y'all bring it?" asked Cassie.

"'Cause it's a *witch's* broom, of course," said one of the girls, but Tabitha didn't see who.

Cassie said, "Well, I think it's cool."

The comments were too near the truth for Tabitha's comfort. So, change the subject. "Where's Joey? Shouldn't he be here by now?" *He better not be off in the woods with one of the girls "getting charged up." Not if he wants me to trust him.*

Not that he's been around that much lately.

Joey hadn't met her at lunch the day after the incident with Reverend Billy. He hadn't asked her to talk about *The Book of Mormon* since that day. In fact, she'd seen him only from a distance at school.

"Is he with Beulah?" she asked.

Patsy shook her head and gave Tabitha a dubious, everybody-knows-that grin. "She always comes with Magnus. The queen with her king."

Tabitha nodded. *They always enter the clearing hand-in-hand, like sweethearts. Or, as Patsy said, like a king and a queen. Together.*

"What's gotten into her lately?" asked Linda, a young blonde, tall and slender, like a willow tree. In the bonfire light, her glasses glinted from underneath her hood. She, like Tabitha, was one of the minority of girls in the Circle who were not on the cheerleading squad. Tabitha didn't know the girl well, but Linda had the reputation of being a bit of a bookworm, although like every other girl in the Circle—except for Tabitha—she also had the reputation of being "easy."

"Her daddy's missing," said Cassie. "Probably dead. He's been gone since Tuesday night." Cassie didn't look particularly troubled by this pronouncement. It didn't even seem to carry the tenor of juicy gossip. To Tabitha, it almost seemed as if Cassie was irritated, annoyed.

"No!" Linda, on the other hand, looked horrified. "The Reverend?"

Patsy harrumphed. "Some Reverend. That man catted around like ol' Elias Thibodeaux."

Cassie's lips twitched, further deepening the impression that she was annoyed by Reverend Billie's disappearance. "He didn't come home Tuesday night. And he missed Wednesday night services. He'd never do that. The man's too much of a glory hound."

"No!" Linda put a hand to her mouth. "Poor Beulah."

"I think," Tabitha began, "Beulah's doing okay."

Beulah hadn't mentioned her father on Wednesday, not to Tabitha, at least. And Tabitha wasn't about to bring up the subject herself. Beulah had been unusually, but understandably, quiet. Tabitha had supposed Beulah's feelings about her father were *complicated*, to say the least.

Two nights earlier, on Thursday, during the ride home from rehearsal, Beulah had finally brought up the subject of her father's disappearance. Her tone had flitted from worried to sad to venomous to hopeful to everything in-between.

Tabitha had, of course, kept her comments to a minimum. But she did ask, "Are you and your mom going to be okay?"

"Moneywise?"

I didn't even think about money. Of course, they need money. Without Billy's income, what are they going to live on?

Tabitha nodded. "Yeah. Does your mom have money in the bank?"

Beulah laughed bitterly and shook her head. "She's got the household account. But that's only what Daddy gives her to operate on. Like a dang allowance. She'll burn through that in a month. Or less. Daddy's got the rest in his name and his name only."

Oh, no! I've made things worse.

No. *A shudder ran through her.* They can't be worse than they were. *"So, what are you going to do?"*

"Daddy's got this big safe in the house. It's got loads of cash in it. He thinks nobody knows the combination." One side of her pink lips rose in a half-grin. "But I do. I watched them install it—hiding in Daddy's office, of course. I heard him repeat the combination to himself a few times. Then, I tried it out." The half-grin became a complete smile, though the smile never touched her eyes. Beulah's eyes looked haunted. "He's got a fortune in there. Or he did. When he didn't come home, when

he missed Wednesday night services, I raided the safe. Now, the money's all hidden away."

"Wow."

"Hundreds of thousands. Mama and me'll get by. For a while."

"How's she doing? Your mom?"

Beulah shrugged. "Drunk. She's almost always drunk. Nothing much has changed there."

"So, how are you doing?"

"I'm glad he's gone." Beulah's words came too quickly, as if they'd been rehearsed. "The son of a bitch. No reflection on my grandma, but he's a son of a bitch. Or he was." She was silent for minute. "I miss him too. Even after what he, ya know. He was my daddy." She glanced over at Tabitha. "Heard about your daddy and what happened. Y'all ever miss him?"

Tabitha shook her head, slowly at first, then more vigorously, like a cat shaking water from its fur. "Not one bit. I hate him." I don't want to see or hear from him ever again. *"Hate his guts."*

"I bet. Y'all broke his arms. Both of 'em. With the Power, wasn't it? Y'all're strong, girl."

"Yes, but... I didn't mean to. He knows about me and the Power. I don't know how—"

"Really? He knows? How'd he find out about the Power?"

Tabitha shrugged. "How would I know? It's not like he told me. How did Magnus find out about it? Or Joey?"

Beulah huffed once. "By touching me. Magnus, he figured it out. From the shock. The tingle. Joey? The same."

Tabitha frowned and looked inward. "Maybe that's it. Dad felt it over the summer. I'd never shown any ability before then. Maybe he figured it out like they did."

"Maybe. It's not like it's in a book somewhere. Least, not so's I've heard about."

Tabitha nodded. Then her still-burdened conscience goaded her to say, "He tried to grab me. He wanted to use me. I reacted."

"Ya know, y'all're the only one can do it—summon the Power at will."

Tabitha looked out the window, away from her friend. "I wish. I tried. I tried to force it. Tried to make it come when I wanted. It only comes when I'm angry or maybe scared."

"Well, that's something at least."

"But it's so unfocused. And violent. Like a bomb. I can't control it. And it hurts people."

"Well, Miss Tabitha, that's a good thing, at least in this case."

"But what if someone I love, someone innocent is there? I could kill them." What if my mom had been coming through the woods when the rock exploded?

What then, huh?

"Seriously, though," Beulah said, returning without warning to the former topic,

"I'm gonna be okay. I'm gonna be better."

"I hope so." I really do. *"I know you will. You're a survivor."*

"Ladies!"

Every head snapped in Joey's direction. He strode into the light of the bonfire. He wore his robes, but kept the hood down, off his head. His wide smile shone brightly in the firelight.

And he was alone.

Tabitha breathed a small sigh of relief. *Alone.*

"Hey, Joey!" Patsy called. "Thought y'all'd forgot about us."

Joey's mouth opened in mock horror. "And miss the opportunity to worship my goddesses? No way!" He bent at the waist in a low bow. "I live to serve you." He pointed at the broom in Tabitha's hand and grinned. "Hey, cool broom."

"Good!" said Linda. "Let's get started! I gotta feel me some Power tonight!"

Joey straightened, beamed, then held up a hand. "One moment, my goddesses. I need to speak with Tabitha a minute. Alone." He held out a hand to her. "May I?"

Tabitha smiled, nodding. She took his hand, and the two of them walked out of earshot of the rest of the Circle.

Tabitha could feel the Power flowing into him, but he didn't appear to be channeling it anywhere. And although he held her hand, his grip lacked any sense of tenderness or familiarity. They were just holding hands as if it meant nothing.

Tabitha felt a pang of loss.

"You've been avoiding me all week," she said, keeping her voice soft.

"I know. It's my fault. I…It's just that…" His voice trailed off.

After Reverend Billy. "After what we did—"

He shook his head and turned to face her. "That's not it. I mean, at least, I don't think so. It's…Beulah."

"Beulah?"

He smiled, and there was a hint of sadness in that smile. "Yeah. She *needs* me."

"But she's got Magnus. She…" *Oh, no! I sound desperate. Don't sound desperate!*

"Yeah, but Magnus, well, Beulah needs to get away from here. She needs to start over. Away from the memories."

"Have you discussed this with her?"

His lips spread into a tight, thin line. "Naw. I'm not even sure she'll want to go. Bein' a mixed-race couple is hard. And it's gonna be harder in Mississippi. The times, they are a-changin' and all that. Anyway, I'm gonna try to get her to go with me. I, uh, got offered a scholarship."

"Really?" *But it's too early.* Tabitha hadn't even begun filling out applications.

A sheepish grin spread across his face, although there was a hint of pride there as well. "Yeah. Academic scholarship, not athletic. Ole Miss. That's, uh, the University of Mississippi to you Yankees." He winked. "Even if you *are* from Maryland, you're a Yankee 'round these parts." He winked. "But it means I'd have to take early admission, you know, start next semester. Mr. MacDonald, he pulled some strings. He's got some contacts down there."

He rubbed a hand through his tightly curled hair. "He's got contacts lots of places, I suppose. But I don't think he thought it would come through like this—at least not this early. They might be looking at me for football too. In fact, I'm a little bit suspicious it might be a sneaky, backdoor way of recruiting me for football. NCAA's got rules against that. But..."

He shrugged his shoulders, and his face took on a dubious expression. "But, let's face it—most college athletes don't get to make a career of the NFL or the NBA. And I can't *play* forever." He shook his head slowly. "Naw, I'm gonna go into physics. That way I can really study the Power and how it works."

The Power. It always comes back to that.

But I'm stronger—far stronger than Beulah. "That's great." Tabitha thought she'd imbued her words with sufficient sincerity. "But what about—"

"I do love her, you know, as *weird* as our relationship is." He put his free hand against Tabitha's suddenly wet cheek. Finally, there was palpable tenderness in his touch. "She's not *you*. But, I think she needs me." He shook his head. And Tabitha could see tears welling in his eyes too. "You don't." He swallowed as if he had a lump in his throat. "You don't need me."

I do. I do need you.

"I can't stick around. Not after... I need to get Beulah away from here." He chuckled a little. "She's got enough credits to graduate too. You wouldn't know it, the way she acts and all, but she's a good student. But I'll be around for a little while. So, we can still pal around. And if you need me, just say the word."

The word! The word!

Tabitha's chest ached as if breathing was painful. *Let's just be friends? Is that it?* "We can still talk about *The Book of Mormon*." The statement sounded almost like a question.

He hesitated, then nodded. "Sure. Maybe. After next Saturday. After the play. We're all too busy."

Tabitha's lips twitched, settling into a wistful smile. "Sure. After the play."

He brushed away the tears that had escaped his eyes. "You're the best." He squeezed her hand. "Hey, listen, girl."

Girl? Not goddess or even Tabitha? "Yeah?"

"Be careful. Magnus. He wants you. He wants you bad. He's done so much for me; for all of us, but he's not exactly what he seems." He looked as if he wanted to say more, but then let go of her hand, cutting off the flow of the Power. He turned away from her and strode quickly back toward the rest of the Circle.

Tabitha stared after him. She didn't weep. She felt too hollow, too dead inside for tears.

The chill of the night air reached with icy fingers through her white robe and jacket beneath and into her bones. She shivered.

Joey doesn't want me. But Magnus does. He wants me badly.

More than the cold, that thought sent tremors though her spine. She clutched the witch's broom to her chest.

"How does he do it?" Joey peered intently at the empty air in the dead center of the Circle. "I can make the air move, and I can't see *that*. Why not photons?"

Tabitha, at the other end of the ring of girls, felt the surge of the Power as Joey's frustration peaked. The flow of the Power, no matter how it might be channeled or for what purpose, filled her with joy, with electric pleasure.

It filled her aching, crushing emptiness.

The earlier part of the gathering had gone well enough. They had flown, spinning high above the trees in the cold November air. Joey had stacked stones into a small pyramid. He had sent the bonfire blazing like a pillar of light, reaching high into the night sky. He'd even made Tabitha's broom dance and spin at the center of the Circle, reminding Tabitha of Mickey Mouse and the broomsticks in *Fantasia*.

Joey was improving, at least so far as his *control* of the Power went, but there was no increase—there never had been an increase—in strength.

He's at his limit and he knows it. We all know it.

But Joey, she knew, was only the preshow, like a lesser-known singer warming up the audience of giddy female admirers before the *real* rock star appeared. *Like watching Ricky Nelson while waiting for Elvis.*

But Elvis is dead. No, the real "King" will be here soon. And when he does come…

As much as she didn't want to be in that place, in that moment, with the boy who'd just dumped her, Tabitha had a mission that night. A mission of discovery— discovery, if not absolute unmasking.

Who are you, Magnus? You better not be who I think you are. Because if you are Mike Kilmore, it's going to kill Mom.

Joey says, "He wants you." Well, if you want me, Magnus, and you're using my mom to get to me.

A flash of gold among the trees caught her eye—a flash of gold and two ghostly shapes.

Magnus strode into the clearing, his face hidden behind his golden mask and his body cloaked in his white robe and hood, his hand firmly clasping Beulah's. *As always.* He did indeed carry himself like a king. Beulah, however, did not appear as if she felt regal at all. She walked at Magnus's side, but the usual spring, the bounce to her step when she and Magnus made their customary grand entrance, was missing. It was as if she wished she were somewhere else.

Or perhaps, with someone else.

Tabitha felt the Power drop off abruptly when Joey's head turned toward the Circle's High Priest. Then the Power ceased altogether as Joey let go of the hands of the girls on either side of him. His time over for the night, Joey stepped out of the

Circle and faded away into the darkness. By the time the gathering concluded that night, he would be long gone.

Gone. Like he'll be gone from my life.

Abandoning me. Just like everyone else.

Magnus and Beulah stepped into the gap left by Joey's departure. Still holding Beulah's hand, Magnus knelt. And in a Power-amplified voice which held not the slightest trace of a Missouri accent, he intoned, "My goddesses! Blessed be your names! May I worship you? May I serve you this night?"

Almost as one they responded, "Serve us. Serve the Divine Feminine."

Tabitha did not join in the ritual response.

If we're supposed to be the goddesses, why do they look at him with worship in their eyes?

Magnus rose to his feet. His head swiveled as if he were scanning the Circle, looking for someone in particular.

Looking for me.

Magnus, towing Beulah behind him, made a beeline for Tabitha.

Perfect.

He stopped in front of her and extended a hand. "With your permission, my lady?"

Even in the fading light of the untended bonfire, Tabitha could see Beulah did not look happy.

Something's wrong between her and Magnus. Is it me? Is she jealous? Maybe Joey's right. Maybe she just needs to get away.

"My lady?"

Tabitha snapped her attention back to Magnus and his outstretched hand. *Here goes. Please, please, please don't be Mike Kilmore.*

She took the proffered hand. The Power flowed from her—stronger, so much stronger than with Joey. She ignored it—or rather tried to—and focused on the hand itself.

Strong. Big. Calloused. Could be. Could be any man with big, rough hands.

She stared up into the eye-slits of the golden mask, seeking to pierce the darkness within. And could, of course, see nothing.

The expressionless face of the mask stared down at her.

Who are you? "Mike?" she said aloud.

Magnus said nothing. There was no movement, no twitch in his hand.

"Kilmore?" she said even louder. *Surely, he can hear me.* "Is that—"

"Mike Kilmore?" Magnus cocked his head. "The man dating your mother? The sheriff's deputy? Is this man bothering you, my dear?"

Tabitha's mouth hung open. *What?* "Uh, no. Are you?"

"Because if this man is bothering you, I…we can see that he bothers you no more."

No. This isn't going right. "No. That's not it." *So freaky talking to that blank mask.*

"You need have no fear, my dear. I will protect you. Say the word and—"

Tabitha shook her head quickly. "No. That's okay. He's not bothering me."

Magnus nodded. "Does he make your mother happy?"

Tabitha glanced at Beulah. Beulah wasn't looking in Tabitha's direction. Her eyes were downcast.

A crowd of girls had gathered around them, listening to the conversation. And it suddenly struck Tabitha that she'd never seen Magnus hold a conversation with any of the girls of the Circle—not one-on-one. No one, expect Beulah.

"Does he?" Magnus asked again. "Does this man make your mother happy?"

Tabitha nodded. "Yes." *Deliriously happy.*

Magnus nodded. "That is good. She deserves to be happy. She is a woman. She is a goddess. She is weak in the Power, but she is special nonetheless. Precious."

"H-How…How do you know he's dating my mom?"

"I know many things." The voice was as devoid of expression as the mask.

Tabitha glanced at Beulah again. And that time, Beulah met her gaze. In the treacherous light of the bonfire and within the shadow of her hood, Beulah's eyes appeared hollow, sad.

Tabitha gathered her courage around herself like a blanket—a very thin blanket that did nothing to keep out the chill. "Who are you?"

"I am your devoted servant, my dear." The mask was blank, but the voice sounded amused.

"But are you—"

"My face must remain a secret. For now. In time, perhaps, you will know."

"We need him." That was Patsy, appearing at Magnus's side. "We need a man who can channel." She laid a hand on his shoulder. "Without him, the Circle is nothing."

The hooded and masked face turned toward Patsy. "Oh, no, my dear. *You are everything.*"

"He'll show you his face," Patsy said, "when you're his favorite. Like Beulah." She stared at him intently, a smile curving her lips. To Tabitha, it looked like a knowing smile—a smile hiding a secret.

Patsy is a favorite? I thought Beulah was the only one.

Tabitha snapped her eyes back to Beulah.

Beulah, however, was glaring at Patsy with undisguised loathing such as only a jealous teenage girl can muster. "Let's get started," Beulah said.

"Yes, my dear." Magnus gently pulled Tabitha to his side. "Let us begin!"

And the Circle began to form. With each girl added to the link, Tabitha felt the Power surge exponentially.

Who are you, Magnus? Are you Mike Kilmore?

She felt no closer to an answer than she had before. *What exactly did he say? Gotta think it through.*

But with the Power flowing through her, electrifying and overwhelming her senses, she found it hard to think about anything other than the sheer joy of feminine might.

Maybe alone, I'm a bomb. But here, like this… I can do anything.
Anything.

And she gave herself over to the rapture of the Power.

The Circle, though incomplete, began to rise into the air. A few girls were left behind on the ground. But presently, they were lifted into the night to join the rest.

The Circle closed, and the Power surged. It flowed warm and tingling into her and through her and into the strong, rough hand of Magnus.

Magnus. Powerful. Strong. Stronger than Joey.

He wants me. He wants this. My Power.

But he wants me.

Are you Mike? Are you going to hurt Mom?

Is there anything I could possibly do to stop you?

From deep inside the dark well of her soul, from a murky, selfish place, arose a thought. *If you are Mike…It's me you really want. Not Mom. Me.*

I can have you. All I have to do is give you what you want.

Self-loathing washed through her, mingling with the Power, like a sweet cake frosted with an icing made of manure.

Got to protect Mom.

Nothing else matters.

But other words echoed through her, soft and dark, like the whispers of an incubus in the night. *He wants me. Not Mom.*

Me.

"Tabitha brought something." Patsy approached the three of them—Tabitha, Magnus, and Beulah. Magnus still held Beulah's hand. The Circle had broken up for the night. The bonfire had been thoroughly doused, and most of the girls were heading off to their cars, heading home after a night of Power-driven revelry.

In her hands, Patsy held Tabitha's broom.

No! Mine!

Tabitha resisted the urge to snatch it out of Patsy's hands—and to slap the smug grin off the redheaded cheerleader's pretty face. Tabitha merely held out her hand for the broom.

Still grinning, Patsy handed it over. "It looks like a witch's broom, doesn't it?"

"Indeed," said Magnus. "It is fascinating." His masked face snapped toward Tabitha. "Would you like to ride it, my dear?"

Tabitha blinked. "Ride it?"

Magnus nodded. "Yes." He swept his free hand across the moonlit sky. "Like a mythical witch, riding her broomstick through the night, silhouetted against the moon."

"Ride it?" she repeated. "Like a witch?"

"Certainly, my dear." Although Tabitha couldn't see his face, the voice carried a smile. "It would be my pleasure."

Tabitha gave a small, nervous laugh. "S-sure. I guess." *That would be so-o-o cool!*

Magnus reached for her hand, squeezed it.

Tabitha felt the Power flow through her again and into him.

But Magnus didn't release her hand. "Um, are you going to fly with me?" *The broom's big, but not that big.*

Magnus chuckled. "No, my dear." He let go of her hand.

She still felt the tingle of the Power as she and the broom were lifted gently into the air. She felt as if strong arms were holding her, pushing her, molding and gently bending her, until she found herself sitting sidesaddle upon the broom. She had expected the broomstick to be uncomfortable, pressing into her legs and bottom, but the pressure was minimal. *It's not really the broomstick that's carrying me anyway. It's him.*

Mike?

She wasn't sure. Some things about the man reminded her of Mike Kilmore, others did not.

Magnus is a persona. A mask. Not the man himself. Not who he really is.

What is there? What exactly reminds me of Mike Kilmore?

But that thought completely slipped from her mind as she began to soar high into the blackness of the night. She gripped the broom tightly, but she needn't have bothered. Unseen hands held her up and steady.

And warm.

And safe.

I should be scared out of my everlovin' mind. But I'm not. He's holding me. He won't let me fall. He needs me.

He wants me.

She soared and swung and looped like a bird, like an aerobatic stunt plane at an airshow. The air blew back her hood, then whipped through her long, black hair, streaming it out behind her. And on she soared through the night sky, beneath the moon.

Like a roller coaster! The best roller coaster in the world!

And through it all, she felt the Power. She wondered briefly why she should still be feeling it. *It's because it's being used on me, maybe? And I'm sensitive to it?*

Who cares? It feels so good!

"Whee!" The cry sprang unbidden from her lips. It seemed to echo through the night. As if amplified by the Power.

Molly knew loneliness well. She and loneliness were old, if noncordial companions. But since Mike Kilmore had entered her life, she found solitude too familiar. Unbearable.

I wish Tabitha would come home. Really? Are you ready for that?

With Mike in Cape Girardeau for a district priesthood meeting and Tabitha out with her friends, Molly had spent the evening practicing how to break the news to Tabitha about the engagement. She gazed wistfully at her engagement ring. She'd been wearing the ring all week, when she was out in public, at least. At home? Not a chance.

I'll tell her tonight after she gets home. We'll settle in for a scary movie and some hot chocolate. I'll tell her then.

She thought she heard a high, keening noise from outside. *It's off in the direction of White Lettie's cabin.*

She heard it again.

That sounds like a scream!

Molly scrambled to her bedroom window and peered out. Silence, except for the thundering of her heart.

Probably just an owl.

She looked up at the moon, high above the trees and saw something. Something impossible.

A dark silhouette traversing across the moon. A shape out of a children's story or a bad horror movie. A witch on a broom.

Molly peered into the darkness, staring intently at the moon but the witch did not return.

What was that? Tabitha! Come home soon!

Tabitha squealed with delight as she maintained a white-knuckled grip on the broom.

"This is so cool!!!"

But after another minute or so, it wasn't so cool. *When's he going to take me down?* Roller coasters were fun, but the rider had a sense of how long the ride was, where it ended. But Tabitha had no control—none at all. And no end was in sight.

"Okay!" she called. "You can let me down now!"

Can he even hear me?

But apparently Magnus had heard, because her wild ride slowed and calmed, and she began to circle toward the ground. She settled comfortably to earth, being raised gently to her feet.

She still clutched the broom in both hands. She was sure her knuckles were white, but no one could tell that in the moonlight.

"My turn next!" cried Cassie, bouncing up and down on her heels.

"Hush." Patsy waved a dismissive hand at the blonde. "Y'all ain't the favorite. 'Sides, it's Tabitha's broom. Come on, y'all," she said to the remaining cluster of girls. "Fun's over. Let's go home."

Patsy and the remaining girls removed their robes, waved, and shuffled off into the night toward their cars, but not without a whine or two of protest from Cassie. Other than Tabitha, only Beulah and Magnus remained, the two of them holding hands as always. But they appeared to be in the midst of a disagreement.

No words were spoken, but Tabitha could see Magnus attempting to pull his hand from Beulah's, and Beulah appeared to be struggling to hold on to him. He wrenched his hand free, and Beulah uttered a startled cry.

Magnus seemed to straighten, to stand taller than before. He turned to Tabitha and bowed at the waist. "Well, my dear? Are you pleased?"

Tabitha saw Beulah step away, distancing herself from Magnus. *Yep. She's upset with him.* "Uh, yeah. It was cool. I, uh…" She pointed off into the woods. "I gotta get home."

Tabitha could still feel the Power flowing through her. Although the sensation was pleasurable, filling her whole body with a tingling thrill, she wondered why she could still feel it. *Is he still doing something to me? Still channeling at me?*

She pulled off her robe, switching the broom from hand to hand as she did so. As she was dragging the robe over her head, she accidentally touched the tip of the broom. She jerked her thumb free, dropping the broom.

The tingle of the Power instantly vanished. Weakness caused her to stumble, but she managed to keep her feet. *Like turning off a light switch.*

Yanking the robe free from her head, she bent to retrieve the broom and saw Magnus on the ground. He was sitting, propped on his hands. Beulah reached for him.

"Are you okay?" Tabitha offered her hand to help him up.

He gripped her hand. And the Power flowed through her. "Thank you, my dear. I must've stumbled." He took Beulah's hand as well and rose to his feet. "I don't know—"

"Hey, y'all!" Patsy's voice came from the direction of the cars. "Look what we found!"

Letting go of Magnus's rough, strong hand, Tabitha turned in the direction of the voice.

The Power. Why is he still channeling at me?

Of course, the warm tingle of the Power felt good, but…*What is he doing to me?*

Five figures approached, four of them dragging the fifth between them. The figure at the center appeared to be struggling, and the girls were holding tight to its arms. "Let go of me!" the figure cried in a familiar voice.

"We got us a spy!" cried Patsy.

Tabitha realized with terrible clarity just who that spy had to be. *No!* In all the worry about discovering Magnus's identity, she'd forgotten all about— *Miss Tulane!*

No! I told you to stay away!

"Let me go!" pleaded the struggling captive. "Please!"

The voice sounded like Suzanne Tulane's, but gone was the practiced alto control and the carefully crafted cadences which marked the history teacher's voice. Suzanne wore black—black jacket, black pants, black sneakers, and a black knit cap. The teacher certainly looked the part of a spy.

"Well, well," said Magnus. "What do we have here?" He strode toward the girls and their unwilling guest. Beulah followed close on Magnus's heels, clutching at his hand.

After a few steps, he acquiesced and accepted Beulah's hand.

"Let her go!" cried Tabitha. "Please!"

"Nonsense, my dear," said Magnus. "We cannot risk exposing our secrets." He stopped abruptly in front of the prisoner. "I know you! Miss Tulane, isn't it? From the high school. My dear Miss Tulane, why in the world would you spy on us?" He waved his free hand in a dismissive gesture. "You may release her, my goddesses. I have her now."

"Got that right," said Patsy. "She ain't going nowhere now."

The girls released their grip on Suzanne's arms, and the teacher remained frozen in a posture of struggling against invisible hands. Suzanne's face, however, was not frozen. Lips and eyes moved with frantic terror.

"What're we gonna do with her?" asked Cassie.

"Please!" cried Suzanne. "Let me go. I wasn't hurting anyone."

"Please, Magnus," Tabitha pleaded, moving quickly to Magnus's side, opposite Beulah. "Just let her go!" She laid a hand on his robed arm, feeling the hard muscles beneath. "Please."

Magnus ignored both her words and her touch. "You didn't answer my question. Why were you spying on us?"

Suzanne swallowed once, twice, then took a deep breath and seemed to seize control. "I know what you're doing here." The voice was calmer, sounding more like Suzanne's carefully practiced alto.

"And what, pray tell, is that?" Magnus sounded amused.

Suzanne flinched. "You are celebrating the Divine Feminine, the true power of womanhood. I wish to join you. I wish to join the Circle."

"I see." Magnus inclined his head. "And are you willing to be tested?"

Worry shrouded Suzanne's face. "Tested?"

NO! "Please, Magnus. Just let her go. She doesn't..." *Doesn't what? Want this?* But Tabitha sensed the terrible truth. Bradley Thibodeaux's obsession with being female would not allow Suzanne to stay away. "Just please let her go."

"I'm going to release you now," said Magnus. "Please do not try to run."

"I won't." Suzanne's face was resolute. "I promise."

Magnus nodded. "Very well."

Suzanne's body remained upright, but the unnatural rigidity, the attitude of struggle vanished. The arms fell to Suzanne's sides.

Tabitha turned to her teacher. "Please, Miss Tulane. Just leave. Go. You don't want this."

But Suzanne smiled. "Oh, but I do."

Magnus extended his free hand. "Give me your hand, my dear. Let me test the

Power within you."

Suzanne extended a hand.

"Please, go!" Tabitha pulled Magnus's arm, attempting to restrain him. "It's not too late." *He'll know!*

But it was too late. With an almost beatific smile, Suzanne put a hand in Magnus'. Magnus said nothing for several seconds.

Maybe he'll just think there's too little Power to feel.

Suzanne emitted a nervous titter. "So, do I pass?"

"Who are you?" said Magnus.

Suzanne flinched, gasping as if in pain. "Stop. You're hurting me." Suzanne attempted to pull free of Magnus's hand. "That's too hard!"

Tabitha pulled frantically at Magnus's arm. "Let her go!"

"Ow! Stop!" Pain was written on Suzanne's face as the teacher continued to attempt to wrench free.

"I *know* you," said Magnus. "I know that face. I know who you are."

"Stop it, Magnus!" Tabitha yelled. "I—I *command you!*"

"Not now, my dear." Magnus's tone was firm, unyielding.

He's not going to stop!

BOOM!

All of them—except Tabitha herself—tumbled across the clearing. They lay on the dirt, unmoving. With an inarticulate cry, Tabitha lurched forward.

I've killed them!

But even before she could reach them all, they began to stir. There was moaning and some crying, but they all seemed to be pushing themselves to their feet or to a sitting position. No one seemed to be screaming or cursing in pain.

"What?" Patsy's eyes were wide with awe. "How did y'all do that?"

Magnus's mask betrayed nothing, but he seemed to be staring at Tabitha as well.

And the flow of the Power had ceased.

Tabitha hurried to Suzanne's side, pulling and dragging the teacher upright. "Go!" Tabitha said. "Get out of here!"

"But the Divine Feminine," wailed Suzanne. "I'm a woman!"

"No, you're not!" Magnus bellowed. He and Beulah had risen to their feet, holding hands. Magnus pointed an accusing finger at Suzanne. "You haven't the slightest spark of the Power which all women possess. *All* women. But you? You have nothing. Nothing at all. You're not a woman. And you never will be." His voice was terrifying, amplified by the Power. The voice of doom. "You're not even a man anymore. You're nothing."

Suzanne uttered a wordless cry.

"Run!" Tabitha cried.

Suzanne, finally yielding to Tabitha's frantic pulling, turned, and stumbled toward the trees.

"You Thibodeauxs!" Magnus's amplified voice boomed through the clearing. "You think you can buy anything in this world with your damned money. Well, you can't buy womanhood, Bradley!"

Suzanne howled then—the terrifying, wailing cry of a lost child—but kept on stumbling toward the trees.

Magnus called, "Run away, Bradley! Your secret's out now. You mock the very essence of sacred womanhood."

Tabitha glanced back and saw Magnus and the rest of the girls linking hands in a straight line. They floated slowly toward Tabitha and Suzanne. Magnus's golden mask gleamed in the moonlight.

Tabitha turned, stopped, and faced them. "Let her go!" She held the broom in front of her with both hands like a weapon. She mustered all the anger she could, but the anger couldn't quite overcome her terror.

However, she knew she still had one trump card to play. "Let her go, or I will never let you touch me, touch my Power again. Do you hear me? You want me? You better let her go. You better leave her alone!"

The line of floating figures, some robed, some not, with Magnus at the center, slowed, and halted. They settled lightly to the ground.

"As you wish, my dear." Magnus inclined his head in a slight bow. "It makes no difference. No matter how he has mutilated his body, Bradley cannot escape himself." He released Patsy's hand and waved dismissively. "No, Bradley is no longer entitled to that pronoun. *It* cannot escape *itself*."

Tabitha gritted her teeth and tried to look fierce. "Just leave her alone. I mean it. Otherwise, I'm done with you *and* the Circle."

From behind her, Tabitha could hear a car starting, then driving away, tires spinning on the dirt road.

But in her mind, all she could hear was the echo of Suzanne Tulane's howl of loss and despair.

I told you to stay away! Why couldn't you just stay away?

But even as she asked the question, she knew the truth. Because Bradley's obsession left him no choice.

But now her secret is out. What will she do?

28

"Just a bird. An owl." Molly paced around the living room. "That's all it was."

She stopped her pacing and fought the urge to go to the window yet again. *Tabitha, where are you?*

She checked the clock. *Not even eleven yet. She's not late.*

Maybe Mike's home.

Molly went to the phone and dialed his number. *Please be home. Please be home. I need you.*

After several rings, she heard, "Thanks for calling, but I'm not home right now. Or maybe you caught me in the shower or something stupid. Not that taking a shower is stupid or anythin', but…Well, heck, since you went to all the trouble to call me, I'd like to return the favor. So, go ahead and leave me a message after the beep. Oh, and be sure to leave me your number. Thanks."

But when Molly heard the beep, she quickly hung up.

She growled in frustration. *Don't be such a baby.* "It was just an owl." *And my eyes were just playing tricks on me. Not a witch on a broomstick. They don't exist. Okay, witches and Satanists exist. But they don't fly through the air on brooms.*

She sat on the sofa and tried to calm herself. She looked at her ring for the umpteenth time that night. Gold, with a largish diamond in a square setting, with tiny emeralds at the corners—the physical reminder of Mike's love and commitment. A wave of warmth swept over her, calming her.

I'm going to tell Tabitha. When she gets home. It'll be okay. She'll be okay.

Worry and doubt seeped back into her, leeching the warmth away. She shivered.

More hot chocolate? No, better wait 'til she's here. Any more right now, and I'll be peeing all night.

She gazed around the room, looking for something, anything to distract herself. Her eyes alighted on the cold and empty fireplace.

Perfect.

She arose and hurried over to the hearth. She slipped out of her bathrobe and set it on a nearby chair. She knelt and set about lighting a fire. Her Girl Scout training came back to her, and soon, she had a small fire crackling merrily in the fireplace. Kneeling by the hearth, she admired her handiwork.

I should do this more often. She brushed her hands together, dusting off the ash.

She imagined herself sitting by the fire, cuddling with Mike, feeling his strong arm around her, holding his powerful, rough, calloused hand. She imagined him kissing her neck, nibbling on her earlobe...

The door opened, and Tabitha entered. She carried White Lettie's broom and wore her book bag over her shoulder. The bag bulged as if stuffed to the gills.

And it was obvious she'd been crying. Tabitha tried to hide her face by keeping it turned away, but her telltale mascara was a mess.

"Tabby-Cat!" Molly sprang to her slippered feet and rushed toward her daughter.

Tabitha didn't glance at her. "What are you doing up?" Tabitha's voice carried a dangerous undercurrent of anger.

That stopped Molly in her tracks before she'd closed half the distance between them. "I always wait up for you. You know that. Besides, we've got 'The Invisible Man' at midnight." Her voice dropped to a whisper. "I made hot chocolate."

Tabitha shook her head. "Not tonight. I'm too tired." She moved to get past Molly.

But Molly wasn't about to let it go at that. She put a hand on Tabitha's arm and gripped it gently. The girl flinched at her touch, but didn't attempt to escape.

"Tabby-Cat," Molly said, pulling her daughter toward her, "what's wrong?"

"Nothing."

Molly kept her tone firm, but soft. "Tabitha, you've never lied to me before. I trust you."

Tabitha flinched.

So, maybe you have been lying to me. Molly's heart ached—and not just with the pain of knowing her precious daughter might have broken her trust. "Please don't lie to me now."

"Mom," Tabitha kept her mascara-streaked face averted. "I can't."

Molly released her hold on Tabitha's arm. She began to pull the bag off Tabitha's shoulder. Tabitha slapped a possessive hand over the bag. "No. I've got it." Tabitha removed the bag and set it on the floor against the wall.

What are you hiding in there?

Tabitha propped the heavy, ancient broom against the wall.

The girl allowed Molly to help her out of her jacket. *No objection there. Nothing in the jacket. But something in the bag. Something she doesn't want me to see.*

"Tabitha, what's in the bag?" Please don't let it be drugs. Tabitha didn't smell of cigarettes or pot or booze.

"Nothing." Tabitha heaved with a huge sigh. "It's just a costume."

"Let me see it, please."

"No."

Molly drew a deep breath. "Tabitha, let me see it. Don't make me go searching your room."

Tabitha turned to Molly, a look of shock and horror on her face. "You wouldn't!"

Molly put her hands to her sides. She was trembling with a dozen emotions she couldn't begin to name or catalogue, except for one—acute sorrow. "I never have. But I would. Especially if I thought you were lying to me."

Tabitha looked her mother full in the eye, her expression blank. "It's just a costume. There are no drugs, if that's what you're thinking. I don't *do* drugs. I've *never* done drugs." She paused, taking a calming breath. "And I'm not lying to you."

A costume? What kind of costume? And for what? "Let me see it, please."

Tabitha's blank expression hardened, her lips drawn into a tight line. "No."

How far can I push this? What if she bolts? What if she walks out? Runs away? If I stand my ground, the risk is…No. "Now, please."

Their eyes locked, a silent battle of wills with neither combatant gaining or ceding an inch of ground.

"Tabby-Cat," Molly began, her voice calm as a pond on a breezeless day, "I love you. I promised to protect you. No matter what. Even if I have to protect you from yourself. So, please let me see what's in your bag."

Tabitha stared at Molly for a moment, then dropped her eyes. The battle—or at least that skirmish—had ended in a retreat. Tabitha bent and picked up her bag. She stepped around Molly and went to the dining table. She opened the bag and pulled out a bundle of white cloth. She quickly shoved the bundle under her arm. She then dumped the rest of the contents onto the table.

Molly went to the table first. She examined the items briefly. Hairbrush, various items of makeup, a couple of pens, a small spiral notebook, a wallet, pads, and a roll of breath mints. *No birth-control pills. At least not that.* Just the normal items any teenage girl would carry—except for the white bundle which Tabitha had not as yet surrendered.

Molly turned back to her daughter.

Tabitha held on to the bundle all the more tightly.

Molly extended a hand.

Anger flashed in Tabitha's eyes. Her lips pursed.

But she surrendered the bundle.

Molly unfolded it slowly, examining by feel for hidden pockets. She found none. But when she had unrolled the garment. "A robe?" She blinked at the wrinkled white robe and a memory stirred.

White figures. Phantoms. Tabitha's involved with them.

But the robe wasn't all white. Around the bottom hem, it was stained with dirt. "You're wearing this?" She lowered the garment. "Out in the woods? At your wienie roasts? Your bonfires?"

Tabitha said nothing, keeping her eyes averted and downcast.

"What are you doing out there?"

Tabitha's lips moved, but Molly couldn't hear the words.

"What are you doing out there in the woods, Tabitha?"

"I said, I can't tell you."

"And why not?"

"Because I made a promise." Tabitha looked up and met Molly's eyes. "And I swear we're not doing anything bad. No drugs. No sex. No alcohol. No anything. I promise you."

"But why this?" Molly shook the robe.

"It's just part of the club."

Anger and terror merged, roiling together inside Molly—anger at Tabitha's evasive answers and terror for her daughter's safety—physical and spiritual. Anger and terror merged and produced frustration. "What club?"

"I can't tell you. I made a promise. And if you make a promise, you have to keep it." She lowered her voice and her eyes. "At least that's what you taught me."

Molly recoiled as if struck. *How dare she?*

She dares, because that is what I taught her. Molly softened her voice. "These are the robes of those phantoms. The ones who broke into our home."

It was Tabitha's turn to recoil. She glanced up at Molly, saw the look in her mother's eyes, and then lowered her gaze once more. Slowly, Tabitha nodded. "They were afraid you'd shoot them. So, they were looking for the gun." She looked up, meeting Molly's gaze. "That's all. They shouldn't've done it, but that's all it was."

Okay. I can buy that. It's plausible. "What kind of club is it?"

Tabitha sighed, but she averted her gaze again. "It's all girls, Mom. A-And just two boys. We're not doing anything bad. I promise. I'm not breaking any commandments. Not a single one. But I promised to not talk about it. Please don't make me. Promises must be kept."

This is it. This is what she's been holding back. Do I dare push her any further?

Molly decided to take a different tack. "So, what are you so upset about? You've been crying."

Her daughter met her gaze again. Fresh tears threatened in Tabitha's eyes. Her lower lip trembled. Then the tears spilled down the girl's mascara-stained cheeks. "I got dumped tonight."

Molly's heart melted at her daughter's anguish. She dropped the white robe and drew her daughter into her arms.

Tabitha buried her head in Molly's shoulder and sobbed quietly, but she kept her arms at her sides.

Molly kept silent for several seconds, then she said softly, "Was it Joey?"

Tabitha nodded. "How did you know?" It was barely a whisper, but Molly caught the words.

"I just figured. He's the only boy you really talk about. But I didn't know you two were that close."

Tabitha shrugged slightly, then put her arms around her mother. "We weren't. Until recently. He was reading *The Book of Mormon*. I hoped…"

Molly stroked her daughter's hair with one hand. "I'm sorry, honey."

"Thanks."

"Is that all that's hurting you, Tabby-Cat? I mean, I know it's *enough*, but…"

Tabitha gave a great shuddering sigh. "Can we sit down?"

Molly nodded and let go. "I have hot chocolate on the stove."

Tabitha wiped at her eyes. "That'd be really nice." She plodded to the sofa and plopped herself down. She sat with her head bowed, her black hair draped around her face like a shroud.

Molly went to the stove and reheated the chocolate. "I have marshmallows. Do you want any?"

Tabitha nodded, then stared into the fire.

The chocolate was soon steaming again. Molly filled two new mugs, ignoring her own used mug on the coffee table. She added a generous helping of miniature marshmallows to each cup, then put a spoon in each.

Soon, mother and daughter were sitting side-by-side on the sofa, sipping quietly and staring into the fire.

Give her a minute. She'll let it out.

Tabitha sighed wearily. "Mom, I have a friend. A friend with a terrible secret. And it's going to come out. The secret, I mean. Tonight. Tomorrow. Monday for sure. And it's going to destroy…my friend. My friend will have to move away."

A terrible secret? And why does she keep saying it like that? "My friend?" It sounds so strange. "She's pregnant or something?"

Tabitha laughed, low and bitter. "Nope. Not pregnant. That'd be bad enough, but not pregnant."

"A boy then?"

"I really can't talk about it. Not my secret to tell."

She's used those words before. "But it's going to come out, you said."

Tabitha nodded, then shook her head. "Not from me. I promised."

And you keep your promises. In spite of the circumstances, Molly felt a small swelling of pride. "I'm sorry, honey. That's a terrible burden."

Tabitha nodded again. "Yeah, but it's worse for my friend."

They stared at the fire. It had burned low and needed tending. Molly put her mug down beside the empty mug she'd used earlier. She went over to the fire, rearranged it with the poker, then placed two fresh, split logs on it. The fire snapped and crackled happily as if to say, "All will be better in the end."

Keeping her back to Tabitha to make her words seem less confrontational, Molly said, "About this club."

"I'm not going back."

Molly rose and turned toward her daughter. "You're not?"

Tabitha shrugged, keeping her eyes on the fire. "Probably not." Abruptly, she groaned and threw up her hands. "I don't know. Right now, I just don't want to. I'm done. It's not… It's not fun anymore."

"Is this because of Joey? Is he part of this club?"

Tabitha nodded and looked in Molly's general direction—but she didn't meet Molly's eyes. "I'm not supposed to say. Anyway, he's not the only reason." Her eye went wide. "What is that?"

Startled, Molly followed her daughter's gaze.

My ring!

Instinctively, she covered it with her right hand. But it was too late. "I was going to tell you. Tonight. I—"

"Is that an engagement ring?" Tabitha stared at Molly, openmouthed. "Mike? I mean, Brother Kilmore?"

Molly's sheepish smile did nothing to hide her embarrassment. "Yeah. He proposed."

Tabitha shook her head, disbelief written plainly on her face. "But…" She couldn't seem to find the words to frame a question. Or an objection.

Molly moved quickly to the sofa, sitting a little distance from her daughter, giving Tabitha some space. She turned toward Tabitha. "It's okay. You know I got a temple annulment years ago. It took almost six years after the divorce, but—"

"Mom, do you really know who he is? It's been so fast. You don't know…"

Molly placed a hand on Tabitha's shoulder. The girl flinched slightly, which Molly chose to ignore. "I know it's been fast. It's been a whirlwind, really."

"You don't know him." Tabitha's jaw was set, the muscles in her neck taut. She set her mug down on the coffee table with an audible thud. Brown liquid and a single melting marshmallow splashed over the side. The spoon clinked. She turned to glare at her mother. "Do yourself a favor next time you see him. Do us *both* a favor. Ask him a question and watch his face. Watch it real close. Ask him, *'Are you Magnus?'*"

Molly gasped.

Tabitha bolted to her feet. Molly stared at her in mute shock as Tabitha gathered her belongings, stomped to her room, and slammed the door.

The décor of the room—like that of the entire house—was, in a word, girly. Pinks and flowers and lace abounded, from the wallpaper to the curtains to the furniture upholstery to the carpet. Even the chandelier which hung from the ceiling on a stout chain was done all in pink crystal.

Suzanne Tulane paced the pink carpet of the living room, wringing hands slick with sweat. "What am I gonna do? What am I gonna do?"

The controlled alto tone of Suzanne's voice was gone, replaced by a low, trembling tenor.

"Everyone's gonna know. Everybody! Teenage girls can't keep a secret. Why would they? Girls gossip. By Monday, it'll be all over the school. All over town! Teenage girls can be so cruel." Suzanne's voice dropped to a whisper. "They were always cruel to me."

Suzanne stopped, staring into the mirror above the mantlepiece. The reflection that stared back looked awful. In spite of the hair and the tear-streaked makeup, the face looked at once alien and familiar. Grotesquely familiar. A mask. A cracked mask unable to hide the despised, disgusting countenance behind it. For the eyes behind the mask, the eyes staring back, were all too familiar.

The eyes of Bradley Thibodeaux.

"I hate you. I hate you. I hate you! I HATE YOU!"

Suzanne screamed and pounded on the mirror with both fists—fists just a bit too large. Mannish fists, in spite of the long, red-polished nails.

"I hate you, Bradley! Why did you come back? Why can't you just go away and leave me alone!"

The reflection opened its too-red-lipstick-coated lips. "Y'all can't buy womanhood. You're a fraud, Bradley. A pathetic, grotesque fake."

"NO! I'm NOT Bradley. I'm Suzanne! I'm a woman! A woman. A woman."

The reflection shook its head, the red hair floating in disheveled waves. "No, you're not a woman. And you never will be, no matter how much money you spend, no matter how many surgeries you have." The reflection scowled. "No matter how you mutilate your body. No matter how much makeup you slather on your face. You have no womb, no ovaries. You have a Y chromosome. But you know that, Bradley, don't—"

"Stop calling me that!"

"You know what, Bradley? Mama was right about you. Y'all're sick. And you're not even a man anymore. You're an *it*. Just a disgusting, mutilated, former male."

"NO! I'm a girl! I've *always* been a girl!" Suzanne burst into fresh sobs and sank to the floor.

"I'm a girl. I'm a g—"

BANG!

Suzanne squeaked in fright. It took a moment to identify the loud noise. *Front door!*

But I locked it!

Suzanne's head snapped toward the hallway just in time to see two figures, robed in white and clasping hands. Like ghosts, they floated eerily through the air.

Suzanne recognized one of them—Patsy Moody, her lips curved in a wicked smile, ripe with gloating malice. The other figure wore a golden mask, blank and expressionless.

Suzanne tried to move, to scramble away, but was frozen, as if bound by unseen hands. Suzanne tried to scream, but was unable to utter a sound. *No! Leave me alone!*

Suzanne stared up in mute horror at Magnus and Patsy looming above, suspended a foot or so in the air. The invisible force held Suzanne immobile, gagged, and completely helpless. Then the Power shoved, roughly flattening Suzanne against the pink shag carpet.

"So, Bradley," intoned Magnus, shaking his head, "this is what you did with the Thibodeaux fortune." His voice was toxic venom mixed with the acid of sarcasm. "You thought you could purchase womanhood. And then, in the height of your arrogance, you returned to Blue Beech Ridge. Didn't you think someone might recognize you? I must admit, you did pull it off for a while, fooling everyone. Even me."

"Y'all're sick," Patsy said. "Y'all make me sick. Being a woman is sacred, divine. You just can't *take* it. Y'all's a freak. I wanna puke. Puke all over y'all." She spat at Suzanne. "And by tomorrow, the whole town's gonna know."

Magnus shook his head. "Your very existence is an offense against nature. A mockery of sacred womanhood."

Please! Please let me go! I'll leave. Leave town. Just let me go! Suzanne's bladder threatened to empty itself.

"Do you remember the story of White Lettie?" asked Magnus. "Of course, you do. You grew up in this town. White Lettie was raped, accused of witchcraft, and then hung in the town square. And she couldn't say a word to defend herself—just like you, Bradley. You wanted to join us, Bradley, to be a witch? Well, I can't grant you that honor, because you are not female, Bradley. You are simply emasculated, a eunuch, cosmetically mutilated to look like a woman. Hanging is too good for you, but perhaps that might be a way for you to end your miserable existence. But the rape?"

Magnus inclined his golden, blank face toward Suzanne. "Now, *that* is a service I *can* perform."

Morning dawned, and all was quiet in the Tulane house. The room had been straightened—all signs of violence had been removed, except for a scrap of torn underwear hidden under the sofa.

Near the center of the room lay a wooden chair, tipped on its side. And from the pink-crystal chandelier, hanging on its stout chain, dangled an improvised noose made of curtain rope.

And from that rope hung a corpse. The corpse was dressed in an elegant blue evening gown and wore one very expensive high-heeled shoe. The matching shoe lay some distance away on the fireplace hearth, as if it had been accidentally kicked off during the death throes—the frantic thrashing of the body as it struggles for breath—for even in the event of a voluntary suicide by hanging, in the end, involuntary impulses will cause the self-determined victim to fight for life. The corpse's makeup and hair were impeccably done, although the eyeshadow might be considered a bit heavy.

On the coffee table lay a note written on pink stationary, scented like strawberries. The note was unsigned, because the writer hadn't been able to decide what name to use. The paper was blotched with salty tear stains, one of which had smeared the ink slightly. However, the writing was still quite legible. The message itself was simple, written with a trembling hand. It consisted of a single sentence—

"I don't know who I am anymore."

"So, what, exactly," asked Molly as they drove to church the next morning, "do you know about Magnus?" She kept her eyes on the road and, of course, both hands firmly on the wheel.

Tabitha, normally ebullient and full of life at home, had been unusually reticent that morning. She'd been quiet ever since the blow-up the previous night. Molly knew Tabitha didn't enjoy going to church in their little branch, knew she didn't really have any friends there—except for Angelica Goldsmith, but no friends her own age. So, Tabitha's silence on a Sabbath morning wasn't unusual, but Tabitha hadn't uttered even a single word.

And that was far from normal.

"Tabitha, I asked you a question."

Tabitha turned her face toward the window.

She's still mad. Mad at me. Mad at me for getting engaged to Mike. But to think Mike could be Magnus? How does she even know about Magnus? What does she know?

Magnus—the shadowy figure who sought control over Tabitha. But Molly knew nothing about his motivations, the reasons why he was stalking her daughter like a mountain lion stalking a lost lamb.

But she wants me to ask Mike if he is Magnus...

"Tabitha, please answer me."

Tabitha turned back to Molly and stared at her with an intensity that almost pulled Molly's attention from the road. "You tell me first," Tabitha said. "What do *you* know about Magnus?"

Molly drew a deep breath to calm herself. She resisted the urge to point out that she'd asked first. Barely resisted the urge. "I know only that he *wants* you. That he's after you. I don't know who he is. Or why he wants you." She paused. *Do I tell her the rest?*

Yes. Molly continued, "I know he's financing the play. He's using the play to keep you here."

"Is that so?" Only, it didn't sound like a question—Tabitha obviously knew as much already.

"Tabitha, what else do you know? Who is he?"

Tabitha shrugged, then turned her face forward, toward the road. "I don't know. Honestly, I don't."

"Have you met him—this Magnus?"

"I told you, I don't know who he is." Tabitha's tone carried annoyance with a distinct undercurrent of evasion.

She's not lying, but she's not telling the whole truth either. "Okay. But you've heard of him."

"Yeah."

Molly waited for her daughter to say more, but Tabitha offered up nothing else. "A-and you think Magnus is Mike."

Tabitha shrugged, staring straight ahead. "Maybe."

"Why? Why do you suspect Mike Kilmore of being this boogeyman?"

Tabitha snorted, then laughed. Heartily. She turned a bright smile to her mother, apparently forgetting for the moment to be angry. "Boogeyman?" She burst into laughter again. "Really?"

The laughter was infectious, and Molly couldn't help but chuckle. "What else would you call him?"

"I guess that fits well enough."

"Tabby-Cat, what do you know?"

Tabitha sobered, but the ghost of a smile lingered at the corners of her mouth. "Pretty much what you said. I don't know who he is, but I've got my suspicions."

"Mike Kilmore."

Tabitha nodded, but said nothing.

"But why?"

Tabitha sighed and shook her head. "You're not going to like it."

"Tell me." *Whatever it is, you are my priority. But what about Mike? I love him. But I love my baby girl, too.*

Tabitha squared her shoulders, as if gathering her courage. "I know Magnus wants me."

"Why?"

"I can't say."

"Can't? Or won't?"

"Right now?" Tabitha sighed. "Right now, it's the same thing. I can't."

Because it's your secret. Or somebody else's. Your promise. "So, Magnus wants you."

Tabitha nodded. "And"—she screwed up her face as if chewing something unpleasant— "he might be using you to get to *me*."

Mike? Using me to get to Tabitha?

But Mike's words flashed through her mind—*"And I love that little girl of yours—not the same as I feel for you, of course—but I love her like my own kin."*

No. Mike loves me. He loves me.

But a worm of doubt began to chew its way into her heart.

"You have to admit," Tabitha said, "this all happened really fast. The engagement—all of it."

Molly shook her head in vehement denial. *Mike loves me. He does.*

"I'm just worried about you," Tabitha said. "I don't want you to get hurt. Again."

But that's not all, is it?

An ugly, nasty feeling bubbled up in Molly, like bile in her throat. *You want him for yourself, don't you?*

She bit the venomous thought back down. "I appreciate that, honey. I do." *But if you think he wants you...* "I can see why you're concerned."

Tabitha's expression was earnestness in perfection. "So, ask him, okay?"

Molly nodded slowly. "I will. I promise. I'll ask him today. Sometime during church."

Tabitha nodded and turned her face away once more.

They rode the rest of the way to the chapel in the same wordless silence with which they'd passed the morning.

But Mike Kilmore wasn't at church. That month being Mike's month to conduct in sacrament meeting, President Roylance had to lead the meeting in his stead, announcing from the small pulpit that Brother Kilmore had been called away on police business.

Tabitha scowled at this news. *Figures.* She stole a surreptitious glance at her mom. *Probably running Suzanne Tulane out of town. Tarred and feathered. On a rail.*

For her part, Molly appeared annoyed, but perhaps a mite relieved.

Now she can put it off, Tabitha thought with a bitter grimace.

Throughout Sunday school and Young Women, Tabitha listened for whisperings about Suzanne Tulane and the big secret. But she heard nothing.

None of these kids are part of the in crowd, she thought as she sat through the combined Young Women class. Angelica Goldsmith wasn't teaching that day. She was absent too. *So, maybe they haven't heard yet. I bet it's all over Beulah's church.*

I wonder who's preaching services over there with her dad gone? They've got to have an assistant pastor or something. Maybe they're not even having church today.

Wish I wasn't. This sucks. This whole day sucks rotten eggs.

I hope Suzanne's all right.

She pounded a fist on her knee in frustration. *This whole thing sucks.*

As they drove home, the subject of Mike Kilmore and Magnus didn't come up at all. But Molly dropped another bombshell. At least on that day it was a bombshell for Tabitha.

"We're having company for dinner," her mom announced.

Tabitha looked at her mother askance. *Company? We never have company. Not once since we moved here.* "Who?"

Molly appeared to swallow a lump in her throat. "Fergus MacDonald."

"Mr. MacDonald? My teacher?"

Her mom nodded. "Yeah. He's been so helpful—to me, at least. And we had a falling out. Now that it's all resolved, I wanted to do something nice for him. He's very lonely. He doesn't have any real friends, I think."

"Of course, he doesn't have any friends, Mom. He's a creep. A creepy old man."

Molly shook her head. "No. That's just the way he's perceived. He's quite nice once you get to know him."

Tabitha rolled her eyes. "He's a creep, Mom. He's always eyeing all the girls. He insists on these creepy, long handshakes. He's just creepy!"

Molly chuckled. "You don't know him. Not really. And you should really learn to vary your vocabulary. You used some variation of 'creepy' at least five times in the last minute."

Tabitha's indignant expression almost made Molly chuckle.

"But, Mom," Tabitha protested, "it's the best word to describe him. He's just creepy!"

Molly sighed and adopted the tone she used when lecturing a particularly obtuse student. "How about, eerie, disturbing, scary, weird, freaky? Hmm?"

"More like disgusting, nasty, gross. He's a creep, Mom—especially to the girls."

Molly shrugged. "Maybe that's just his school persona. Did you ever consider that? Anyway, we'll see how he acts tonight." She paused. "I'm making quiche Lorraine. How does that sound?"

Tabitha harrumphed. "Sure, you'll make my favorite when creepy old Mr. MacDonald comes for dinner." But the girl couldn't quite hide the grin that threatened to curl her lips and brighten her eyes.

Molly, however, grinned mischievously. "Well, perhaps we should have him over more often?"

Tabitha scowled. Then she began to whistle.

Molly recognized the tune, and immediately disapproved. "'Old MacDonald Had a Farm?' Really?"

Tabitha stuck her tongue out. Then went on whistling.

Fergus MacDonald pushed his wheelchair back from the dinner table and patted his belly. "That was heavenly, Miss Molly!" He sighed, a smile of contentment on his face. "I'm stuffed to the gills!"

Tabitha kept a barely civil and neutral expression on her own face. *You ate four pieces, you old goat.*

Her mom beamed with obvious pleasure. "I'm so glad you liked it."

"You used Swiss cheese, am I right? A true quiche requires Swiss cheese."

Molly's smile widened. "Yes. And just a bit of goat cheese."

MacDonald's eyes widened. "Goat? I'll bet you didn't get that down at the Piggly Wiggly!"

Molly shook her head, but the smile remained. "My visiting teacher raises goats. She brought me some."

"I see!" The old man nodded vigorously. "That'd be Polly Perkins, now wouldn't it? She's the only one I know of who raises goats 'round these parts. And she's a Mormon."

He knows Sister Perkins? He knows what a visiting teacher is? How does he know so much about Mormons?

Molly pointed an affirming finger at him. "You got it!" She put both hands on the table and pushed her chair back. "How about dessert?"

Dessert? We really are going all out. I understand he's lonely...

MacDonald patted his belly again. "I couldn't but, what do you have?"

Probably just ice cream. Or a frozen pie.

Molly stood, obviously confident her dessert would be well received. She smiled. "Crème brûlée."

Seriously? That's my favorite! She hasn't made it since before we moved.

The old man shivered with obvious pleasure. "Ooh. That sounds divine. Yes, please, Miss Molly! By all means!"

"Coming right up!" Molly spun about, her Sunday skirt swirling, and hurried to the fridge.

I didn't even see her make it. She had to've made it in advance.

Let's be honest, here. I spent the better part of the afternoon hiding in my room. I didn't help with dinner at all, except to set the table.

But I don't feel the least bit guilty. I don't.

She sighed. *Sometimes, Tabitha, you most definitely suck.*

Her mom served the tasty cream dessert prepared in individual bowls. Tabitha craned her neck to peek inside the fridge, and yes, there was a fourth bowl.

She was hoping Mike Kilmore would show up.

The dessert was certifiably yummy, earning Tabitha's silent—yet official—seal of approval.

To judge from the nonverbal noises issuing from Mr. MacDonald as he partook, his gastronomic senses were overwhelmed. When he finished, he said, "Miss Molly, you are lovely, intelligent, and a great cook. Not to mention, sexy as hell." He winked at her, and, to Tabitha, at least, the wink was as lascivious and creepy as always. "You are going to make a perfect bride for your young man, if I may be so bold."

The crème brûlée suddenly sat very unsteadily in Tabitha's stomach. She suppressed a shudder. *At least he hasn't tried to shake my hand. For the first time ever. Maybe, not in front of my mom.*

The old man beamed contentedly. He pushed his wheelchair back from the table slightly. "I have some news that might interest you." His smile took on an air of someone about to bestow a surprise—a gift worthy of Santa Claus himself.

Molly leaned forward. "What is it?"

"I have it on very good authority that we'll have in our audience for Saturday night's performance"—he paused, rubbing his hands gleefully together—"a Broadway theatre agent. He'll be here, it would seem, to observe our Miss Tabitha!"

Tabitha blinked stupidly. *What?*

"An agent?" asked Molly. "For Tabitha? My Tabitha?"

The old man turned to Tabitha, grinning from ear to ear. "Yes, indeed! What do you think of that?"

"An agent?" Tabitha echoed. *To see me? Why?*

"That's wonderful!" Molly said. "Fantastic! But how do you know?"

The old man straightened in his wheelchair, sitting as tall as he could. He looked suddenly like the old Marine he was reputed to be. "Because I arranged it. I called in a favor. Or two. Or three."

A favor? Like he did for Joey? But why would he do it?

"Broadway!" Her mom sounded ecstatic. "That would be perfect. I'll be the first to admit New York's not the best environment, but it'd get Tabitha away."

Out of this town, she means. Away from Magnus and the Circle. She doesn't know about the Circle, not really. But she fears Magnus. I don't blame her.

Tabitha couldn't help but smile. *Wouldn't that put a monkey wrench in Magnus's plans?*

Does Mr. MacDonald know about Magnus? Mom heard about him from someone. Was it Mr. MacDonald? Why would he help me? I avoid him like the plague.

Is it because he likes Mom? He does know she's engaged, right? And he's way too old for her. Creepy as all get-out.

Mr. MacDonald chuckled. "Ironic, isn't it? Using someone's own plan against him?"

What does that mean?

An urgent knock at the door startled Tabitha. She saw her mother jump as well. Mr. MacDonald seemed unaffected.

"Excuse me," said her mom, wiping her mouth on a napkin.

Tabitha rose more quickly. "I'll get it." She left the table, grateful for the distraction, thankful for anything that got her attention off Old Man MacDonald.

The knock was repeated, and it seemed to Tabitha as if there was an impatience to the sound.

Whoever you are, thank you.

She opened the door, revealing the imposing figure—imposing and breathtaking, especially framed by the blackness of the night—of Mike Kilmore. He looked harried, and his eyes had a haunted look as if he'd seen something he wished he hadn't.

"Hello, Sister Moonshadow. May I come in?"

Tabitha began to nod, but he was already pushing past her.

That's not like him. Or Magnus. He's always polite. To a fault.

Mike spoke up. "Molly, I'm sorry I wasn't there this morning. I had to—" He stopped, frozen, like an inactivated golem, staring at the table.

At Mr. MacDonald and Brother Kilmore did not look happy to see the old man. "I see you have company."

Molly jumped to her feet. "It's okay, Mike. I saved you dessert. It's crème brûlée. Mike, this is—"

"I know Mr. MacDonald." Mike, usually the epitome of Missouri charm, sounded upset. In fact, he sounded royally pissed. "We know each other quite well." He turned his attention to Molly, though his expression softened only a little. "What's *he* doing here?"

Molly's own expression darkened. Tabitha recognized it as the face she wore when she was dangerously close to a rare outburst of fury. "He's here as my guest."

"Actually," MacDonald said, "I was just leaving. Thank you, Miss Molly, Miss Tabitha, for a lovely evening."

"Oh, no, Fergus," Molly said, placing a hand on his shoulder and glaring daggers at her fiancé, "you don't need to go. Mike is just—"

"Nonsense, Molly," MacDonald said, cutting her off, "there is some bad blood between the deputy and myself. But I'm sure he'll tell you *all about it.*" He reached up and placed his hand atop Molly's. Molly looked down at him and they locked eyes. "But know you this. It's all a pack of lies. Every damned word of it."

The old man spun his chair about and wheeled himself to the still-open doorway. He deftly retrieved his coat and woolen hat. Then he was out the door, without another word, and soon was crunching down the driveway to his car.

Mike stepped to the door and shut it, closing off the cold night air and any further sight of the old Marine.

When he turned around, Molly was in his face.

"That was so rude!" she cried. "He was a guest in my house!"

Mike pointed behind himself. "You don't know him like I do."

But Molly was having none of it. "That's no excuse! That old man has been so kind to us. He—"

"That old man is the most virulent anti-Mormon in Butler County. And believe me, there are some *nasty* anti-Mormons in these parts. But he takes the cake."

Anti-Mormon? Mr. MacDonald?

Molly shook her head. "I know all about that. He used to teach Sunday school lessons about—"

"He used to be in the branch presidency!" Mike snapped. His face was livid. Tabitha had never seen him angry, much less furious. In the face of his rage, even her mom took a step back. "He was excommunicated, Molly. For seducing a teenage

THE WITCH OF WHITE LADY HOLLOW ~

girl. It was before my time, but that's what happened."

Tabitha's jaw was almost on the floor. *He seduced...*

"B-but he's a teacher!" Molly spluttered. "Surely the school—"

"The school didn't know anything about it." Mike plopped down at the dining table in an unused chair. His face twisted into a sneer, and his gaze seemed to be focused on the past. "And when they *did* find out about it, they discounted it—blew it off completely. Because the accusation came from a *Mormon*."

"That's awful," Tabitha said, soft and low.

"Yeah." Mike thumped the table. "But not that uncommon 'round these parts, unfortunately. Those arrogant, self-righteous sons-of— uh, y'all know what I mean."

Yeah. I do. "So, Mr. MacDonald really is a dirty old man."

Mike Kilmore grimaced. "*Used* to be, at least. As far as I know, he's been a regular Boy Scout ever since. 'Cept for the anti-Mormon part. But in this county, that pretty much makes him a hero."

Wait a minute. "But he's paralyzed, in a wheelchair. How'd he…"

Her Mom shook her head. "It's just his legs, honey. That part of him still works. He told me so himself."

Tabitha looked at her mom with horror and disgust. "He told you so?"

Molly shrugged. "It wasn't as weird as it sounds. He got married after his accident. They had a child."

Mike growled, low in his throat—a sound which sent shivers of ice up Tabitha's spine. "The poor girl was pregnant. He tried to get her to abort it. That was illegal back then. The girl refused. He kept hounding her about it. Then she had a hard and premature labor. There were complications. She and the baby—a little girl—they died."

"But how?" Molly wrung her hands. "He's my friend. He was my friend. How do you know? How do you know it was him?"

"The girl's mother," Mike's teeth were clenched. "She caught them together. There was even a police investigation. Statutory rape, you know. But even *they* blew it off. The sheriff at the time hated Mormons too. And that was the end of it. Except for the Church disciplinary council. He denied it, but the girl and her mother testified. Two witnesses. You know what I mean. He was excommunicated."

Tabitha felt sick. *How am I supposed to face him at school? At rehearsal? He and his crew built the set. They're everywhere!* "That's horrible."

Mike looked up at her. "The seduction and the statutory rape are bad enough. But his actions led directly to her death. And the death of her little baby." He shifted his gaze to Tabitha's mom. "That's two lives lost." Tears appeared in his eyes, spilling down his chiseled, handsome face.

Molly sat down. She took his hand, brought it to her lips, and kissed it. She caressed his cheek with her other hand, not drying his tears—she was simply comforting him.

"I know"—he swallowed hard—"we're not supposed to value one life over another, but women, girls, they're special. We—men—we're supposed to protect them. Cherish them. Honor them." He looked from Tabitha to Molly, his eyes now red, his cheeks streaked with tears. "We're—I'm supposed to protect you. Cherish you. Honor you. You—women—are divine."

Tabitha gasped. Women are divine? The Divine Feminine? "Mike, uh, Brother Kilmore?"

He turned a sad and weary smile on her. "Mike is fine." He looked at Molly's ring—not hidden, but on display. "She told you? We're engaged?"

Tabitha nodded quickly. So did her mom.

Then Tabitha shook her head. "No, that's not what I…"

"I don't expect you to call me daddy or anything, but you can call me Mike, okay?"

Tabitha grimaced. *That doesn't matter right now. This is too important. I have to know.* She stared at Mike intently. "Mike, are you Magnus?"

Molly gasped.

Mike Kilmore's jaw dropped. He blinked. Then he closed his mouth, seeming to shake off the shock. "Magnus? What do you know about Magnus?"

Molly groaned. "More than we do, apparently, but she's not saying much. It's part of some promise she made."

Tabitha ignored her mom. "Mike, I asked you a question."

He closed his mouth, his lips stretched into a tight line. He met Tabitha's gaze with red eyes suddenly devoid of emotion.

His face like a mask. A golden mask.

He shook his head slowly, but kept his blue eyes riveted to hers. "No. I'm not. Now, it's my turn. I asked *you* a question."

Tabitha stared right back at him, unblinking. *Don't look away. If I look away, if I blink, I'll miss it.* "I've said all I'm going to say."

"Tabitha, I'm not asking you this as your prospective step-father, as your church leader, or even as your friend. I'm asking this as an officer of the law."

Tabitha blinked, and cursed herself silently. "Is this a matter of the law? Has some law been broken?" *Gotcha.*

Mike took a deep breath through his nose, then released it slowly. "Touché, as they say. Not yet. But it may be."

Tabitha narrowed her eyes. "And when it does—no, *if* it does, you get back to me."

Mike glanced away, withdrawing from the field of battle.

Are you Magnus? You said, no, but I don't know what to believe.

Mike sighed and put his head on the table, face-down, as if he was mentally and physically exhausted.

Tabitha looked at her mom. Molly shook her head, then mouthed, *Not Magnus.*

Tabitha shrugged slowly and dramatically. She mouthed, *We don't know.*

Molly shook her head again.

Mike let out a long, loud sigh as he raised his head. "I know I wasn't invited, but do you have any grub? Haven't eaten a thing all day."

Molly stood and let go of Mike's hand. "Sure. It's cold by now, but I've got a slice of quiche left."

He looked at her without comprehension. "What's…"

Molly smiled an indulgent smile, as if she were addressing a delinquent pupil. "Quiche Lorraine. It's like a French ham and cheese omelet pie. Sort of."

He grinned, but his eyes didn't have their usual sparkle. "Sounds great!"

"And I have crème brûlée for dessert. It's like a—"

Mike waved, cutting her off. "I know what crème brûlée is." His smile widened, and the twinkle returned to his eyes. "And you mentioned that when I came in." His grin morphed into a sheepish grimace. "Before I caused a scene and interrupted your dinner party."

Molly set down a plate with the last slice of quiche on it, along with a cloth napkin and a fork. "Well, I *was* going to invite you, but you weren't at church and you didn't answer your phone."

He rolled his eyes again and let out another deep sigh. He shook his head. He picked up the fork and looked at it. But Tabitha could see he wasn't really looking at the fork. He was focused on something or someplace far away. He put the fork down again without taking a bite. "I'm not supposed to comment on an ongoing investigation, but it'll be all over town by tomorrow anyway." He paused. "Heck fire. What difference does it make? What difference does any of it make?"

He looked from Tabitha to Molly. "Y'all'd better sit down."

They both took their seats. Molly placed her hand on Mike's again. He grasped her hand and squeezed gently.

He grimaced, screwing up his face in disgust. He looked down at the food on his plate. "It's not the quiche or whatever. I'm suddenly not all that hungry." He shook his head. "You know, sometimes I hate my job. When you can help people— Well, that's the part I like. But when people are beyond help, all you can do is try to get them justice after the fact. Y'all know what I mean?"

Neither of them answered, but Mike probably didn't expect them to. He continued, "I got called out to a crime scene this morning. Technically, suicide's a crime, but you can't go after the perpetrator, can ya? But you gotta go investigate. That's what I do."

But you gotta go investigate. That's what I do."

Suicide? Horror gripped Tabitha's spine with its icy claw. "Who? Who died?"

He gazed at Tabitha, then Molly, then back to Tabitha again. "It was your teacher, Suzanne Tulane."

"NO!" *It's all my fault!* Tabitha's breathing became rapid and shallow. *I told her to stay away! All my fault. I should've tried harder!*

Mike reached across the table with his long, muscular arm. He put his hand on Tabitha's shoulder.

She flinched a little, but didn't pull away from his touch. *No! No! No!* "How did it happen?"

Molly said, "Tabitha, we don't really need to know the details."

Tabitha glanced at her mother, then focused on Mike. "I need to know. How did it happen?"

Mike sighed, but he met Tabitha's gaze without hesitation. "She hung herself, sometime late last night. She climbed onto a chair, tied a noose to her chandelier in the living room, put her neck in the noose, and kicked the chair out from under herself. She left the window curtains open and the light on. She wanted someone to find her quickly, I guess. A neighbor saw it early this morning and called it in."

Molly covered her mouth with her hand, but she still managed to say, "How awful! Are you sure it was suicide?"

Mike nodded, then looked at Molly. He lowered his eyes to his untouched plate. "Yeah. She got herself all dolled up, put on a fancy dress, and she left a note."

"What did it say?" Tabitha asked. "The note?"

"It said, 'I don't know who I am anymore.'"

Molly asked, "What does that mean?"

Mike shook his head, and his shoulders drooped as if he was carrying the weight of the world on them. "That's where the real crime comes in." He took a deep breath, then continued, "We've got a coroner in this county. Stinkin', worthless, elected official. He came out, examined the body for all of fifteen seconds. Meanin' he just looked up and said, 'She's dead. Cause of death, suicide by hanging.' Then he left. He did his job and nothin' else. Stinkin', worthless Thibodeaux."

Worthless? That's right. But what about me? I'm worthless too. I should've done more!

"So," Mike said, "I have a friend. A doctor. He's a surgeon now, but he interned as a forensic pathologist back in St. Louis. I call him in when County Coroner Thibodeaux does his usual piece of sh— crap job. He examined the body. And, well, Miss Tulane was raped. Sodomized, actually."

"No!" Tabitha fought to control her breathing. *Don't pass out, you idiot!*

"My friend," Mike continued, "he found blood on her underwear and panty hose. Only it was just in the back. No damage to the... I'm sorry, ladies. Are you sure y'all want to know?"

Tabitha nodded.

So did Molly.

Mike shrugged. "There was no damage to the vagina. No evidence of vaginal rape. Just sodomy. It was pretty bad too."

The blood seemed to have drained from Molly's face, but she squeezed Mike's hand. "Is that why she?"

Mike shrugged again, then shook his head slightly. "Partly, probably, but it's more complicated than that. My friend...he got all quiet-like. Then he shook his head and said, 'Mike, the victim isn't female.'"

"What?" Molly cried. "What do you mean, 'not female'?"

Mike looked Molly in the eye. "I mean, Suzanne Tulane isn't wasn't a woman. She—I mean, *he* had had surgery. They call them 'transgender.' He was changed, plastic surgery everywhere so he could pass as a woman. We searched his house, found estrogen pills and progesterone and something else—I forgot the name—but it's a testosterone blocker. These poor souls take these pills to stay feminized. Like to keep from having facial hair or a masculine sounding voice or—"

"You're kidding!" Molly said.

Mike shook his head, but he looked at Tabitha.

He knows. He can tell I'm not surprised.

He fixed his eyes on hers. "What do you know about this, Tabitha?"

Tabitha gritted her teeth. "I can't tell you. I promised."

"If you promised Suzanne Tulane, she, I mean *he* can't hold you to that promise anymore."

Tabitha lowered her eyes.

And she told them. She didn't mention the vision or the iron thimble which used to belong to Bradley Thibodeaux's mother—she didn't tell them *how* she knew, but she told them who Suzanne had been.

Mike nodded. "Bradley Thibodeaux. Well, that's one mystery solved."

"Who's that?" Molly asked.

Mike met her gaze. "The last of the old-money Thibodeauxs. The missing heir. He took off with the family fortune when he came of age. Left the rest of the family destitute. Well, now we know how he spent the money."

Molly shook her head, disbelief written plainly on her face. "He spent the fortune to become a woman?"

Mike chuckled bitterly. "That's the he— heck of it. His rapist knew. He knew Bradley or Suzanne or whatever. The rapist *knew* the victim wasn't a woman. And I think that's why he raped him… her," he growled. "This is confusing as all get-out. The rapist did it…the way he did it, because he knew the victim wasn't really female."

Magnus! It had to be Magnus! He raped Suzanne.

She looked hard at Mike Kilmore, at her mom's fiancé.

Mike, you sound so sincere, but…are you Magnus?

"Well, he never fooled me," said Jay Ellis in a stage whisper loud enough to be heard by the entire first-period history class. "Not for one dang minute!"

Shortly before Jay's pronouncement, Vice-principal Hardin had walked into the classroom, one very long minute after the bell had rung, and had announced that, in light of the sudden passing of Miss Tulane, he, Hardin, would be their history teacher until arrangements could be made for a permanent substitute. He had told the class of freshmen—plus Tabitha, of course—to silently read a textbook chapter they had already studied two weeks earlier, and then walked out, promising to return "shortly."

This, of course, was taken as implicit license for the class to explode into gossip like a murder of crows squabbling over fresh roadkill.

The story was already all over the school—if not all over the town.

And everybody and their proverbial dog seemed intent on declaring, just as pimple-plagued Jay had done, that he or she had known all along Miss Tulane was no "Miss" at all. To hear each and every protestor, *none* of them had been taken in.

"Why, everyone could see it," proclaimed Jay, his whisper louder than before. "Didn't look nothin' like no lady. Hell, Ol' Bradley Thibodeaux wasn't even pretty at all, not even with all that makeup he wore. Downright ugly, if y'all ask me. Made me sick just to look at him!" He laughed once. "Warn't no *him* anyway. Just a damn *it*!"

This was met with a chorus of agreement from the rest of the freshmen students, *especially* from the boys in the class. They were tripping over each other, vying to be the loudest to assert their lack of credulity and their profound disgust.

And Tabitha could stand it no longer. "Oh, really, Jay?" she said with heartfelt, scathing contempt, glaring at the acne-riddled adolescent. "Is that why you were slobbering over *him* in class last week?"

Jay's face turned so red, his zits became tiny islands of white in a sea of crimson. "That's a damn lie!"

Tabitha raised her eyebrows and laughed scornfully. She turned away from Jay and addressed the rest of the class. "So, how come you were staring at him, at his legs and his breasts like you'd never seen a girl before? Your tongue was hanging out, and you were panting and drooling like a dog after a bone. He turned you on, Jay. Didn't he?"

Several of the girls cackled with laughter, pointing fingers at the hapless Jay. Some of the other boys joined in, mocking and adding vulgar comments questioning Jay's sexual proclivities.

Jay spluttered, seemingly unable to form coherent retorts beyond repeatedly yelling some variant of, "Shut up!" Tears of rage and humiliation welled in his eyes.

"Don't worry, Jay," Tabitha said, muting the chorus of jeers. "You weren't the only one." She swept a hand around the room. "All you boys were gawking at him. He got you all hot and bothered. Mark"—she pointed at another boy—"I distinctly heard you call Miss Tulane a fox. 'Foxier than Farah Fawcett,' you said."

More shrieks of laughter and scorn came from the girls. The fingers of derision were pointed at other adolescent males, who blushed and protested loudly.

The laddies do protest too much, methinks.

No longer the exclusive object of contempt, Jay wiped furiously at his tears. Then he glared daggers at Tabitha. "Bitch!" he snarled. "Mormon bitch! Who gives a *damn* what y'all think, ya damn Mormon? All a bunch a liars an' whores!"

The crowd hushed, dividing their attention between the apoplectic boy and the object of his fury.

Jay pointed an accusing finger at Tabitha. "Mormon witch!"

And suddenly, all eyes were on Tabitha. And there was a distinct aspect of fear to their stares. They had all heard the story about Tabitha's first day at school.

Then Tabitha heard whispers—real whispers that time, meant to escape her hearing. But she caught "Ol' Waddle" and "scared" and "broke the door."

And she caught "Mormon" and "witch."

Don't get mad. Don't explode. Don't be a bomb.

She closed her eyes and tried to calm herself. When she opened her eyes again, they were all staring at her, still whispering, but more cautiously than before. None of them had moved their desks—at least not far—but they were definitely *leaning* precipitously away from her.

That's right, boys and girls. Be afraid. I'm like the Hulk. And you wouldn't like me when I'm angry.

However, Tabitha's anger was no competition for her grief and disgust.

Why are we even having school today? Why are we going on with life as if nothing happened?

"That's right," she said, keeping her voice even and calm. "I'm a Mormon. So what? A person is dead."

"But—" said one of the girls. Tabitha had no idea what her name was.

Tabitha glared at her, and whatever the girl had intended to say died in her throat. Then Tabitha's eyes swept the room. "Like I said, a *person* is dead—a human being. One we all liked. And she's dead. Dead. All you boys thought she was sexy, a fox.

287

All you girls admired her, even envied her, and wanted to be like her. Does it matter if Suzanne or Bradley or whatever was a man or a woman? She or he was a child of God. And that child of God is now *dead*. And all you little punks are worried about is proving you weren't a bunch of fools. Well, you *were* fooled. We all were. And you're all *lying*."

"Damn Mormon," murmured Jay. "Y'all ain't even Christian. Who the hell cares what you say?"

"That's right," said the nameless girl, more loudly than before. "Y'all ain't no Christians. Y'all're all liars. An' sluts! Pastor Billy says—"

Tabitha gritted her teeth. "Pastor Billy Martineau was a monster."

Stay calm. Stay calm. Stay calm. Or I could kill them all. "And you want to talk about sluts?" She laughed bitterly. "The *Reverend* slept with half the women in this town. Probably some of your own mothers and sisters. Maybe even some of you."

The unnamed girl's eyes went wide, and her jaw dropped. The blood drained from her young, pretty face.

Bingo. Darn it.

A wave of pity washed over Tabitha. *You poor thing. You didn't deserve it. And it's not your fault. But you know what, kid? There's someone else who deserves our pity even more right now.*

"Christians?" Tabitha shook her head. "There's nothing *Christian* about a *reverend* sleeping around, seducing wives and mothers and-and children." She realized she was staring at the girl. *This isn't just about you, kid.* Mercifully, she shifted her gaze to another girl and then to Jay. "There's nothing *Christian* about lying and hating—hating Mormons or people like Miss Tulane. Or anybody else. The *Christian* thing to do would be to mourn her...or him. To pray for him, to beg God to have mercy on Bradley Thibodeaux's poor, tortured soul. And on your own."

"Y'all ain't no Christian," snapped another girl, her nose in the air.

You wouldn't stick your nose in the air, honey, if you knew you had boogers hanging out.

Tabitha gathered her books. "Well, if that's what being Christian is all about, you can have it. It stinks." She stood. "Me? I'm glad I'm one of those unchristian Mormons who do our level best to follow Jesus Christ."

"Going somewhere, Miss Moonshadow?"

Tabitha nearly spilled her bag as she wheeled around.

Vice-principal Hardin stood in the door.

"I-I was just—"

"You were just going to take advantage of the situation to skip out on class." He pushed his glasses up the bridge of his nose, and his expression hardened. "Go to the office. Now."

"It's not her fault."

Turning her head back in the direction of the voice, Tabitha was amazed to see it was the "nameless" girl who had come to her defense.

"Tabitha was just..." The terrified girl glanced from Tabitha to Mr. Hardin. "She was just defending Miss Tulane and—"

"*Miss* Tulane," said the vice-principal in a voice brimming with menace, "was a liar and a deceiver and a damned faggo—." He bit off the nasty word. He seemed to chew on it for a second as if he wanted to vomit up what he could neither spew out of his mouth nor swallow back down. "A deceiver. And I— And *we* do not tolerate deceivers in this school." His face twisted into a sneer. "Now, Miss Thibodeaux, y'all may join your friend in the office. Get out of my sight, both of y'all. Now!"

Tabitha made for the door, but halted a few feet short of the exit.

Mr. Hardin had not moved. He was still blocking the door. He glared at her with unmasked hatred and loathing.

And Tabitha was terrified. She was uncertain if the man was going to strike her physically or if he simply meant to prevent her from obeying his command.

He won't hit me. Not in front of all these witnesses. He won't.

But he could expel me. Kick me out of school. And the play.

It was the fear of losing the play which allowed Tabitha to find her courage.

Not the show! Not Eliza.

Strategically, she lowered her eyes. "Please, Mr. Hardin. I'm trying to obey you. Please let me pass."

One second passed. Two. Three.

He stepped aside.

Tabitha fled from the room.

Halfway down the long hall, she slowed her pace and tried to calm her breathing.

"Tabitha! Wait up! Please!" The voice was muted but insistent.

And Tabitha recognized it. *Miss Thibodeaux.* She halted and turned, waiting for the younger girl to catch up. As the freshman approached, Tabitha observed the girl was in tears.

"I'm sorry," the girl said. "I'm sorry I got y'all in trouble."

Tabitha rolled her eyes. "I got *myself* in trouble. It's not your fault." *None of this is your fault.*

The girl shook her head, wiping away tears and smearing her mascara. "Yeah. It kinda is. I'll tell him—Mr. Hardin—it was my fault."

Tabitha turned back toward the way she'd been going. "You don't need to do that. It'll just make him angry. Angrier."

They walked a few steps in silence, then Tabitha asked, "What's your name?"

"Mary-Sue. Mary-Sue Thibodeaux." Then she gave a tiny, nervous laugh. "I mean, half the county is Thibodeauxs."

Tabitha chuckled softly. "That's not your fault either." She glanced at Mary-Sue.

The girl's face bore a weak smile. "I'm sorry 'bout what I said back there. 'Bout Mormons and all. It's not fair. It's not…Christian."

Wow. Never expected that.

Tabitha managed a weary smile. "We're all doing the best we can. That's what Jesus wants us to do. We do the best we can, and He makes up the rest. That's what Mormons believe."

"Thanks. You're nice." She paused. "I wish we could be friends."

Tabitha put an arm around Mary-Sue's shoulders, only slightly annoyed the freshman was slightly taller than herself. "Sure. Why not?"

"Really? Me? Friends with a senior? The big star of the school musical?"

Tabitha chuckled. "It might surprise you to know that seniors and high school actresses and Mormons, step into our skirts one foot at a time."

The open door of the school office suddenly loomed barely a half-dozen yards ahead. Tabitha had lost track of where she was going and what she was doing. And what possibly devastating punishments lay ahead.

If I still get to be in the show.

Mary-Sue slowed her pace. Tabitha slowed with her.

Mary-Sue slowed her pace. Tabitha slowed with her.

The girl seemed as reluctant as Tabitha to face the music. "I'm, uh, really looking forward to the show. I love the music from *My Fair Lady*."

"Me too."

Mary-Sue halted. She grasped Tabitha's hand. "Y'all were right about Pastor Billy."

Tabitha gasped. "No! I'm so sorry. So, so sorry." She wrapped her arms around the girl. She could feel Mary-Sue's hitching, silent weeping.

After a moment, the girl said. "I'm not pregnant. I got my period, but I'm afraid. Of him. Of Pastor Billy."

Tabitha hugged her more tightly. "I'm so sorry. I don't think Pastor Billy's coming back."

A louder sob escaped the trembling girl. "Are you sure? How can you be sure?"

"I just am." *I hope.* "Trust me."

Mary-Sue squeezed Tabitha, clinging to her as if the girl was drowning and Tabitha was her only lifeline in a dark and tempestuous sea of misery.

Tabitha watched the second hand on the generic, black clock on the wall, ticking slowly, inexorably toward second period. The two of them, Tabitha and Mary-Sue, had been forced to await the wrath of Vice-principal Hardin in punitive silence.

Please, Heavenly Father, please don't let him take away the show. We're so close! I'm so close! I know I shouldn't be worried about it—not with Suzanne. Not with what happened to her, but it means so much to me.

I think Suzanne would want us to go on with the show. I do. I think she would. Art Thou listening? Dost Thou care? I know I'm being selfish. I know it. But, please? Art Thou there?

Her prayers and questions continued; a steady stream of every question, hope, doubt, cascading through her mind like water down a mountain.

And Magnus. Is Mike Kilmore Magnus? Is Mom engaged to Magnus? Did Mike rape Suzanne? I'm sorry. I'm sorry about the Circle.

I'm sorry for my doubts.
Art Thou there?
Do I matter?
Please protect my Mom! She doesn't deserve this. If she's engaged to Magnus...
If he hurts her, it'll be my fault. Well, it'll be Magnus's fault, but it'll be because of
me.
Please be merciful to Bradley. Please.
Art Thou there? Are Thou real?
Do I matter?
Do any of us matt—
"Tabitha?"

Both Tabitha and Mary-Sue jumped. Tabitha stared up into the astonished face of Angelica Goldsmith.

"Tabitha, what are you doing here?"

"Ange— Miss Goldsmith!" Tabitha glanced at the school secretary watching them over the rims of her glasses. Tabitha held her breath.

The secretary scowled at her with her too-red lips. Then waved at her impatiently and dismissively.

Tabitha released the breath. "I'm"—she glanced quickly at Mary-Sue—"We're in trouble."

Angelica rolled her eyes. "Well, I can see that. What happened?"

"Oh, Miss Goldsmith," cried Mary-Sue, her voice choked with fresh tears, "it's all my fault. We were talkin' 'bout Miss Tulane in class—Mr. Hardin wasn't there—then he was there—everybody was pickin' on Tabitha—me too—I mean, I was pickin' on her too, and I said those nasty things about Mormons and all—other people were sayin' 'em too, but I said 'em too and—" She clasped her hands together and extended them toward the English teacher in nigh-hysterical supplication. "Oh, Miss Goldsmith! Mr. Hardin's gonna cancel *My Fair Lady*, and Tabitha won't get to play Eliza Doolittle, and it's all my fault!"

Tabitha had tried to interrupt, to protest, to wedge a single syllable of contradiction into the rush of the younger girl's panic, but her efforts had been fruitless.

As Mary-Sue took a moment to draw a sobbing breath, the English teacher focused on Tabitha. "Is this true?"

Tabitha nodded, barely keeping back her own tears. "Yeah. Except for the part about it being all Mary-Sue's fault." Eyes wide, Tabitha shook her head vehemently. "I'm so, so scared!" *He could cancel the play!*

Then Angelica Goldsmith did something so unexpected, Tabitha was convinced the English teacher had lost her ability to comprehend the English language—Angelica smiled.

"Didn't you hear me?" Tabitha asked, tears now falling in earnest.

Angelica nodded, still smiling. "Oh, I heard you all right. Both of you." Then she shook her head. "Not a problem. You just leave this to me."

At that very moment, Vice-principal Hardin stormed into the room. His eyes first focused on Tabitha, narrowing in the confident, controlled, and nigh-gleeful anger of an all-powerful magistrate about to lower the full weight of his authority upon the head of some helpless miscreant. Tabitha had seen that savage joy in the eyes of many a bully over the years. She'd seen it in the eyes of Randy, her father's current boyfriend, when he used his position in Jerry's household to bully her.

And despite Angelica's assurance, Tabitha was very afraid.

"Now, Miss Moonshadow," he growled happily, "in my office." His grin was all teeth.

Angelica Goldsmith tapped his shoulder. "Excuse me, Mr. Hardin. May I have a word?"

He glanced at her, just long enough to register her presence, then shook his head. "Not now, Miss Goldsmith. I have a disciplinary matter to attend to."

Angelica smiled. It was a sweet smile, but there was a wicked curve at the edge of her lips, as well as a mischievous gleam in her pretty eyes. "Now, George. This won't take a minute."

He rounded on her. "I said, not now. And I meant not now."

Angelica showed some teeth, and her smile shifted from wickedly sweet to gleefully feral. "Believe me, George, if you don't speak to me now, you will regret it for the rest of your career—however mercifully short that may be—if not the rest of your life."

And with those words, she sauntered into his office without a backward glance.

He stared at her openmouthed and speechlessly flabbergasted.

But he followed her into his office.

Angelica peeked out the door, winked at Tabitha, then withdrew from sight.

The door closed.

Hardin's roaring voice could be heard clearly by those sitting outside. "How dare you speak to me that way in front of students! I'll report you to the school board! I'll have you and your Mormon ass fired so fast—"

Angelica uttered a few words which Tabitha couldn't catch.

And then both voices began to speak in muted tones, although the diminutive English teacher did most of the talking.

True to her word, Angelica emerged from the office after barely a minute. She smiled sweetly, innocently at Tabitha and Mary-Sue.

Vice-principal Hardin stepped out of his office. His face had taken on a pallor worthy of a cadaver. "Miss Moonshadow, Miss Thibodeaux, you may go. I *apologize* for my conduct and my hasty words."

Tabitha blinked in stunned incomprehension.

"We...can go?" squeaked Mary-Sue.

Mr. Hardin nodded. "Yes. Off to class now." He disappeared into his office and closed the door—a bit hastily it seemed.

Angelica extended a hand to Tabitha and said, "Walk with me to class?"

Tabitha nodded, then remembering the freshman girl, turned to Mary-Sue, and said, "Bye."

The English teacher dragged Tabitha out of the office and into the deserted hall. And Tabitha allowed herself to be led away. "What just happened?"

"Come with me to my classroom, please," said Angelica with a knowing smile. "We've got just enough time before the bell."

"But…"

Angelica put a finger to her lips. "Mum's the word." But she continued to grin all the way to her classroom.

Once inside the room, with the door closed, Angelica burst into peals of laughter. "Did you see— Oh, man! That was priceless! Did you see his face?"

Utterly confused, Tabitha did not join in Angelica's mirth. "Yeah. He looked like he'd seen a ghost."

Angelic nodded heartily and laughed some more. "Yep. He did! The ghost of his career *and* his worthless reputation." In an instant, however, she sobered completely. "You have to keep this a secret. You promise?"

Tabitha nodded, but slowly and with reluctance. *So tired of secrets.*

Angelica jerked a thumb toward the door. "Did you know he's married?"

"Who? Mr. Hardin?"

The English teacher nodded. "Yep."

"I never thought about it."

"Well, he is." Angelica looked as if she wanted to spit on the floor. "Although, you wouldn't know it. He has three kids—he and his wife."

"Okay?" *What's she trying to say?* "So what?"

"Well, he *hit* on me. My first day here."

"Hit on you?"

"Yep. Walked right into my classroom, when I was setting up, and he asked me out on a date. I refused, of course. I didn't know he was married at the time, but I'm like you—I'm only interested in dating someone who can take me to the temple."

Like me? I think that's still what I want. I hope it is, but… After Joey…

Angelica shuddered. "And that's when he put his hand on my butt."

"He did? Oh, barf!"

Angelica snorted. "Well said. 'Oh, barf.' I tried to slap him, but he deftly stepped out of my reach." She looked at her hands. "Don't have much of a reach. You can relate, I'm sure."

Tabitha grimaced. "Never been hit on by a teacher, but, yeah." *Tommy.*

"When I found out he was married, it really made me sick. But he's pretty much untouchable. Nobody believes a woman teacher, especially a Mormon. You know, he's an elder in that Assembly of God church?" She shuddered again.

Reverend Billy's church? No surprise there, I guess. "So, what did you say to him today?"

"He was having an affair with Suzanne." Angelica paused, letting that sink in.

"You're kidding! Oh, that's…" *Awful. Disgusting. Pathetic.* Tabitha's breathing quickened. "That's just…"

"Yeah. It's just a *lot* of things."

"How do you know?"

Angelica shrugged. "We were friends—Suzanne and I. Not too close, but we talked. She told me. I mean, he told me—Suzanne did. He, meaning Suzanne, was proud of it. Like he'd *accomplished* something."

"What? Having sex as a-a w-woman?"

"Well, Suzanne said he—George Hardin—wasn't her first, but I think it was like Suzanne's first…relationship. Even if it did last only a few months. And it was with a married man. And it had no future."

"Does anybody else know?"

Angelica shook her head. "I don't think so. Apparently, they were pretty discreet. I advised her to break it off. 'Think of the children, his wife,' I said. But the way he, Hardin, came on to me, he would've just taken up with someone else. George, I mean. He would've. Anyway. It seemed to make Suzanne happy. Sort of. I don't think Suzanne was in love, but she was in love with having a man to…"

Angelica burst into tears. She sat down at one of the student desks, then buried her face in her hands. "I thought I was all cried out last night. But I miss her. I miss my friend. I don't have that many friends in this town."

Tabitha laid a hand on Angelica's shoulder. Tears spilled from her own eyes as well. "I miss her too."

Angelica drew a few broken, stuttering breaths, then quieted her sobs and wiped her tears away, smearing her mascara. "Anyway, I told George I knew about the affair. *That* got him. He might survive news of an affair, but an affair with a-a-a man? With Suzanne?" She shook her head. "Not in *this* town. He'd be tarred-and-feathered and ridden out of town on a rail. They might even lynch him."

Tabitha blew out her breath slowly. *Not that farfetched.* "It's happened before in good old Blue Beech Ridge." *It happened to White Lettie.*

"Maybe not all that," Angelica said, "but he'd be done here in any case."

"So, that's why he let us go?"

Angelica shrugged. "I'm not going to blackmail him. But you can't say anything to anyone."

"I won't." *Another awful secret.* "I promise."

"But, yeah. George Hardin will mind his p's and q's around me now. And he'll leave you alone too, I suppose."

The bell rang, ending first period.

Angelica pointed at Tabitha's eyes. "You better take a minute and touch up your eyes." She gave Tabitha a wan smile.

Tabitha nodded. "You too."

Angelica stood and pulled Tabitha into a fierce hug. "I miss her."

Tabitha nodded. *Me too.*

Angelica Goldsmith pulled out of the embrace. "I need you to spread the word. Rehearsal is still on tonight. We'll talk—as a cast and crew—about whether we *should* go on with the show, but we *will* go on. It's what Suzanne would've wanted."

We have to go on.

I need this show. It's like the only normal thing left in my life.

Tabitha pulled her compact mirror out of her bag and began repairing her makeup. "First rule of the theatre—the show must go on."

Life must go on, Molly thought as she and Mike sat across from each other in a booth at the A&W, sharing a specially made root beer milkshake.

I didn't know Suzanne Tulane well. We only met a couple times. Maybe I should feel guilty with him being dead, and me just enjoying a moment like this with the man I love.

But I don't feel guilty. This. This is what I want. Two straws—one milkshake. Like two teenagers in love, dreaming of the day we can get sealed in the temple of God.

And, of course, what comes after…

As they both sipped from the same shake, leaning in, Molly looked up into Mike's blue eyes.

Such beautiful eyes. How could they be the eyes of a rapist?

Mike returned her gaze, his eyes twinkling, amused, filled with mutual delight. He managed a grin, even with his lips securely closed around his straw.

I could stare into those eyes all day, thought Molly. *No, I couldn't. Because if I did, I'd end up in serious violation of the law of chastity. I love you. I do. So, how can I do this? How could I ever doubt you?*

But I do doubt you. And I can't shake it. And Tabitha's my baby. That outweighs everything else—even my love for you.

So, I've got to know.

But I need to handle this just right. Tabitha's the actress—she could carry this off. But me? I'll probably just botch it. Gotta catch him off guard.

"Mike"—she maintained eye contact, trying to keep her teenager-in-love expression intact—"are you Magnus?"

His eyes opened wide. His smile vanished as he released his straw. Then he sat up. "Why do y'all keep asking me that? First Tabitha. Now you?"

She sat up as well. But her eyes still bored into his, though any vestige of affection was gone. *Because you're too blasted perfect. Because I love you. Because I need you.*

But I must protect my little girl. "Because Tabitha is my daughter."

His face was as blank as an unpainted canvas. "If you already doubt me, what could I possibly say to convince you otherwise?"

That's not a denial. It's almost an accusation.

He narrowed his eyes and stared back with laserlike focus. "I am not Magnus. I can't say it any plainer than that. I only want to protect Tabitha. I would never, never hurt her."

Molly's lip trembled. "I want to believe that." *I really, really do!* "I love you, Mike."

"Molly, have you, have you prayed about this? If you think I'm a danger to your sweet daughter, then pray about it."

Molly's fist thumped the table. "I have prayed! Don't you think I have?"

"And what answer did you get?"

She shook her head, clenching her teeth. "Nothing. Nothing, yet. I—"

His soul-piercing stare never wavered. "Then you're not askin' the right question. Or you're afraid of the answer."

Molly swallowed, the sweet and creamy taste of root beer shake turned to bile on her tongue. "Please take me home." She glanced at the ring, the lovely diamond ring which no sheriff's deputy should've ever been able to afford. "I need to pray."

And pray she did.

But no answer came. No "stupor of thought." No answer at all. Just a feeling of gnawing fear.

When Tabitha had arrived home after rehearsal, having gotten a ride from Beulah, Tabitha had calmly, matter-of-factly informed Molly that, despite Suzanne Tulane's death, the cast and crew had decided to "go on with the show."

But Tabitha had said little else as she prepared for bed then disappeared into her room.

Molly knelt at her own bedside again and continued pleading with her Father in Heaven for guidance.

What should I do? Should I break off the engagement? If Mike is Magnus, who can I tell about it? I can't go to the police. He is the police. What would I say anyway? I just don't know what's going on!

Should I confide in President Roylance?

She listened for a response, listened with all her soul.

Nothing.

What should I do? Help me, Heavenly Father. Please!

And then it came—clearly, as if she were hearing a voice in her mind— *"Stay close to Mike Kilmore."*

Molly quivered.

Stay close to him? Because Mike will protect her—protect my Tabitha?

Or I am supposed to watch him—to be there when he makes his move? To stop him?

But that was all. Plead though she might, no further answer came to her.

Magnus ran his hand over the curve of Patsy's hip. Unlike that little bitch Beulah,

Patsy had come when he called. She snuggled closer to him in his bed, pressing her naked, sweaty flesh against his.

"What're y'all thinkin' about?" she asked. "Y'all thinkin' about that Bradley Thibodeaux freak? What y'all did? What we did? That was *nasty*. Kinky." She giggled. "Real kinky!"

His lips twitching in self-reproach. *Should've left little Bradley alone. He'd have run away if I'd just left him alone. Damn him. This's all his fault.*

I let my anger get the best of me. But it's still Bradley's fault. Damn Thibodeaux spawn.

Patsy nibbled on his earlobe as she scratched his chest lightly with her painted fingernails. "It's all working out, ain't it? Goin' according to plan?"

He scowled. "I am losing the mother. She no longer trusts me."

"But we're almost there, ain't we? Just five more nights. Just 'til Saturday, right? Then it all comes together."

He nodded slowly. "Just five more nights. And then Molly Moonshadow will have served her purpose. Then we shall have Tabitha. Then we shall have the prize."

"And then we can dispose of the old lady."

"Indeed, my dear. Then we can dispose of her."

Patsy giggled.

Magnus suppressed a grimace of distaste. *Such a damnably annoying sound.*

You're powerful, you redheaded little fox. Almost as powerful as Beulah, though neither of you holds a candle to Tabitha's nuclear fire. But you have sufficient strength in the Power to meet my needs for the present.

And that makes you useful. For now.

Good in bed. Definitely good in bed. Enthusiastic. Delightfully buxom. Athletic. Flexible. But that giggle? Annoying as hell.

Once I have my prize, though—in just five more days, as you've so conveniently pointed out—well, then I can dispose of you too, my dear.

Yes, once I have Tabitha, all the rest of you idiotic little whores can go straight to hell for all I care. In fact, I may speed you on your way.

Yes, that would be perfect. No wagging, gossiping little tongues. No inconvenient witnesses. It seems I need to make a small change in the plan. A slight addendum, as it were.

Easy enough.

He grinned, baring his teeth. "Yes, indeed, my dear. Utterly disposable."

All of you.

Brutal night, Tabitha thought. *Absolutely brutal. But good. Almost believe we're ready.* She and Beulah sat together, along with the rest of the cast and crew of *My Fair Lady*, in the front-row audience seats. She was exhausted.

They were all exhausted.

"Okay," said Angela Goldsmith, flipping through the scribbled-on pages of her notepad, "double notes tonight. We'll do the tech rehearsal first. Then the run-through." She exhaled wearily through pursed lips, then grinned. "But we did well tonight. Very well, overall. Some glitches, but we'll get those worked out."

Tabitha and Beulah exchanged a high-five. Then Tabitha turned and high-fived Billy Hammond—her Professor Higgins.

I've grown accustomed to his face. It wasn't a romance, but it had become something just short of that. *As soon as the play's over, this will be over too. But it's been nice while it lasted. Sweet. Comfortable. When you play opposite someone, you either grow to despise each other or you grow accustomed to each other.*

Maybe in the next show, if we end up together again...What am I thinking about? He's got a girlfriend, and I'M NOT DATING ANY MORE NON-MORMONS!

Especially after Joey. *Well, that wasn't really dating. Just some kissing. Some wonderful, breathless kissing. But he's going away with Beulah.*

Beulah had told her as they rode in together. Beulah and Joey would finish the semester, and then they'd head off to the University of Mississippi.

And they'd try to make a go of it.

Tabitha had wished them well, and, deep down, she'd even meant it. Joey and Beulah had so many strikes against them. No diplomas, at least not yet—which would make it harder to get jobs down there—and an interracial relationship. The Deep South was, to say the least, not the best place to be a mixed-race couple.

I hope they make it.

Me? I still have to finish stupid freshman history class to graduate, under the loving tutelage of Mr. Hardin.

"Tabitha? Eliza?" Angelica sounded slightly irritated. "Care to join the party?"

Tabitha grimaced. "Sorry. What'd you say?"

Angelica gave her a stern look, with just the hint of a smile. "I said you missed your lighting in the last scene. Those are Fresnel lights. They don't move. You must step *into* the light. And stay there. Do you understand?"

Tabitha nodded quickly. "Got it."

"Okay," said Angelica. "So, on to the run-through…"

The notes for the full run-through went quickly. "And that's it," Angelica said. "Good job, everyone. Tomorrow's Thursday. Full-dress rehearsal. I know some of you asked about parents coming tomorrow. But, no. Sorry. Besides, we might have to run some parts of it again later. Then we open Friday night."

Three performances. Friday night, Saturday matinee, and Saturday night. Then it's all over. Back to a life that makes no sense anymore.

Everyone stood to gather their belongings and head home. For Tabitha, that meant making a beeline backstage for White Lettie's broom. But Angelica stopped them. "Before you go, I have a couple of announcements to make."

Some of them groaned their inarticulate protest, but all took their seats once more.

"First of all," Angelica began with a wink to Rebecca Hargrove, the choir teacher and accompanist for the show, "V.P. Hardin has authorized funds for us to hire an *orchestra* for the show."

A collective gasp went up from the assembled students.

Angelica nodded. "That's right. An eighteen-piece orchestra from Cape Girardeau. They'll be here tomorrow."

"But tomorrow's dress rehearsal!" cried Scott, a.k.a. Colonel Pickering.

Angelica nodded, smiling. "That's right. They're professionals, so we don't need to worry about them being able to play the music. But we need everyone to stay after school tomorrow to rehearse with them." She held up both hands to silence protests. "Don't worry about dinner. V.P. Hardin has *generously*"—she grinned wickedly at Tabitha—"and out of his own pocket, I might add, paid for pizzas for everybody."

Pizzas? Mr. Hardin? Generously? Tabitha returned the sly grin. Then she grimaced sourly. *Probably from Pizza Hut. Not good pizza. She sighed. Still, pizza paid for by Mr. Hardin? That'll make it taste a little better!*

She winked at Angelica Goldsmith. *I thought you weren't going to blackmail him?*

Angelica responded to Tabitha's wink with a mask of complete innocence. The English teacher turned her attention back to the rest of the kids. "Can I count on all you cast members to be here? It's important. Mr. MacDonald says we'll need the stage hands too."

Amid a mixture of groans, nods, and some pronouncements of "cool," everyone consented.

Angelica nodded with satisfaction. "Good. Now, for the second announcement. You may not like it, but"—Miss Goldsmith's sly grin gave the lie to that notion—

"another group has volunteered to strike set for us after the final production on Saturday night." When a number of voices were raised in surprise, disbelief, and joy, she raised her hands to silence them all. "I know. I know. You were so looking forward to staying late and tearing down the set after the last show. But we'll just have to grin and bear it."

"Who's gonna strike set for us?" asked Jason. He tapped rhythmically on the top of his hat. They hadn't been rehearsing in full costume yet, but the Alfred P. Doolittle's wedding top hat was as much a prop as it was a costume piece. And they'd been rehearsing with all props for more than a week.

Angelica indicated the gray silk top hat in Jason's lap. "Make sure you put that away before you go. You know the rules—no props or costumes at home. Since we lost…" A hush blanketed the theatre. Several people wiped surreptitiously at suddenly moist eyes. They hadn't discussed Suzanne's death since the meeting on Monday night—at least not during rehearsal. It was as if they'd all entered into an unspoken, informal covenant of silence on the subject of the costume mistress's tragic end.

Angelica bit her quivering lower lip. "I'm sorry. I didn't mean to… It's hard on all of us. And it's complicated. Our feelings are complicated." She dabbed at her eyes. "But we're going to push through to the end. And we'll do it well. We're going to dedicate our final performance to Suzanne Tulane."

Nods and sniffles were universal.

"But the school?" said Billy, shaking his head while wiping his nose. "The administration? They won't like it."

"Then the administration"—Tabitha rose to her feet—"can go straight to hell." *Wow. I can't believe I said that.* "Suzanne Tulane was…" *What? Sweet? Nice? Infectiously enthusiastic?*

Yes. All of those things. Whatever else he was, Suzanne was nice. "She was nice."

"Amen." Beulah joined Tabitha standing. "Amen." She placed a hand on Tabitha's shoulder and squeezed.

Billy nodded. He wiped at a tear. Then he clapped. He stood slowly, applauding all the way.

One by one, the cast and crew stood and clapped. And wept. And hugged.

After nearly a minute, Angelica Goldsmith slid off the lip of the stage. "We should've done this on Monday." She glanced over at Miss Hargrove, who, with the advent of the orchestra, would no longer be playing the piano. "And I'm probably going to get in trouble for this." Her eyes swept the students. "Will you join me in prayer?" Without waiting for consent, she knelt and bowed her head.

"We ain't supposed to pray in school," said a girl, one of the stage hands. She wore a conspicuous crucifix about her neck. "The school…" Her voice trailed off.

Miss Hargrove knelt next to Angelica. Through a tearful grin, she said, "The school can go straight to hell too."

Tabitha knelt. Beulah dropped to her knees as well. Her hand sought and found

Tabitha's.

In a matter of seconds, they were all on their knees. And shortly thereafter, each of them was joining hands with another.

To Tabitha's mild surprise, there was not one word of protest at the idea of a "Mormon" prayer.

Angelica smiled. "Thank you. All of you." She squeezed her leaking eyes shut. "Dear Heavenly Father…"

The waning moon peeked through a hole in the clouds as Tabitha and Beulah walked quickly through the parking lot of the school theatre. They had lingered longer than the other kids and were the last to leave. Tabitha had her bag over one shoulder and the broom carried over the other like a hobo's stick with the broom's bristles acting the part of a bundle.

Beulah waved a hand at the witch's broom. "Y'all ever going to get a car of your own? I mean, y'all can't ride that thing. Not without—" She gasped. "Oh, I'm sorry. I didn't mean to bring it up again…"

Tabitha shrugged, causing the heavy broom to wobble slightly. "It's okay." She paused. "I'm not going back."

Beulah nodded. "I figured."

They both knew what Tabitha meant. *The Circle.*

Beulah started digging her keys out of her purse. "Me, neither."

Tabitha stopped in her tracks. "You're not?"

Beulah pulled the keys out and held them, staring at them, contemplating them as she stood still in the crisp November night. "No. I'm not." She raised her head to gaze at Tabitha.

The harsh, yellow lights of the parking lot cast the blonde's face into shadow, but the spectral gleam of the moon caught in and reflected in her eyes. "I didn't realize it until just now—not 'til you said it—but I'm done." She shook the keys, pointing with one of them as if it was a weapon or a wand. "I've done a lot…a lot of bad with Daddy, with the Circle. And with Magnus." She shook her head slowly and decisively from side to side. "I don't want to do bad stuff anymore."

"What about the Power?"

Beulah shrugged. "I've got Joey. It's not the same." She wiped away a tear. "It'll be enough."

Tabitha's heart ached. *Joey.*

"Did y'all kill Daddy?"

The air in Tabitha's lungs seemed to freeze. "Wh-what?"

A single yard separated them. Beulah took a step closer. She pointed the key at Tabitha accusingly. "Did y'all…Did you, Tabitha Moonshadow, kill my daddy?"

Tabitha swallowed the bile threatening to erupt from her throat. She shook her head. "No. I just scared him. That's all."

Beulah nodded, her expression unreadable in the uncertain light. "Scared him?"

Tabitha nodded. "He ran away."

"You and Joey?"

Tabitha hesitated, then nodded. "But your father was alive and-and unhurt when I... when we were done with him."

Beulah nodded, paused, then nodded some more. She pointed the key at the ground. "I killed Sergeant Thibodeaux. That deputy sheriff." She lowered her head, casting her entire face in shadow.

Tabitha stared, openmouthed, at her friend.

"Well," Beulah said, "me and Magnus. Me and the Circle. He was a rapist—Daniel Thibodeaux was. Raped a few women. 'Specially black women. Used his authority as deputy and his gun. He deserved it, I guess. Deserved to die for what he'd done." She raised her head again, so her eyes were glinting in the moonlight once more. "But I didn't hurt Miss Tulane. I didn't help Magnus hurt him. That wasn't me."

Help Magnus? Why would she help Magnus rape Suzanne?

"That was probably Patsy," Beulah said. "She's the one that's strongest after me. And after y'all, of course. I'm not the one to point fingers and all." She lowered her face again. "I've done enough bad. I don't wanna be Daddy's baby girl anymore."

Beulah's body trembled as she sobbed.

Killed Sergeant Thibodeaux? That awful man? The Circle killed him? Murdered him? Magnus murdered him?

"I'm sorry!" Beulah cried. "Sweet Jesus! I'm sorry!" She sank to her knees. Her hands hung limp at her sides.

Tabitha stumbled forward and knelt beside her. She dropped her bag and the broom to the asphalt. Tabitha wrapped her arms around her friend.

Beulah sobbed all the louder, her body quaking violently in Tabitha's arms. After a moment or two, Beulah returned the embrace, clinging to Tabitha like a lost child clutching at her mother. "I'm sorry."

Tabitha managed to free a hand, so she could stroke Beulah's hair. "Sh. Sh. It's okay. It's okay."

Slowly, by small degrees, Beulah cried herself out.

And Tabitha held her.

When Beulah finally loosened her hold on Tabitha, she whispered, "Thank you."

Tabitha pulled back slightly. *She's thanking me?* "What for?"

"For sending Daddy away. For setting me free. Of him." She pulled out of the hug entirely, taking Tabitha's hands in hers. As close as they were, even in the darkness, Beulah's tear-streaked face was clear enough to see. "Now"—she swallowed—"now, it's up to me. I have to walk away. From Magnus, from the Circle—"

"Y'all're gonna walk away from us?"

Tabitha snapped her head up, then left and right. They were surrounded by the Circle.

They were not wearing their robes. Magnus wasn't there, but all the girls were there. All of them.

They're not holding hands. Why would they? They can't channel without Magnus or Joey.

Patsy stepped forward, her red ponytail—black in the moonlight—bouncing jauntily behind her head. "Y'all think y'all can just walk away?" She shook her head. Her teeth gleamed in the darkness. "Y'all can't leave the sisterhood. Our secrets are y'all's secrets. And y'all's secrets are ours."

Beulah stood, wiping hurriedly at her eyes. "I won't tell anyone. I won't. Y'all know that. All y'all know that."

Tabitha gripped the broomstick in her right hand. She got to her feet. *Don't make it look like a weapon. Can't fight them all off. Can I?*

"Actually," said Patsy, "Beulah, y'all can go. Magnus don't need y'all anymore. He's got me now. So, y'all can go. Run away, for all we care."

It's me they want. "Beulah," Tabitha said, fighting down a tremor in her voice, "get behind me."

"Tabitha." There was naked terror in Beulah's voice.

"Just do it," Tabitha said, clenching her teeth.

Beulah complied.

Tabitha drew herself up to the fullness of her diminutive stature. She held the witch's broom in front of her with both hands. And there was no mistaking her fighting posture. "You've seen what I can do. At least some of you have." She stared straight at Patsy.

Patsy shuddered.

"That's right," Tabitha continued, gathering her courage. And her rage. *Get angry. Quick.* "So, back off. Now." She paused. "We're going to get in the car and leave." She glared daggers at Patsy. "Beulah, please get our stuff."

Beulah gathered up her bag and Tabitha's.

"Y'all can't just leave," Patsy said.

"Oh, watch us." Tabitha bared her teeth in a feral grin. She hoped Patsy could see it. "Now, back off. Maybe I won't just blow you up or break all your bones. Maybe I'll just knock you down. Hard. Put some road rash on those pretty faces of yours."

Some of the girls took halting steps backward.

Patsy took a step back as well, but she extended both hands toward Tabitha. "Come on, Tabitha! Why're y'all doin' this? We're friends, right?"

Tabitha nodded. "I thought so. I really did. You took me in when no one else would. So, why are you threatening us?"

Patsy smiled, showing a mouthful of teeth. "I'm not threatenin' y'all, girl. Y'all're free to go. To go and come as y'all please, of course." The smile vanished. "But not to leave the Circle. We are Sisters. We are goddesses of the Circle. We are the embodiment of the Divine Feminine. Y'all can't never leave that."

They won't hurt me. Magnus wants me too badly. But Beulah? Patsy's so jealous of Beulah. Already taken her place. "We can't ever leave? So, what's that supposed to mean? We can't graduate? Go away to college? Get married? Have families?" She waved the broom around, pointing it at the girls in front of her. "We have to stay here and be…" *Magnus's puppets? No. Don't say that.* "…the Circle for the rest of our lives?" *Surely, they've thought about that. Right?*

"What's wrong with that?" asked Patsy. "Ain't nothin' like the Power. Feelin' it. Usin' it."

Tabitha took a deep breath. "Fine. So, tell me, Patsy, Sister of mine? Were you there when Magnus raped Bradley Thibodeaux, when he raped Miss Tulane?"

A few of the girls gasped, putting hands to shocked mouths. A few. But not all. Not Patsy.

You were there. You bitch. "Did you help him, Patsy? Did you help Magnus…" *What's the word?* "…sodomize Miss Tulane?"

Patsy's teeth shone. "Hell, yeah."

Rage bloomed in Tabitha. And she knew exactly what to do with it.

"Isn't that your car?" She pointed with the broom at Patsy's 240Z. The sporty Datsun was cherry red, although one couldn't see the bright color in the dark.

The Circle parted as Patsy and the girls turned to gaze in the direction indicated. *Say goodbye to your cute little car, Patsy.*

Tabitha focused on the car, ready for the explosion that, with any luck, would obliterate Patsy's treasure.

No! Not yet. "If I wanted to, I could blow it to bits." Tabitha nursed her rage, but shifted her focus past the gap in the Circle and into the trees beyond the parking lot—far to the left of the car.

Patsy shook her head. Hesitantly. "Y'all can't do that."

"I can't?" *Hope this works.* "Watch the trees."

Now. Now. NOW!

BOOM! CRACK!

They all jumped—even Tabitha. Several of the girls screamed.

And all eyes were focused on the flattened, broken trees—more than a dozen destroyed.

Even in the moonlight, Tabitha could see that Patsy's eyes were wide with shock. And terror.

It worked! Wow. So much damage. Those trees. Just like Magnus did.

Ignoring a twinge of guilt at what she'd just done, Tabitha grabbed Beulah's hand. "We're going now."

Patsy said nothing.

Tabitha led Beulah toward her car. "And you're going to leave us alone. Magnus won't let you touch me. But if you touch Beulah…or my mom, I'll destroy you."

Don't hurry. Don't let them know how scared I am. Tabitha did her best to appear leisurely and in control as she and Beulah got into the car. Somehow, Beulah got the message too. They both trembled as they moved, but Tabitha was certain the other girls couldn't see it.

As soon as the car doors were closed, Tabitha said, "Drive."

Beulah's eyes were riveted straight ahead as they rolled toward the parking lot exit. "Where?"

"My house. You're staying the night with me."

As the darkness of the road enshrouded them like grave clothes, Tabitha finally released a breath she hadn't known she was holding.

"Wow." Beulah's tone was filled with awe and fear. "Just...wow."

"Yeah." *It gets worse, stronger every time. Lucky I didn't kill someone. I could've killed them. Could've killed them all.*

And what frightened Tabitha most—more than the threat from the Circle—was that for a brief moment she had *wanted* to.

Stay close to Mike. She snuggled closer to him on the back seat of his car. *To be any closer, we'd have to ditch our clothes.*

Stop it.

As first counselor in the branch presidency, the weekly Wednesday night Young Men and Young Women meetings were part of Mike's responsibilities. And lately, Molly had been going with him to those meetings.

Mostly they just chaperoned as the youth led their own program. That night, the youth had engaged in a joint activity, all of them learning how to "disco dance."

Molly and Mike had even joined in. The kids weren't all that enthusiastic, but Mike had really gotten into the spirit of things. Molly had laughed and "gotten her groove on."

Afterward, they sat out in the parking lot—in the cozy back seat of his sexy Mustang. "Watching the kids leave," Mike had said. "And we can actually sit together in the back seat. Not like the bucket seats up front."

It would be safer to sit up front, not back here like a couple of hormonal teenagers.

The November air was frigid, but Mike had a blanket. "For emergencies. In case I get stuck in the snow."

That made sense enough, but Molly suspected he didn't mind a chance to cuddle.

And so, they sat, huddling and cuddling under Mike's "emergency blanket" in the back seat of the perfect make out car. *Just like the song—"I wanna huddle and cuddle, as close to you as I can get!" Only Mike is the "teacher's pet."*

Not exactly make out point, but the kids are all long gone. And it's just us. And I don't want to be anywhere else in the world right now.

I'm so confused.

Who are you really, Mike? Are you the kind, wonderful, sexy hunk of a man I think I know and love desperately, or are you a monster?

"You know," she said, breathing in the heady scent of his Old Spice mixed with good, clean, masculine sweat, "if this were any place other than the church parking lot, I'd be suspicious of your motives, Brother Kilmore."

He chuckled softly. "I'd be suspicious myself." He sighed and squeezed her hand. "I'm real glad you decided to trust me again." He kissed her earlobe, sending a shiver through her entire body. "Prayer's a miraculous thing."

"How can you be so sure I prayed about it?" *And how can I think about prayer when you're doing that?*

"Because I know. I know you, Molly Moonshadow. You love your precious gal. You'll do whatever it takes to protect her."

Including let you rip my heart out? I love you, darn it. I want you. I need you. But...

"And I promise you," he whispered in her ear, his hot breath tickling the delicate hairs inside, "I will protect her too. I'll find this Magnus, and when I—"

The radio mounted on the dashboard crackled to life. "Bravo-Charlie-Two, this is Bravo-Charlie-Dispatch." The voice was electronically distorted, but discernibly female.

Mike growled like a dog robbed of a bone. "Dang it."

He threw off the blanket, disentangling himself from Molly. "'Scuse me."

"Bravo-Charlie-Two, this is Bravo-Charlie-Dispatch. Do you copy?"

Mike somehow insinuated himself between the two front seats—without crushing Molly—and grasped the microphone. "Copy, Dispatch, this is Bravo-Charlie-Two. Go ahead."

"Sorry, Mike, but there's been a report of an explosion at the high school."

Mike turned his wide, horrified eyes to Molly. "Copy, Dispatch. Call the fire department." He wriggled himself fully into the driver seat. "On my way. Bravo-Charlie-Two out."

Molly scrambled to get the door open, intending to move to the front passenger seat. But Mike had already started the car. "Just you stay put."

As they roared out of the parking lot, Mike unrolled his window and set a small flashing siren on the roof. "Hang on." The siren began to wail.

Molly looked at her watch, frantically angling it this way and that, trying to catch enough light to see the time. *Tabitha's done by now. She's gone. She's not there. She's not there!*

Please, Heavenly Father, let my baby be safe!

Molly slid across the seat in a most unladylike pile of arms and legs as the car swerved hard around a corner, out of the parking lot and onto the highway.

Molly burst through the front door of the cottage. "Tabitha? Tabitha?"

When the deputy sheriff had dropped her off—at Mike's insistence—Molly had recognized Beulah's car parked in front of the house, next to her own car. And that sight had given her hope.

"Tabitha?"

Tabitha emerged from her room, wearing her long winter nightgown. Behind her, stood Beulah, similarly dressed for bed.

"Mom?"

Molly threw herself at her daughter, enfolding her in a bear hug. "You're okay!"

Tabitha wheezed, patting Molly's back. "Yeah. I'm fine. Can't…breathe."

Molly pulled back, still trembling. She gripped Tabitha by the shoulders. "You're okay!"

"Yeah." Tabitha grinned. "I'm okay. I invited Beulah to stay—"

Molly shook her head, grinning like a lunatic. "There was an explosion. At the school, they said. Only it was just the trees. I—I was so worried."

Tabitha grimaced sheepishly, and her eyes flickered away, as if trying to look at Beulah. "Yeah. Freaky, huh?"

Molly's jaw dropped. "You saw it? You were there?"

Tabitha shrugged. "Sorta. It was dark. There wasn't a flash or anything. Just… BOOM! And the trees cracked and…"

"We were in the parking lot," Beulah said. "I didn't see it. Not 'til after. I heard it, though. I, uh, hope y'all don't mind me staying the night…"

Molly barely spared a glance at the tall blonde—her hands and eyes were too busy examining Tabitha, checking for broken bones.

Tabitha brushed her mother's hands away. "I'm okay, Mom. We're okay."

Molly stepped back, biting her bottom lip and trying desperately to hold back tears. She wrapped her arms protectively around her middle. "How about some hot chocolate?"

"I'm okay, Mom. Really—"

"Hot chocolate?" Beulah smiled. "Why, that'd be lovely, Miss Moonshadow."

Molly looked at her and smiled. "You're always welcome here, Beulah. And call me—" As soon as those words were out of her mouth, she regretted them. Not proper. But it was too late. *Well, she's almost an adult anyway.* "Call me Molly." She noted that the nightgown the tall girl was wearing was too short for her—not immodest, just too short. *It's one of Tabitha's nightgowns. So, this wasn't a planned thing.*

Do her parents know she's here? Wait. Isn't her father that pastor who disappeared last week?

"Can I light a fire?" Tabitha asked.

Molly couldn't resist. "I don't know. *Can* you?"

Tabitha grimaced with annoyance and rolled her eyes. "*May* I light a fire?"

Molly grinned and inclined her head. "Yes, my dear, you *may*. If you can."

Beulah visibly started.

Was it something I said? Molly thought back quickly, replaying the words in her mind, timed with Beulah's reaction. *"My dear?"* Was that it? Why?

Later, as they sat sipping cocoa before a small, crackling fire, Molly also began to replay her time with Mike that night.

He'd been so loving, so affectionate, but then that radio message had come.

Then he was all business, stern, even angry. Worried about Tabitha? *He had become a different person, almost as if he'd put on a mask.*

And when they arrived at the scene, he was out of the car immediately, with only a "Stay here!" to her.

She had, of course, not heeded his command.

More than a dozen trees, several of them at least a foot thick at the base, had been broken off. It looked to Molly as if some of the broken trees had been blown back several yards from their shattered stumps.

The scene, lit by the red-and-white flashing lights of the fire trucks and the red-and-blue sirens of the three sheriff vehicles, was surreal, otherworldly—like something out of a sci-fi movie or the aftermath of an atomic blast. It seemed surreal, because something was missing.

No smoke. No smell of burning. No heat.

Just a lot of broken trees.

And there was Mike. He was everywhere, with his flashlight, examining the bizarre scene. Occasionally, he would shout an order. Most of the time, however, his voice was calm, though distinct, as if he expected everyone to understand his every word. And obey.

And one thing more had struck Molly—there was one aspect of Mike's conduct which set that Mike a world apart from the Mike she knew and loved. Her Mike was forever catching himself right on the verge of using rough language, correcting or substituting words more suitable for "mixed" or polite company. Molly had assumed that in the field, with the types of people Mike had to deal with day-in and day-out, he was accustomed to being looser, more forceful, even cruder with his language. His constant struggle to temper his speech in her presence was—to Molly—one of his more endearing qualities.

But there, Molly had seen Mike in his element, dealing with a crisis, dealing with his fellow officers. But there had been no swearing, no rough language. His folksy, almost clumsy manner had vanished beneath his professional veneer.

Like putting on a mask.

Or taking one off.

And his Missouri accent was completely gone.

Tabitha hadn't shared a bed with anyone since she'd been a little girl—on those dark nights right after her dad had left. Tabitha had sobbed quietly, alone in her bed. Her mom had come in. She'd sat on Tabitha's bed. Mom had stroked Tabitha's hair. And Mom hadn't told her not to cry or to hush. She hadn't lied to Tabitha, saying everything would be all right or she knew how Tabitha felt. She had just *been* there.

And if that weren't enough, on some nights, her mom would climb into bed with her. Tabitha would curl up in a fetal ball and weep. Her mother would wrap her arms around Tabitha and hold her while she cried.

Sometimes—perhaps most times—Tabitha was sure her mother was crying too.

But there had been no one else—except the once—the night Randy, her father's horrible boyfriend, had tried to rape her. Tabitha had escaped, barricading herself in the bathroom.

But both had been very different from her present situation.

She had invited Beulah to stay the night. For Beulah's protection.

For their *mutual* protection.

The double bed was wide enough, and Beulah kept to her side, but the girl's presence made it difficult for Tabitha to relax.

Beulah, however, had fallen asleep quickly.

She's used to it. She has shared a bed with lots of guys. At least that's the way she tells it. But not always by her own choosing.

Tabitha shuddered.

Beulah moaned.

Tabitha tried to relax, tried to hold still.

Beulah's moaning grew louder, rising and falling. Soon the sounds took on a stuttering, irregular tempo, as if Beulah was trying to say something.

Talking in her sleep?

"Not tonight, Daddy. Please! I *did* him. Like you made me. Ain't I done enough?"

Wide awake and terrified of what else she might hear, Tabitha tried to cover her ears. But her efforts were useless.

Soon Beulah's agonized words were inescapable. "Sound waves. Photons. Invisible. Music." A sob. "Tappin' his feet. No! Y'all don't need me. Y'all don't need me anymore."

Is she talking about Magnus?

"Y'all don't love me anymore. If you ever really did. Y'all don't need me."

Did she love him? Does she love him? Love Magnus?

"No! I won't. Just leave him alone."

Suzanne? She's talking to Magnus about Suzanne.

"Please stop! It hurts! I don't wanna do it. Not tonight. Not me, Daddy! Look at his foot! Photons. Invisible. Music. I didn't kill him, Mama. He's just gone. Didn't kill him. Tabitha didn't either. Put down the bottle, Mama! Put down the damn bottle. Just for once! See what's right in front of you. Right in front of your nose! He was *doin'* me, Mama! Y'all knew. All along. And y'all didn't care! Just so long as y'all could have the damn bourbon!" Beulah's body shook with sobs in her sleep. "He-he was doin' me, Mama! He was doin' me." Beulah groaned. "No, Mama. Didn't *entice* him. No. I was eleven. Eleven! Go back to your bottle. Leave me alone."

Beulah seemed to quiet then, lost in an uneasy sleep of quiet weeping, broken only by the occasional hitching breath.

Tabitha let her own tears flow. *Where were you, God? Why didn't you protect her? She was just a little girl.*

Why didn't you protect me?

"At least," Beulah continued suddenly, "he said . . . loved me. Loved me. Did y'all ever say that, Mama?"

It's starting all over again. A man who says he loves me. Okay, he didn't say he loves me. But he wants me.

And he's a monster. I won't let him use me. I won't let him hurt Mom.

But what if I'm wrong? What if Mike isn't Magnus? If I accuse him...

I already accused him, and she's still going out with him.

Heavenly Father, what do I do?

"No!" Beulah screamed. "The music! He can do anything! Can't stop him! I can't!" She began to thrash in the bed. "Not my fault! Not my fault! Can't stop him! NO!!"

Beulah sat upright, screaming and shaking.

Tabitha sat up beside her. She encircled her friend's shoulders with her arms. "It's okay. 'Sokay."

Beulah clutched at Tabitha's forearms with hands curled into claws. "I'm...I'm s-sorry."

An urgent knock at the dock.

Both Tabitha and Beulah squeaked.

"Tabitha?" Her mom's voice. "Are you okay?"

"It's okay, Mom."

Beulah opened her mouth, but Tabitha gave her a quieting squeeze.

Tabitha shook her head, looking at the shivering blonde. Beulah looked like a zombie, her hair badly mussed, her eyes wide, tears running afresh down her cheeks.

Tabitha pursed her lips and made a quiet shush. "Beulah just had a bad dream."

A pause—a pregnant gap in time—as Tabitha prayed her mother would take that explanation and leave. *She has a key. She could open the door. She's probably already heading for her jewelry box to get it.*

"Okay," her mom said. "I'm here. In my room. If you need me."

Tabitha swallowed hard, then cleared her throat. "Thanks, Mom. You're the best." *I'm glad you're there. You make me feel safe. Well, safer.*

Tabitha pulled gently on her friend, urging Beulah to lie down again.

Beulah allowed herself to be pulled.

Tabitha hauled the blankets up, covering both of them.

"Will y'all..." Beulah shivered. "Will you hold me 'til I go to sleep?"

"Sure." Tabitha put an arm around Beulah's shoulders.

"Thank you." Beulah shifted herself, drawing closer with her back to Tabitha. "I don't deserve you. Y'all're the best friend I've ever had. Some ways, the only friend, the only female friend, at least. I don't deserve it."

"Well, you're my friend." *Deserving has nothing to do with friendship. It doesn't even have anything to do with love. We love, because we must. We love because others need us.*

"I ain't been a good friend. I've been an awful friend. Magnus, he wants you. He's bad. And I helped...helped him get you. I'm so sorry." Her voice was calm, and she didn't break into fresh tears or sobs.

Which mildly surprised Tabitha. *Maybe she's all cried out. I would be. Maybe.*

"Beulah?"

"Um-hm?"

"Can I ask you something?"

Beulah stiffened. "I can't tell you. I can't."

"But I haven't—"

"Y'all're gonna ask me who Magnus is. I can't tell you."

Tabitha paused, drawing in a deep breath, holding it, then letting it out slowly. "Why not?"

"Because he'll kill me. He'll kill anybody who gets in his way."

"How? The Power?" The faces of the Circle, shadowy, eyes and teeth glowing in the moonlight, filled Tabitha's mind.

"Oh, yeah."

"But you and me and Joey, we could stop him. Maybe I could stop him." *I'm a bomb.* "You saw. The trees."

"Yeah, and I saw what y'all did on Saturday night too. Knocked us all down."

"So?"

"But it ain't just that. Magnus—he's powerful in other ways."

"How?"

"He's got more money'n God. He's been stealing and blackmailing from all the richest men in town ever since he discovered the Power. An' I helped him do it. Some of it, anyway. He's got dirt on everyone. Every last one of 'em. He doesn't need the Power to kill us."

"We could run away. Leave."

Beulah shook her head. "Even if we ran away, he'd have us killed. He's got connections. He knows people. He's like a big spider. Even from this tiny, backwater town, he can find us. Anywhere." She paused. "Only reason he'll let Joey and me run away is 'cause he don't need me anymore. He has you."

"But he *doesn't* have me." *Not yet.*

"And if I tell you who he is, he'll kill us—me and Joey. Even Mississippi ain't far enough away from Magnus. He won't kill you. He needs you, now more'n ever. But he'll kill your mom."

"But—"

"Please don't ask me. I can't say. I *won't* say." She was silent for the space of several breaths. "Told y'all I was a bad friend. I don't deserve you."

Tabitha resisted the urge to nod, recalling the scripture— *"Charity seeketh not her own."* Instead, she shook her head. "Doesn't matter. You're my friend. That's all that matters."

Beulah began to weep again. The sobs were quieter than before, but she still shook with the force of them. She curled up into a fetal ball, with only her shoulders pressed against Tabitha.

As her mother had done for her so many times, Tabitha stroked Beulah's tangled hair. She said nothing more, she made no false promises of safety, she didn't say everything would be all right. She just held her friend silently until, at last, Beulah succumbed to the merciful oblivion of quiet sleep.

"You knocked 'em *dead*!" Angelica beamed, bouncing on her heels like an overexcited child. Her diminutive stature only affirmed that image in Tabitha's mind. *If she's happy, we must've done pretty darn well, thought Tabitha. It certainly feels like we did great.*

Those prolonged standing ovations were a good sign too.

One of the director's arms still held the flowers the cast had bought and presented to her at the end of the final show—two dozen yellow roses. Angelica squeaked in ecstatic delight. "Great, fantastic, *stupendous* job, everyone!" She wiped at her eyes, smearing her makeup even worse than before. Then she scowled at the black smudges on her finger. "Crap. Knew I shoulda worn waterproof."

This struck Tabitha as incredibly funny. She guffawed with laughter.

Angelica looked at her in mild amusement. "It's not *that* funny."

But Tabitha's hilarity was infectious, spreading through the cast and crew. Most of them were probably unsure what they were laughing about—not that it mattered. Some of them even clapped.

As Tabitha's laughter died away, she thought, *We're just relieved. All that work, all that tension—and it paid off.* "We did it." Still in costume, she unpinned and removed her hat. Then she raised it toward "the fly" above them with its myriad ropes and lights and suspended scenery backdrops. "We did it!"

The cast and crew of *My Fair Lady* joined her, fists and hats pumping in the air. "We did it!"

It's over.

She knew, in the morning, that simple sentence would carry with it a sense of loss—but not that night. *We did it!*

"Tabitha!"

She wheeled around to see her mom emerging from stage left, dashing toward Tabitha, black evening gown, high heels, and all.

Molly seized Tabitha in a tight embrace, laughing and crying at the same time.

"Oh, sweetheart! You were magnificent! Flawless!"

Tabitha would've returned the embrace, but her arms were pinned at her sides by Molly's bear hug. Still, she did her best to pat her mother's waist. "Thanks, Mom!"

"This was the best one of all!" Molly had been to all three performances—Friday night, the Saturday matinee, and the final performance. All three had been sold-out, but Molly had somehow managed to be in the audience each time. That night, she'd been in the front row.

"That was amazing!"

Tabitha peeked over the top of her mom's shoulder—she was just barely able to do so because of the high heels on her costume shoes—and there was Mike Kilmore, grinning at her.

Mike had worn a suit each night, but this particular black suit with its matching bow tie looked almost too formal—almost like a tuxedo. The effect was spoiled, however, by the brown cowboy boots he wore. But boots or no, he was stunningly handsome, his smile bright enough to light up the already well-lit stage. "This little town hasn't seen *anything* like what all y'all did tonight! Miss Tabitha, if I was wearin' a hat—which, of course, I'm not—that'd be rude and all, me wearin' a hat and sittin' right smack dab in the front row—but if I were wearin' a hat, it'd be off to you. You"—he made a sweeping gesture, almost as if he *were* waving a hat, taking in all the assembled cast and crew—"all y'all were just…incredible."

He stepped around Molly, coming alongside mother and daughter. "Can I get in on this hug?"

Tabitha hesitated for a moment. *Are you Magnus?*

Molly hesitated a moment longer. She pulled back slightly and looked at Tabitha. Molly still wore a smile, but her eyes silently communicated concern.

Tabitha responded with the slightest of nods.

They opened up their embrace, allowing Mike in.

He encircled them in his strong arms, squeezing gently. "My girls, if I may be so bold. No. My *ladies*. My *fair* ladies."

Molly managed a stifled chuckle. "Oh, you big goof!"

He laughed. "That's me!" He kissed Molly on the lips briefly, then he planted an exuberant kiss on the top of Tabitha's head. "I count myself the luckiest man alive. You realize that?"

He stepped back and looked at them both in turn, his eyes finally fixing on Tabitha. "You were…I just don't have the words. You were just, well, the best I've ever seen."

Tabitha felt her cheeks burn. Of course, she reveled in the accolades which came from a performance well executed—but that was from a distance, from an audience on their feet, applauding thunderously, while she bowed from the safety of the stage. But one-on-one, in person, she had difficulty accepting such praise. "Thanks." *You can't be Magnus. You're just too nice.*

But appearances can be deceiving, I've learned that much.

Mike bent at the waist, bowing. He took her hand in his, flinching slightly—they both flinched—as skin touched skin. And Tabitha felt the unmistakable flow of the Power—just a trickle—but it was there.

Mike Kilmore brushed her hand with his lips.

Then he straightened and flashed his million-dollar smile. "Well done, my fair lady."

Tabitha suppressed the urge to yank back her hand, to sever him from the Power. She fought to keep a smile firmly engraved on her face. "Thank you."

She looked up into his eyes, and the Power surged slightly. The Power felt pleasurable.

And terrifying.

Magnus.

She felt someone grasp her free hand. Grateful for the distraction, she turned away from Mike, pulling her hand free from his.

But when she turned, she saw it was Mr. MacDonald clasping her left hand in both of his. "Well done, Miss Moonshadow! Well done indeed." Tabitha had avoided the creepy old man as much as possible, especially after Mike's revelation about the science teacher's lecherous past. But MacDonald had caught her off guard.

He patted her hand, lingering as he always did whenever he managed to ensnare her or any other girl he considered pretty.

He seduced a girl, got her pregnant. She committed suicide. He was excommunicated.

But Mike told us all this. And Mike is Magnus. Can I trust anything he says?

MacDonald let go of her hand.

Tabitha glanced quickly over her shoulder. Mike and her mom stood hand-in-hand, both grinning with vicarious joy, seemingly unaware of the old man's presence. *Gotta get Mom away from him—away from Magnus. He's a monster. He'll hurt her. Can't let on that I know. Gotta...*

She gasped. *The Power!* Tabitha shivered. She could still feel the Power pulsing within her.

How? He's not touching me. Nobody's touching me.

Is he channeling at me? But whose Power is he using? Mom's? Does Mom have the Power? All women have it—at least that's what Beulah said—but does Mom have enough of it to—

"Tabitha!"

She snapped her attention back to Mr. MacDonald, taking half a step back, staying out of the old man's reach.

MacDonald grinned at her. "Forgive me, Tabitha, but there's someone here I want you to meet." He twisted his head to the left and pointed at a portly little man with bright orange hair and a red, pencil-thin mustache. The man stood at the side of the old man's wheelchair, grinning like the Cheshire Cat. "Tabitha Moonshadow, may I present Morty Corrigan? He's the agent I told you about."

The flame-haired man stepped forward. He stood only a few inches taller than Tabitha. He had a wide, toothy smile and too-friendly eyes that reminded Tabitha more of a shady used-car salesman than her idea of a professional theatre agent. He snatched at her hand, gripping it in a fervent handshake worthy of a Mormon missionary. "That was a *helluva* performance, Tabitha! A *helluva* performance. May I call you Tabitha? You can call me Morty." He continued to shake her hand with gusto. "Boffo! Ya-know-wudda-mean? And just seventeen!"

Tabitha finally managed to extricate her hand. "I'll be eighteen in March."

His grin widened 'til he resembled a wolf drooling over a tender lamb. "Even better. Won't have to worry about all those silly child-labor laws." He glanced past her, then back again, winking. "Won't have to get mommy's permission either."

Tabitha twisted around, looking for her mom and Mike. They were there, still holding hands. But they weren't looking in her direction. At that moment, they seemed to have eyes only for each other.

Gotta save Mom.

"Can you dance?"

Confused, Tabitha turned back to the little man. *What did he say?* "Huh?" was all she managed as she blinked stupidly.

Morty nodded, still flashing a mouth full of teeth beneath the thin, red mustache. "Can you dance? You know, tap? Ballet? Kick? Can you dance?"

Uh-oh. She shrugged and gave him a sheepish grimace. "A little."

He frowned, but nodded at the same time. "Okay, so no triple threat. At least not yet." He gave her another wink and a crooked smile. "We can get you dancin' lessons. You speak French?"

"What?"

His wide grin bespoke well-practiced, if somewhat strained, patience. "Do. You. Speak. French?"

Tabitha nodded slowly, squinting at him as if *he* were speaking in a foreign tongue. "I took two years of French in school, but I haven't—"

His eyes lit up like twin spotlights. "Perfect! Kid, I'm gonna make you a star." He raised a hand as if tracing letters on an imaginary marquis. "Tabitha Moonshadow! Great stage name, by the way. Won't even have to change it."

Tabitha glanced at Mr. MacDonald. The old man's stare looked as ravenous and predatory as the fat, little theatre agent's.

Tabitha's mouth felt dry, her palms moist. A cold bead of sweat slid down her back. "Mom?" She turned again, looking for her mother, but Molly and Mike weren't there anymore. *Where'd they go?*

The crowd of cast, crew, family members, and well-wishers had thinned considerably. But her mother and the man she was certain was Magnus were nowhere to be seen.

"Mom?"

"I'll go find your mother," said Mr. MacDonald, placing his hands on the wheels of his chair. "I have to go supervise the set strike anyway. The volunteers should be here soon." He sighed dramatically. "Seems a shame to tear all this down. So many hours of blood, sweat, and tears—not to mention love—but, hey, that's show biz!"

He began to roll away. "I'll leave you two to talk. Congratulations, Tabitha. You've really earned this. The opportunity of a lifetime!"

Tabitha almost called out to him to stay. *Don't leave me with this guy! As creepy as you are, old man, this guy really gives me the willies. But Old MacDonald's right. This is the opportunity of a lifetime. And that means dealing with creeps like this.*

A trickle of the Power continued to tingle within her. *Where is he? How's he doing that? Whose Power is it? It's gotta be coming from Mom, but—*

"Listen, kid." Morty put a hand on her arm. The flesh of his hand was slimy, as if he'd put on too much hand lotion. "I've got an inside track on a new Broadway musical. It's called *42nd Street*—you know, like the old movie?" He waved dismissively with his free hand. "Before your time. But it's gonna be *dynamite*! I got a mind to present you as the star—the 'naïve newcomer' they need. You certainly got the look. Fresh, innocent, and *sexy* as hell. We gotta get you dancin' lessons for that one. But with your knock-'em-dead voice and your cute-as-a-button, virginal looks—not to mention your impressive acting chops—I *know* I can get you in. On the other hand, well, listen, kid, I know a couple-a guys in Paris—French types. Gonna make a musical based on *Les Misérables*." He pronounced it, "Less Mizzerabulls." The agent winked at her. "You know, the old Victor Hugo book? The huge one? Maybe you read it in school?"

He didn't wait for an answer. "I know it sounds real highbrow, but if the show does well in France, it'll go to London—in the King's English, of course. I got a feelin' it's gonna be *huge*." He tapped his temple. "Ol' Morty's got an instinct for these things. Trust me, kid. I know what I'm talkin' about. Anyway, these Frenchies—they want a couple of short, petite, innocent-lookin' gals with huge voices who can play the female leads. If it goes to London, you got the English accent down pat. And if you can do French…"

He laughed suddenly—fast, low, and nasty. "Do French." His grin took on a lascivious nature. He squeezed her arm, then slid his slimy hand down toward hers. "Fresh. Innocent. And *sexy* as hell."

Tabitha recoiled in revulsion, but managed to keep her face neutral. "I gotta find my mom."

As she turned away from him, she heard, "I'm gonna make you a *star*, kid! Ol' MacDonald was right about you. I'll be in touch!"

"Mom?"

Where are you? I need you. I need to get you away from Magnus.

She spotted Beulah. And Joey. Beulah had already managed to change out of her costume and back into street clothes. But she still wore her stage makeup, making her look decades older.

Despite the myriad emotions roiling in her gut—and the tingle of the Power—Tabitha felt a twinge of annoyance. *Never wear stage makeup outside the theatre. It's unprofessional.*

Then she felt irritation at her own annoyance. *Like that matters right now.*

Beulah waved, then motioned for Tabitha to join them.

Tabitha hurried over. "Have either of you seen my mom?"

Beulah shook her head. "They were just here—your mom and…" Her voice trailed off as if she was rethinking what she'd been about to say. "But I don't see them now."

Joey's happy smile tugged at her heart—regret for what might have been. "Great job tonight!" he said. Then he leaned in and whispered in her ear. "Change of plans. Beulah and I are leaving tonight. Right now. My mama's in the car outside, and we're all packed. We'll try to get word to you later."

Tabitha looked at Beulah with wide eyes.

The tall girl nodded. "Yep." She threw her arms around Tabitha, then whispered, "I'm gonna miss y'all. Thank you. You saved me. Saved my life."

Tabitha let out a deep sigh and squeezed back. "Be safe. I'll miss you too." She gave Joey a sad, wistful smile. "Miss you both."

Beulah nodded. "Safe. Yeah. Don't you say nothin' else. Not now. Not here. Bye." She pulled out of the embrace, grabbed Joey's hand, and the two of them pivoted and walked quickly up the aisle toward the exit.

Tabitha suspected they were attempting to make it look as if their departure was casual and unhurried, but she detected an urgency to their gait. To her eyes, it was unmistakably a bid for freedom.

Be safe. Get out of here before he sees.

She turned, scanning the nearly empty theatre for any sign of her mom and Magnus. Mr. MacDonald sat in his wheelchair on the stage, and his back was to her. *Probably saying goodbye to the set he designed. It was a great set.*

Angelica Goldsmith sauntered up the aisle toward her. She carried her bouquet and wore her winter coat, a stocking cap, and a bright, if weary, smile.

Angelica Goldsmith sauntered up the aisle toward her. She carried her bouquet and wore her winter coat, a stocking cap, and a bright, if weary, smile.

Tabitha cast her eyes about the theatre again. *Where are they?* She could still feel the tingle of the Power. It was slight, almost tenuous, but it was still there. *He must be able to see me to channel it at me, right? He's not doing anything to me—not that I can tell. But he has to be able to see me. That's how it works, right?*

He has to be here somewhere.

"You were so great tonight!" Angelica's declaration sounded as if it carried a pound of joy and a ton of relief. "I'm so proud of you. Did you hear there was a theatre agent in the audience? Did he talk to you?"

"Yeah, he did."

"Oh, good. I heard he really liked you."

Tabitha suppressed a shudder at the memory of the slimy hand on her arm. "Have you seen my mom and…Brother Kilmore?"

"Over there. Second row." Angelica indicated the audience seats off to the side. She enfolded Tabitha in a quick, one-armed hug. "Gotta run. You were fantastic. We'll talk tomorrow at church."

And with that, she was off.

Tabitha zeroed in on the trio sitting in the otherwise deserted theatre seats. She recognized her mom and Mike.

And Morty Corrigan.

The agent was gesticulating enthusiastically as he talked with her mom and Mike. Molly's face was half-eclipsed by the back of Mike's head. Mike, however, was facing away from Tabitha.

Not looking at me. But I can still feel the Power. He must see me—be looking at me. That's what Joey said. And Mike's not. That means…it's not him.

Mike is not Magnus!

Relief washed over her, nearly causing her legs to give way.

Mike is not Magnus! Mike must be able to channel, but he just doesn't know it. That's why he gets shocked whenever we touch.

But if he's not Magnus… Suddenly, her weak knees stiffened as the temporary relief drained out of her like water through a sieve. *Then who?*

She spun around wildly, looking for the mysterious and once-again-unknown Magnus. When she'd been convinced that Mike was the Circle's High Priest, at least then she had thought she knew who the enemy was. But with that certainty ripped out from under her like a rug, she didn't know where she stood. Panic seized her as she frantically searched every shadow, hunting for the glint of a golden mask.

Like he's going to wear the mask here. He'd be unmasked. But who? Where?

She could see no one, except her mother, Mike, and the toadish theatre agent. Even Mr. MacDonald was nowhere in sight.

Where is Magnus?

"Tabitha!"

She turned toward her mom.

Morty Corrigan was stomping away, and he didn't look happy. As he stormed up the aisle, he cast a murderous look at her mom. Then he gave Tabitha a hearty thumbs-up and a too-wide smile.

A tremor of revulsion shook Tabitha. She rubbed at her arm. It still felt oily where the little man had touched her. *It looks like Mom shut Ol' Morty down. Good.*

But he's not really going away, is he? No. I've got worse problems than a handsy agent right now. Even if a creep like Morty might be the key to my career on the international stage…

Molly waved. "Go get changed, honey. I feel a definite SNORBS coming on!"

"Okay." *Magnus is here somewhere. He has to be. He's watching me, even if I can't see him.*

Mike Kilmore turned and grinned at her. "Better hurry up, before the A&W closes!"

But at least it's not Mike. At least Mom's safe.

One of the theatre doors slammed as Morty Corrigan made his dramatic exit, and both Mike and Molly glanced in that direction. However, Molly soon turned her attention back to Tabitha.

Tabitha grinned at her mom, pointed at Mike, then gave her mother a thumbs-up.

Molly blinked at her, uncomprehending. Then her face lit up in a wide smile.
Tabitha mouthed, "Not Magnus."
Molly seemed to sag with relief.
Mom's safe. But am I?

"You turned him down? Are you crazy?" Fergus MacDonald stared wide-eyed and openmouthed at Molly as she waited for Tabitha to get changed. "You know what's at stake here!"

"Yes, Fergus," Molly said. As much as she had come to distrust the old man, it gave her no pleasure to see him so worked up. "I do know what's at stake."

MacDonald's face soured into a frown. His knuckles turned white as he gripped the armrests of his wheelchair. "It's that man of yours. That lying policeman."

He hadn't said the word "Mormon," yet the unspoken epithet seemed to hang in the widening gulf between them.

Standing in front of the old man's wheelchair on the stage, Molly glanced toward the back of the theatre. Mike had gone out, into the hallway to retrieve their coats. *He should be back by now. Maybe he went to the car to grab his radio. He better not get called away again. Not like Wednesday night. He's our ride home.*

But Tabitha says he's not Magnus! I don't know how she knows, but I believe her. She knows! Thank you, Heavenly Father!

He's a good man. And he's all mine!

MacDonald grunted with disgust. "That man has poisoned you against me. It's all a pack of lies."

She shook her head. "No, Fergus. That man, that agent. What was his name? Corrigan?" Her nose twitched as if she could still smell Corrigan's pungent cologne. "Morty. He was a pig. A wolf. Oh, he tried to disguise it, but he wants Tabitha. He wants to *use* my baby."

"But he'll get her out of this town! Away from Magnus!"

"I'm not throwing my daughter into the jaws of one wolf just to get her out of the paws of another."

"But Magnus!"

Molly threw her hands up. "I don't even know who Magnus is! *You* don't know! He's just some boogeyman. You even suggested *Mike* was Magnus. My fiancé!" She leaned toward the old man and fixed him with a withering stare. "But he's not. And I think between the pair of us—Mike and I, that is—we'll be able to protect my daughter."

Molly heard what sounded like girlish laughter. She turned her face to the other side of the stage. A couple of dozen teenage girls had gathered, milling about. They seemed to be watching Molly and the old man with interest. MacDonald had referred to them as "volunteers" who'd be dismantling the sets.

The old man pounded an armrest with a fist, drawing Molly's attention once more. "You don't know what you're up against!"

"And neither do you." She straightened and spun on her heel just as Tabitha scampered onto the stage. "We're done here, Fergus."

Tabitha looked pale and agitated. She held the broomstick in one hand and had gathered her long skirt in the other, holding it up to her knees as if she intended to run.

Or flee.

"Tabitha!" Molly rushed to meet her daughter. "What's wrong?"

Tabitha's head swiveled as her wide eyes searched the cavernous theatre and stage. "Let's get out of here!" She let go of her skirt and grabbed Molly's hand, tugging at her.

"What's wrong?" Molly repeated, staring at her daughter's terrified face.

"He's here!" Tabitha said. "Magnus! He's *watching* me." She looked about wildly. "He could see me. In the dressing room!"

"You saw him?"

Tabitha shook her head, her eyes wider, more frightened than before. "No! But he's here. I know it!"

Molly pulled her daughter's hand, turning toward the empty theatre, toward the exit. "Then how can you—"

Molly's voice died in her throat.

They were surrounded.

The girls—the "volunteers"—their hands joined, encircled them. And at the front of the circle, facing Molly and her daughter, holding the hand of a girl on either side of him, stood a tall figure. The figure wore a long, white robe with a deep hood. His face was obscured by a golden, expressionless mask. And although Molly had never seen him or even heard a description of his appearance, she knew at once who he was.

Magnus!

"Mom!" Tabitha's voice rose to a near shriek. "Look at his feet!"

Molly looked, and the air in her lungs turned to ice.

Beneath the robe were a pair of brown cowboy boots.

33

"Get behind me, Tabitha." Her mom tugged at Tabitha, at the same time trying to place her own body between Magnus and her daughter. Molly kept her voice calm as she repeated, "Get behind me."

Tabitha, however, was scared out of her mind, rooted to the spot. "It's no use!" she wailed. "As long as he can see us, he can do anything he wants!"

I can blow them away! Tabitha thought. *Rip them apart. Kill them.*

But Tabitha could barely focus. The Power roared within her, every nerve trembling with an ecstasy so intense, she could think of little else.

Stop him! Scared enough. Angry enough. Unleash it!

Tabitha strained to mentally aim all her anger, all her fear on Magnus. *I'll hurt Patsy and the rest of them, but I have to protect Mom.*

Now!

But nothing happened.

Tabitha had never felt so much of the Power before—not by herself at least—only when linked to the Circle had the Power been so intense. But she wasn't linked, wasn't touching anyone.

And she couldn't release it.

Angry. Scared.

What's going on? What's he doing to me?

"Tabitha," the Power-amplified voice of Magnus boomed from everywhere and nowhere, "why would you leave us, my goddess? I love you. I love you with all my heart, might, mind, and soul. I *worship* you. And I will serve you all my days. How could you even think of leaving me?"

Magnus and the Circle rose off the stage and into the air, half a dozen feet or more—not terribly high, but they were above, while Tabitha and Molly were below. And Magnus could see her perfectly.

Nowhere to hide! Now! Unleash it NOW!

Nothing.

She pointed at Magnus with the broom, aiming the heavy stick like a wand. Or a bazooka. *Now! Now! NOW!*

Not working!

Terror pounded through her veins, mingling with the joy of the Power pulsing through every nerve—pleasure and fright causing her to vibrate like a high-pitched string on a violin.

Molly took a step forward—toward Magnus. "How could you? Mike! I *loved* you! How could you do this to us?"

"Molly!" MacDonald yelled. "Get out of the way!"

Tabitha jerked her head to the left. MacDonald was beside and behind them, sitting in his wheelchair. And he held a gun.

He held the weapon in his right hand. With his left, he supported his right forearm, steadying the gun. His wheelchair was turned at an awkward angle, so he was leaning over the side to aim. "Get out of the way, Molly!"

He can't get a clear shot!

The old man's hand was steady, his eye focused and calm. But his left foot nervously tapped against the footrest of the chair.

His foot? Tapping his foot?

"Mike!" Molly cried. "Please! Don't do this!"

"Mike!" Molly cried. "Please! Don't do this!"

The words Beulah had cried in her sleep came back to Tabitha in a horrible rush—*Look at his foot!*

Tabitha forced herself to focus on the old man's foot. His paralyzed foot. *Look at his foot!*

"Get out of the way!" MacDonald yelled.

Molly jerked to the right suddenly, stumbling, as if she had been shoved aside.

MacDonald grinned. "Got you, you pompous son of a bitch!" He took a breath and aimed the gun.

And in that terrible instant, the truth crystallized in Tabitha's mind. All of it. She struck out with the broomstick, connecting with the old man's wrist a microsecond before the gun went off, booming like a crack of thunder.

The Circle crashed to the ground—all of them.

The stage floor shook with the impact of their bodies on the unyielding, hard wood. Even as the gunshot continued to echo through the theatre, Tabitha heard the sickening crunch of breaking bones. Then she heard screams of pain coming from the girls of the Circle.

She saw Mike Kilmore lying on his side, crimson blossoming on his chest. The golden mask had fallen from his face. A white strip of cloth went around his head, across his jaw, holding a gagging wad of cloth in his mouth.

"Mike!" Molly screamed—a brief outburst of shock, then she stumbled toward him.

Tabitha thought, *Please, don't be dead!* But that was all the attention she could spare for Mike Kilmore at the moment.

She turned toward Fergus MacDonald.

The old man clutched at his right wrist with his left hand. He growled curses under his breath, then focused his clear eyes on her. "You little bitch. You broke my damn wrist."

The gun lay on the boards of the stage floor.

But Tabitha wasn't worried about the gun. She knew that wasn't the old man's primary weapon.

Not the gun—just for show. I'm the weapon.

MacDonald hissed painfully through clenched teeth. "Let's get rid of that damned stick, shall we?"

The broomstick was ripped out of Tabitha's hands. It tumbled end-over-end 'til it crashed to the stage several yards away.

The Power still throbbed within Tabitha. When she'd hit the old man, breaking his wrist—and hopefully saving Mike's life—the strength of the Power had dropped off, nearly causing her to crumple to the floor. But it was back. Sending pulses of pleasure through her.

Not channeling at me. Channeling through me.

He's been channeling through me this whole time. Ever since he shook my hand after the show.

"I can see it now," MacDonald said, nodding in approval. "You've figured it out, my goddess. Bravo. You always were one of my brightest students."

The old man placed his feet, one at a time, onto the floor. The footrests folded up, moved by the Power. MacDonald rose from his chair, standing on his own feet. The chair itself rolled back a foot, leaving Magnus standing without visible support.

Magnus stepped toward her.

And for the first time, without the robe to cover them, Tabitha noticed the movements of his feet and legs were slightly *off*—like the motions of a puppet hanging from unseen strings.

Unmasked at last, Magnus's face split into a leering grin. "I have you, my dear. You're mine. You. Your Power. I don't even need to hold on to you or maintain contact anymore, not once I have ahold of *it*." He shook his head slightly and whistled with appreciation. "You're that strong, my dear. Yes, you are. And I think you're getting stronger." A tremor of pleasure seemed to run through him. "Stronger every time! Ooh, my dear. The things I can do with you!"

Lights flashed above them—fireworks without sound.

With his good hand, he pointed at the mute explosions over their heads. "I can manipulate the unseen! Photons. Air molecules. Sound waves!" And suddenly, the bursts of light were accompanied by distant booms and pops.

Then the fireworks and the manufactured sounds ceased.

He pointed with his left hand at his right foot. "I've even begun to repair the damage to my spine!"

Tabitha became aware of her mother's voice. "Hold this here. Keep pressure on it." *Talking to Mike? He's alive?*

"I *want* you, Tabitha," the old man said, his eyes blazing with desire. "I don't need *them*." He swept his left hand—his good hand—in the direction of the Circle around them.

The girls—most of them—lay weeping, sobbing, clutching at broken legs and shattered knees and ankles.

Magnus shook his head. "I don't need them at all." He glanced up, and with the sounds of cracking and snapping wood, a huge piece of scenery—the grand staircase from the ballroom scene—fell from the ceiling. Girls screamed, vainly raising their hands to protect themselves.

The massive wooden staircase crushed several of them.

More scenery rained down, strategically targeting every girl in the Circle.

"No!" Tabitha pleaded. "Stop! Please!"

But Magnus gave her cries no heed.

In a matter of seconds, all the members of the Circle lay crushed and bleeding, dead or dying. Even if the girls *had* turned on her at the end, her former friends didn't deserve to die for the betrayal. *Not like that.*

Only Tabitha, Molly, and MacDonald remained.

Don't let Mike be dead, Heavenly Father! Not because of me. Magnus murdered them. Murdered them all. With my power.

Used me. Used me to kill them.

Magnus surveyed his grisly handiwork and nodded in approval. "Goodbye, my dears. You have served me well, but"—he turned his face to Tabitha—"I don't need them anymore. I only need *you*. You and your *limitless* Power."

"Leave her alone!" Molly, trembling with terror and shock at the carnage all around, stepped between Tabitha and MacDonald, blocking Tabitha's view of the old man—the man who'd deceived them all. "I swear, Fergus, if you touch her, I'll—"

Molly flew to the right, like a rag doll tossed aside by a giant, invisible child.

Tabitha saw the broomstick rise from the stage. "Please!" she cried. "Don't hurt her!"

Molly clambered quickly to her stockinged feet, apparently having lost her shoes in the fall. She started toward them again.

MacDonald laughed as the broom flew and struck Molly in the left shin with a sickening crunch.

"No!" Tabitha screamed. She lunged at the old man, but she froze in midair, trapped and held as if by unseen hands. Imprisoned by her own Power. She hung, helpless, a few inches off the floor. She could move her body, though. She flailed madly at the air, but to no effect. She couldn't get to the ground. "Leave my mom alone!"

But Tabitha watched in horror as the iron-cored broom swung again, crashing into and snapping Molly's other leg. A scream of agony escaped Molly as she crumpled to the floor.

"I don't need you, either," MacDonald said, curling his lip at Molly, "you pathetic old cow." Then he turned a triumphant face to Tabitha. His victorious grin morphed into a lascivious leer. He licked his lips. "You see, Miss Molly. I like my ladies *young*."

Tabitha felt herself rotate, her body straightening to an upright posture, though she still couldn't reach the ground. She glanced at Mike Kilmore. He lay on the stage, still on his side and still partially covered by the white robe. He held a wad of the now-crimson cloth to his chest. His chest trembled with his struggle to breathe.

Still alive.

Tabitha focused all her anger on the old man who'd wounded her mother and Mike. "I *hate* you, you old creep. And I'm going to kill you for what you did to my mom. And to Mike."

Mike's a good man. All he ever wanted to do was to protect me and Mom. And I doubted him.

Rage swelled in her, bitter as bile and hot as magma. But she still couldn't release the Power.

If I could just unleash it—if I could blow you to bits, I would. But I can't. Not while you're channeling my Power. Stealing my Power. Using my Power. Using it to maim, to kill.

Helpless. At your mercy.

"You know," said MacDonald, running his eyes over her body as if drooling over a particularly juicy steak, "I *wanted* your cooperation. I wanted your *love*."

Tabitha spat at him.

Even though Magnus and his leering face were barely a half dozen feet way, the spittle fell woefully short. But all the same, Tabitha's act of defiance and contempt had an effect on the old man. His expression hardened. "However, my dear, I don't need you to be a *willing* Power battery. I can *take* it any time I want." He took one more marionette-step closer. "Just like I can take *you*."

Tabitha felt her arms pressed to her sides, her legs trapped and forced straight. She could no longer move her body.

"I could take you right now," MacDonald said. "Right here. In front of your pitiful, ineffectual mother." He stepped right up to Tabitha, reaching out a hand as if to stroke her face. He chuckled low in his throat. "Yes." His rough, calloused fingers caressed her cheek. "Right here." He gripped her hair in his fist. "Right *now*."

He pursed his lips, pulling her face toward his.

And with a cry, his head jerked downward, away from Tabitha and toward the floor. In his surprise, he let go of her hair.

Molly held his leg in a death-grip, dragging him down. She was on her knees, her lower legs bent at unnatural angles. Her face was streaked with tears, her mouth twisted in agony. And she howled with pain as she forcibly dragged MacDonald away from her daughter.

As the old man's concentration broke, Tabitha felt herself freed from her invisible bonds. She dropped the few inches to the stage. "Mom!"

MacDonald growled. "Bitch!"

Molly flew into the air, straight up and out of sight.

Tabitha heard her mother scream from somewhere above them.

Pulling himself up to a sitting position, MacDonald laughed. "Can you see us, Molly? From your perch up there?"

Tabitha looked up. Her mother clung to a rack of lights. *A fall from that height— it'd kill her. Have to stop him.*

Tabitha lunged at Magnus, fist raised to strike.

And she was slammed backward to the floor.

The impact caused the air in her lungs to explode. She lay, convulsing, fighting to draw a breath.

Air!

She clawed at her gut, at her paralyzed diaphragm. With a loud gasp, she drew a painful, life-sustaining breath.

Then her arms were flung wide, pinned to the floor. Her legs were jerked apart. Her long skirt slid up, lifted by invisible, irresistible Power.

"NO!" Molly screamed. "Please! Stop! I'll do anything! Please don't hurt my baby!"

Magnus laughed. "Watch, Molly. Watch me as I make your little girl a real woman."

BOOM!

The gunshot was so loud, so unexpected, it stole the air from Tabitha's lungs again.

MacDonald fell to the stage, his legs collapsing from under him. And Tabitha was free.

As she struggled to flip herself over with her wobbling limbs, to get to her hands and knees, she looked for the shooter.

Mike Kilmore. Somehow, he had gotten to his feet. He'd removed his gag. He clutched the red-soaked fabric of the robe to his chest, he held a gun.

The weapon trembled in Mike's outstretched arm. He kept shaking his head and squinting as if trying to clear his vision, to get another clear shot at Magnus.

The old man was bleeding from a wound to his withered thigh. But he gave no notice to his bleeding, nerveless leg.

All his focus was on Tabitha.

He dragged himself along the floor with his good left hand and his right elbow. Not yet able to crawl, Tabitha kicked at the grasping hand.

But the old man gripped her ankle.

"NO!" she screamed as the Power flowed through her.

Through her and into Magnus.

She kicked free of his grasp, but MacDonald had what he wanted.

The Power continued to flow.

MacDonald snapped his head toward Mike, and the gun flew out of Mike's hand. It arced through the air and thudded to the stage floor beside Magnus.

Then Mike himself flew backward. He collided with a broken scenery column. Mike lay still.

Magnus turned his face back to Tabitha. He bared his teeth in a wolfish grin. "Now, where were we, my dear?"

One chance.

Tabitha thrust her hand into the pocket of her skirt just as invisible bonds seized her once again.

"Are you watching, Molly?" MacDonald jeered loudly. "She's mine. In spite of all your pathetic efforts—yours and your Mormon sheriff's. She's mine. My prize."

"No!" her mother called from high above them. "Please! Stop! Please!" Then, as Magnus used the Power—Tabitha's Power—to yank Tabitha's arms out straight again and force her legs apart, Tabitha heard her mother say between audible sobs, "Tabitha! I love you. No matter what happens, I love you!"

"I know, Mom!" Tabitha replied. She fought to free her fingers from Magnus's invisible grip. She fought to unwrap the bit of torn cloth she held in her fist. Fabric ripped from her pocket.

Magnus's face loomed over hers. "I love you too. I *worship* you, my goddess." His body was poised several inches above hers, floating. There was no need for him to lift her skirt that time—her own hand had yanked it upward when she'd ripped out her skirt pocket. Her legs were exposed to him. Something warm and wet hit her on her bare thigh. The sensation reminded her of drops spilling from a cup of hot chocolate. *Blood. From his thigh.*

Bleeding on me.

She pushed aside the wave of revulsion and horror that rolled over and through her. *Don't think about that.*

Tabitha glared at him. *Keep focused on my face, you bastard. Focus on the rest of my body. Just don't look at my hand.* She spat at him again, and that time the spittle hit him on the chin. "You don't know anything about love or-or worship or women. You only want to possess us, use us. And when we're no longer useful, you throw us away. You kill us." *Like you killed my friends.*

She managed to wiggle her thumb just a little. *Yes. That's it.* Laboriously, she pushed with her thumb at the fabric in her fist. *Almost there.* "You use us and dispose of us. Just like Elias Thibodeaux and White Lettie. You don't love me." *Just a little bit more!*

Magnus chuckled as he lifted her sweater with his good hand, exposing her bra. "But I *do* love you, Tabitha. You are *everything* to me. You will give me back my legs." He reached for her bra as if to lift it. "And then, together, we'll have our revenge on this town. On the Thibodeauxs. On the whole damn world." He hooked a thumb under the front of her bra. "And I don't even need your cooperation. I don't need your help. It would've been nice, but as you see"—he chuckled—"you are mine. Your Power is *mine*." He sighed and smiled in triumph. "All *mine*."

"Wait!" *Need more time!* "H-hear me out. Fergus? May I call you Fergus?"

He paused, still hovering, floating just above her, his thumb still hooked under her bra, his blood still dripping on her leg. He licked his lips. "Yes, my dear?"

"Spare my mom. Spare Mike. A-and I'll g-go with you. Willingly. I'll promise you. And you know—everybody knows—" She thought of all the girls of the Circle lying around them, crushed, mangled. She couldn't even hear them crying anymore. *Dead. All dead. Because of me.*

"Yes, my dear?"

"Everybody knows, I keep my promises."

He pursed his lips. "Yes, I do believe you, my dear. But I have the problem of *witnesses*, you see. I will have to eliminate them. You know that." He shrugged his shoulders. "As much as I would savor your cooperation, this *conquest*, if you will, has its own rewards. Besides, my dear. It's not *your* Power anymore." His hand and his thumb tensed, ready to yank triumphantly upward. "It's *mine!*"

The Power surged in her—pleasure, almost to the point of pain.

Come on! I can feel it. It's right there! Tabitha jerked her thumb just a little. "No, Fergus," she said, forcing a smile. "It's mine. And you can't have it." She wiggled her thumb once more, and the flesh of her thumb came into contact with the iron washer.

The Power vanished—like a light switch suddenly shut off.

The old man collapsed atop her. He roared in agony as his broken wrist crunched to the wooden stage floor.

Tabitha's world went white.

Not now! Not a vision!

She held her six-year-old daughter in her arms. "If the monster breaks my legs, I'll crawl. I'll bite. I'll scratch. Whatever it takes. I will protect my little—"

Tabitha wrenched her thumb from the iron. She brought her knee up hard, into the old man's groin. His growl of pain rose to a high-pitched squeal.

She shoved with her hands, and rolled Magnus off her. Tabitha rolled over, away from MacDonald, and scrambled to her knees.

Get away! Before he touches me again.

Then she was on her feet, pulling down her sweater. Her skirt had already dropped back to its proper place, the fabric clinging to her where Magnus's blood had dripped down her leg. And as soon as her body was covered and her Power out of MacDonald's reach, she felt a different kind of power. She felt in control.

MacDonald lay on the floor, unmoving, his good hand between his legs. His right arm was outstretched, the broken wrist bent back in an unnatural position. Blood oozed from his wounded thigh, pooling on the floor.

"Tabitha!"

Tabitha's head snapped up. Her mother clung to a light rod above. Her legs shook, twisting like wind-chimes dangling in the wind.

"Mom! Hold on!"

Molly sobbed. "I can't! I'm losing... Tabitha, honey—I love you! You— You did— So proud..."

"Hold on!" *Where's the rope for that one? I can lower it. Where is it?*

THE WITCH OF WHITE LADY HOLLOW ~

But she had no idea which rope would lower that particular lighting rod.

Left? Right? Where?

"Hold on!" Tabitha cried again. "I'll get help!"

"I can't!"

Mike!

Tabitha pivoted and dashed toward Mike's crumpled body. He lay against the broken scenery column.

Don't be dead! She knelt beside him.

His chest shuddered as he gasped for breath, and his left hand still held the soaked cloth to his wounded chest. "Go," he croaked. "Get help."

Tabitha shook her head. "Nobody's here." *If those gunshots didn't get anyone's attention...* "There's just you. I need *you*. You can help me save Mom."

He shook his head weakly. "Can't. Go. Get help."

Tabitha gripped his free hand. She felt the tingle of the Power flowing into him. She tried to give him a reassuring smile. "No. You can help. Do you feel that? That tingle?"

He nodded. Barely.

"That's the Power. *My* Power. But *I* can't use it to save Mom. Only you can do that."

"H-how? I don't know how." Mike looked at her. There was pain in his eyes, but they were clear and focused. "Tell me how...what to do."

She nodded. Tears welled in her eyes, blurring her vision. *You're a good man.* "Don't look at me. Look at Mom. Focus on *her*."

Obediently, his eyes shifted away and up. They refocused. "O . . . kay."

Tabitha recalled Joey's explanation of how the Power worked. "Just focus on her. Imagine holding her. Imagine lifting her. Imagine lowering her safely to the floor. Can you do that?"

"Tabitha!" Molly cried. "Mike! I-I love you. I love you both so much! I'm sorry!"

Tabitha tried to ignore the anguish, the hopelessness of her mother's words. "Can you do that, Mike? Please?"

Obediently, his eyes shifted away and up. They refocused. "Okay."

Tabitha recalled Joey's explanation of how the Power worked. "Just focus on her. Imagine holding her. Imagine lifting her. Imagine lowering her safely to the floor. Can you do that?"

"Tabitha!" Molly cried. "Mike! I-I love you. I love you both so much! I'm sorry!"

Tabitha tried to ignore the anguish, the hopelessness of her mother's words. "Can you do that, Mike? Please?"

Mike coughed—a horrible gurgling sound. Blood oozed afresh from between his fingers. But he nodded. "Yeah."

And Tabitha felt the Power flow. It surged. Molly screamed. Tabitha shut her eyes tight and the Power ceased to flow.

She opened her eyes; Mike's eyes were closed. But he still breathed.

Tabitha twisted her head. Her mother lay in a twisted heap on the stage, unmoving. Tabitha released Mike's limp hand, clambered to her feet, and lurched toward her mother's body. She knelt at Molly's side.

"Mom!" Tabitha's wail filled the theatre. "Mom! Oh, Mom! I'm so sorry!"

Molly's eyes fluttered, then opened. "T-Tabby-Cat?" Molly reached up and placed her hand against Tabitha's wet cheek. "How? How did you?"

Tabitha threw her arms around her mother. "Mom!"

"I don't understand." Molly's arms encircled her daughter. "I just, floated down. Like a feather. Like an angel caught me."

Tabitha laughed and squeezed her mom and wept tears of joy. "It was Mike! He's like Magnus—like Mr. MacDonald. He can channel my Power."

"Mike? Like Magnus?"

Tabitha shook her head, squealing with unbridled happiness. "Ooh, no. Not like Magnus. Mike's *good*. He's a good man."

Molly nodded. "A good man. I love him."

Mother and daughter froze as if the same thought had hit them simultaneously. *Mike's hurt!*

Molly let go of Tabitha. "Call an ambulance! Quick!"

Tabitha looked at her mother's broken legs, but shook her head.

Molly said, "Don't worry about me! Get help! Now!"

Tabitha nodded and scrambled to her feet. "There's a phone backstage—in the office!"

She turned to dash for the phone.

Then she froze.

A few yards away, in front of a backdrop of broken scenery and the mangled corpses of teenage girls, Fergus MacDonald sat on the stage floor in a pool of his own blood.

He grinned like an insane cartoon coyote as he held the gun in his left hand.

And he pointed it straight at Molly.

The gun in Fergus MacDonald's hand did not waver. He kept his eyes on Molly, but he addressed Tabitha in a very confident, steady tone. "I know what you're thinking, my dear. You're thinking, 'The old man's right-handed. If he shoots, he'll miss.'"

Tabitha shook her head quickly. "I wasn't—" But that had been exactly what she'd been thinking—or at least hoping.

"Did I ever tell you," he said, "I was wounded in the war? Not my legs. That came after. But I bled red-white-and-blue for the good ol' U.S. of A. a myriad of times. I even took a Jap bullet at Guadalcanal. I was lucky with that one. Just tore up my arm a bit." He chuckled softly. "'Just a flesh wound,' as they say on the boob tube. But in truth, I only had my arm in a sling for a couple of months. One of the lucky ones. They wanted to send me home." His crazy, toothy grin vanished as he scowled and shook his head. "Wouldn't hear of it. But I had to learn to shoot a sidearm. With my left hand. I got pretty good at it too. Qualified as marksman. Dead-Shot Lefty, they called me."

The grin returned. "So, if you think I can't hit your mother in the heart at this range, think again."

"Fergus," Molly began, raising a hand to him, "please. I'll—"

The old man didn't nod—neither his focus nor his aim wavered. "You'll do anything, Molly. Yes, I know. But you have nothing I want. You're just a bargaining chip. A tool. A means to an end. That's all you ever were. Too old by far and too weak in the Power. Oh, you're pretty enough. I'd've slept with you willingly. More than willingly. I have a hunch you'd be a *tigress* in bed. But only if it'd gotten me close to my real target."

"Okay," Tabitha said, inching to the right. *If I can get between him and Mom.* "I'll go with you."

"Take one step more in that direction, my dear," Magnus said, "and dear old mommy is dead."

Tabitha froze.

However, her mother started to crawl, to drag herself toward the old man. Toward the danger. "And then what, Fergus?" She couldn't mask the pain in her voice, the obvious struggle to form every word, but she somehow managed to make her voice sound calm. "If you shoot me, you'll lose your bargaining chip. You'll lose your only hold on Tabitha."

Magnus laughed then, and the gun wobbled. For just a moment.

And for a moment, Tabitha tensed, readying herself to jump, to put her body between her mom and danger. But she *believed* the old man—she *believed* his aim would be dead-on. *Can't take that chance.*

MacDonald's laughter died. "You have no idea, Molly. The joy of the Power. The sheer bliss of holding, possessing the Divine Feminine! You're so weak. You have no clue." He licked his lips again, reminding Tabitha once more of a coyote. "But Tabitha does. Don't you, my dear? You want it." He spared her the briefest of glances, but the lust in his eyes was palpable. "Just as badly as I do! You *need* it. Need my touch. Don't you, my dear?"

"Stop calling me that," Tabitha growled. "I'm not 'your dear.' I'm just a tool to you. An object. What's your plan, huh? To keep me chained up in your basement? Like a slave?"

"Like a treasure in a vault." He breathed out slowly through pursed lips, as if savoring a vision of delight and ecstasy. "Like a goddess in a temple. Like the Oracle of Delphi. To worship. To worship you with my body and my soul as you give me knowledge and power. It will be heaven on earth. Our own celestial kingdom." He chuckled once. "If you still believe in all that Mormon crap. *They* don't value you in that damn church. They don't care about you. They don't love you. You're just a *woman* to them. Second class. Worthless, except for sex and babies."

Get angry. Focus on him.

She was angry. She was scared. And she was focused.

But can I kill him? Even after all he's done, can I just kill him? To save Mom. And Mike—if he's still alive—I could kill you, old man, to save them.

I can.

I'm a bomb. I can—Mike!

Her eyes were drawn to Mike Kilmore. He was still lying against the broken scenery column, his chest still rising and falling in uneasy, uneven hitches. And Tabitha saw the danger. Mike was also only about forty-five degrees to the side of Magnus—well within the possible blast zone. *What if I hit Mike?*

MacDonald's mad grin transformed into a sneer of contempt. "You can't even hold the priesthood, for whatever that's worth. But you *do* need a man. A *special* man."

"Yes, she does," Molly said.

Stop it, Mom! Stop talking! I need to think! I need to concentrate.

But Molly kept right on talking, and she kept crawling slowly forward. "She needs a special man. A woman *does* need a man. If she wants to have a baby, she needs a man. If she wants to marry in the temple of God, she needs a man. If she wants to use this Power you're talking about—"

MacDonald's eyes blazed. "Yes! She needs a *special* man! She needs me! I'm that special man! Without me, she's nothing!" His eyes narrowed. "Stop right there, Molly. I see what you're doing. Don't think I don't. Stupid bitch."

Molly froze.

"Just sit where you are," said Magnus. "Sit!" He chuckled. "Sit, girl. Sit!"

Molly eased off her knees to the floor, but a whimper of pain escaped her as her broken legs shifted.

"Good girl," Magnus said, obviously delighted at his cleverness. "Good dog. Good old *bitch*!"

Edge to the left. If I go to the left, Magnus won't care. Then I can get a clear chance at him. And I won't hit Mike. I hope.

I just need time. Keep him talking!

"Yes," Tabitha said, taking another small step to the left, "I need a man. But it should be *my* choice. If I get married and have a baby, that's *my* choice. If I want to *allow* a man to channel *my* Power, that's *my* choice. My choice. *Mine.*"

Magnus seemed either unaware or unthreatened by Tabitha's movement. "Correct, my dear. And if you fail to make the right choice, the only logical choice…"

Tabitha took another step. "Then you'll just *take* it, right? That's theft. That's *rape.*"

His smile widened, showing all his teeth. "Some women—I think *all* women—fantasize about rape." He pursed his lips. "Ooh, the thought of having a man just take you? Take you against your will? Deep down in your heart, you know you want it!"

Just a couple steps more. "Did Suzanne want it?" But can I do it? Can I really just kill him?

She realized with a start she wasn't angry enough anymore. *Trying so hard to keep him talking, distracted, to act calm, rational…Get angry. Come on! Get angry!*

His lip curled in disgust. "Bradley Thibodeaux wasn't a woman."

There it is. "He was a child of God!" *Angry enough.*

"He was a faggot!" MacDonald roared.

Look at me, you monster! Take your eyes off Mom! "And you raped him. What does that make you?"

Magnus turned his blazing eyes on her.

Tabitha gathered all her rage, all her hatred for Fergus MacDonald and—

"Tabitha, stop!" Molly cried.

Tabitha gaped at her mother, wide-eyed. "Mom?"

Molly frantically waved both hands back and forth. "Please don't. You're going to do something, right? Something with... with the Power? Kill him?"

Tabitha couldn't believe her ears. *So close!* "Mom!"

Molly shook her head vehemently. "Don't do it, honey! Whatever it is you can do…don't do it."

"But he deserves to die!" Tabitha swept one arm to her left and the other to her right, taking in the entire stage, the carnage that surrounded them. The stench of blood and urine and even feces fueled Tabitha's rage. "He killed them all. With a thought. With *my* Power! He murdered them. They were my friends! It's all my fault!" Tears streamed from her eyes. "I killed them!"

Tears fell from Molly's eyes as well. "Oh, no, honey! You didn't. *He* did that."

Tabitha stomped a foot in frustration. "Then he deserves to die!"

Molly nodded. "Yes, he does. A hundred times over. But not"—she extended a pleading hand toward her daughter—"not at your hand. You don't want that on your conscience. I don't want you to have to live with that."

Every door in the theatre began to open and slam repeatedly. At first, the slams were chaotic, but in moments, they joined together, crashing as one in a symphony of violence, as Tabitha's volcanic rage boiled toward eruption. "He stole it from me! He took what was mine and used it. How's that any different from rape? Huh? How's it any different? He. Raped. Me!"

Stop slamming! And with that thought, the doors stopped thundering.

"Yes, honey." Molly's voice shook with pain, but she didn't shout. She didn't yell. "He did. He violated you. But that was just your Power. It wasn't you. It wasn't you, honey. Don't do this. Don't let him steal *you*. Don't let him take your soul. Please."

Tabitha heard a thud.

Tabitha and her mother snapped their attention back to Magnus. Fergus MacDonald lay slumped over. The gun had fallen from his limp hand. The pool of blood in which he lay had grown, spreading all around him.

The gun! Get the gun away from him.

Tabitha took a hasty step toward the old man, then stopped. *If he's still alive, if he grabs me… If he touches me…*

She cast her eyes about for the broom. She spied it, dashed to it, and snatched it up. Then she used White Lettie's broom to sweep the gun out of MacDonald's reach.

She picked up the gory weapon with disgust. She shook it briefly, gingerly, trying to get the some of the blood to drip off. Then she carried the gun quickly to her mother. "Here. Sorry it's gross."

If Molly was creeped out by MacDonald's blood on the gun, she didn't show it as she took the weapon and aimed it at Fergus MacDonald. "I'll keep him covered."

"I'll call an ambulance."

Tabitha dashed from the stage, weaving her way between two crushed and mangled corpses—corpses she'd once known as friends.

When Tabitha scurried back to the stage, assured that medical help was on its way, she found her mom at Mike's side. Molly hadn't moved him—Tabitha was certain her mom knew better than to move the wounded man and risk further injury—but Molly herself was applying pressure to Mike's chest wound, using fresh cloth torn from the robe. Most of the robe had been ripped away, leaving Mike clad in his now-ruined, too-formal black suit and brown cowboy boots.

Molly was talking to him, low and pleading. "Stay with me, Mike. Please don't leave me. You saved me. You saved us both. I love you so much. Please don't go." Molly wept as she spoke, and her voice trembled. "Dear Heavenly Father, please don't take him from me. Please!"

Tabitha knelt at Mike's other side. He still breathed, but his breathing was more rapid and shallow than before. She took Mike's hand and joined her mother in prayer. "Dear Heavenly Father," she pleaded, "please help him. I know I don't have the priesthood. I can't give him a blessing. I can't heal him. But if Mike can wake up, if he can use my Power, maybe together we can stop the bleeding inside. Maybe we can keep him alive 'til help gets here."

She looked over at the corpse of Fergus MacDonald. The old man lay where he'd fallen. The lake of blood had ceased to grow. Tabitha was certain Magnus was gone. *Gone to judgment. And hell.*

She turned her eyes back to Mike Kilmore and continued her prayer. "Wake him up. Please let him wake up. Let me save him. *Help* me save him."

She squeezed Mike's hand.

And weakly, he squeezed back.

Tabitha felt the tingle of the Power. *Thank you, God!* "Mike, listen to me. Focus. Think about the bleeding in your chest. Think about it stopping. Think about stopping the bleeding. Imagine it. Make it happen. Please, Mike. Use the Power. Come on! Make it happen!"

And she felt the Power flow. It felt *very* good. Sweet. Joyful.

Mike's breathing eased just a little. His eyes opened.

"Mike!" Molly cried, blubbering. "Oh, Mike! Stay with me! Help's on the way, Mike. Stay with me." She closed her eyes, squeezing out fresh tears. "Thank you, God! Thank you!"

The ghost of a smile flickered at the edges of Mike's pale lips. "Y'all didn't think, y'all'd get rid-a me…so dang easy." He swallowed. "Hurts like h— uh, hurts like *heck*. But"—his eyes flickered toward Tabitha—"that Power stuff feels good. Almost sinful good." He winked at her. Or at least, he tried to wink.

Tabitha blinked through her tears. "Just concentrate on stopping the bleeding. Concentrate on keeping yourself alive."

"Yes, ma'am." He looked at Molly. "You okay? Your legs…"

Molly laughed. "My legs hurt like *hell*. But you saved my life. You saved us both."

Mike really did smile that time. "Just got 'im in the dang leg." His smile vanished. "MacDonald?"

Tabitha squeezed his hand. "Dead. He bled to death. Could'nt feel it, 'cause it was in his leg. You killed him." *I didn't have to do it.* She looked at her mother, choking with love for Molly. *The monster broke your legs, and you still crawled to protect me.*

The Power surged, flowing into Mike. He was still pale, but he looked better, stronger. His breathing, though still shallow, was definitely stronger. "You okay, Tabitha?"

Tabitha nodded. "I'm great." *Now that you're gonna be okay.*

He grinned. "My girls. My ladies." His eyes focused on Molly's face. "What's a fella…gotta do to win a kiss, huh? Get himself shot or somethin'?"

Molly grinned, then bent and kissed him gently on the lips. "I love you, Mister. Don't you *dare* even *think* of leaving me. I'm gonna marry you. Even if I have to push you into the temple in a wheelchair."

Tabitha gasped at the word.

So did Molly.

Wheelchair? Tabitha stole another glance at MacDonald's corpse lying in its gore, then at his abandoned wheelchair.

Her eyes met her mother's. *He's still dead.* They'd both seen too many movies where the dead villain suddenly pops up and grabs the girl. *Still dead.*

Molly said, "It's okay. We're safe. We're all here. We're all alive."

Molly said, "It's okay. We're safe. We're all here. We're all alive."

Tabitha nodded, resisting the almost ghoulish need to survey the charnel house around them. *Not all alive. My friends…I don't have any—*

Mike squeezed her hand. His grip was stronger than it had been a minute before. "They were your friends, weren't they?"

Tabitha nodded, wiping futilely at her tears with her free hand.

Mike nodded, then bit his lip. "Ouch. Shouldn't-a done that." He locked eyes with her. "I'm sorry. They, uh, I guess they were involved in some bad stuff, but they were just kids."

Tabitha let out a hitching sigh. "Yeah. Most of them, though…I don't think they were involved in, the-the bad stuff. They were just…girls. Like me."

He shook his head, grimaced, then shook it again with more caution. "They were girls. Girls are special. Each and every one of 'em. But there ain't— *isn't* any girl as special as you two are." He squeezed her hand, and Tabitha felt a new surge of the Power. "You know, I never, well, it was rude of me...and I should've. But, I'm asking now." He smiled.

And as pale as he was, that million-dollar smile was still enough to make Tabitha quiver. "What?" she asked.

His grin widened—from a million dollars to a billion. "May I have the honor of being your father?"

Tabitha's mouth hung open. "What?"

"I mean," he said, "I know you already got one and all, but…"

Tabitha bent and kissed his pale forehead. "Please, Mike. Please be my dad."

And in that moment—though Tabitha had felt many conflicting emotions about this good man, though she had once fantasized about him in romantic ways—in that singular moment of clarity, Tabitha knew *exactly* who she wanted this man to be to her. And she knew she would never again call or even think of Mike Kilmore by any name but one. "I would love for you to be my one and only daddy."

Molly Moonshadow officially changed her name to Molly Moonshadow Kilmore on Friday, the first of June 1979. On that day, she and Mike were sealed for time and eternity in the Washington, D.C. Temple. And thus, Molly became a June bride.

During the very long drive from Blue Beech Ridge, Missouri to South Kensington, Maryland, where the temple was located, Mike had pointed out, "It's like in that old song from Seven Brides for Seven Brothers." He had belted out in a hearty, rich baritone, singing of how a bride who marries in June is a bride all her life.

To which Molly had sung back that a bridegroom who marries in June gets a sweetheart as his wife.

And Tabitha, sitting in the back seat of Mike's Mustang, had smiled. "You just wish we'd done that one instead of Camelot for the spring musical. Besides, it's not like there's a stage version anyway."

Mike had chuckled. "Too bad. You'd've made a swell Dorcas. Or Millie."

Tabitha had rolled her eyes. "Guinevere was a lot more fun. And besides, I'd never be able to do all that dancing."

A few minutes after the marriage sealing was performed and officially witnessed by Mike's father and nephew, a wide-eyed Tabitha was escorted into the sealing room. And there she was sealed for eternity as a daughter to Michael Kilmore.

It had taken special permission from the First Presidency at Church Headquarters in Salt Lake City. However, once Tabitha had turned eighteen and was no longer a minor, she had petitioned for the sealing, even though her biological father was still living. Her petition had been granted, and Tabitha, Molly, and Mike had officially become an eternal family.

In the temple, Tabitha had worn an elegant white dress bought especially for the brief covenant ceremony. And she had looked beautiful in white, especially with the contrast of her long, coal-black hair hanging down the back. The dress had short sleeves, but Tabitha had chosen a pair of long, white evening gloves to go along with it—just as she'd worn in *My Fair Lady*. She couldn't wear the gloves in the temple, of course. Molly had rather cryptically informed her that gloves couldn't be part of the sealing ordinance. "You'll look beautiful without them," her mother had said. "But you can wear them at the reception." And Tabitha did look lovely in white.

But she didn't hold a candle to the bride.

Molly was stunning, radiant, and overflowing with a joy she had never expected to know again. She had been adamant that her dress be simple enough to be worn *in* the temple as well as *out*. This meant long, full-length sleeves and no train, of course. Tabitha had told Molly she was sorely disappointed about the lack of a train, saying "I wanted to carry it like the Von Trapp girls in *The Sound of Music*!"

But "simple" or no, Mike had insisted on paying a fortune for genuine pearls to be sewn onto the already luxurious, silk gown. "You're worth every penny, Molly Moonshadow!" he'd said.

When Molly had questioned how in the world they could afford such an extravagant—though apparently temple-suitable—wedding gown, Mike had been typically evasive. Mike was never particularly forthcoming when it came to the source of the funds in his sizable savings account. However, he had promised to reveal the secret *after* the wedding. "Don't y'all worry your pretty heads about that. I came by it honestly. No bribes. No extortion. No nothin'. Scout's honor!" He had even made the Scout sign with his right hand.

Mike had, of course, looked like a hero on a cover of a typical romance novel—or at least, a *Mormon* romance novel. His shirt wasn't ripped, nor his chest laid bare. "I know y'all'd like to parade me around without a shirt, darlin'," he'd said, "but this here chest's got one big, da— uh, *nasty* scar on it." Instead, he wore a white suit which was almost too-formal, but not so fancy it couldn't be "worn to church"—assuming, of course, wearing white suits ever came back into fashion. He also sported a pair of white cowboy boots he'd ordered for the occasion—and would probably never wear again.

The surgeon had been able to save most of his left lung, but Mike still wasn't fully recovered and would probably never be at his physical peak again. "I can't chase down and tackle two dozen bad guys a day anymore," he'd say when asked about his recovery. "After the first dozen or so, I leave it to the *young* pups."

As for Molly, both her legs had healed well. However, she would walk with a slight limp for the rest of her life.

Late on a Saturday night in May, as the three of them—Molly, Mike, and Tabitha—had sat on the sofa watching the original Frankenstein *and munching on popcorn from a large metal bowl, Molly had pointed at the hunchback Fritz on the TV. She'd said, "That's me—limping everywhere."*

Without missing a beat, Mike had responded, "Fine by me. I'm kinda fond of your cute, little limp. I like the way it makes your butt wiggle. Especially when you wear high heels."

Molly had, of course, done her best to appear shocked. And failed utterly.

Tabitha had groaned and rolled her eyes. "Honestly, you guys!"

However, a few minutes later, during another scene between Dr. Frankenstein and his deformed assistant, Molly had snuck a glance at her daughter. Tabitha had met her eyes and given her a mischievous grin. "Hey, Mom, maybe you should grow a hump on your back too. Mike might like that even better."

Somehow managing to keep a straight face, Molly had said, "Not 'til after the wedding. Otherwise, we might not make it to the temple."

Spilling the popcorn everywhere, Mike had nearly busted a gut laughing.

When he finally quieted down, Tabitha had sighed dramatically. "That's it. Frankenstein is ruined forever." She had unsuccessfully stifled a giggle. "Too sexy for this family."

And the laughter had started all over again.

Although a small reception was planned for the chapel back in Poplar Bluff—after the honeymoon, of course, and after Mike's planned move into the cottage in the Hollow—the main reception was held at the Annandale Stake Center in Virginia. The event was well attended, mostly by Molly's friends and family in the D.C. area.

Not a single person remarked on the absence of the bride's ex-husband—who had, of course, not been invited.

By seven o'clock, however, both the bride and groom were ready to "split the scene." Standing in the reception line for the second and final round, with no one else waiting to congratulate the happy couple, Mike tugged at his collar for what seemed like the twelve-thousandth time. "Wish they'd crank up the air-conditioning," he said. "Is it just me, or is it a hundred degrees in here?"

Molly sighed and fanned herself with her free hand—the one not holding his. "Virginia in June. But I think the AC's working." She squeezed his hand, leaned in, and whispered in his ear, "I just think you're anxious to get to the hotel."

He gave her a wink and a lopsided grin that made her heart flutter. "You know it, woman." He glanced at his watch, then growled in irritation. "How soon y'all think we can we ditch this shindig?"

Molly muttered, "Not soon enough, in my opinion."

"What'd y'all say, Mrs. Kilmore?"

Molly turned and kissed him, lingering perhaps a few seconds longer than propriety permitted. "You heard me, Mr. Kilmore."

He put his lips next to her ear. "You drive me crazy. You know that?"

Molly suppressed a groan. *Just you wait, Mister, 'til I finally get you alone.* "You know that we have one last matter, one last bone of contention that must be resolved before, you know, we can even *think* about…"

"What're y'all talking about?"

She managed to give him a look of severity which would've made her actress daughter proud. "You promised me, Mike."

"What?" He appeared to be truly distressed. And confused.

"You promised me you'd tell me how we could afford this extravagant wedding. And a week at Disney World? In the honeymoon suite of their most expensive resort? When I thought, when I suspected you were"—she hesitated only slightly before uttering the name which was almost never mentioned between them—"Magnus. Where'd all this money come from? What are you hiding from me?"

He actually blushed. "It's a little embarrassing."

Molly's lips curled into a wicked grin. "Well, we're married now. No secrets. So, spill it, Mister!"

"It's just…Well, you're gonna think it's not a particularly *masculine* thing."

She raised an eyebrow at that. "Oh, really?"

"It's just, you know, I've been a bachelor for a long time. Well, all my life, well, especially since I got back from my mission…"

If he gets any redder, he's going to burst a blood vessel. "Come on. What is it?"

"Well, I've just been *dreaming* of this day for a long time. Long before I met y'all, even. I've just been saving up. For my wedding. For my honeymoon. You know—a wedding fund. Like a hope chest, only in a bank. I know it sounds kinda *girly*, but…"

You? Girly? Are you serious?

He threw up his hands in exasperation. "I mean, what else was I gonna spend money on? I knew what I wanted outta life. And you"—he pointed at her—"you are *everything* I ever wanted, everything I ever dreamed of. You are perfect."

Molly threw her arms around his neck and kissed him long and passionately. *Propriety be damned.*

"Oh," Tabitha said, "will you two just *go* already?"

Molly turned her flushed face to her daughter, expecting to see irritation in Tabitha's expression.

However, Tabitha wore an impish grin. "The fact is you're both driving me crazy. So, just get outta here!"

"But the bouquet," Molly said. "The garter. The cake."

"Then do it!" Tabitha cried. "Five minutes. Ten, tops. Then you're out of here!"

Mike chuckled. "Hey, Molly. I like this kid. I think we should keep her." He reached out to Tabitha and encircled her in his strong arms. "I love you, my little girl."

Tabitha put her arms around her new father's neck. "You're stuck with me now, Daddy." She stood on tiptoes, raising her high heels another inch off the floor. It still wasn't enough. He still had to bow his head so she could kiss his cheek.

Skin-to-skin contact, Molly thought. *He'll feel the Power.* Molly sighed. *That's a bond between them I'll never really know. Oh, when they take me flying, yes. But not one-on-one. Not just Mike and I. Not like the two of them.*

Mike had learned to detect the Power within Molly, but Molly's spark was weak compared to Tabitha's—a candle flame to a nuclear fire. But Mike, as it turned out, was stronger at channeling than even Fergus MacDonald had been. Mike had learned to fan Molly's tiny flame. He'd learned to make her *tingle.*

That's all it was, though—a tingle. He'd never be able to lift more than a feather or, perhaps, a dropped book—not with Molly. Molly shivered. *Oh, that tingle is more than enough. He loves me. And he loves my,* our *daughter.*

And oh boy, does he make me tingle!

In the end, it took twenty-five minutes to conclude the festivities and allow the bride and groom to change into travel clothes for the drive to the "undisclosed hotel." Mike didn't want anyone attempting, as he put it, "some back-east version of a shivaree." Molly had been in total agreement on that score. Once they were on the plane to Disney World the next day, they'd be safe. But as long as they were in town on their wedding night…

Personally, Tabitha suspected her mom's true reason for the secrecy was that she didn't want Jerry showing up. In her mind, Tabitha could no longer call the man who'd sired her "Dad"—"Jerry" was good enough for him. As far as Tabitha was concerned, she had only one man she would ever call "Dad" or "Daddy"—the only man who had ever risked his life and sacrificed part of his own body to protect her and her mother.

Just like Mom did.

Tabitha watched the Mustang pull out of the stake center parking lot. She waved, even though she was fairly certain her parents couldn't see her.

She was happy for her mom. And for Mike. "Daddy," she said aloud. "I love you, Daddy. Thank you for making Mom so happy."

I'm going to miss you both.

They'd gone flying for the last time—or at least the last time for a while—the night before. Mike had suggested they fly over the capital city itself, over the monuments. But Tabitha wanted to fly over the temple. So, Tabitha, Mike, and her mom—holding hands and sharing the joy of the Power—soared over and around the Washington, D.C. Temple, with its white-marble walls and golden spires. They had hovered right in front of the statue of Moroni with his trumpet.

Tabitha had sighed happily, looking at the golden statue's face. "I'm going inside there tomorrow." Tabitha felt a sense of awe and reverence that made her quiver.

"We're all going inside," her mother had said. "All of us."

Mike squeezed Tabitha's hand. "We're going to be a family. An eternal family. You, your mom, and me."

Tabitha felt a surge of the Power. And she trembled. I'm really going to miss this. Especially at BYU.

Tabitha sighed. *Better get changed myself. Then find that nephew—my cousin now, I guess.* She turned and walked slowly back into the building.

Mike's nephew had been there, in the sealing room when she'd been sealed to her new dad. Her mom had said he was there as a witness for the sealings. "The ordinance needs two priesthood witnesses. Just like you had witnesses when you were baptized." Not that Tabitha remembered that particular detail about her baptism when she was eight years old.

As for the witness at the sealing that morning—the younger of the two men—Tabitha remembered he was cute—black hair, blue eyes, chiseled jaw—almost like a younger version of Mike. But at the time, she'd barely given him a second thought. She'd been so overwhelmed by the simple, elegant beauty of the temple—and the poignant feelings stirring within her just from being in that sacred place. This, she had thought at the time and had ruminated on several times after leaving the House of God, this is why I'm here. This is what it's all about—being a woman, being part of an eternal marriage and a family. It's like the Power—only better. We work better as man and woman when we are joined together. This is what I want. What Mom and Dad have.

She'd actually met the nephew while standing in the reception line. He'd been on the other end of the line, of course, but there were breaks when they didn't have to stand in a straight line and greet guests. And during the first break, Mike had introduced the two of them.

His name was Joshua Kilmore. "Josh," he'd said when they shook hands. "Nobody calls me Joshua. Except my mama when she's mad." He'd smiled then.

And Tabitha's impression that he was cute was reinforced to the point of making her knees wobble slightly.

They'd talked for all of a minute—long enough for her to learn he'd just barely returned from a mission to Scotland and he'd be returning to BYU in the fall. When she had informed him that she'd be starting at BYU as well in the fall, he'd asked her if he could "look her up."

Tabitha scanned the cultural hall of the church, searching for Josh. *You better be here, mister. You're my ride to the airport!*

She had money enough for a cab, of course—Dad had made sure of that—but she thought it would be a lot more fun to talk to a cute guy than be ignored—or perhaps worse, not ignored—by a cabdriver.

Not that she couldn't protect herself.

In the months since the "incident," Tabitha had slowly learned to focus her explosions. She couldn't lift anything with the Power or do anything really useful, but she could limit the scope and force of her Power blasts. "Not useful for much," she'd told her mom.

344

But Mike had piped up immediately with, "You'll be safe. Nobody'll dare mess with you. Or if they do, y'all'll show them the error of their ways."

Tabitha had smirked. "Nobody talks to me in this town anyway. Except you two and Angelica."

And other than Angelica Goldsmith and the choir teacher, Miss Hargrove, she had no friends in Blue Beech Ridge.

While no one talked to her, people talked plenty about her. They whispered behind her back. They called her names. "Mormon" and "Witch" and worse things. Some even called her "White Lettie returned."

Tabitha had learned to live with it. She'd been accepted to BYU and had won a full-tuition Presidential Scholarship. She was content enough that she'd meet friends there.

Friends who knew nothing about the Witch of White Lady Hollow or the deaths of Fergus MacDonald and all the girls of the Circle.

Even with the tragedy—or perhaps, because of it—Camelot had been scheduled for two full weekends, with matinees on both Saturdays.

And all performances had been sold out.

She spotted him. He sat at one of the many circular tables, chatting with a pretty blonde over wedding cake and punch.

Tabitha waved at him with a gloved hand. And he waved back.

He'd already changed from his rented black tuxedo into street clothes. *Better tell him I'll be ready quick.*

And it wouldn't hurt to interrupt his conversation with that girl.

She walked toward him.

He rose from the table. He had a small smear of white frosting near the corner of his mouth. Somehow, it made him look even cuter.

"I'll be changed in a jiffy," she said.

His countenance appeared to fall. "Oh, now that's a darn shame. You look…" He shivered as he blew air through pursed lips. "Well, you look stunning. Like that. Takes a man's breath away."

Tabitha felt heat rising in her cheeks. She lowered her face, but not her eyes. Surreptitiously she watched him through her lashes. He was grinning—apparently pleased with the effect of his compliment. "Well, uh, thank you. Um, don't forget— you're my ride to the airport."

He bowed slightly in the courteous fashion of a true southern gentleman. "Your chariot—otherwise known as my VW Bug—awaits your pleasure, Miss Tabitha Moonshadow." He had Mike's manners, but no trace of a southern or Missourian accent. In fact, he sounded vaguely Scottish.

Probably something he picked up on his mission.

"I'll, uh, be quick." Tabitha snuck another glance at him as she scurried away. His eyes were following her, and his grin never wavered.

The blonde appeared suitably annoyed.

As she changed clothes in the ladies' room, Tabitha thought to herself, *He's just a cute boy. Nothing more. Just a cute, Mormon, returned-missionary, temple-worthy man. He's not Mike. And besides*, she told herself as she stepped into her customary long, black skirt, *it'd be weird to marry someone exactly like Daddy. Wouldn't it?*

But on the ride to the airport in the Volkswagen, which smelled of old motor oil, she discovered Josh was very different from his uncle. For one thing, he had no interest in being a cop. He was studying physics and astronomy at Brigham Young with an eye on going to work for NASA. "I'm on an Air Force ROTC scholarship. Gonna be a pilot and get some experience."

He stole a glance at her. "What would you think of marrying a military man?"

Tabitha looked at him askance. "Marrying? We just met!"

He chuckled, blushing. "I, uh, I know that. And I'm not proposing or anything. But I *do* think, heck I *know* I want to ask you out when we get to the Y. And, well"— he ran a sweaty hand through his hair—"isn't the whole purpose of dating to find an eternal companion?"

Tabitha laughed, both in amusement at his obvious discomfort and in relief. "I suppose. And I think a military man would be just fine. I'm going to major in theatre, but I have no illusions about acting on Broadway." *Not after meeting Morty Corrigan, the Broadway agent from hell. If that's what I have to deal with, no thank you. Community theatre or local professional productions will be enough. I hope. So, moving around with an Air Force officer-husband would be okay, I suppose.*

"Well, now"—the grin had returned to his face—"that'd be Broadway's loss. Uncle Mike says you're *amazing!*"

It was Tabitha's turn to blush. A little. "Does he?"

"Oh, yeah! He raves about you. He's very proud of you."

Tabitha bit her lip.

"In fact," Josh went on, "he flat-out suggested—strongly, I might add—that I check you out. He says you'd be quite a catch!"

"Oh, did he?"

He winked at her. "One thing I've learned—you can trust Uncle Mike."

She smiled then. *Yes, you can trust Mike. My daddy.* "My mom's lucky."

He chuckled. "Not to hear Uncle Mike tell it. According to him, he's the lucky one. He really loves her. And she's a *beauty*." He paused. "I can see where you get your looks."

Tabitha felt the heat rising in her cheeks again.

When they arrived at the airport, pulling up to the unloading zone, Josh said quickly but firmly, "You stay right there. Please let me get your bags. And your door."

Tabitha waited obediently, smiling, as he scrambled out of the Beetle, opened the trunk of the car—located at the front—and unloaded her two suitcases to the curb.

Then he was at her door.

In a courtly fashion, he extended a hand to help her out of the low-riding car. She carefully gathered her skirt, then took his hand.

He jumped back, releasing her hand and staring at his own. "Holy…" Then he looked at her in amazement. "What was that?"

Tabitha froze. *You've got to be kidding me!*

"Wow!" he said. "Did you feel that? It was like electricity or something. Like static electricity. Shocking" He stared at her as his eyes narrowed in curiosity. "But *nice.*"

Guess the gloves were in the way before. Giving him a knowing smile, brimming with secrets, Tabitha reached for his hand again.

He took hers, flinching only slightly. Then he grinned from ear to ear.

As he helped her from the car, he said, "I have to say, Miss Tabitha Moonshadow, that is one electric handshake you've got."

When she got safely to the curb, she stood there for a long moment, still holding his hand. She could feel the Power flowing into him as he smiled in wonder.

"What is that?" he asked, his eyes wide and his smile as broad as his face.

"You'll have to 'look me up' at BYU to find out." Then she winked at him.

He shivered. "Can't wait! Uh, in the meantime, can I get your phone number?" Reluctantly, he let go of her hand. Then he dug a card out of his wallet and handed her a pen.

She wrote down the phone number for the cottage and returned the pen and card to him.

He took her hand again, and she felt the Power flow once more. That time, he didn't flinch at all. "By any chance," he said with an embarrassed grin, "do you like old, scary movies?"

The End

Acknowledgements

This project has been fun, exhausting, dangerous, and emotionally draining, but worth every fun, exhausting, dangerous, and tear-drenched moment. And it wouldn't have been even remotely possible without the invaluable help of a number of wonderful individuals. First of all, it was Alison Barton who got the whole ball rolling with the story of her ancestress. Annalyn Osborn, herbalist extraordinaire, provided expertise on, well, healing herbs. Medical knowledge (including research) was generously imparted by Dr. David Palmer, M.D., Dr. Steve Devenport, M.D., Dr. Evan Black, M.D., and Dr. William D. Voss, D.O. I even worked up the courage one evening to approach Dr. Mack Wilberg, D.M.A., Musical Director of the Mormon Tabernacle Choir, for advice on 19th Century American folk hymns, and he very graciously bestowed his knowledge and wisdom and helped give Lettie a voice. Joshua Bishop, J.D.M.P.A and Randy Marshall (who doesn't want me to list any capital letters after his name) provided their legal expertise (free of charge, I might add). My dear friends, Alex Lindstrom, Dr. Eric Huntsman, Ph.D., Dr. Luke Howard, Ph.D., and Cliff Park were subject-matter experts on a variety of topics. My dear eternal companion, Cindy L. Belt was my sounding board and sharer of secrets during the whole of this project, as well as my first line-of-defense when it came to proofreading. Mable F. Belt, Melissa Cox Meibos, Adam Ward, David Belt (my dad, not me), Bryan Belt, John Abercrombie, and Alex Morris graciously served as beta readers, reviewers, and essential critics. My acting and singing dynamo of a daughter, Rachel Belt Aylworth, in so many ways, inspired Tabitha (even though Rachel can dance up a storm). I must give a long-overdue thank you to the good people of Poplar Bluff of 1978. To my nearly five hundred brothers and sisters in the Tabernacle Choir at Temple Square and Orchestra at Temple Square, you have inspired me and helped me to feel the Spirit. Finally, I must gratefully acknowledge the guidance, inspiration, and love I received from my Heavenly Father as I attempted to navigate the dangerous waters of the themes explored in this story.

It's been one hel— *heckuva* ride. Thank you all—all y'all—so very, very much.

About the Author

C. David Belt was born in the wilds of Evanston, Wyoming. As a child, he lived and traveled extensively around the Far East. In Thailand, he once fed so many bananas to a monkey, the poor creature swore off bananas for life. He served as a missionary in South Korea and southern California (Korean-speaking), and yes, he loves kimchi. He graduated from Brigham Young University with a BS in Computer Science and a minor in Aerospace Studies, but he managed to bypass all English and writing classes. He served as a B-52 pilot in the US Air Force and as an Air Weapons Controller in the Washington Air National Guard and was deployed to locations so secret, his family still does not know where he risked life and limb (other than in an 192' wingspan aircraft flying 200' off the ground in mountainous terrain). When he is not writing, he sings in the Tabernacle Choir at Temple Square and works as a software engineer. He collects swords, spears, and axes (oh, my!), and other medieval weapons and armor. He and his wife have six children (and a growing number of grandchildren) and live in Utah with an eclectus parrot named Mork (who likes to jump on the keyboard when David is writing). There is also a cat, but she can't be bothered to take notice of the parrot, and so that is all the mention we shall make of her.

C. David Belt is the author of *The Children of Lilith* trilogy, The Sweet Sister, *Time's Plague*, and *The Arawn Prophecy*. For more information, please visit www.unwillingchild.com.

Printed in Great Britain
by Amazon